SUMMER LOVE

SUMMER LOVE

Janelle Taylor
Jill Marie Landis
Stella Cameron
Anne Stuart

Zebra Books
Kensington Publishing Corp.
http://www.zebrabooks.com

ZEBRA BOOKS are published by

Kensington Publishing Corp.
850 Third Avenue
New York, NY 10022

First Printing: June, 1997
10 9 8 7 6 5 4 3 2 1

Printed in the United States of America

CONTENTS

Straight from the Heart

Janelle Taylor

One

Thunk! Ka-bang!

Kimberly Harden clamped onto the suddenly spinning steering wheel and held hard as her little compact shimmied through a yawning rut outside Betsy's rustic mountain cabin. Rain poured so heavily over the windshield she felt as if she were in a car wash. Kim held her breath, her heart hammering painfully. She half expected some new awful thing to happen. When all remained still except for the harsh tattoo of the rain on the roof of the car, she exhaled on a deep sigh.

She'd made it here in one piece!

A smile quirked her lips. So, okay, the weather was a total nightmare. So what? She needed this weekend away like she'd never needed anything before. Life could be pure hell and since her less-than-amicable divorce she'd experienced that side of it more than she'd believed possible.

Her ex-husband was a lying louse. The vision of him gloating in the courtroom as his attorney denounced her in the most wickedly awful and untruthful terms was so indelibly etched in Kimberly's mind that it could still bring tears to her eyes and quicken her heartbeat.

And yes, she'd won custody of Bobby because all of Alan's lies had proven to be just that—lies. But those untruths had scraped against her heart and soul, leaving little wounds which couldn't quite seem to heal over.

Digging in the backseat for her bag, Kim tried not to think

of the custody trial. There were so many things about it that still hurt. Her disillusionment was complete. And it certainly hadn't helped when Stephen Wright of Jackson, Wright and Smith Associates—and an extremely attractive divorced father to boot!—had taken Alan's case. Okay, so he wasn't the actual trial attorney—rat-faced Robert Jackson won those honors. But it had been *Stephen* who'd referred Alan to Robert. *Stephen* who'd believed all Alan's lies. *Stephen* whose green eyes had made Kim drift into romantic schoolgirlish dreams that still had the power to make her blush.

"Beast," she muttered between her teeth.

It was good to get away from all that. Darn good.

When Betsy, Kim's good friend and mother of Bobby's best friend, Chad, had offered a free weekend at her parents' cabin, Kimberly had jumped at the chance. She knew the cabin. Remote, yet cozy. Miles away from civilization, but close enough to make the trip back to Portland in half a day. Kim had been here before and all her memories were warm and wonderful, the kind that brought a smile to her lips and a sense of well being that was soul deep. Powerful medicine. A much needed tonic.

To hell with Alan, she thought as she gathered her purse with her overnight bag and climbed from the car. Now all she had to do was negotiate this terrible weather until she got to the front door. Then she was home free.

Placing her bunchy leather purse atop her head, she ran for the front door. A light shone from somewhere inside, dim and yellow, and Kimberly's radar went on alert. *Oh, no!* Was someone here? She was supposed to have the place to herself.

The tail end of a red Jeep Cherokee peeked from the side of the house. Heart sinking, Kimberly wondered what was up. Raising her hand to knock, she was startled when the door swung open on its own and a man stood silhouetted in the light.

"I'm sorry . . ." she murmured, stepping back.

His intake of breath was a warning, standing the hair on her arms on end. "Mrs. Harden?" he asked in that rough, smooth voice she'd come to loathe.

Alan's attorney! Stephen Wright!

"Oh, my God!" Kimberly, reacting on pure instinct, dropped everything and ran for her blue compact as if the devil himself were at her heels.

A series of swear words crossed Stephen's mind, unspoken but vehemently uttered nonetheless. What was *she* doing here? "Wait!" he yelled. When she didn't heed him, he ran through the pouring deluge, catching up with her at the car door. He made the foolish mistake of trying to grab her arm. She jabbed an elbow in his solar plexus that turned his next words into a sharp gasp. "Kimberly!"

"Don't touch me," she shot back. "Let go!"

Since he was practically doubled over and clutching his chest, her words were unnecessary. "I'm—not—"

"Well, you were. I can't believe you're here! What are you doing? Stay away from me."

"Don't worry," he managed to answer, annoyed. He drew a deep breath and glared at her. "I was just trying to keep you from getting soaked to the skin."

"Too late."

"Yeah, well, whose fault is that?"

"Stay—there," she said, when he shifted his weight from one foot to the other.

Stephen shook his head. Unbelievable! Throwing up his hands in mock surrender, he glared at her through the curtain of rain. Instantly his mood lifted. She looked like the proverbial drowned rat.

"What are you smiling at?" she demanded suspiciously.

"You," he admitted.

"Well, I'm glad you see something funny in this."

"I do. As a matter of fact, I think this is a damn riot. I came up here for a weekend of sun and fun in the mountains, and look—a summer storm like you've never seen! And we're both standing out here as if there's not a torrential downpour likely to drown us in ten minutes flat!"

Her hand was on the car door. She clenched it over the handle and pushed several times. Water poured over her as if the heavens above were already flooded and spilling the overflow onto Mother Earth. "I'm locked out," Kim said.

Stephen threw back his head and laughed. Her car keys were in her purse which she'd thrown down just outside the cabin door. "Well, then come inside. You can dry out and we'll figure out what's going on."

"Oh, no! I'm leaving. I'll get my keys."

"You can't leave," he told her.

That earned him a glare that could cut through steel. "Watch me!"

"The roads are flooded at the base of the mountain," he explained. "They closed them about an hour ago."

"They?" she repeated blankly, blinking against the rivulets of water that ran down her face. Her blonde bangs pressed limp and dark against her forehead and raindrops starred her lashes.

Stephen scowled to himself. He'd known Kimberly for several years and he'd always found her attractive. A small surge of warmth ran through him, then his good mood rapidly evaporated. "The Highway Patrol. This flash storm's created a hellish mess. I take it you weren't listening to the radio."

Kimberly didn't hear him. "Flooded? What does that mean?"

"Well, in layman's terms—" he began, but she cut him off.

"Are you saying I'm—*stranded*—here?" She thrust her bangs from her face, staring at him in dismay. "Is that what you're saying?"

"For a while, at least."

"What about you?" she asked, aghast.

"Well . . ."

Her dawning look of horror said she'd grasped the consequences. "You can't be here. You can't be staying here. One of us has to leave!"

"There's nowhere to go," he pointed out reasonably.

"There has to be. I won't—I can't stay here. We can't be here together," she added, as if he were completely dense and she was working hard to explain the situation.

Stephen's patience snapped. He could understand her hostility toward him, but it wasn't helping anything. "Since I didn't bring my ark with me, I'm stuck. Maybe you've got a better idea."

"Oh, funny."

"I'm going inside," he said, turning away.

He would have liked to grab her arm and propel her with him but her harsh words and stubborn stance warned him not to come near her again. At the cabin, he glanced back. She was still standing in the deluge.

His mouth clamped in irritation. He understood her frustration and anger and general dislike of him, but it didn't make it any easier.

Swearing softly to himself, he propped open the door with a small wooden block, a silent invitation. Glancing up, he saw her shoulders slump as she sagged against her car, and in a wave of memory that last terrible scene flickered across the screen of his mind.

You don't know anything about me, she railed at him in a whisper on the courtroom steps. People swarmed around them, parting as if they were an island in a stream. *I will never forgive you or Alan for trying to separate me from my son. I didn't believe there were people as cruel as you in this world but I believe it now . . .*

Gritting his teeth, Stephen walked to the river rock fireplace to warm his hands, wishing the heat from the spiraling flames would reach that cold, miserable spot in his soul. He could have reminded her that he hadn't been the trial attorney, but the excuse had sounded so feeble he hadn't been able to voice it.

Instead he'd taken the brunt of her anger and been only partially vindicated when she'd said even worse to Robert.

Betsy had warned him he was making a mistake. "You don't know Kim," she'd said tartly as she gathered some papers from his desk and marched from his office. As his aide, she had complete knowledge of all his cases, and as his friend, free rein of her tongue.

"I know her husband is a self-centered egotist, and that's why I turned him over to Robert."

"If you know that about Alan, why do you believe what he says about Kim?"

"I just don't like liars, even when they lie for the right reasons."

"Kim's no liar."

"You don't think she'd lie to keep her son?"

Betsy's jaw tightened. "Any woman would lie to keep their children from a louse like Alan Harden! You don't know the whole story."

"Then enlighten me," he invited.

Betsy had glared at him. She'd seemed about to say more, but then she'd looked at him in that motherly way that really got him and said instead, "It's her story, and I'm not sure you're the guy who should hear it."

He knew what that meant. His own failed marriage to Pauleen had everybody in Riverside, a small suburb of Portland, certain they knew what kind of man he was. It was his own fault. He should have blabbed about Pauleen's problems to anyone who would listen, but he hadn't. He'd let Pauleen spin her own web of lies because she'd given him Jason.

Still, he'd needled Betsy. "Because her husband retained me as his lawyer?"

"Because you're a bit of a Neanderthal," she had said with a smile. "Lovable, but a Neanderthal. Sorry, sweetie . . ."

Warmed by the fire, Stephen's soaked jeans steamed gently. It was way too warm for a fire, but with this blasted rain, it had seemed like a good idea. He glanced toward the open doorway. Sooner or later Kimberly Harden was going to have to walk across the threshold.

Then what? he asked himself. *And what's she doing here?*

As he thought about it, another realization hit: there was only one bedroom in the cabin.

"I don't believe it," Kim said aloud for about the twentieth time. It was incredible. Stephen Wright was *here.* At the cabin. At Betsy's cabin.

And she was *stuck* here!

"No, no, no!" Kimberly yanked on the car door handle again, wishing by some miracle it would open by the sheer power of her will. She did not want to have to go back to the cabin, not even for her keys. But there was nothing else to do.

Bypassing ruts filled with muddy rainwater, Kimberly slogged her way through the welcoming doorway. The aroma of burning oak and fir reached toward her. In fact the whole room glowed with steamy warmth; a cozy retreat in the mountains away from the pressures of work and the events of the past eighteen months. If it hadn't been for the man staring into the flickering flames and pulsating embers she would have found the haven she'd been dreaming of ever since Betsy offered her this weekend away. But the wide expanse of Stephen Wright's shoulders and the rain-darkened strands of his thick brown hair were an unwelcome intrusion.

Blast! she thought furiously. *I could wring his conniving neck!*

"You probably ought to change," he said without turning around. "You're soaked to the skin."

Kimberly was so livid she couldn't find her voice for a moment. "No, thank you," she said firmly. "I'm just fine."

Now he turned, his eyes raking over her without much interest. "I came in the same way."

"What does that mean?"

"Without a coat."

It took a considerable amount of will not to look down at the summer blouse and khaki pants she'd thrown on before she tore out of town this afternoon. Sure, it had started to rain but it was summer, after all, and it wasn't cold or anything. She'd figured it would let up. And yes, she knew showers were in the forecast, but tough. She was in "vacation mode" and with every mile that passed beneath the wheels of her car her mood had lifted. The weather hadn't bothered her at all.

Her blouse was now drenched pale blue linen. Glancing down, she was embarrassed to see her bra defined as clearly as if she were part of a Madonna video. Snatching up her suitcase she bolted for the one small bedroom, biting back a cry of annoyance at the sight of his black bag tossed on the quilted spread of the only bed. He'd carelessly thrown a shirt and slacks and pair of jeans across the spread, and a faint musky scent of male cologne invaded everything.

Kimberly quickly changed into a black short-sleeved sweater and her own jeans. Removing her socks, she stood barefoot against the plank floor, wishing absurdly that she hadn't spent the time the evening before painting her nails. They looked so, so, *feminine.*

How could this happen? she asked herself.

Betsy! For a wild moment Kim wondered if Betsy had planned this encounter. She was always on Kim to meet a new man, have a few laughs, get out of her routine of work, work, work.

"You've got a great kid, there," Betsy told her one afternoon. "And you're a terrific mom."

"But . . ." Kimberly filled in.

"But you've got to make time for other recreation as well. You're a secretary by day, and a mom by night, and you're the best. Now it's time to look a little further."

"How much further?" Kim was leery.

"You need a date."

A date . . . Just thinking about it made Kim shudder. When she and Alan had first split up, she'd actually entertained the idea of going out to dinner with another man, enjoying a quiet drink or a movie, or just a stretch of fun, uncomplicated conversation. She'd looked at other men, but was too inhibited to think of actually "dating" them. Her one mistake was telling Betsy what she thought of Stephen Wright.

"He's too good looking to be as nice as he is. There's got to be a flaw there."

It was two summers past. She and Betsy had been sharing a bottle of white wine over a picnic dinner in Betsy's backyard, while the Reed boys and Bobby were spraying each other with the hose. Betsy's husband, Ray, had a water pistol and was involved in the game.

"Stephen and Pauleen are divorcing," Betsy said. "But I'll tell you, it's more her than him."

"What do you mean?"

"I mean, that woman isn't what she seems." She leaned forward, the wine talking for her, since Betsy was careful what she said about her boss. "She's a witch, and you can spell that with a 'B'."

Since Kimberly's marriage had headed down that same path, and Alan had called her the same name, Kim didn't quite trust Betsy's judgment. "It always takes two."

"Not always."

"So, you blame their divorce solely on Pauleen?" Kim had always been a bit in awe of Pauleen Wright. The woman was a blonde beauty with style, grace, and a razor-sharp wit. She and Stephen were among the elite of Riverside's social set. The local paper was quick to report "Wright" sightings.

"Pauleen's not what she seems," Betsy said.

"What is she?"

But Betsy, maddeningly enough, pressed a finger to her lips and shook her head. "I can't talk. Stephen would fire me in a heartbeat! But trust me, Kimmy, he's a good guy. You just need to get to know him and, hey, he's going to be available very soon!"

Now, thinking back, Kim actually moaned aloud in humiliation. She *had* been attracted to him. So much so, in fact, that until Alan decided to go for custody—just to hurt her and get himself in the spotlight again—Kim had actually entertained fantasies about Stephen Wright that were darn near X-rated.

"Oh, I can't stand it!" she whispered, covering her face with her hands. In a fit of nervous energy she grabbed her hairbrush and attacked her wet hair with a vengeance, brushing downward in harsh strokes.

Five minutes later, her once-tangled hair now straight to her shoulders, her feet still bare since she hadn't had the foresight to bring more than her favorite pair of suede flats—now forever ruined—Kimberly walked into the living room.

Stephen had retreated to one side of the hearth, his shoulders propped against the wall, one foot resting on a block of fir. A quick glance up at her and then he looked back down, as if he were as uncomfortable as she was.

Oh, sure, Stephen Wright, attorney extraordinaire. Society page's darling. Like she was going to believe that.

"So, what are you doing here?" she asked.

"Betsy offered me the cabin for the weekend, and I took her up on it."

"Hmmmm . . ."

"What does that mean?"

"It means she offered *me* the cabin for the weekend," Kimberly informed him.

"Then you must have gotten your weekends mixed up."

He was so certain he was right and she was wrong. Kim smiled faintly. "Nope. She's taking care of my son while I'm here."

Stephen stared at her silently for several long seconds. "She's taking care of my son this weekend."

"What?" Kimberly's lips parted.

"Betsy's taking care of Jason this weekend, too."

"I know, I know. I just . . ." She let her voice trail off. Maybe Betsy *had* set this up. No! No, there had to be another explanation. When Betsy had offered her the cabin, she'd originally slated it for the following weekend. They'd been at a Little League game and when Kim asked if this weekend were free instead, Betsy had distractedly said, "Sure." Then Betsy had agreed to take care of Bobby as a matter of course since their two twelve-year-olds were inseparable.

Kim shook her head. "But she must have realized we'd be here together if Jason's at the Reeds' for the weekend, too."

"You'd think so," he admitted.

"Oh, I don't believe this!" Thrusting her fingers through her hair, Kim fought back a rushing torrent of emotion. This couldn't be! Fate could not be so unkind.

Well, at least Bobby's having a blast, she thought unhappily. Stephen's son, Jason, was good buddies with Betsy's eldest son, Matt, so sometimes all four boys ended up together at the Reeds', which thrilled Bobby to the core because, as he often said, "Jason Wright's the coolest guy on the planet, bar none, Mom."

Like, oh, sure to that one, too. Still, one had to be cautious when dealing with junior-high admiration. Throughout the long custody battle Kim had done her best to discourage Bobby's opinion of Jason without alienating him. Bobby, however, simply could not be dissuaded. And in all honesty, Jason was a nice kid; a product of Stephen Wright's ex-wife, Pauleen, Kim decided, no matter what Betsy thought of Stephen.

"I'm calling Betsy," Stephen suddenly said. In one lithe movement he was away from the fireplace and to the phone. His sudden proximity to Kim had her shrinking inside herself. The man was all shoulders and chest and possessed that peculiar kind of male grace that belied his six-foot-something frame. He absolutely pushed every one of her buttons without even trying!

She watched him hit the speaker phone button and dial Betsy's number, and all the while she attempted to rein in her rollicking pulse. It bugged her that he had this effect on her even though she couldn't stand him. She might have found him attractive once, but she sure as heck didn't now!

"Hello?" Betsy's disembodied voice filled the cabin, sounding a bit frazzled.

"Hey, Bets, it's Kim," she jumped in before Stephen Wright could say anything. "I'm calling from the cabin."

"Oh, yeah? Oh, Kimmy! Oh, my God!"

Kim's gaze locked with Stephen's. The light must have belatedly switched on inside Betsy's head. A quiver raced down Kim's spine as she stared into Stephen Wright's green eyes. "Yeah, well, don't worry, Bets. It's my fault," she said. "I didn't give you a chance to check your calendar before we changed the dates."

"But you couldn't have known. This is the worst weather in forty years! Floods everywhere. You should see the news. I know you don't have a TV there, but check the radio. All this incredible rain and, hey, we're used to rain here in Oregon. It's just amazing!"

"Betsy, I know about the weather—"

"Did you forget I'm here, too?" Stephen asked Betsy.

Kim caught a whiff of that familiar cologne when he shifted his weight. She leaned further away, wishing she could move to the other side of the room, but unwilling to leave the speakerphone.

There was a long pause. Then a gasp. Then a torrent of apologies. "Stephen! Oh, no. I can't believe it. Oh, I'm sorry. Kimmy, my God! Oh, my God!" She broke into a fit of laughter. "I'm sorry. I'm so sorry. Oh, wow . . ." Another pause. "Maybe you can draw straws and see who has to leave!"

"Neither one of us can leave," Stephen drawled sardonically. "As you said, there's a flood out there. The roads are closed."

"Closed?" Betsy repeated. Then, noticing her friend's silence, "Kimmy?"

"Right here, Bets."

"Are you okay?"

Kim knew what she was asking. Betsy was aware of how she felt about Stephen Wright these days; Kim had been pretty clear on that. "I'm okay," she assured her friend.

"Oh, well . . ." Betsy half laughed. "Kim, you remember that swimming class we took?"

"Yeah."

"How to be a lifesaver, or something? You could maybe put it into action and swim back."

Kim narrowed her gaze at the phone. Catching sight of a small movement out of the corner of her eye, she dared a glance at Stephen's face in time to glimpse the quirk of a smile. It was instantly gone. "I'm not the one who's leaving."

"Looks like we're both staying," Stephen stated.

Oh, no, Kim thought. *Not in this lifetime.*

"Well, good," Betsy said with such cheer that Kim's mood darkened even further. "Hope you kids have a great time. By the way, if you run out of food, the pantry's bound to have something in the way of—"

The phone clicked hard. Something popped loudly and the lights went out as if pulled by a master switch. Only the orange glow of the fire remained, casting dark and dangerous shadows along the pine walls.

"I think we just lost electricity," Stephen stated with a touch of irony.

"Really."

"There go my microwavable burritos for dinner."

"This place doesn't have a microwave," Kim retorted, her mind whirling from too much information. "So Betsy's taking care of Jason this weekend, too. Where did she think you were?"

"At home, I suppose." He sounded indifferent. "Jason spends half his time at the Reeds' anyway and Betsy and I just leave messages on each others' phones about where the kids are."

Her eyes were adjusting to the dim light. She saw him run a hand over his face. Was he as stressed as she was? Impossible!

"I could use a beer. Want one?" he asked.

"No," she said, thinking the idea sounded marvelous but unwilling to make even the smallest concession. This was the

man who'd tried to help Alan steal her son! He was no friend.
No ally. She wasn't about to share a beer with him like they
were old buddies.

As he went in search of his drink she walked to the fire,
examining its orange and scarlet glow against her bare feet.
Wiggling her toes, she sought for some kind of control. She
was anxious and uneasy, deservedly so, and there was an un-
happiness inside her, too. Oh, sure, she'd eventually won custody of her son in court, the one thing Alan had promised her
she couldn't do, but memories were sometimes so sharp and
unkind.

Alan's mocking voice crowded inside her mind. "Wright'll
get me Bobby. He promised. No problem. It's what he's best
at. Screwing women and taking what he wants from them!"

Well, of course, she'd known that wasn't true. Stephen
Wright had been the model husband during his marriage to
Pauleen, everyone knew that. If there'd been the slightest in-
discretion the town gossips would have reported it. But instead
every word uttered and printed about Stephen and Pauleen had
been filled with superlatives. And why not? They'd been one
of the most attractive couples in town: he so tall and dark, she
so slight and fair. And when they'd split up, citing irreconcilable
differences, none of the acrimony that had surfaced in her own
divorce had appeared. Pauleen and Stephen were as sane and
reasonable throughout their divorce as they'd been bright and
beautiful during their marriage—no matter what Betsy inti-
mated.

Still, Alan's words had hurt—almost as much as the slap and
shove he'd used against her that one awful night. She hadn't
wanted to hear anything bad about Stephen Wright any more
than she'd wanted to tell the world about her husband's physical
abuse. But she'd had to face both, for Alan had employed
Stephen as his attorney, and she, Kim, had been forced to reveal
the ugliest part of her union to all and sundry.

Things deteriorated from there. Alan claimed she was lying
about his physical abuse. She'd set it up as a means to get Bobby.

Ask anyone in town. Everyone knew Alan Harden was a good guy. Wasn't he Little League coach? Hadn't he helped out on the telethon to raise money for the schools? Didn't Harden Electric help build the snack hut at Laurel Park?

Accusations. Questions. Long, sideways looks. Kim had endured it all and somehow managed to keep her chin up. In the end she'd won Bobby away from Alan, but what a price! Bobby's trust in adults had taken a definite beating.

And Stephen Wright's part in this drama was enough to make her want to scream and inflict some physical abuse of her own!

Drawing a deep breath, Kim closed her eyes and ran her fingers through the lush strands of her blonde mane. Okay, it was Robert Jackson who'd tried the case, but that was small comfort. She didn't care about Robert Jackson. She'd never fantasized about him. And besides, Stephen could have refused Alan's case. He could have kicked her egotistical ex-husband right out in the street. But no, his law firm had hung right in there, and Kim considered any association with Alan a total betrayal.

Men, she thought, pressing her hands against her scalp, as if the very thought might explode out of her brain. *They're all in it together.*

"Here . . ."

The voice behind her nearly shot her out of her skin. Kim whipped around, furious. "Why don't you just scare the liver out of me!" The fire in her aquamarine eyes lessened a little as she realized he was holding out a long-necked beer for her. Condensation dripped down the label and onto his thumb. Almost mesmerized by the cool invitation, Kim managed to mutter a stiff, "I said I didn't want one."

"Oh, for Pete's sake, take it. It's hot in here."

That it was. It might be wet outside and rumbling with thunder and wind, but it was a summer storm that lashed against the cabin and the air was fairly warm. The fire, though cheery, was throwing off more heat than either of them needed. In fact the whole room felt close and sultry.

"Thanks," she said tightly.

His lips twisted. "Don't mention it." With that he took a
long swallow, and before Kim looked away she saw his throat
contract several times. Now why that movement should seem
so sensual she didn't quite know, but it was several moments
before the image cleared from her brain and by the time it did,
she realized she'd missed something in the conversation.

"I'm sorry, what?" she asked, as he was waiting for some
kind of answer.

"I said you can have the bedroom."

"Oh. Good." She glanced around the living room. There was
one overstuffed chair and a claw-footed love seat, but nothing
remotely big enough for his huge frame. "I could sleep here,"
she offered.

"Don't worry. I doubt I'll be sleeping anyway."

"Why not?" she asked, before she could help herself.

"I never do."

"What does that mean?"

Stephen took another swallow from the bottle. "I'm just not
much of a sleeper these days."

"Oh." Kim sipped at her beer, marveling that it tasted so
wonderful. She really didn't like the stuff much, but once in a
while, when she felt overheated and tense, nothing tasted better.
"I've got a couple sacks of groceries in my trunk," she suddenly remembered. "Of course we don't have an oven . . ."

"Well, I could grill the burritos over the fire," he suggested.

Kim tried to picture that in her mind. Stephen, leaning over
the fire, a cast-iron frying pan over a roaring flame filled with
frozen fast food. "I'll get the groceries."

"Give me the keys and I'll get them. You don't have any
shoes on."

They both glanced down at her pink-painted toenails. Kimberly could feel a flush traveling up her neck and she cursed
herself for being so sensitive. "The keys are in my purse," she
said, walking to her bag and pulling them out. He was right

behind her, so close she could feel his body heat adding to the warmth of the room.

As soon as he was jogging through the rain, she downed a huge swallow of beer, then two more, hoping the liquor would run through her veins and smooth her frazzled nerves.

"How long do you think the roads will be closed?" she asked when he returned. He was carrying her grocery sacks as if their combined weight, which had had her staggering, was feather-light.

"I don't know."

"Got a guess?"

"A day, or two maybe."

"A day or two!" Kim sank onto the love seat. "I can't wait that long."

Stephen left the sacks on the kitchen counter and rescued the beer he'd left on the table before returning to the living room. She was facing the fire, and now she could feel him somewhere behind her right shoulder. She swallowed again, wondering if the rush to her head was a result of drinking too fast or her own taut nerves.

"We can't stay here like this," she tried again.

His answer was a very male snort. She glanced back and caught him just finishing a long draught of beer, emptying the bottle. Dangling the bottle's long neck with his right hand, he swiped his mouth with the back of his left. To Kim, who'd only seen him in formal social situations or "attorney" mode, this turn to rugged indifference was both unsettling and unsuitably appealing.

You hate him. Remember that.

"Something has to be done," she muttered, returning her gaze to the fire.

"Got a suggestion?" he asked.

"Nope."

"I do."

"You do?" Carefully, she hazarded another glance his way.

He, too, seemed entranced by the dancing flames, but spying her movement, his gaze swept upward, meeting hers.

"Another beer," he said, turning to fulfill his own request.

Kim narrowed her lashes at his retreating back, half-inclined to nail him with some perfect barb. Inspiration did not strike, however, and she was still working up a comeback when he offered her another dewy bottle.

"I've still got a ways to go on this one," she said frostily.

"Yeah, well . . ." He shrugged and with several long steps, flopped onto the love seat, his legs stretched so far forward that his ankles straddled her two feet. It was peculiarly intimate and Kim, pretending an indifference she didn't feel, sidled toward the overstuffed chair, dropping into it with what she hoped was same unaffected casualness.

Silence stretched between them, but it wasn't the easy, familiar kind between friends. Kim had to struggle not to fidget. "Aren't you hungry yet?"

"Actually, no."

"Well, I am." She jumped up and found her way to the kitchen where Stephen had lit the oil lamp Betsy normally used as a centerpiece on the tiny kitchen table. Shadows walked along the cabinets and counter as she dug inside her sacks for the frozen hamburger, now half-thawed, and a loaf of bread. There were no buns; she'd planned on fixing spaghetti for herself, along with some "salad in a bag," her new favorite meal. Now, it looked like she would have to settle for hamburger patties on wheat bread.

"Need some help?" he called.

"No, just be a male and sit there," she muttered under her breath.

"What?"

"No, thank you," she called a bit louder.

Alan had never helped in the kitchen. Once in a while he would invite some people over—someone he wanted to impress—and make his mother's famed Hungarian goulash. Never mind that it was Kim's recipe he'd adopted and that she did the prep on the meat and vegetables. Never mind that Alan's mother was as far from Hungarian as Pluto from the sun. Never mind that Kim was left with clean up while Alan's guests sat around afterwards over brandy and ribald talk that she found more than mildly offensive. But that was how Alan believed clients should be wooed, and to her disgust, it often worked. Harden Electric contracted for some of the major builders around Riverside, and Alan knew how to schmooze with the best of them.

With extra fervor she pounded the half-frozen ground round into patties and arranged four of them in a black cast-iron skillet. A few seasonings over the top and she returned to the living room, ready to create a "gourmet" sensation.

Her mouth went dry at the sight that met her eyes.

Stephen Wright was still stretched out in the love seat, his long jean-clad legs slightly apart. He'd taken off his shoes and socks and unbuttoned his shirt, a concession to the steamy heat. His eyes were closed and his head lolled back against the cushions. His beer was propped between his thighs, forgotten, one hand curved laxly near its neck. He looked younger, less intimidating, his brow relaxed in sleep, his lips fuller, those lines of discontentment bracketing his mouth erased. The curve of his jaw drew her interest as if by a magnet.

Somewhere deep inside Kim something came alive. Something long dead, or maybe never given birth before.

Shaking all over, she dropped the skillet on the pine coffee table with a clatter. Stephen jumped up as if he'd been stabbed.

"What the hell?" he demanded, towering over her as she fought for composure. Then, worried, "Kim, are you all right?"

Her heart beat in her ears. She couldn't answer.

And then he reached a hand out to tip up her chin and stare searchingly at her and Kim, in a state of pure emotion, sensed traitorous tears spring to her eyes. As if that humiliation weren't enough, her body quivered when, almost in amazement, his thumb captured one tear and he watched it melt against his own skin.

Two

"What is it, Kim?" he asked softly.

Of all the things Kim could handle, pity and caring were the hardest. If someone was nice to her, that's all it took to start the waterworks, and Stephen's concern coupled with her own strange reaction were enough to do her in.

It didn't help that he was *touching* her either!

"I'm all—right. Just—don't—"

Stephen's eyes searched her flushed face. Quietly, he said, "Don't what?"

"Don't touch me."

He frowned. But it was as if her words were an invitation, not a warning, for his hands reached for her shoulders and slid downward until they rested just below the short sleeves of her black sweater. Kim's breath caught in her throat. He seemed lost in concentration, feeling her skin. Her heart kicked painfully. This wasn't right. She shouldn't *feel* these things!

Tense as a bowstring, she slowly pulled her arms free of his grasp. For a moment it seemed like he might actually resist her efforts, but then he took a step back. They stood in silence.

"I don't want to be here with you," she heard herself say, the words fast and scared. "I didn't want any of this. I'm sorry, I just—don't."

"Did I say I did?"

"I just don't want you to think—" Kim broke off helplessly.

"Think what?"

"That I'm . . . that this is . . . okay."

The Stephen Wright she'd feared, the one Alan had threatened her with, the one who had obviously given him his courtroom reputation, suddenly appeared. One moment the man was approachable; the next he was cold as a distant star.

"What do you mean *this?* Did you think I was going to kiss you? Make a pass? Put you in some kind of compromising position?"

"I'm already in a compromising position!" Kim declared. "I don't want to be here with you. I don't trust you. And after what you did, I'll never be able to even *like* you!"

"After what I did?"

She nodded. It took all her courage not to step back, away from him a few paces. His very nearness was intimidating.

"After what I *did?"* he repeated again.

"You tried to take Bobby from me!"

Silence fell. Her accusation reverberated in shock waves. It almost felt as if she'd slapped him. "You may not have been the courtroom attorney, but you took Alan's case," she fumbled on. "And I don't want to hear that a job's a job. That's no excuse. You represented Alan." Her throat was dry as salt. "And he's no kind of father, and certainly no kind of husband."

Stephen stared down at the petite blonde-haired woman who stood in front of him—so small, yet so defiant. He was angry at the weather for stranding him here with her. He was angry at himself for being so susceptible. And he was angry at her for being right.

His defense sounded pathetic even to his own ears. "I didn't know what kind of man Harden was when our firm took the case."

"When *you* took the case," she corrected.

"I passed on being his attorney," Stephen reminded her.

But Kim was having none of it. "Oh, really? That wasn't Jackson, Wright and Smith representing Alan?"

"It wasn't Stephen Wright," he snapped back, stinging. He wanted to tell her that he'd spent his time in the background, listening to what went on, keeping well out of it. He'd never been particularly concerned that Harden would end up with Bobby; his bid for custody was too weak, especially since Kim appeared to be a model wife and mother. And though he didn't really like the man personally, he'd found him at least tolerable—until Betsy had let it slip that Alan had struck his wife.

It had been late in the trial. Betsy, who was generally good about separating her personal life from her professional, overheard Robert Jackson shaking hands and saying good-bye to Alan. Like Mount Etna about to explode, she'd suddenly clenched her fists and turned bright red, literally shaking with the effort to contain herself.

"What's got into you?" Stephen asked her.

"I'd like to wring his lying neck!"

"Who?" Stephen looked around, then spied Alan Harden's retreating back through the open door of his office.

"I know what he did to Kim. She tried to hide it, but I know."

Fascinated, he simply waited. Betsy tried to clamp her lips together, but in a rush, she spewed out, "He *hit* her! Slammed her into a wall. When I saw the bruises I knew what had happened."

The rush of emotion Stephen felt was totally out of proportion to the circumstances. Yes, he was infuriated. Yes, he was disgusted and sickened. But the need to comfort and hold Kim and wrap himself around her was an unwelcome yet overwhelming desire. He was left speechless, spent, as if he'd run a marathon. And it took all of his not inconsiderable will to hide the freight train of emotions that rushed through him from Betsy Reed's knowing eyes.

But she was too upset herself to pick up the vibes. "If he gets custody of Bobby, it'll kill Kim."

"It won't happen."

"How do you know? Our firm is representing him, for crying out loud!"

"Harden's a bad witness," Stephen responded bluntly. "Robert said as much to the man's face. He blusters and talks big. The judge would award custody to Kim even if she weren't the best choice."

"You're sure?" Betsy gazed at him pleadingly.

Yes, he'd been sure. Certain to the tips of his toes. But it still had been a relief to hear the outcome in Kim's favor. When she'd blasted him on the courtroom steps he'd had no defense of his own. He'd deserved some of it because when Alan had first brought him the custody case he'd painted Kim out to be some kind of self-serving bitch. Though Stephen had known better, he'd half believed the man. His own experience with Pauleen was partially to blame, and he'd made himself believe it was Kim who'd been lying, not Alan. Still, it was no excuse, and he'd taken Kim's verbal battering as his due.

And so, now what? he asked himself, gazing at Kim in the firelight. She'd turned her face away while he'd traveled through this lightning introspection. Now she stared fixedly at the flames, a means of shutting him out and pulling away without physically moving.

If he were ever going to be given the opportunity to explain himself to her, this was it. Yet, there really was no excuse. He hadn't taken Alan Harden's case but he also hadn't thrown him out on his ear. And when Betsy had blurted out Harden's true nature, Stephen hadn't charged after him and rendered the man serious physical harm (his first, most burning desire). Instead, he'd quietly warned Robert about a rumor he'd heard and let Jackson handle Harden any way he chose. Confronted with his abuse, Harden blustered and whined and denied, and Robert Jackson went ahead with the custody suit.

It was the way some cases went.

Still, the whole thing had left a bad taste in Stephen's mouth, and at some level he'd wanted to clear it up with Kim. And here, *here,* was the perfect opportunity. So, what was stopping him?

"I'm not really hungry," Kim suddenly said. "I think I'll just go to bed."

He had a sudden vision of her lying between the sheets, hair tossed in a silken heap across the pillow, eyes closed, breath soft and even, her expression gentle and sweet. He imagined her naked, her skin smooth and lustrous.

"You sure you want the love seat?" she asked, her face still averted.

"It's fine," he answered shortly.

"I'm smaller. It would be easier for me to curl up here."

"I'm not interested in sleeping right now. Go ahead. I'll be perfectly fine."

Now, she darted him a look, questions hovering in her eyes. But she was clearly too upset to delve into what was eating at him, and for that he was glad. *She* was eating at him. He hadn't wanted any woman since his divorce, though scores had thrown themselves at him as soon as they learned he was unattached. He hadn't even wanted to date. Pauleen had cured him of that—he'd thought forever.

But Kimberly Harden got to him. In ways he didn't want to think about.

So, now, when she hesitantly said goodnight and slipped away, Stephen found it was all he could do not to let his gaze follow after her, devouring her. The soft click of the door closing brought him back to reality.

Muttering a few pungent obscenities beneath his breath, he worked his way through the shadowy room back to the kitchen in the hope of finding another beer.

Kimberly lay on her back with her hands folded beneath her head, staring at the bedroom ceiling. There was no such thing as total darkness. From the window grayish outdoor light threw a square of faint illumination across the foot of her bed and lightened the walls. Shadows danced from the stiff breeze that gusted outside and rain fell in a steady symphony.

She couldn't sleep. Not at all. Her mind was busy, her thoughts fragmented. But her overall feeling was one of, what? She didn't know. Cautiously, she tiptoed through the mess in her head and suddenly tripped over luscious thoughts of Stephen Wright.

With a groan of self-loathing, she snatched up the pillow and buried her face in its smothering softness. Then she pounded on it with one fist. *You are such an idiot!* She couldn't stand the man. He'd sided with Alan! It wasn't fair that he was so outrageously attractive.

Why? Why? Why?

Removing the pillow, Kim sighed hugely. She'd never been stupid about men. Well, okay, she'd misjudged Alan. She'd fallen for his charms—limited as they now appeared to be—but she could excuse herself because she'd been so young. Now, there was no excuse. She knew the kind of man Stephen Wright was, and he would never be the man for her.

Still . . .

She looked across the room to where she'd folded up his clothes and set them atop his bag. She should have pushed the bag outside the door but there it stood, mocking her. If Stephen wanted anything from it he was going to have to knock on her bedroom door, but so far that hadn't happened.

What time was it? she wondered. She'd gone to bed shortly after seven. *When was the last time you did that, my girl?* And now she was wide awake and wishing for dawn. As soon as it was light she might be able to leave. More wishful thinking, as it hadn't stopped raining all night and it was bound to take a while for the floodwaters to recede.

She tossed and turned for what had to be at least an hour, then finally out of pure frustration and exhaustion, she stopped avoiding the issue picking at her brain and faced it full on: She was attracted to Stephen Wright. Kim actually winced as she mentally said the words. She felt like a traitor to herself. How could she be? How could she?

Easy. She'd been attracted to him before, why not now? She'd first met him several years earlier; they were loosely involved in the same circle of friends. Betsy, of course, was the main connection, and when she first introduced Kim to Stephen at a barbecue at her house he'd still been with his wife, Pauleen. Kim, sensitive to her own still-fresh divorce, had eyed Stephen and Pauleen Wright and wondered what kept them together. Sure, they were the quintessential beautiful couple, but Pauleen seemed so stiff and discriminating. The corners of her mouth never lifted, and there was a restlessness about her, as if she couldn't wait to leave. Her tension was palpable. Stephen, on the other hand, had clearly been having a great time. Kim had warmed to his conversation. She knew he was a lawyer, and she learned that he was acquainted with Alan—Riverside was small enough, and Harden Electric was big enough, that it was almost a given the two men would have met.

Pauleen had had too much to drink and that ended Kim's first meeting with Stephen; he took his tottering wife home. Still, her attraction to him had remained, like a haunting melody. Oh, she didn't want him then; he'd been married, for crying out loud! But she'd enjoyed the mellow tones of his voice and the amused quirk of his mouth as a woman appreciates any attractive male. Kim had been starved for that kind of easy camaraderie; she'd never really had it with Alan, and it was darn difficult to find. That evening she'd been sorry to see Stephen leave, but then in the course of her frenetic life, she'd dropped him from her thoughts. Betsy brought his name up upon occasion, of course, but one day the word "divorce" was mentioned in conjunction with Stephen Wright. *That* caught Kim's attention.

"They weren't meant for each other," was Betsy's blanket assessment. And then, because she was loyal and true, "He deserves better."

Kim had wanted to query her further without seeming overly curious, but Betsy, a friend who generally loved to speculate on people, could sometimes be as closemouthed as a clam. Kim sensed that she was protecting Stephen, which was admirable but downright frustrating! Kim knew her own appreciation of the man could easily turn into an out-an-out attraction.

And it would be the first time she'd actually wanted to date another man since she'd met her ex-husband—a lifetime ago!

But, no . . . Stephen and Pauleen Wright might be divorcing, but he was in no mood for dating; Betsy was clear on that. She then alluded to the messiness of the split up and became like a mother hen clucking over her injured chick. What Stephen thought of Betsy's concern, Kim never knew, but she decided to keep her interest in him to herself.

She saw him at several social functions during this transition. Once he'd even had a beautiful woman on his arm, though Betsy, unsolicited, remarked that the woman, Samantha, had clamped onto Stephen when he'd walked through the door and that he was doing his best to disengage her.

Kim learned this was true when at the hors d'oeuvre table she was suddenly right next to him, and he desperately looked like he needed a rescue.

"Hey, there," he said to Kim, the dark-haired beauty still fervently clutching his sleeve.

"Hi," was all Kim managed to answer. As far as scintillating conversation went, she scored a perfect zero.

The would-be girlfriend broke in right there. "Stephen, come over here. I want you to meet a friend of mine. He's thinking of switching law firms, and I promised that I'd bring you over to him A.S.A.P."

"Can't do it right now," Stephen answered politely.

"Oh, sure you can!"

"I'll be there in a minute. I'm involved in a conversation."

Kim was surprised. After a moment of consternation, the lovely brunette flicked Kim an assessing look, then reluctantly released Stephen's arm. Stephen gave Kim a sideways glance as he filled his plate. "Sorry I had to use you as an excuse. I know the guy Samantha wants me to meet, and believe me, I can wait."

"It looks to me like it's Samantha who's wanting a private meeting," Kim said. As soon as the words were out she flushed with embarrassment. It wasn't often she unthinkingly betrayed the thoughts that brushed across her mind. Her boldness shocked her.

Stephen's head turned to gaze at her sharply. Spying her flooding color, he started to laugh. "You're right!" he declared.

"I'm sorry. I—that was uncalled for. I feel like an idiot."

"No, no. It's okay. I haven't been socializing much these days, and I think I've lost the ability to politely get out of sticky situations. I mean, look, I had to depend on you for help."

"Depend away. I absolutely hate being trapped in something I can't get out of without coming off like a jerk."

"I can't believe you ever come off like a jerk." He gazed into her eyes. He seemed about to say something—a compliment, perhaps?—but then Samantha reappeared.

"Come on, Stephen! Come now. Hurry, hurry, hurry!" Her attempts at cuteness fell completely flat, but her insistence was rapidly putting Stephen in exactly the sticky social situation one couldn't avoid. Samantha yanked on his arm and he graciously followed, but not before glancing back to Kim and pretending to strangle himself, his tongue lolling out of his mouth and his eyes rolling upward. Kim laughed and he pulled himself out of the pantomime just as Samantha looked around suspiciously.

Betsy clapped her hands together in delight when Kim related the story to her later. "Don't you just love him!" she declared. "Oh, Kimmy," she added, as the bolt hit her. "He's perfect for you!"

"Whoa. Hold on. I don't even know if he's actually divorced yet."

"Totally divorced," Betsy informed her. "And ready to date again."

"He said he hadn't been out in many social situations."

"Hey, that was a bad marriage. He's still suffering from it."

"What was wrong?"

Betsy pressed her lips together. "You know, it's not for me to tell."

"Since when did you get so hung up about gossip!" Kim laughed.

"I would give my back teeth to talk about Stephen Wright, but he asked me to keep his affairs private. He's very private himself."

Kim was unrepentant. "Hey, this is your best friend you're talking to."

Betsy looked about ready to explode with the desire to tell all. "Oh, stop it! If and when enough time goes by, believe me, you're first on my list. Meanwhile, I'll plant the seeds that you're maybe kind of interested—"

"No!" Kim cried adamantly. "Betsy, no! I don't want him to think I'm chasing him!"

"See, you're as bad as he is. I could help you both."

"Don't. Please. I mean it."

Betsy had merely sniffed in supreme knowledge that both Kim and Stephen were being ridiculous over this clearly budding romance.

And then . . . Alan had chosen the new tack to try and wrest Bobby from her, just out of plain meanness, and he'd let her know that Stephen Wright had agreed to be his lawyer.

Now Kim shivered, a mass of emotions. What was it about being attracted to Stephen that made his actions seem like such a betrayal when, as he'd pointed out, he was just being businesslike? Had she invested more of herself in the relationship than she should have, even at that first germ of the feeling? Probably. She always led with her heart, not her head.

Well, it hardly mattered now. As soon as the sun broke through tomorrow she was going to find a way out of here. Scrunching her pillow into a new, comfortable shape, Kim settled down to serious sleep, except that it kept eluding her. Nerves, she realized, and a lack of dinner.

Once the thought crossed her mind she was famished. She'd smelled the burgers cooking over the fire and listened while Stephen moved back and forth from kitchen to living room, apparently putting together the rest of his meal. The thought of a juicy hamburger suddenly overpowered her. Food. Her stomach growled at the thought. She felt like she hadn't eaten in a week.

Throwing back the quilt, she stopped mid-motion. The image of Stephen Wright sprawled across the love seat pinned her to the bed. Could she sneak past him without waking him?

It was so quiet she could hear the tiny creaks of the house and the faint crackling sparks of the dying embers. Eventually giving into hunger, she padded barefoot to the bedroom door. It squeaked upon opening. Kim grimaced at the sound. She really didn't want to wake him.

Two steps into the living room, she gasped. He was standing in front of the fire watching her sneaking arrival.

And all he had on was a pair of boxers.

Stephen eyed Kimberly with a mixture of frustration and amusement. "Couldn't sleep?" he asked. Unlike him she wore a sleepshirt that covered her from chin to just below the knees. Across the darkened room her bare legs glowed softly white, their shape defined. For some reason Stephen couldn't get his mind off them. He remembered her sitting on the love seat earlier, legs crossed.

You're a total pervert! he told himself.

"Why aren't you asleep?" she asked.

"I told you, I don't sleep much."

"But you're not even lying down." Her voice sounded like an accusation. She reluctantly stepped forward, and he realized she was looking anywhere but at him.

His own near nudity finally registered. Well, tough. He was hot, and it wasn't exactly like he'd planned this midnight meeting. She could just deal with it.

"I thought about getting something to eat," she said, sidling toward the kitchen.

"The lamp's kind of low on oil. Let me light some candles," he suggested, leading the way ahead of her. He'd found several in drawers and had used drinking glasses as candlesticks. As he lit them, they illuminated the kitchen with eerie pools of light, their listing shapes within the glasses giving them a drunken look that added to the general feeling of strangeness and intimacy.

Kim eyed the candles with more interest than necessary. Stephen could feel how much she wanted to keep distance between them; she practically moved an extra yard away whenever she had to get by him.

"I had a couple of burgers," he told her.

"I know," she said a trifle testily. "I could smell them."

"You should've had one."

"I wasn't in the mood then."

"Well, they're cold now."

"Thank you for that information. I don't think I could have come up with it on my own."

"What's eating you?" he demanded, glancing around at her. She'd circled past him and was standing in the shadows somewhere behind his left shoulder.

"Nothing."

She crossed her arms over her chest, but the movement only defined her breasts. Stephen tried not to stare, but the lovely picture she made only fueled his fantasies—which bugged him to no end.

Annoyed, he purposely moved into her space. "I could stir up the fire and give them a reheat. I don't guarantee they'll be any good, but hey, there aren't a lot of options here."

"Maybe I'll just have wheat bread and salad," she answered, stepping back until her hips pressed against the counter.

Something snapped inside Stephen; some long held fury at the fates for making everything so difficult. He'd simply had it with convention. Moving closer, he stood right in front of her, not touching, but staring down at her so that her breath caught in alarm and she shrank back against the cabinets.

"What—what are you doing?" she asked shakily.

"I don't know," he admitted.

"Well, don't do it!"

"I'm just tired of all the problems and I just want to forget them."

Kim's hands were clasped in front of her chest, as if this gesture would ward him off. "Fine. Great. Forget away. But you're really—crowding me!"

"I'll just reach around you to the cooler and pull out the rest of the salad. I saved you some." With that he slid an arm past hers and dragged the cooler out.

Kim stood frozen for a moment, then said icily, "Would you mind putting some more clothes on?"

Stephen pretended surprise. "Does this bother you?"

"No. I just—" He waited, staring down at her. "Actually, as a matter of fact, it *does* bother me." She hazarded a direct glance upward. "You bother me."

"Well, you bother me, too."

"I didn't mean it like that," she said swiftly.

"Like what?"

"Good grief, you really are an attorney. Questions, questions, questions."

"You're just avoiding answering."

"Look, I came out here to get something to eat, but you know what? I'm not hungry anymore. You have killed my appetite." She squeezed past him.

It was all Stephen could do not to trap her full body against the counter. He was amazed at himself. He couldn't ever remember behaving so badly.

But when Kim glanced back at him over her shoulder, lips soft in the candlelight, expression lost and a little miserable, his control completely broke. Against all of her wishes, he dragged her close. "I'm sorry," he whispered against her hair.

Her body quivered in his arms. He half expected her to slap him, but all she did was heave a trembling sigh. She struggled to talk; he could feel her effort. But she was unsuccessful.

Seconds ticked by. The contours of her body melted against his. His lips brushed her ear. Her forehead fell to his chest, as if her bones had given way. He held her tighter, heard her uneven breathing mixed with his own. Thoughts danced in his head. Desires. He was on the verge of sweeping her into his arms and carrying her Rhett Butler-style to the tiny bedroom until she whispered faintly, "I can't."

"Kimberly . . ."

"I don't even like you very much," she said with a touch of humor.

He rested his chin on the crown of her head, struggling for control, for the same lightness. It would break the spell, something she obviously desperately wanted, "I can live with that."

"Goodnight, Stephen." Slowly, she pulled herself from his arms. "See you in the morning."

His name on her lips seemed to echo in his mind. She didn't say it often. Had he ever heard it? It distracted him for so long that she'd moved from the kitchen to the living room before he could respond.

"What about your wheat bread and salad?" he asked, catching sight of her as she stepped across the threshold into the bedroom.

"Somehow I think it'll be there for me tomorrow."

The door closed softly behind her. And Stephen Wright spent a very uncomfortable evening on a too-small love seat in front of a dying fire while his mind tortured him with a continual rerun of those moments when Kim was in his arms.

Three

Kimberly's wish for sunshine was completely ignored by the gods of weather. Rain plummeted with renewed force as soon as dawn broke. She watched from the living room window, her arms folded across her chest, her thoughts dark. She could hear the water from the shower, probably icy cold, but Stephen had taken his bag and braved the possibility anyway.

Kim longed desperately for a cup of coffee. She'd brought instant. All she had to do was build another fire and heat some water over the coals, yet for some reason it sounded like a monumental task. She was weary all over. Lack of sleep definitely had something to do with it.

And why couldn't you sleep?

Kim snorted in disgust. What in God's name had come over her last night? For a heartbeat, locked in the security of Stephen's arms, tantalized by the possibility of lovemaking by candlelight, she'd forgotten herself completely. She'd forgotten whom she was with! When he'd gathered her close, instead of running away she'd stood in robot-like anticipation, mesmerized by every touch and downright faint with desire.

The memory embarrassed her. Groaning, she buried her face in her hands, then dug her fingers into her scalp, wanting to rip her hair out by the roots. The incessant rush of the shower invaded her thoughts. She could picture him naked under the unforgiving spray, his muscles sleek and wet.

"You are completely crazy," she told herself.

Pacing the room, Kim wished there was some way she could

call Bobby. The sound of her son's voice was bound to be a reality check. He was so good and exuberant and full of pep. She needed that right now. Instead, she was trapped here with no means of communication.

The taps suddenly shut off. The thought of Stephen Wright appearing damp and half-naked galvanized Kim into action. She threw more wood on the fire and shoved newspaper beneath it. She'd just struck a match when she heard the bathroom door open, and she turned and looked without thinking.

He wore a pair of jeans, low on his hips, and a towel draped around his neck. His hair was wet and tending toward a curliness she hadn't noticed before. Raking fingers through that wet mane, he threw her a questioning look.

"What?" he asked.

"What do you mean?"

"Why are you looking at me that way?"

"What way?"

Stephen merely lifted a brow at her attempts to divert him. He strode into the kitchen, and Kim broke seven matches before she managed to set fire to the newspaper. Blast the man. He completely disarmed her.

When the flames took hold, Kim situated a sauce pan full of water precariously atop the logs. Earlier she'd munched on a dry piece of wheat bread and eaten the rest of the salad. So much for breakfast.

Stephen appeared from the kitchen with more bread, butter, and jam. He gazed at the pan full of water with interest. "Coffee?"

"Hopefully,"

"Did you get anything to eat?"

"Yep," Kim responded.

"Good. Wouldn't want you wasting away."

Why couldn't he wear a shirt? Kim asked herself. What was this bare chest thing all about? It irritated her that she was so susceptible to it. She'd never thought of herself as someone who obsessed over men's bodies, but she sure as heck was obsessing over this one!

"You're frowning," he pointed out. With animal grace he slipped the towel off his shoulders, absentmindedly dried his chest, then tossed the towel to the edge of the love seat.

"You're half-dressed," she snapped back.

"I'm going to put a shirt on as soon as I'm totally dry." He looked amused.

"I just don't feel comfortable, okay?"

"Still think I'm going to make a pass?"

He made the idea sound ridiculous, but last night's memories were still very fresh. "You came pretty close in the kitchen last night," she reminded him.

He inclined his head. "Yeah, well . . . I won't do that again. I'm sorry," he apologized once more.

She wished he'd ranted and raved and acted like he didn't know what she was talking about. To throw down the gauntlet and chivalrously concede wasn't working for her. Now it was Kim who felt like the guilty party.

"Do you think this rain is ever going to stop?" she asked, walking back to the window.

"No."

That brought a smile to her lips. "So, we're stuck here forever with no electricity and a diminishing supply of wheat bread?"

"I've got a few beers left. We should last 'til the end of the month."

"You're a real comfort."

"The water's boiling."

Kim hurried back to pull the saucepan from the logs. While Stephen watched in silence she measured instant coffee into the two mugs she'd scrounged from the kitchen, then poured the hot water over it. The smell of the melting granules was as aromatic as a cup of fresh coffee. Kim breathed deeply, although she would have sold her soul for a latte at that moment.

Handing Stephen his cup, her fingers touched his. She pulled

back, then was surprised when he grabbed her wrist, holding
her in place. In shock, her aquamarine eyes searched his for
an answer. "Thanks," he said softly, releasing her.

Kim moved to the chair, perching in it cross-legged. "If
you're trying to intimidate me, you're doing a darn good job
of it."

"What?"

"You're in my space!" she declared, uncomfortable with her
own feelings.

"You're in *mine.* I was here first," he pointed out.

"Oh, right," Kim returned dryly. "You had dibs. I forgot."

Stephen grinned wholeheartedly. Unabashedly. From the
pure joy of Kim's disgruntled sarcasm. If she'd thought he was
disarming before, this sent her pulse charging like a bull
through the gate.

"I'll try to behave," he said, "but I gotta tell you. I feel great
today, like some weight's been lifted that I didn't know was
there."

"Really."

He nodded. "And you know why?"

"I'm afraid to ask," Kim murmured, but secretly she couldn't
help wondering if it might have something to do with her. Not
that she wanted it to, she reminded herself. This was not a guy
to lose your heart to. He was not a man to be trusted.

"I've been looking forward to this weekend since before
Betsy even offered me the cabin. I've wanted to get away for
months, maybe years. But there's always been something, or
someone, with other plans."

Kim didn't answer, her own hopes dashed a little.

"And I thought I wanted to be alone," he went on, "but now
I don't know. It's nice having company."

"I don't like the idea of being trapped with you."

"Not even just a little?"

His audacity was just short of self-adulation. He was teasing
her, but she didn't want to be teased. She didn't know what
she wanted, and he made her feel off-balance and testy.

"Not even a smidgeon," she lied.

His grin grew to Cheshire cat size. He saw right through her. Kim turned away. She had to get out of here soon, or she would lose her sanity. As much as she denied it, she felt the same lifting of that weight that he did.

"How was the shower? Still warm?" she asked hopefully.

"Bearable."

"Ice cold, huh?"

"You'd be better off to heat more water on the fire and add it to the tub."

"Maybe I'll do that later," she murmured, her mind already skipping ahead. She needed something to do. If she had to sit around here with nothing to think about but him, she really would go crazy.

When he got up from the love seat and went into the kitchen, she silently eyed his progress. She heard water running, then he returned with a huge tub which he arranged on the burning logs.

"Oh, don't worry about it," Kim sputtered. "Really. I'm okay."

"Might as well heat it up," he answered.

His ability to just take over bugged her. Everything bugged her. Striving for neutrality, she said, "My son thinks yours is about as cool as it gets."

That brought a half-smile to his too sexy lips. "Jason's a pretty good kid."

"Pretty good? Bobby would be offended that that's all you could say about him. Jason is 'The Best' and 'The Coolest.' Everything is a superlative when it comes to your son."

"He just got his driver's license, and he thinks he's 'The Best' and 'The Coolest,'" Stephen said with affection. "All he wants to do these days is run to the grocery store, so that I don't have to."

Kim smiled. "How thoughtful of him."

"Yeah, isn't it, though? It couldn't have anything to do with the car." His expression grew sober. "Pauleen wants him to come live with her. She wants to send him to a private school."

"Oh." Kim tried to read his thoughts. "So, that's what you're going to do?"

"Over my dead body."

She could feel the roil of emotions just below the surface of this conversation. She understood the tension. "Your divorce wasn't so amicable, was it?"

He hesitated, his gaze narrowing on her face as if he were considering whether to trust her or not. Kim, who'd managed for months to make him out as some kind of monster who'd tried to steal her child from her, had picked up on the vibes of his own shredded marriage. Her lips parted; she wanted to say something, an apology perhaps? But Stephen's gaze dropped to her lips and stayed there, searing in its intensity and driving whatever she'd planned to utter right out of her head.

"I don't want to talk about my ex-wife," he said flatly. "We stayed together for too long, for all the wrong reasons."

"I understand. I don't know why I stayed with Alan. I was just too afraid, I guess, you know, to make a change even though there was nothing there. Nothing left." Kim heard herself babbling, but couldn't stop. Stephen was watching her in that intense way that seemed to reach down inside and yank on her emotions. "I had to get out, and I finally did, and then I was alone and it was okay. Except for Bobby. Just the two of us, you know."

"But then Alan sued for custody," Stephen put in when Kim suddenly stopped.

That stopped her cold. She blinked several times, unable to speak. Stephen set down his coffee cup and came to stand over her chair. He squatted down, so close she was enveloped by the clean spicy scent of his soap and the heat of his skin. "I didn't know he hit you," he said softly. "Betsy told me after Robert took Alan's case."

"He didn't really hit me. He pushed me," she said quickly, still too mortified over the event to talk about it openly.

"Same difference. I . . . met with Robert about Alan . . ." Stephen admitted.

"Robert knew and he still represented him?"

"Robert had a client whom he couldn't really trust. He suggested Alan give up the idea of custody. He knew he'd lose. But Alan was hell-bent on going to court."

"I hate hearing about it," Kim said bitterly.

"Then let's not talk about it anymore. But for the record, Alan Harden deserves to be strung up." Stephen was deadly serious.

Kim gazed at him, her eyes burning with unformed tears. It wasn't meant to be an invitation. It wasn't meant to be anything. But her expression shimmered with gratitude, and Stephen, used to a woman who drank and belittled and trampled over emotions, couldn't resist this trusting, sincere beauty. Before Kim could respond, she was surrounded by a pair of strong, sinewy arms, her face pressed against his muscular chest, her ears deafened by the thunderbeat of his heart. Her mouth opened against his skin, a whispered "thank you" in her mind. But her tongue encountered warm skin and crisp whorls of chest hair and her brain shut down completely.

He kissed her crown. His palm caressed her face. One hand slid down her back and pulled her upward until she slid from the chair against him and they tumbled together to the pine heartwood floor, neither conscious of anything but the feel of the other.

For Kim, it was complete abandonment, something she'd never experienced before. She went with it, letting his hands discover her, letting her own wanton fingers travel over him, pulling him tight. One moment they were talking, the next they were writhing in each other's arms, the transition so quick that conscious thought simply couldn't catch up.

His mouth found hers. Kim's lips parted wantonly. His tongue discovered the warmth inside, stabbing delicately until small mewing sounds that would later bring a hot flush to her cheeks issued from inside her. Her fingers moved down the firm muscles of his back, reveling in the taut feel of sinewy flesh. The weight of his body was deliciously hard against her, and though her experience with men was limited, she reacted as if she were a slave to desire.

Their kissing grew in intensity until Kim was breathless with aching need. She wanted to be totally possessed. She wanted to block out the world and wallow in sensation. And she wanted Stephen Wright.

His hand traveled down the small of her back and over her hips. She was conscious of his heat and hardness and quickness of breath.

And then fingers slid beneath her shirt and tugged upward and his hand covered her breast, massaging through her bra. Melting with weakness, she would have given in right then and there if a spark from the fire hadn't popped out, live and hot, landing on Stephen's arm.

He jerked reflexively, laughed, brushed it aside. "Damn," he muttered, gently pushing Kim aside as he got to his feet and kicked the glowing ember back toward the hearth. Kim watched through desire-drugged eyes, but when he turned back to her, reason had returned.

"I can't do this," she whispered again, pulling her knees up to her chin. Stephen stretched out beside her, an open invitation.

"Why not?"

"I've never been with anyone but Alan."

"Good grief, Kim. It's high time you started living."

She looked at him squarely. At his sexy mouth and cool green eyes and burnished muscles. "By having an affair?"

"Starting a relationship," he amended. "I've been attracted to you since the moment we met," he added softly.

She wasn't secure enough to admit she'd felt the same way. "I don't want to do something I'll regret."

"How do you know you'll regret it?"

"Oh, believe me, I know." Her lips twisted as her mind spun ahead to various scenarios: Stephen, telling her how wonderful she was in one breath, breaking off their relationship with another; Stephen slowly stopping calling her; Stephen, another lovely beauty on his arm, catching sight of Kim and making a point to just say hello. Men like Stephen Wright married women like Pauleen, whether they were compatible or not, but they chose unsophisticated women like Kimberly Harden for "nice" affairs.

"What's going on in your head?" he asked, reaching forward to twist a thick strand of her blonde hair around his finger.

"I don't want to be a number."

"A number?"

"Yeah . . . just a number."

His brow furrowed. He pulled her closer and Kim was unable to resist. She watched his lips target hers until they were just a whisper away. Then his breath caught. "You mean a notch on a bedpost?" he asked, his voice revealing his displeasure.

Kim didn't answer. He pulled back, waiting. She could see she'd irked him. "We live in the same town."

"So, first I'm the evil attorney that tried to take your son, and now I'm the heartless love-'em-and-leave-'em sex fiend?"

"That's not what I meant."

"The hell it isn't!" he growled.

"Okay, it is what I meant," Kim answered recklessly. "I don't want any of this."

"Fine. Neither do I, anymore." He jumped to his feet. Kim, disconcerted, did the same. "I'm . . . I'm . . ." She tried to apologize and couldn't find the words. He didn't bother to turn around anyway, just strode furiously toward the bedroom. *Her* bedroom.

Blast the man! Somehow this was his fault. "I'm leaving," she tossed out, following after him to make certain he heard her.

She practically slammed into him just inside the bedroom door. He was pulling a shirt over his head.

"The roads are closed," he bit back, as if she were a complete moron.

"Maybe they're open now. How do we know? We're cut off from communication."

"I wouldn't count on the roads being passable until electricity's restored."

"Well, how do you know?"

"Educated guess," he told her flatly.

It didn't help that the jade green of his casual shirt made his eyes all the more sensual and mysterious. She tried to concentrate on his rock-hard jaw instead, and the anger that made it that way.

Just to be contrary, or because she was a glutton for punishment, Kim didn't know which, she said breezily, "I think I'll check it out for myself."

"If you get stuck, don't expect me to come after you."

"I won't!"

With that she sailed past him into the bedroom, threw her gear into her bag, and headed for the door. Stephen was once again standing in front of the fire when she reappeared. As she hauled her suitcase from the room he shook his head at her as if she were a naughty girl.

"Don't be ridiculous," he started, but that just ticked Kim off.

"Somebody has to do something," she snapped, "and it might as well be me."

"Then, I'm going with you."

"I'm not helpless!"

"You're just stubborn, then?"

She glared at him. Now, he was really irritating her. "If I wanted your help, I'd ask for it."

"I'm coming with you," he stated in that masculine way sure to infuriate any woman.

Since arguing with him wasn't working, Kim simply hitched up her suitcase and headed into the rainy morning. She slogged toward her car. Stephen made one aborted attempt to take her bag from her, but when she held on with a death grip he gave up. They reached the car together and Kim unlocked the door.

By the time she managed to stow her suitcase in the backseat and had struggled behind the wheel she was thoroughly soaked and out of breath. Apart from rain dampening his hair and shoulders, Stephen Wright looked cool, calm, and capable.

With a twist of her wrist, Kim turned the engine. Her little compact started up eagerly. Putting the car into reverse, her toe touched the accelerator. The engine revved but nothing happened. She tried again. The memory of that loud *ka-bang* when she arrived made her nose wrinkle.

"Are we stuck?" Stephen asked.

"I'm stuck," Kim answered shortly.

"Oh." He rubbed his nose with his finger, and Kim eyed him suspiciously. Was he hiding a smile? A moment later, he asked, "Want to try my Jeep?"

I'd rather walk! "Yes," Kim muttered with ill-grace, which seemed to strengthen his need to rub his nose. He *was* smiling. No, he was flat out grinning!

"Let's leave your suitcase for now and just check it out," he said reasonably, and Kim, who knew she'd been behaving badly, nodded and followed him to the red Jeep.

He started the engine and slowly backed away from the cabin. Rain washed the windshield, the wipers flailing wildly in an attempt to keep the glass clear. In silence they slowly worked their way down the rutted, muddy track to the two-lane road that was the main highway down the mountain. Stephen turned on the radio and before they'd traveled one mile they heard the report: The roads were still closed.

In silence, he brought the Jeep to a standstill. They sat in the middle of the road, wipers beating furiously, news reporter blabbering on about the weather. Stephen turned to her and arched his brow in silent query.

There was nothing to do but head back.

Kim felt like an utter fool. Nothing seemed to be going right. Worse, as they approached the cabin, it felt like fate was leading her inexorably into a romantic trap.

"When do you think the roads will be open?" she asked.

"Anybody's guess." He pulled the Jeep up next to her compact, climbed out, and started around the back to open the passenger door.

Kim pushed open her door, avoiding his efforts to help her from the car. Why all these tiny things should matter baffled her a bit, but instinctively she knew she was fighting the battle of the sexes.

Or maybe her own rampant desires . . .

He watched her tiptoe around muddy puddles. The rain had abated to a light drizzle, but Kimberly felt it soaking her nonetheless.

"What are you doing?" she asked as he leaned inside the Jeep.

"Gotta get something."

She could see him digging in the glove box. With a shrug she hurried to the cabin door, dodging the worst of the rain puddles. In the safety of the threshold she glanced back.

He was carrying a cell phone.

"What?" she demanded as he eased past her, pushing a series of buttons. "You had that all the time!" She followed him inside.

"I think the battery's dead."

"Was it dead yesterday when the lines went out?"

"Probably not," he conceded, unruffled.

"I can't believe you! All this time we could have been in touch with civilization!" Kim was beside herself.

"What was the point of calling then? We'd gotten hold of Betsy. Nobody could do anything about us being here."

His reasonableness drove her crazy. "I could have talked to Bobby," she said.

That remark struck home. He seemed about to say something, then clamped his lips shut. "Maybe the battery isn't completely dead," he said after a moment, attempting to dial.

She waited in silence. She was fast losing patience with him and herself and *everything.* Normally she was so much more in control, but these were not normal times.

After a couple of minutes he shook his head and put the phone on the mantel. His serious face made her wonder if he were growing as anxious to leave as she was. The idea bothered her a great more than it should.

The silence stretched uncomfortably. Kim traversed the room several times before flopping into the overstuffed chair and picking at a loose thread on one of the pillows. Stephen spent a great deal of time stoking the fire until the room was absolutely sweltering. Kim determined she would not complain no matter what, so they both suffered in the heat.

Eventually Stephen took the tub of water into the bathroom and poured it into the bathtub. "You can use it, if you want," he said, and Kim, deciding to take him up on it, grudgingly thanked Stephen as she locked the bathroom door behind her.

It felt wonderful to luxuriate in the warm water. Downright sinful. A half hour later, when the temperature had cooled too much, Kim stepped from the tub and brushed her hair in front of the misty mirror. She eyed her reflection and wondered what to do. Dragging on a pair of denim cut-offs and a cream sleeveless Polo shirt, she stepped back into the living room.

Stephen was nowhere in sight but she heard an engine running outside. Looking through the window, she was amazed to see that her little compact was turned nose out.

"How did you fix it?" she asked when he came back inside, rain- and mud-spattered.

"It was really just stuck. You were just afraid to punch it."

"Oh. Thanks."

"You're welcome." A glint of humor lightened his eyes.

Once more they fell into silence. Kim debated about fixing something to eat but couldn't think of what that might be. Finally, she could stand it no more. She opened her mouth to say something, but Stephen beat her to the punch.

"Do you believe in fate?"

She stared at him in surprise. "Do you?"

"On the whole, no. I think you make your own opportunities."

"I'd say I feel the same way."

"But once in a while, something happens. Something unexpected. An unexpected opportunity," he clarified. To Kim's continued silence, he added, "And when that happens, I think you should grab it, go with it." He shrugged. "Some people might call that fate."

Kimberly nodded.

"That's what we have: an unexpected opportunity. Fate. A chance to know each other."

His gaze was direct, full of promise and expectation. Kim's heart began a dull, hard beat.

"We've got a few hours left here together. I don't want to waste them."

Mouth dry, she asked, "What do you mean by 'waste?' "

A pause. "Don't you know?"

"Spell it out for me. I don't want to misunderstand."

He smiled faintly. "I want to touch you and talk to you and make love to you. I want to spend hours in your arms. I want it so badly that I can't think of anything else. Is that spelled out enough?"

Kim's gaze fell to his open shirt neck. She watched his throat work as he spoke. Inside, she quaked with nervousness. He was waiting for her answer. Waiting for her to choose. He was offering her an affair. The start of a relationship. No, a weekend out of time. Completely removed from real life. His voice was an aphrodisiac. She was powerless. She wanted him. She couldn't speak.

But he was waiting.

"Kim . . . ?"

Four

Breath held, Stephen waited for what felt like the proverbial eternity. Kim couldn't meet his eyes. Her fists were clenched and her slim body shook a bit. Clearly she was taking his offer as a serious one, which it was meant to be, but he was afraid she would overthink it—something he refused to do. He wanted to run with emotion. He was tired of all the years of pent-up feelings, worry, and doubt.

"Kim?" he asked again.

"It's so hot in here I can't think."

"Come here." He didn't wait for her to protest; he didn't listen when she finally did. He led her to the back of the cabin and a covered porch where rain beat a tattoo on the slightly listing roof and puddles danced with bouncing droplets.

His hand was on her arm. He ached to pull her close. Shooting a sideways glance at her, he noticed the lushness of her pink lips and the thick curve of her lashes. Her skin shone with health. He longed to reach over and run a finger down the hill of her cheek.

"Tell me about Pauleen," she said unexpectedly.

"Pauleen?" Stephen hesitated. "There's not much to tell."

"Oh, come on." Kim sniffed in disbelief. "You were the perfect couple."

"Who said we were the perfect couple?"

"Local headlines. People who knew you."

"Nobody knew us," Stephen assured her bitterly. "We were all for show."

"She's a very beautiful woman."

Stephen shot Kim a look of amazement. Kim made a dozen Pauleens. A thousand! She had that wholesome look of a country girl in a denim sleeveless dress picking wildflowers and wearing a floppy hat, yet she had the sass of a waitress used to juggling overeager male patrons.

"Like I said, we were all for show."

"How did you end up with Jason?" Kim asked in a small voice.

So, that was it. Given her own set of circumstances—and his involvement in them—she couldn't understand how he'd managed to wrest Jason away from his mother. Pauleen, by virtue of being Jason's mother, was good; ergo, Stephen was evil.

"Like I always get everything," he said with a trace of bitterness, "by legal trickery and coercion. How could I possibly win any other way?"

She had the grace to blush. Bending her head, she wrinkled her nose in an entirely enticing way and whispered, "Sorry."

And right then Stephen knew he had to stop protecting Pauleen. Regardless of the terms of their divorce and custody decision, Kim had a right to know the truth. Keeping the truth to himself hadn't helped anyone: himself, Jason, or Pauleen.

"You think I had a storybook marriage, don't you?" he asked, his mouth twisting.

"No . . . if it were storybook, it would have had a happy ending."

"Pauleen and I got married for all the wrong reasons." He stopped, wishing he hadn't used the cliché.

"What were they?"

Kim turned to him, her eyes full of warmth and interest. It stopped Stephen for a moment. He wasn't used to someone who was so open, so ready to listen.

"We were young and in love."

Kim's lips parted. "Those are the wrong reasons?"

"All right. That isn't quite true. We were young, and we kept telling ourselves we were in love, and Pauleen was pregnant."

"Oh."

"Looking back, I realize I was ready to get married anyway, and that sort of made the decision. Then we had Jason. Pauleen didn't want any more children, so that was it."

Kim's brows lifted. "Alan didn't want any more after Bobby, either."

"Maybe they should have gotten together," Stephen suggested with a trace of humor, to which Kim smiled. "Anyway, we stayed married, but . . . there was always something missing. Another cliché, but there it is. I didn't think about it anymore. I threw myself into my work—earned myself the reputation of 'shark'—and just kept going.

"Pauleen was unhappy, too. Neither of us addressed it. When the core's bad, you rot from the inside out. That's what we did. I handled it my way, and Pauleen handled it hers."

It was all he could do to keep himself from reaching over and dragging Kim to him. He wanted to hold someone. He wanted to assuage the pain of the past, and he wanted to love someone else. He couldn't remember ever being so honest and insightful about his own feelings.

Kimberly chewed thoughtfully on her lower lip. He could sense how much his words penetrated, and why not? They were coming straight from the heart. "I remember that barbecue at Betsy's. You were so relaxed, but . . ."

"Pauleen drank too much," he finished for her, relieved that she'd stumbled on the truth. Or maybe Pauleen's problem was more obvious than he knew. "That was how she coped. Eventually she checked herself into a treatment center for alcoholism, but it was only temporary help. I got Jason by virtue of being the more responsible parent, and if you want the bald truth, Pauleen was relieved. She fussed about it. Told everyone her 'shark' of a husband had stolen her son."

Kimberly grimaced, remembering Alan's denouncement of Stephen and recalling the way she'd jumped on the bandwagon when she'd heard similar rumors floating around after Pauleen's badmouthing went public.

"But Pauleen couldn't handle Jason. She could scarcely handle herself. So, when we divorced, I got Jason. We're all happier now that it's behind us."

Kim inhaled deeply, expelling her breath on a long sigh. "I asked Betsy about you and Pauleen, but she wouldn't tell me. She said it was your story."

"Well, it's not much of a story." Stephen snorted. "It's just a sad statistic."

"How's Pauleen now?"

"Most of the time—better. But she does have bouts when she's out of control. That's why Jason spends so much time at the Reeds'. He can't be with Pauleen. It makes him, and me, too nervous. They can visit each other, but Pauleen is not responsible and Jason's an impressionable sixteen."

"I don't talk to Alan," Kim revealed. "I mean, yes, we communicate necessary information. Like 'I'm picking Bobby up at six for Little League practice,' and 'Bobby cut his finger and I ran him to the emergency room,' but otherwise, it's best if we don't talk to each other."

"When I think of him hitting you . . ." Stephen took a breath. "I want to kill him."

"You'll have to take a number, because I'm ahead of you in line," she said lightly.

She shot him a soft glance out of the side of her eyes and it was too much for Stephen. Gently, very gently, he drew her into his arms. She didn't resist, and after a long, long moment she let her head fall to his chest, her breath escaping on a sigh. Stephen closed his eyes. This is what he'd missed with Pauleen. This tenderness. This love.

His heart skipped a beat. *Love?* He hadn't thought in those terms in years. Not romantic love. Not the hearts and flowers and stars-in-your-eyes kind of nonsense that he'd felt once during puberty over Jennifer Dalton, the most popular girl in the seventh grade. And, of course, that had been puppy love.

Instinctively he started assessing his feelings, digging deep inside himself to make some kind of rational sense of this. At some level he'd always thought of Kimberly Harden as the kind of woman a man could spend his whole life with; she just came off that way. But on another level, he hadn't really thought of her for him.

Why not? he asked himself now.

He had no answer.

She stirred in his arms. "I've spent a lot of time being mad at you," she admitted.

"I know. You had just cause."

"Actually, no I didn't. I blamed you for Alan hiring an attorney to take Bobby away."

"Alan did come to me first."

She lifted her head. "What? Are you trying to play devil's advocate now? Hey, counselor, just agree with me, okay?"

He was enchanted. "Okay. I agree with you."

His capitulation brought a mischievous light to her eyes. "And you'll keep agreeing with me, right?"

"This sounds dangerous."

"Just keep agreeing."

Stephen eyed her thoughtfully. They'd reached a new plateau in their fledgling romance. An element of trust had sneaked in. "Okay," he said.

"You are my slave."

"Oh, no." Stephen started chuckling. Her scent rose upward. He breathed deeply, filling his head, reveling in the abandonment.

"You are my slave, and you will do as I ask. You will not add another log to the fire when it's just embers, otherwise we shall all swelter to death."

He could hear the laughter in her voice. His arms tightened around her. "The slave would like to kiss the master."

"Forget it. You will also refrain from asking favors."

"What would you have me do, O Powerful One?" His hand,

exhibiting a will of its own in direct opposition to her commands, reached up to cup her chin.

"I think . . . you should . . . stop that . . ."

"Now?"

"Immediately." Her voice caught on a breath.

His hand slowly slid down her cheek and neck, one finger lightly touching the pulse at the base of her throat. Passion beat there. For a moment they stood in silence, Kim gazing at the floor. When she reluctantly lifted her eyes again, Stephen bent down to touch his lips to hers, lightly at first, then with deep need. Kim didn't resist. She let him hold her and kiss her, and her mouth meshed with his hungrily.

It was too much. They were too attracted to each other. They kissed like teenagers who only had a limited time together, making each touch, each moment, each sigh count.

Kim slid her arms around his neck. She wanted complete surrender, complete love. Deliberately, she crowded all her doubts to a small locked corner of her mind.

"I want you," he whispered. His body was hard against hers. He didn't try to hide any feelings, any desires.

Kim nodded, unable to speak. She didn't mean it as a complete surrender, but that's how Stephen took it. He swept her into his arms and carried her back through the cabin. She clung to him, suddenly scared. His gaze read her face, but before she could protest, his mouth swooped down on hers again, reminding her of the pleasures to come.

When her back connected with the quilted bedspread, Kim's sanity returned in a cold rush. "Stephen, wait!" she cried, hands pressed against his shoulders to ward him off.

His green eyes swam with desire. She couldn't look at him. He mesmerized her, and it made her think dangerous, wicked, delicious thoughts.

"I can't just throw caution to the wind."

"Oh, Kim, don't talk," he murmured against the warm skin of her neck. His body stretched out luxuriously beside her, half atop her, legs tangled.

"This is insane."

"Why?" he demanded, lips against her throat.

"Because!"

His mouth cut off more protests. Kim's senses swam under his tender assault. As soon as his lips left to discover the curve of her jaw, the lobe of her ear, she muttered, "I won't like myself later."

"You worry too much."

"There's always a tomorrow," she half choked out. *What was he doing?* His tongue had found sections of her ear she hadn't known existed!

"Just love me . . ."

It was so tempting. *Why not?* her heart demanded. *Why not?* But her head wasn't so eager, so swamped with desire.

Still . . .

Because it was easier than fighting, Kim accepted his kisses and tender touches. His hand drifted downward, massaging her breast, and her heartbeat quickened in anticipation. Squeezing her eyes shut tightly, she tried to force out the drumbeat of warnings that filled her head. *Why can't I just make love to him?* she demanded of herself. *Other people do it all the time. Why not just this once? Why not?*

The answer came swiftly: because she had to be in love with him, and he had to be in love with her. She was pretty sure she was falling head over heels for him, but she didn't believe for a minute that for him this was more than an attraction.

With understanding came action; she pushed him away.

"Kim," he protested with a thick murmur, his own emotions difficult to override. But it was just sex for him, she reminded herself, and with a squirming twist she was out from under him and standing, shaking by the side of the bed.

Stephen groaned and buried his face in the quilt in frustration.

"Look, I'm sorry. I'm not trying to be a tease. I just can't do this. I can't. Sex is for people in love. I'm sorry, that's just how I feel. I wouldn't be able to spend this weekend with you, then go back to my regular life like nothing had happened," Kim struggled to continue. "I'm—sorry."

Heaving a huge sigh, Stephen rolled to his back, sliding her a rueful glance. "You've said that three times. Stop apologizing."

"Well, I feel I have to. I may have sent out mixed signals. I'm—" She caught herself before she uttered it a fourth time.

"I'm beginning to agree with you wholeheartedly," he expelled.

"About what?"

"We can't stay here together."

With that, he shot off the bed with a muscular twist and headed out of the bedroom, through the cabin, and out the front door into the drizzling afternoon.

By nightfall the rain stopped but there was still no sign of Stephen. Kimberly was torn between annoyance and worry. He'd taken off in his red Jeep, and she'd surreptitiously watched from the window as he'd heedlessly bumped and sloshed through puddles on his way.

It was a fit of pique if she'd ever seen one. So what? It wasn't her fault he was feeling horny and frustrated. Well, not totally anyway. He was the one who'd kept pushing everything, and so she'd run up against the wall of her own morals. There was no crime in it. A majority of the world might actually commend her for her values.

So, why was she feeling like she'd made a terrible mistake?

The clouds had blown away as if by magic, traveling across the sky and leaving little patches of blue until, just before sunset, the sky was clear. Now, Kim could see a myriad of stars flung into the black velvet heavens. She sat on the love seat, turned toward the window, trying not to let worry spoil the moment.

Damn the man! This wasn't a lovenest planned for his pleasure and convenience. And it wasn't an *opportunity* for them, either. *Opportunity!* Kim gave a very unladylike snort. She was coming to loathe that word. No, this was merely a mistake. They'd ended up at the same cabin together and were making the best of it. If all went well, the floods would recede by morning and they'd both be out of here.

Hasta la vista, baby!

That is, if Stephen ever returned.

Time ticked by, excruciatingly slowly. Needing something to do, Kim raided their larder, nibbling on several saltines. She didn't even like them all that much. It was Bobby who'd thrown the box into the sack. Kim smiled and reminded herself to thank her son when she saw him again.

What would Bobby think if she were to date Stephen Wright? Kim wondered idly. Probably pass out from pure delight for it would mean more of Jason Wright in his life—heaven on earth if there ever was one!

Where *was* Stephen? If he didn't show up soon, she'd be downright upset! In fact—

Kim gasped as the lights suddenly went back on. "All right!" she cried, thrilled at the prospect of a connection to civilization. Snatching up the phone, she was disappointed to learn it still wasn't working.

Needing something to occupy her time, Kim chose the opportunity to throw together the spaghetti sauce, *sans* meat, and boil the pasta. Salad in the bag was long gone, but there were some apples and pears which Kim arranged on plates. She'd just found the wine cork when she heard the front door open.

"Stephen?" she called, peering around the doorjamb. "My God! What happened to you?"

He was covered with mud from head to foot.

"I made it down to the river, but the water's still over the bridge. We're stuck on this side until probably tomorrow afternoon. I see power's restored on the mountain though," he observed.

"But why are you so muddy?"

"I tried to help a guy get his pickup out of the floodwaters.

No chance. It's just a matter of waiting." He shot her a look. "But it won't be much longer. Just one more night," he added as he headed toward the bathroom.

"Stephen, wait!" Kim called, but he turned on the taps to the shower. She wasn't certain whether he heard her or not, but it hardly mattered. He wasn't going anywhere, at least for one more night.

Suddenly, she was gripped by anxiety. *Only one more night.* Though she'd made lots of noise about wanting to get away from him, those feelings had quickly changed. Now the idea of separating tomorrow and going back to their own lives filled her with dread.

Kim uncorked the wine, lit the candles which still tilted drunkenly in their glasses, set the arrangement of fruit at two places, poured marinara sauce over bowls of pasta, then tipped an Oregon pinot noir into a pair of surprisingly pretty wine goblets. She was waiting at the table when Stephen stepped out of the bathroom, once again wearing a pair of jeans and no shirt.

He stopped short at the sight of her. Kim had changed earlier but had covered up her sundress with a terrycloth apron while she cooked so he hadn't seen the transformation. Now the way he looked at her made her blush.

"You look beautiful," he said after a moment, realizing he was staring.

"Thank you." The dress was a white, sleeveless cotton shift that showed off the soft tan she'd achieved before this sudden deluge had hit the Portland area and turned it into waterworld.

She waited while he put on a shirt, white also, with the long sleeves rolled up. His forearms were sprinkled with masculine hair, several shades lighter than his own dark brown locks. His skin glowed like burnished copper in the candlelight.

"As grateful as I was for power, I chose the candles instead," she stammered, feeling a little foolish at her romanticism.

"This looks great," he said, inclining his head toward the meal.

"I'm not a half-bad cook with a few modern conveniences," Kim said lightly.

"You're not half-bad anyway," he returned. Then, as if embarrassed, he said, "I checked the phone."

"It's still not working, I know."

"I plugged in my cell phone battery charger. It won't be long before we can get through."

"Great!"

Now why did that feel so forced? Kim asked herself miserably as she toyed with her pasta and nibbled at the fruit. Even the red wine, wonderful as it was, wasn't doing anything for her. Stephen, too, seemed self-absorbed and lost in his own thoughts.

"Think we can date when we get back to the real world?"

Kim stared at Stephen, wondering if she'd actually heard the words or had been hoping to hear them so badly that she'd imagined them. "What?" she asked.

"I'll take that as a no," he remarked, his mouth twisting.

"No! I mean, yes! That's what I want."

He grinned at her. "Yeah?"

"Yeah."

"Well, lady, let me tell you something. You're really hard to read sometimes. Maybe I come on too strong, but it just seemed right."

"It did seem right, but it was scary. I just need time."

"Take all the time you need, All I want is a chance."

Kim was positively glowing with joy. One moment everything seemed wrong, then *poof!* She was granted her every wish. "Are you serious?"

"Like a heart attack, serious," he stated strongly. "And I already know we're not going to sleep together tonight, so don't worry, I won't ask."

Kim hid a smile behind her wineglass. "You can't ask, slave," she told him. "Only the master can ask."

"The master has made it quite clear how she feels."

"The master just needs to sort through some feelings and

figure out where this is going." Swallowing a sip, she decided to lay her cards on the table. "The master has to make sure the slave is hoping for some kind of long-term relationship, because that's the only way it works for the master."

"The slave doesn't jump from master to master like some people seem to think he does. The slave would like to hope for something more, too."

"Then anything's possible, slave," Kim said boldly, meeting his gaze.

"Don't tempt me, woman," he growled.

"Master," she corrected.

"Yeah, well, we'll see," he said with pure masculine ego, and they both broke into laughter.

An hour later they'd finished washing the dishes and put them away when Stephen picked up his newly charged battery and inserted it into the phone. He dialed Betsy's number, feeling relaxed and at ease in a way he hadn't been in what? Years? Kimberly Harden was a pure heaven. He could easily fall in love with her. He was halfway there already.

"Hey, who's this?" he asked, when he'd connected. "Chad?"

Kim reached around him for the phone. He twisted to keep her out of reach, and she wrapped her arms around his waist and tickled.

"Get your mom, Chad," Stephen ordered, fighting back laughter. "What?" He went suddenly still. Sensing a crisis, Kim turned around to gaze into his eyes. His suddenly grim expression scared her. "When did they go?" Stephen demanded.

"Who?" Kim mouthed. "Where?"

"The emergency room?"

That did it. On a cry she yanked the phone from his hand. Stephen let her, numb to the core.

"What happened?" Kim demanded. "Chad, where's your mother? Who went to the emergency room? Where's Bobby?"

"Jason and Bobby were in an accident," Chad blubbered.

"Mom and Dad are at the hospital. Nobody could reach you guys. Matt's with 'em, too," he added, referring to his older brother.

"What kind of accident?" Kim asked faintly.

"Car accident. They were just going down the driveway. Jason was taking them out for a Coke. Mom said it was okay, since Jason's got his license now. A car just smashed 'em, but Matt's okay."

"What about Bobby? And Jason?" Her knees were quaking. Dimly, Kim realized Stephen was holding her up.

"They're at the hospital. I don't know."

Stephen pulled the phone from Kim's unresisting fingers. Still holding her close, he asked Chad for further details. Finally, he hung up the phone and led Kim to the love seat where they both collapsed against each other.

"Betsy will call as soon as she knows something," Stephen said woodenly.

Kim couldn't think. She was consumed with fear. If she lost Bobby . . . "What was he doing in the car with Jason?" she asked, her voice trembling. "He shouldn't have been there."

Stephen didn't respond.

Inside Kim an unfair voice told her that she should have stuck with her first instincts. She should never have gotten involved with Stephen at any level. It was bad karma. Some misalignment of the stars. Somehow, being connected to this man was a threat to her and Bobby.

"I wish we'd never gotten this far," she cried half-hysterically. "Bobby and I were fine—without you in our lives!"

Stephen turned his head as if her words physically struck him. Tears welled in Kim's eyes. How stupid she was! But she couldn't shake the feeling. It was a pall, and it wrapped around her and fed her most basic fears.

Romance, which had been thick in the air a few moments earlier, vanished completely. She couldn't think of anything to say to Stephen and clearly, he felt the same way. They drew apart from each other and took turns pacing and waiting. In a dull fog Kim walked to the kitchen and made a pot of coffee that neither of them felt like drinking.

Near midnight Stephen's cell phone purred. He snatched it up and listened intently. As hot as it was, Kim shivered uncontrollably and after a few terse words that told her nothing, he handed the phone to her.

"Hello?" Kim said shakily.

"Hey, Kimmy." Betsy's tired voice brought a new surge of pent up emotion. Kim closed her eyes, fighting new tears and a sense of complete fright. She felt like she was about to self-destruct. "Everything's going to be okay," Betsy assured her. "Bobby bumped his head against the dash, but he was seat-belted in. He's bruised from where the seatbelt yanked against him."

"Is he—all right, then?" she choked.

"Perfectly fine. He's home with us tonight and waiting to talk to you. Here . . ."

"Mom . . . ?"

The sound of her son's voice closed Kim's throat. She could scarcely answer. "Hey, you," she whispered.

"I'm sorry," he said.

"What? It's okay. *You're* okay, and that's what matters."

"Yeah, but Jason's still in the hospital."

Kim's heart jerked hard. "He is?" Guilt raged through her. She hadn't even *asked* about Jason, she'd been so immersed in her own worry and pain.

"His arm broke and the bone was all mangled." Bobby sounded sick. "They had to operate."

She shot Stephen a look. He was staring into the charred remains of the fire, his expression stern. His fingers gripped the coffee cup as if it were a lifeline.

"How is Jason?" she asked Bobby.

"Okay, I guess. When are you going to be back?"

"Tomorrow. As soon as the roads are clear."

"You're not mad?"

"Mad?"

"Because I was in the car with Jason? I know you don't want me to ride with teenage drivers, but we were just going to the store to get a Coke and this guy came around the corner going about ninety!"

"We'll talk about it later," she said. "You're sure Jason's all right?"

"Uh huh. You want to talk to Betsy?"

"Yes, please."

There was a brief hesitation. "I love you, Mom," he said quickly, as if afraid to be heard.

"I love you, too," she said on a choked swallow.

"I am so sorry this happened," Betsy apologized. "I feel like it's all my fault. I told Jason he could go to the store, and I guess Bobby popped in the car with him."

"It's all right. It's fine. Jason's coming home tomorrow?"

"Yeah, I told Stephen. Is he okay, Kim? He sounded so monosyllabic, like he was mad or upset. I don't know what to say to him."

"I'll talk to him."

"I had to call Pauleen. She was hysterical. I think she's at the hospital now, but I'm afraid . . ." Betsy broke off. "Kimmy, she was drunk."

Kim winced. "Oh."

"I had to tell Stephen. Make sure he's okay, huh? I feel terrible. Are you two doing okay?" she asked as an afterthought.

"We're coping," Kim admitted, smitten with guilt. Stephen needed her support, not her accusations. Catching his eyes, she held the phone his way, but he shook his head so Kim finished her good-byes and hung up.

"I'm sorry about what I said earlier," Kim said awkwardly. "It's not your fault, or Jason's."

"I'd say it's definitely Jason's, as he was the driver," Stephen pointed out grimly.

"Please, don't be like that," Kim begged humbly.

"You were the one who pointed out you're better off not getting entangled with the Wrights."

"I didn't mean that."

"Maybe you did, Kim. This whole weekend I've been trying to force a romance between us that you haven't wanted."

"That's not true!" she protested.

"Let's leave it, okay? I'm tired, and I just want time to pass so I can make sure Jason's all right." With a snort, he added, "The good news is my drunken ex-wife is there to make things right."

"Stephen . . ."

Her plea went unheard because he walked outside to the porch. He was still standing there, back turned against her, when Kim finally headed, dejected and sad, off to bed.

It was four o'clock in the afternoon before the water had receded enough for them to return to Riverside. Kim followed Stephen down the mountain and the outskirts of Portland where he turned off to the hospital while she headed on to Riverside and Bobby.

At the Reeds', Betsy hugged her so tightly Kim nearly suffocated. "It's okay," Kim assured her troubled friend.

"Did Stephen go directly to the hospital?" To Kim's nod, Betsy added despondently, "Some babysitter I am."

"Things like this happen. Stop beating yourself up over it. Besides, it could have been so much worse."

"Jason had barely gotten into the street when this car whipped around the corner and hit him broadside. I was so scared!" Betsy recapped the accident, finishing with, "Matt's going to be sixteen in a couple of weeks. I am *not* looking forward to it."

Bobby burst into the room at that moment. At the sight of him, Kim gasped and clapped a hand to her mouth. A bandage was wrapped around his forehead Ninja-style and there was a huge dark smudge beneath his right eye, the beginning of a major shiner. Spying her expression, he grinned like a pirate. "Cool, huh? Jason's getting out today. He's got a cast on his arm. I'm going to sign it 'B. Harden, Crash-Test Dummy.' What do you think?"

Betsy looked pained. Kim started chuckling. She couldn't help herself. While Bobby eagerly awaited her answer, she simply folded him in her arms and squeezed him tight. This was not, however, the reaction he wanted, so he squirmed free and ran from the room, screaming like a banshee with the pure abandonment of a twelve-year-old boy.

"Do you think I should call Stephen?" Betsy fretted.

"Let him call you," Kim suggested. "He will, as soon as he's got a minute."

And will he call you? her needling mind questioned sharply. She had no clue.

". . . should've never let him have a license. He's always been irresponsible. You should've done something before. A long time ago. It's your fault, Stephen. Your fault, and I never, ever want to talk to you again! I hate you! I hate—"

Click.

Stephen glanced down at his finger on the receiver, slightly surprised that it seemed to have exhibited a will of its own. Before the message had gelled in his brain, his finger had cut off Pauleen's angry ranting. She was furious, but then, after a few drinks, she was always furious. People handled liquor in different ways and Pauleen's way was to be as obnoxious and flat out bitchy as possible.

Jason sat in a chair in the living room, pale but upbeat. His left arm was casted from wrist to shoulder, set in an L-shape that made him look as if he were constantly flexing.

"I swear, that guy was *moving.* One minute the road was clear, the next he was there and he just smashed me."

"You're lucky all you got was a broken arm."

"When do you think the car'll be fixed?"

Stephen almost smiled. Oh, to be a teenager and spend all your time worrying about cars. It was a simpler life.

"We'll figure it out."

"Can I drive the Jeep?"

With a glance at Jason's casted arm, Stephen said, "Not in the near future."

Jason's expression darkened, but then he flicked on the remote control and lost himself in some evening television show. Without further delay, Stephen placed a call to Betsy, assured her that everything was fine and that he didn't blame her for a thing, asked about Bobby, then fought the urge to inquire about Kim. Betsy was too distraught to pick up on the vibes, and that left Stephen alone, and lonely, with his thoughts.

Drumming his fingers on the receiver, he considered calling her. She'd been upset, and she'd tried to apologize, but he'd been too raw and bullheaded to listen. Her accusations had hurt, like the ones she'd thrown at him on the courtroom steps. Maybe she was right. Maybe they were star-crossed, destined to only hurt each other.

A moment later Stephen snorted in disgust. Was he nuts? When had he ever buckled under to superstition and nonsense? What was it about this woman that got to him so much?

"I'll be back in a while," he told Jason in sudden decision. Then he stepped outside to an inky night sky and the chance to secure his future.

Cradling a glass of wine, Kimberly curled her feet beneath her on her couch, conscious once more of her painted toenails. She'd remembered the name of the color: Pink Passion. It bugged the heck out of her.

Her fireplace was the gas kind; it could be ignited with the flick of a switch. The air was still warm and thick and full of the heat of summer, but, feeling like a complete imbecile, she'd switched on the fire.

She'd called Alan and told him about Bobby's trip to the

emergency room. He'd chastised her for letting Bobby drive around with some "stupid teenage driver" and Kim had let him rave on rather than explain the circumstances. Alan wouldn't have listened to that part anyway; he was too good at painting his own scenarios.

Now, she just felt like taking a deep breath and putting some perspective in her life. Bobby was safe, Jason would be fine, and Betsy would eventually get over her case of the guilts. As for Stephen Wright . . . she shuddered when she remembered what she'd said to him. She owed him one whopping apology.

B-br-brring . . . B-br-brring.

Kim frowned at the sound of her doorbell. Who?

Stephen! her heart cried out, and she rushed to the door, amazed that it was indeed the man she loved.

The man she loved . . .

"Stephen, I'm so glad you came. I owe you an apology," she rushed to explain as soon as the door was cracked open. "I was so selfish and worried. I guess I've become an overprotective mother ever since—" She broke off in a gasp as Stephen took both of her hands, pulled her close, and kissed her hard on the mouth.

"This is the start of a relationship," he said after several heady moments of kissing. "A serious relationship that could very well end in marriage. Now don't say 'I can't' again, because each time you do, I'll have to kiss you until you stop."

Kimberly closed the door behind them, leaning against it for a moment. Was she dreaming? It couldn't be this good. Her lips curved upward and she said teasingly, "I can't."

His mouth swooped down to capture hers. When he pulled back, he arched one brow, waiting.

"You're awfully cocky for a mere slave," she complained.

"This slave wants an answer: Are we going to start a serious relationship, or not?"

"The master doesn't want to be rushed."

"Tough," he said, grinning. He kissed her again.

"Hey, I didn't say, 'I can't.' "

That earned her another kiss that had her giggling and laughing in his arms.

Footsteps pounded on the stairs and Kim and Stephen broke apart like guilty teenagers. Bobby stopped dead, halfway down.

"Mom! Are you dating Mr. Wright?"

"Yes," Stephen answered, to which Bobby started whooping and screaming in delight.

"You shouldn't have told him that," Kim scolded. "You know he's on his way to call Jason."

"Was I supposed to hide it? Kim, before long, the whole town's going to know it. I am personally going to tell everyone I see."

"Maybe we should start with Betsy," Kim suggested.

"But first . . ." He tugged on her hand and drew her to the couch, cradling her in his arms and burying his face in the sweet-scented lushness of her blonde mane. "I'm falling in love with you," he admitted.

"Oh, Stephen, I've been falling in love with you forever," Kim declared in pure happiness. "I can't believe this!"

"Believe it," he whispered, kissing her softly and tenderly.

By the time they got around to calling Betsy, Kim believed with all her heart that she possessed Stephen's love completely, just as he'd always possessed hers. No more questions or worries or misunderstandings. Their two lives were destined to be one.

Summer Fantasy

Jill Marie Landis

One

I must be out of my mind.

Kylee Christopher tightened her hold on the steering wheel of the black Jeep Wrangler 4x4 and braced herself for a jolt. Leaning forward to wipe the fogged windshield, she pressed her palm against the cool glass and used her hand as a wiper blade. The smeared trail she left in the condensation did little to improve her vision.

The sly smile on the face of the clerk working the auto rental desk at Lihue Airport should have warned her something was up. When he heard she was staying up on Powerhouse Road, he immediately suggested she opt for a Jeep instead of a standard model vehicle.

Leave it to Sylvia to get her into this fix. Kylee swerved to avoid another puddle the size of a small lake and sighed. When her literary agent, Sylvia Greene, suggested she get away and then convincingly recommended a secluded vacation rental on the north shore of Kauai, Kylee had envisioned an elegant oceanfront condo, or at the very least a sprawling hillside retreat—not a trek into the uncharted reaches of a dense rainforest.

The rutted road narrowed and then curved sharply as it wound steadily uphill. Whenever she dared take her eyes off the smeared windshield, the dark emerald jungle appeared to be encroaching closer on both sides. Huge monstera vines sensuously wound themselves around the trunks of the trees close to the right side of the road. On her left, the jungle growth partially obscured the land where it fell away into a deep ravine. She couldn't see clearly enough to tell how far it was to the bottom.

Swinging her glance back to the road ahead of her, she saw an animal lumber into her path. Kylee cursed and stood on the brake. The Jeep swerved. The oversized tires ground into the gravelly mud. The car stopped short of a very fat spotted dog.

Kylee leaned on the horn, expecting the animal to run off, but it didn't budge. Rain beat a steady tattoo on the roof. Her fingers began to echo the beat as she tapped on the steering wheel.

"There's no way I'm getting out to chase you off."

Kylee had mumbled aloud, but her voice was lost in the beat of the rain as she downshifted, intending to head the Jeep straight for the dog at a crawl and hope the creature gave way. She was releasing the clutch when a little Hawaiian boy no more than four years old careened into the road on a rusty, miniature dirt bike.

Kylee slammed on the brakes again.

"What next?" she yelled at the windshield, watching in awe as the dark-haired, nearly naked boy jumped off the bike and scurried over to the fat dog.

She opened the door, stood on the inside edge of the floorboard and ignored the rain that felt like ice when it hit her overheated skin. She blinked twice, then wiped the water out of her eyes and stared harder.

The dog was a pig. The biggest, ugliest, meanest looking pig she'd ever seen, not that she'd seen many pigs up close and personal. Even more amazing, the kid in the Batman underpants was tugging on the pig's ear, trying to get him to move.

The boy shouted something she couldn't understand and the pig finally got the message. It headed back up the steep, narrow drive to the right. The little boy jumped back on the rusted, muddy bike. Pedaling furiously, he rode straight through a puddle, nearly tipped over, then kept going without a backward glance.

Recovering from her surprise, Kylee leaned against the roof of the Jeep and yelled, "Wait!"

She could see the deep ruts going up the driveway on the hillside. The drive wound steeply uphill to a small, ramshackle island home. Dark green, the house blended into the dense growth and might not have even been discernable if it hadn't been for the yard filled with old cars, wandering rust-colored roosters, and a pack of dogs, that had to be related to each other, chained together.

The little boy didn't say a word. He sat there straddling his bike, staring back at her with a broad smile on his face.

"Do you know where *Hale Nanea* is?"

The child shrugged.

"Hale Nanea?" She yelled.

Finally, the boy pointed to the opposite side of the road.

"Hah-lay. Down dere," he hollered back.

Kylee squinted toward the opposite side of the road. All she saw was a smear of jungle. Amid the wild greenery along the road stood a row of tall gingers in full yellow bloom, but there was no sign of the vacation rental the brochure described as "The perfect island retreat in the peaceful Wainiha Valley."

"Where?" She turned back to question the child, but he had disappeared. The only sign of him was the abandoned bike lying in the yard.

"Damn," she whispered, ducking back into the Jeep. She shoved the stick shift into first gear and eased off on the clutch. On the passenger seat, her brand-new, woven straw bag was getting soaked, so she punched the window button, determined to head back down the cursed road as soon as she found a wide enough place to turn around. Once she reached the bottom of Powerhouse Road, she was going to head back to the five star hotel she had seen on the bluff at Princeville about ten miles back.

Just then, a flash of color caught her eye. Red, saffron, and royal blue against the tangle of green. Braking, she slowly backed up until the Jeep was directly across from a pretty, hand-painted sign decorated with a lei of orchids wound around the words, *Hale Nanea*.

Grumbling, Kylee scanned the bushes for some sign of a drive and finally found it. She would have to make a left turn into a steep incline without any notion of what might be waiting at the bottom. Checking to be sure she was in four-wheel drive, she shoved the gearshift into first and started down the hill.

Water was running off the main road in heavy rivulets on both sides of the rock-paved driveway, which had become a sea of mud. She gripped the wheel. The Jeep rolled down, reaching the end of the drive well before she expected it to, and she was forced to slam on the brakes. She took a look around. A small house stood just ahead of her. Behind it was a wall of thick growth. On the driver's side was a larger version of the cottage.

"Just wait, Sylvia," she mumbled to herself, thinking of her hare-brained agent and wondering how she ever let herself get talked into *this*. Living like Tarzan's Jane wasn't exactly what she needed right now.

She opened the car door and discovered the rain was beginning to lighten up. A wide wooden veranda fronted the large house beside her. It was crowded with comfortable looking wicker furniture. A plaque on the wall beside the wide double doors was a reduced version of the one on the road. *Hale Nanea*.

With a sigh of relief, Kylee reached for her purse and the carryall that held her essentials intent on heading for the shelter of the porch. She stepped out of the Jeep. Her new white tennis shoes sank into the red mud.

"What next?" Squashing her way to the veranda, she climbed two of the three low steps and stood on the edge of the porch.

"Hello?" she called out, looking for some sign of life. The inside doors were open, the screens closed. She could see

through to a comfortable room with casual furniture uphol-
stered in fabric with a palms and hibiscus motif, accessorized
with island touches. Woven mats covered the floors.

The porch was unbelievably clean, especially since it was
surrounded by a sea of mud. She could hear water rushing
beyond the curtain of thick trees with shiny green leaves and
fragile-looking yellow flowers that looked like they were made
of crepe paper. The small house in back was connected to the
larger but identical structure by a raised wooden walkway.

Just before she took a step onto the immaculate veranda, she
saw a sign opposite the *Hale Nanea* plaque that read: ISLAND
STYLE—PLEASE REMOVE YOUR SHOES.

She tossed her purse and the carryall toward the nearest chair
without taking another step onto the porch. The skies were still
gray, but the rain had momentarily stopped, so she decided to
unload the car before the next deluge. Trudging back and forth
to the Jeep, she carried up two suitcases, her laptop, printer,
then a box of books and magazines. Luckily, she finished just
before the rain started again.

Kylee paused to rest on the edge of the porch and wiped her
brow with the back of her hand. The humidity was as thick as
a flannel blanket. She was hungry, exhausted, and frustrated.

" '*Complete with all the amenities.*' Ha. Good joke, Sylvia.
All the amenities except for a bellboy," she grumbled aloud.

"You're early."

At the sound of the deep, masculine voice behind her, she
nearly jumped out of her skin. Kylee spun around and found
herself face-to-face with a Polynesian god. Dressed in a faded
tank top that sported a surfboard logo and shorts, he was over
six feet tall with wide shoulders, a tapered waist, well-developed
biceps, and legs that would make a weightlifter drool. His com-
plexion was bronze; his shoulder-length, coal black hair was tied
back in a ponytail. His dark eyes had an exotic, slight tilt at the
corners. His lips were stunning, lush and full, framing a smile
wide enough to reveal perfect teeth. He was definitely half-Hawaiian, if not more.

Kylee had to blink twice to break the spell. For the first time in her life, she knew what it meant to be rendered speechless. She took a step back. The mud on her shoes was beginning to stiffen.

"You must be Kylee Christopher. Welcome to *Hale Nanea*." The god held out his hand.

Like a robot, Kylee offered hers. He shook it.

"I guess the rain on the roof kept me from hearing you drive in. I'm Rick Pau. P-a-u, not p-o-w. Houseboy, chef, caretaker, and gardener. Like the brochure says, I'm here to see to your every need."

Kylee didn't recall the brochure or Sylvia mentioning anything about a Hawaiian god being on hand to "see to her every need."

"Well, Mr. Pau, I wish you had been here to help me unload."

She watched him glance over to her pile of assorted bags and boxes and took the opportunity to study him closer. He was far too handsome for his own good. Probably used that killer smile to get him out of any jam.

"In fact," she went on, ignoring the sparkle in his eyes, "I wish you had put more detailed directions on that little brochure of yours. I was almost hopelessly lost in this jungle, and I nearly ran over a pig in the road. A *pig*. A big one. Not to mention a little boy on a dirt bike."

As he leaned back against the veranda railing, he folded his arms across his chest. The move emphasized all his muscular assets.

"You *are* having a bad day." He continued smiling for all the world as if he were trying to win the Mister Congeniality division of a Gorgeous Island Man contest. Then suddenly he straightened and pushed off the rail.

"Why don't you take off your shoes. Go on in and relax? I'll bring all your things in."

She wanted to be furious at him, she really did, but her conscience got the best of her. The rain wasn't his fault, nor did he have anything to do with the pig or the poor condition of the road. Deep down, she knew exactly what was *really* bothering her and it certainly wasn't Rick Pau.

It was the ever-mounting panic that her Emmy-award winning career as a television screenwriter was on the brink of disaster.

Rick stepped aside and watched the trim, leggy blonde walk into the house. Even drawn back in a severe ponytail, her hair was stunning, long and thick, shot through with golden highlights. She had sensuous curves in all the right places. It would be a long, long time before he forgot the impact she had on his senses when he rounded the corner of the lanai, or veranda, and found her standing there.

Like most tourists who came to the island, she was wearing brand-new clothes; what had once been pristine white shorts nicely revealed her shapely legs. Her pale peach sports shirt had a pricey logo riding over her left breast.

"This is like a movie set," she said while her bright, sea-blue eyes roamed over the interior of the main room. "Right out of *South Pacific.*"

"Did you know the movie was filmed on the island?" He easily hefted the bags and started toward the master suite.

The warm sound of her voice followed him into the other room. "How could I *not* know? It's in every article I ever read about Kauai."

Rick laughed. "The tourist bureau tries to get a lot of mileage out of the locations of film sights around the island. *Jurassic Park,* the remake of *King Kong, Raiders of the Lost Ark,* some scenes from *The Thorn Birds* were even shot here."

"I like these mats on the floor." Obviously not interested in movie trivia, she continued to prowl.

"They're called *lau hala.*" He set her suitcases down and led her back to the main room that opened onto front and rear verandas. He found Kylee standing at the huge window staring out at the picture-postcard view of the Wainiha River, water-filled taro fields, and the ocean beyond. Rick couldn't help but admire her profile as she stood there unaware that he had joined her again.

He walked over to the door and stacked her laptop on top of the box that appeared to hold a printer. "Would you like me to hook these up at the desk?"

"I can manage."

"I guess you plan on doing a little work while you're here."

It wasn't a question. One of his former guests from L.A., Sylvia Greene, had called to tell him that she was going to suggest *Hale Nanea* to one of the writers she represented, a woman who needed to get away. When Sylvia added that she wanted Rick to see that her client had a good time, he had expected someone a bit more . . . well, literary looking. Someone who might have a problem meeting people. Not a woman who didn't seem shy at all and who could hold her own in a beauty contest.

No, Kylee Christopher wasn't what he had expected. Not at all. The effect she was having on him—both physical and mental—was something that hadn't happened to him around any other woman for a long, long time. There was something about her eyes, something deep down inside the blue depths that reflected a lost, tentative side of her, one that didn't mesh with the capable, confident air she had shown so far. She was a woman with secrets. He felt drawn to her, compelled to know her better. He wanted to be the one to help her find whatever it was she was missing in her life. If he wasn't careful, she just might turn his well-orchestrated life, not to mention his heart, upside down.

Rick walked over to a wide desk trimmed in bamboo and gently set down her things.

"I plan on doing a lot of work, not a little," she said in answer to his earlier question.

"On Kauai? You crazy?"

"No, I'm not crazy."

He couldn't help but notice that she didn't sound very certain as she continued to stare out at the steadily falling rain.

"Hopefully this weather will keep up. I won't even be tempted to go outside," she said.

"Oh, it'll rain some in the next three weeks, but just wait till the sun comes out," he said. The beauty of Kauai was almost the best-kept secret in the world.

Before he could stop himself, Rick took one quick perusal of her bare legs and damn, if she didn't turn around and catch him at it. She shot him an icy glare even as she self-consciously tugged on the hem of the white shorts that hit her mid-thigh. He felt as guilty as hell, but could he help it if he appreciated beauty in all its forms?

"Anything else you need before dinner?" He smiled and tried focusing on her eyes, which turned out to be an even bigger mistake. He was drawn to them the way he was drawn to the blue Pacific waters on a sunny day.

Fighting the urge to shiver despite the heat, Kylee ran her hands up and down her arms and turned away to avoid Rick Pau's heated stare.

"No, thank you. All I need is peace and quiet," she said.

She heard him moving across the room. When she turned around, expecting to watch him leave, she found he'd paused beside the door. Her cool dismissal hadn't diminished his smile in the least.

"I'll just leave your dinner on the table in the kitchen. That's my house in back. If you need anything, just call the number on the pad next to the phone in the kitchen or walk on over. The door's always open."

"Thank you," she said, watching him let himself out of the door. When the screen door closed behind him, she let out a sigh. She was alone at last with nothing but the sound of the rain on the metal roof for company. Aside from Rick Pau's sudden appearance, this was just what she wanted. Just what she needed to get her writing back on track. No more excuses.

She cast a wary glance at the laptop in its padded case and decided that after the five-hour flight from L.A. and then the quick, inter-island commute and drive out, it wouldn't hurt to take a shower and slip into some clean, comfortable clothes. She'd been traveling a good nine hours. Waiting a few more minutes before she started working wouldn't hurt.

Hurrying toward the master bedroom, she left both bags on the floor, opened them flat, and then dug out a short, cool, lemon yellow summer shift and carried it toward the bathroom. Upon opening the door, Kylee stood there gaping at a bathroom complete with almost everything, right down to thick, fluffy towels with *Hale Hanea* embroidered on them—everything except exterior walls. Two sides of the room consisted of open air and the tangled jungle beyond.

She knew enough about exotic plants to recognize the ginger that bloomed profusely. The bushes covered with the crepe-textured yellow flowers grew there, too. A lava rock waterfall stood outside, a few feet from the varnished, wooden floor of the deck. Blooming orchids growing in woody coconut halves hung from the tree limbs, adding a touch of magic to the atmosphere. The shower was off to one side of the open lanai, the fixtures plumbed into more lava rock.

She glanced over at the toilet standing in the opposite corner, then at the sink and the sunken bathtub before she turned around and searched the house. There wasn't another bathroom in the entire place. She made a beeline for the kitchen phone.

Rick Pau answered on the first ring. *"Hale Hanea.* Can I help you?"

"There seems to be a little something missing in the bathroom."

"Ah. Miss Christopher. Didn't I put out fresh soap and towels?"

"No walls."

She could hear him laughing on the other end before he said, "No need."

"You don't expect me to shower or to . . . to . . . do *everything* right out in the *open* do you?" She hated hearing her voice rise on every word and tried to get a grip.

"Nobody can see you. The room's completely surrounded by thick *hau* bush and ginger, not to mention the hill behind it. In fact, that's the room that usually gets the most compliments."

"It's totally unacceptable."

"Give it a try." There was a long, pregnant pause.

"Well, if I stay here I guess I'll have to, won't I?"

"Trust me, it's totally private," he assured her.

Kylee simply sighed. She was from Los Angeles, for heaven's sake, where nearly every house and car was fully armed and alarmed and this man expected her to strip down and shower out in the open? He *had* to be kidding.

"Is there anything else I can do?" He was obviously quite serious.

She wondered if anything ever got to Rick Pau and made a mental note to *never,* ever take one of Sylvia's vacation recommendations again.

"No. Thanks." She hung up before he could say another chipper thing and stalked back to the bathroom. Whipping a towel off the rack, she went back into the bedroom to strip off her mud-splattered, damp clothes and wrapped herself up in the towel.

With her lemon shift in hand, she trudged back to the bathroom and simply stood there for a good three minutes, silent, half-expecting to catch sight of someone creeping through the bushes. Birds were singing despite the falling rain that trailed off the metal roof in steady streams. The waterfall bubbled merrily; the hanging orchids swayed in the gentle breeze.

Kylee shrugged and walked over to the handles in the lava wall to turn on the water. *What the heck,* she thought with a shrug. *When in Rome . . .*

* * *

Rick put a mini loaf of freshly baked basil-sourdough bread into the basket he had filled with the rest of Kylee's dinner. A swatch of tropical print fabric lined the heavy wicker. He tucked the material around containers of chilled salmon flavored with dill, a green salad, and some assorted veggies he'd grilled earlier on the barbecue on his lanai. The addition of a chilled bottle of chardonnay and a container of rice pudding completed the task.

Staring down at the basket without really focusing on its contents, he gave up trying and admitted he couldn't get his new houseguest out of his mind.

If the look in those clear blue eyes was any indication, Ms. Kylee Christopher's life wasn't as perfect as the cool, totally put together image she projected. There was something eating away at her that even her standoffish attitude couldn't hide. What he thought he had read in the depths of her eyes was fear—certainly not of him—but from some undefinable source, and for some curious reason, he found himself wanting to be the one to help remedy her situation.

The rain had stopped and the sky was beginning to clear as Rick picked up the basket and walked out of the kitchen of the house that backed up to the Wainiha River. Originally, he'd built the smaller cottage, a mirror image of the large structure, as the guest house, intending to move into the more spacious dwelling when it was complete. But after two years in the cottage, he found that he was so comfortable right next to the river that he decided to establish the main house as a vacation rental and share with others the solitude of the garden spot he had created.

Hale Hanea was usually a honeymooner's paradise, not often rented by singles, yet Kylee Christopher had come here alone, not to sightsee, but to work. It gave him one more facet of her life to think about, one more piece of the puzzle to toy with.

When he reached the wide double doors of the main house,

he immediately saw Kylee seated at the desk that overlooked the taro patches in the field below the house. She had obviously dealt with the open-air shower, for her long hair was still damp. A wisp of a yellow dress showed off her bare shoulders to perfection. She had already plugged in her computer and was seated with her back to him, staring at the blinking cursor on a blank screen.

He shuffled his bare feet against the lanai floor and cleared his throat so that he wouldn't startle her before he called out a greeting.

"I've got your dinner," he explained, opening the door for himself as he carried the basket inside.

"Set it in the kitchen," she told him, not turning around, her attention focused on the blank computer screen.

He carried the basket over to the tile counter that separated the living space from the kitchen appliances, opened the refrigerator, and unpacked the separate food containers.

"Ever been to Kauai before?" Rick asked as he straightened.

"No."

"Let me know when you'd like a guided tour of the north shore." *Nice going, Rick.* The offer was made before he could stop himself. If he wasn't careful, she would be gone before morning.

She made no comment, as she ran her hand through her hair.

"No extra charge," he added.

Her shoulders rose and fell on a sigh. Rick found the corkscrew and uncorked the wine, then shoved the cork back in and placed the bottle in the refrigerator. He straightened, still unable to take his eyes off of her.

"Plenty to see. Lots to do if you like the outdoors. Kauai can be pretty slow for some folks." He left the basket on the counter and walked around it into the main room.

Kylee turned around, her elbow propped on the desk, and pinned him with an icy stare.

"Thank you for your offer, but this is strictly a working

vacation for me, Mr. Pau. I need *absolute* privacy. I don't intend to go anywhere or do anything, just work."

"Rick," he said.

"What?" She looked startled.

"The name's Rick. Mr. Pau always ends up sounding like the name of a World Championship Wrestler when a haole says it. You know. Mr. *Pow!*"

"Haole?" She frowned.

"A stranger." Rick started toward the door. Something in the way she was hovering on the edge of the chair, every inch of her tensed and waiting for him to leave, prodded him to keep talking. He'd love to see her relax. "I left your dinner in the refrigerator. Tonight it's all alfresco. Salmon, vegetables, salad. Some wine."

"Thank you." She finally softened a bit and ran her hand through her hair again, shaking out the damp ends. "That sounds fine. I'm sorry if I was a bit abrupt, but I plan on spending the next three weeks working and really do need privacy."

"Working on . . . ?"

"I'm a television screenwriter."

"I kind of figured it was something like that," he said quickly, glancing at the blank computer screen again.

"I'm on a pretty tight deadline, so if you see my lights on late at night, don't worry. Time gets away from me."

"Working on anything exciting?" Expecting a brush-off, he was surprised at how easily she opened up to talk about her work.

"An M.O.W. Movie of the week. For Charese LaDonne. Something that'll have to go up against Monday night football. Something romantic aimed at the female audience that doesn't want to watch Neanderthals grunt and bash their heads together."

"Charese LaDonne?" He whistled, impressed. The middle-aged actress had been low profile for a while, but there weren't many people who wouldn't have recognized the name of the Oscar winner.

Kylee nodded. "Last year I won an Emmy for Movie-of-the-Week Original Screenplay. Charese loved the show. Her agent called mine and now I'm contracted to do a comeback script for her."

"Pretty scary stuff." He leaned back against the door frame and crossed his arms.

She looked surprised by his comment and then frowned, nodding in agreement. "Yeah. It is."

"Any ideas?"

"Some. I just can't seem to get started."

"Maybe you should take a few days off, see the sights and relax," he suggested. As suddenly as it had appeared, her candidness was replaced by a closed look and an icy tone.

"Are you a writer, Rick?"

Although she was no longer smiling, it pleased him to hear her use his first name. "I've dabbled some," he admitted.

"Then you don't really know what you're talking about. This script isn't going to get finished unless I keep my butt in this chair and write it."

He held his hands up in surrender. "Enough said. I'll get out of your hair."

He didn't want to dwell on her cute butt in or out of the chair. Besides, he couldn't help notice how vulnerable she looked sitting there with her bare feet curled around each other and that anxious, haunted look in her eyes. He would have loved to have crossed the room, to massage her neck and shoulders to try to ease away some of the tension that was so palpable. But he wouldn't dare make a move like that without invitation. Kylee looked volatile enough to pack up and leave at the least provocation and the last thing he wanted was to see her drive away.

As much as he was tempted to linger, when she turned away, Rick slipped out without a good-bye.

* * *

It was dark when Kylee gave up and shut down the computer. Frustrated beyond belief, she found she hadn't even been able to decide what to type for the page headers. Rummaging through the refrigerator, she filled a plate with some of the luscious goodies Rick had left, poured herself a glass of wine, and carried everything out to the lanai.

The jungle surrounding the house was pitch black. She set her plate down on a side table beside the wicker couch and lit three citronella buckets he had conveniently left there to keep the mosquitoes at bay. The flames flickered and, when coupled with the light streaming out through the windows, the wide veranda was enveloped in a soft, butter yellow glow.

Night intensified the rainforest sounds. Bullfrogs croaked out a deep, rumbling chorus. Small brown lizards with suction-cup toes clung to the corners of the windows where the bugs congregated. They chirped and clucked while patiently waiting to attack their next catch. Somewhere beyond the dense growth that lined the property, water rushed downstream toward the beach, singing against the river rock along the way. All in all, the sounds blended into a calming, lyrical melody. There was a serenity about the place that should have soothed and inspired her. Instead, the tranquil atmosphere was beginning to drive her crazy. There wasn't even a single, small screen black-and-white television in the place.

Kylee was forced to admit that she was used to the big city pace and noise; the sound of the nightly newscaster droning on the television with the latest doom and gloom statistics; murder and mayhem; the rush of traffic, not water. The smell of smog, not the scent of flowers. By the time she finished the delicious evening snack and set the plate aside, she had convinced herself that her hectic L.A. lifestyle stoked her well-honed competitive edge.

Obviously, coming to Kauai to work had been a big mistake.

"Clear your head. Get out of L.A. and you'll see, the script will come together."

Good old Sylvia and her advice. Usually her agent was right

on with her suggestions, but this one had obviously material-
ized out of left field. Kylee started to stand up and call Sylvia
to tell her that the getaway idea wasn't working until she realized it was already eleven o'clock in California, far too late to
give her agent a piece of her mind.

Kylee leaned back against the plush sofa cushions and sighed,
then she curled up her legs beneath her and stared off toward the
small cottage at the back of the property. There was a light burning in Rick Pau's front window, but she saw no other sign of life.
She wondered if he might have a television hidden away back
there, then realized after the waspish way she'd reacted to him
earlier, she didn't dare go asking any favors.

For a while she sat there staring out at the night while the
lilting strains of guitar music accompanied by a man's voice
singing in Hawaiian drifted on the breeze. The haunting, seductive sounds drew her, lured her into walking across the lanai
until she stood against the railing and looked over at the small
cottage. Rick Pau had obviously been blessed with talent and
good looks.

While she admired the music as much as Rick's ability to
make it, she wished she had learned to play an instrument, but
having been raised in a series of foster homes, her only con-
sistent childhood pastime had been reading.

Later, in her teens, writing had become her passion. Jour-
nalism classes, writing competitions, submissions to small
presses and literary journals had filled her life and took the
place of the family and love she never experienced.

Early on, she discovered she had a gift for screenwriting, for
melding a concept into a storyline of action and dialogue. Without firsthand knowledge of a loving relationship, she became
driven to write. Now, at twenty-five, her work took the place
of a husband and children.

Writing filled the void. It was and had always been her life,
which made her even more terrified to think that now, at the
peak of her career, she might be blocked.

She *was* her work. It defined who and what she was. What

would she do if she never wrote another word? What would she become? Pushing away from the rail, she warned herself not to think so negatively. This inability to come up with an idea, this lack of words, was just a phase.

Sylvia was right. She had just needed to get away, change her environment. Things would be all right tomorrow. She'd be right back at it again in the morning and before she knew it, the first draft of her screenplay would be stacked up on the desk beside the computer.

The night air was thick and humid, alive with mosquitoes. She moved back into range of the candle smoke that kept them at bay. One by one, she blew out the candles and then walked back into the house. Shutting off the lights, she made her way into the master suite and undressed in the dark. As she slipped between the crisp, clean sheets, she lay there listening to the sound of Rick Pau's soothing voice, wondering about the meaning behind the haunting sound of the Hawaiian words. The air was close and hot. She tossed and turned as geckoes chirped and mosquitoes whined against the screens. Kylee sighed and resigned herself to a long night.

What seemed like minutes later, she awoke to the sound of roosters crowing in the bush outside the bedroom window. With a groan, she rolled over and stared at the clock on the rattan table beside the bed: 5:00 A.M. Although it was overcast and drizzling outside, the weak daylight didn't seem to dampen the roosters' enthusiasm.

Extracting herself from the tangle of sheets, she stood up and realized the aroma of freshly brewed coffee was wafting through the house. She shoved her fingers through her hair, pulled on a pair of shorts and a black jogging bra. Bleary-eyed, she headed for the kitchen.

There was no sign of Rick Pau, but the table was set for one and a bright display of tropical blossoms in a pottery vase made a pretty centerpiece. A note printed in bold handwriting was

taped to the coffeepot. She pulled it off and read as she reached
for a ceramic mug.

> *Aloha kakahiaka.* Good morning. Spinach quiche and
> croissants are in the oven. Hope you got lots of work
> done last night. Rick.

Kylee groaned again. *Work?* Who was he kidding? She poured
her coffee, kept it black and reached for the phone. It was eight
o'clock in California. Sylvia was a notorious late riser. *If she
isn't up yet, she can wake up to the sound of my voice,* Kylee
thought as she punched in her calling card numbers.
She was delighted when Sylvia Greene picked up the phone
sounding groggy.
"Greene Literary Agency."
"It's Kylee. Very funny, Sylvia. You could have warned me."
Over the line came the sound of rustling bedclothes and the
protesting mew of a cat. Kylee pictured Sylvia wrestling
around, trying to sit up in bed.
"Kylee? Where are you? Did you find the place all right?"
Unable to stand still, Kylee carried the cordless phone out
onto the lanai. Through the gauze of rain she could see Rick's
cottage a few yards away. He was on his own wide veranda,
doing sit-ups no less. She tried to turn away, but she was mesmerized by the sheen of sweat on his warm, honey brown skin
and the way his abs flexed and unflexed with every curl. She
tried to imagine what those muscles might feel like were she
to run her hands over them—
"Kylee? I said, what do you think of the view?" Sylvia's
voice jolted her back to reality.
"Oh, the view's just *great*," Kylee said, slapping away a mos-
quito on her thigh before she turned around and padded back
into the house. "I am beginning to have a sneaking suspicion
that you set this whole thing up on purpose, Syl."
"Set *what* up?"

"I'm stuck out here in the mud with the devastatingly handsome houseboy that you so very slyly failed to mention."

"Houseboy?"

Kylee had to give the old gal credit. She actually managed to sound like she hadn't a clue.

"Rick Pau. You didn't tell me he was such a knockout and apparently single."

"Oh. Yeah, well. I guess I forgot." Sylvia yawned and didn't try to hide it. "I just loved the house. I really thought you would, too."

While Sylvia went on and on about how much she had enjoyed the place during her own stay, Kylee opened the oven door, reached for a warm croissant and bit into the flaky, buttery flavored bread. She munched away and then, when Sylvia paused to take a breath, she informed her, "There are no bathroom walls, Syl."

"So? It's in a jungle for god's sake."

"It hasn't stopped raining since I got here."

"So? We live in a desert. Soak it up for a while. It's good for your skin."

Kylee sighed.

"He *is* handsome, isn't he," Sylvia admitted, not bothering to clarify.

"Yeah, he is that," Kylee mused, polishing off the last of the croissant.

"Maybe a little injection of passion would do you good."

Kylee almost choked on a swig of coffee. *"Passion?"*

"You know, the stuff of which you write? Passion. Lust. Romance. Your script *is* for a movie of the week aimed at the women who want to avoid the NFL playoffs. Remember? It's *supposed* to be steamy, PG-rated erotic. A woman's fantasy. Why not do a little physical research while you're there?"

Kylee tensed. "I don't need a physical relationship. I don't need any relationship at all." She found herself drifting over to the door again and glancing over at Rick's lanai. He had flipped over and was doing push-ups now. Push-ups. The exercise helped her conjure up all sorts of images.

"Kylee? Kylee, are you still there?"

She spun away from the door, wiped the perspiration from her forehead with the back of her hand, and then held her hair up off the nape of her neck. She'd give anything for even a whisper of a breeze.

"I'm here."

"So how is it going? You're all settled in, ready to write? What time is it there? Six o'clock? What are you doing up so early?"

"Roosters." There was no way she was going to admit that she hadn't written word one on the script yet and didn't know if she was going to do any better today. "Listen, Sylvia, I've got to get going."

"Say hello to Rick for me," Sylvia trilled. Then, in her best old Hollywood style, she oozed, "Bye, bye, dahling."

Kylee hung up the phone, grabbed oven mitts and pulled the quiche out, then turned the oven off. When she straightened, there was a quick knock at the side door.

Rick Pau, his rippling abs thankfully covered in a faded, ripped tank top, stood watching her from the other side of the screen.

"Want to go for a jog? I was just on my way and thought you might like to join me."

"A *jog?*" She scooped her hair back off her face but it fell over one eye again. "I don't jog. Besides, it's raining."

"It's always raining."

"I noticed."

"How was breakfast?"

"Fine," she said, watching him through the screen. "Actually, I haven't had any of the quiche yet, but it looks delicious. Where'd you get it?"

He laughed. "I made it."

He cooks, too. Kylee was beginning to think he was too good to be true.

"How's your script coming along? I saw your light on late last night." He hunkered down to tie his running shoe.

A bout of anxiety made her head swim and her stomach lurch. "Fine," she managed. "It's coming along just fine." She knew a panic attack when it hit her, even though she'd never taken time to allow herself the luxury of one before.

Rick got to his feet and paused, watching her closely. Too closely.

"Are you all right?"

"Sure. I think . . . I . . . it's probably just jet lag."

He was out of his shoes before she could blink. Opening the screen, he stepped inside and walked over to her. Rick reached out and put his hand against her forehead.

"No fever."

"No kidding. I said I was all right."

He was so close she could study each of his lush eyelashes. *It should be illegal for a man to have such beautiful eyes,* she found herself thinking. He continued to hover, watching her with concern and something more, something she didn't want to think about—a look that made her cheeks feel flushed and her pulse jumpy.

She swallowed, backed up a step, and found herself pressed up against the kitchen cabinet. "Sylvia said to say hello."

Rick smiled and leaned back against the round tabletop. "Now there's a lady who knows how to have fun."

"Meaning?"

Kylee didn't even want to imagine young, virile Rick Pau playing gigolo to her agent. Sylvia was tops in her field and a great friend in the bargain, but even a succession of Beverly Hills facelifts couldn't hide the fact that Syl had seen sixty up close and personal quite a few years back. Rick Pau didn't look a day over twenty-nine.

"Meaning, you might need to take time to get out in the fresh air, take a walk or a swim and clear your head."

"That's impossible. I'm on a deadline."

"How can you create if you're uptight? I think you need to relax and get into the beauty of the island. Slow down. This is

Kauai, one of the most inspiring places in the world. You have
to let the island work its magic."

"Do you have a degree in psychology?" Her tone was cool,
her words clipped.

He assessed her for a long, quiet moment. Kylee dropped
her gaze first.

"No, I don't, but it doesn't take an expert to see that you're
pretty stressed out."

"Thank you so much. I feel a lot better now." With his dark
brown eyes staring into hers the way they were, she could
hardly think. Unfortunately, when she did, she recalled Sylvia's
suggestion that she do a little physical research. What would
it be like to kiss Rick Pau? Were his lips as conditioned as his
stomach muscles?

As if he could read her mind, Rick abruptly shoved away
from the table and cleared his throat. "Listen," he said, "I'm
going to a luau tonight on the other side of the island. One of
my cousin's kids is turning a year old. If you'd like to go with
me, see the real thing instead of a tourist luau—"

"No thanks. Really." She tried to ignore the wave of loneli-
ness that hit her. She had no idea what it would be like to have
one cousin, let alone a number of them with children.

He shrugged off her refusal. "Just thought I'd ask. I'd better
get going."

Thank god, Kylee thought.

As soon as the screen closed behind him, she let out an inaudi-
ble sigh of relief. Rick picked up his jogging shoes and carried
them over to the steps where he sat down to put them on. Kylee
turned away and began rummaging through the lower cabinets
and drawers. The anxiety attack she had suffered earlier reminded
her of a writer friend, one of Sylvia's other clients. Rita Mainville
tended to suffer panic attacks near the end of every deadline and
had plenty of suggestions for first aid remedies of all sorts.

In an end cupboard, Kylee located a neatly folded stack of
paper bags. She chose a small one to set on the desk beside
the computer in case she wound up hyperventilating.

Two

Three long, torturous days later, the rain finally stopped just as Kylee finished struggling through the first ten pages of her script. The day was half over. She was pacing the confines of the house when she decided it was the peace and quiet that was driving her stark raving mad. Carrying her work out onto the lanai, she began to read through it while seated in one of the comfy chairs. By the time she finished, she was certain the first draft was definitely nothing more than a pile of dog doo.

Frustrated, she tossed what little there was of the script onto the small bamboo end table beside her and then weighted it down with a citronella candle before she stood up and stretched. Glancing over at the cottage set against the trees, she wondered what in the world Rick Pau did to amuse himself during the long, rainy days. Complying with her wishes, he hadn't interrupted her at all in the last few days except to leave her meals in the kitchen. Once he had come by to ask if she needed anything special from Hanalei, the little town up the road.

She wanted to tell him to bring back a fresh idea.

As much as she would have liked to avoid thinking of him, she couldn't seem to get Rick out of her mind. The more he adhered to her wishes and stayed away, the more she found herself wondering what he was doing, listening for the sound of his pickup truck coming and going or the strains of guitar music that often came from his house.

She glanced over at his place again and thought it looked decidedly magical against the backdrop of green. All around the yard, crystal raindrops still clung to the leaves and blossoms on the thick foliage sparkling like rainbow-hued gems in the sunlight.

Just then, the sound of an automobile on Powerhouse Road drew her attention. Rick's beat-up pickup was parked in the carport beside his cottage, so she was surprised and curious when another truck came barreling down the steep drive and ground to a halt amid the mud and gravel. It came to a stop right in front of her lanai.

Inside the cab sat three middle-aged women who waved cheerfully at her as they hopped out and collected six-packs of sodas and beers from the back of the pickup. Kylee waved back and watched them hurry up the steps to the covered walkway that connected the two houses. The blonde woman leading the way called out, "Aloha, Rick!" and Kylee heard him respond in a deep, resonant voice, *"Komo mai!* Come in, come in. You're right on time.*

Three-to-one odds, Kylee mused. Probably just what a man as handsome as Rick Pau was used to. Ignoring the sound of laughter and frivolity issuing from the cottage, Kylee stood up and stretched and wandered back inside, intent on reading through a stack of recent issues of *Variety* she'd packed along, that and pouring a glass of iced tea.

From her kitchen she could hear the sound of Rick singing in Hawaiian. Upon opening the refrigerator door, she discovered the light was out inside and glanced over at the microwave. Sure enough, the clock wasn't on. The electricity was probably out in the entire house. After removing the tall glass tea pitcher, she banged the refrigerator door closed and wondered at her bad humor.

"No way," she mumbled to herself when the thought struck her that she was actually feeling put out at the women having such uproarious fun in Rick's cottage. "No way," she mumbled. Surely she couldn't be jealous, she decided, quite appalled at the notion. His dark eyes and hair and his megawatt smile gave him looks any woman might swoon over, but even if she had been the swooning type, she didn't even know the man.

Besides, *she* certainly wasn't looking for any *Fantasy Island* romantic interlude.

Kylee poured the tea into a tall glass filled with ice and decided to take a stroll through the rest of the house to see if the electricity was out all over or if perhaps just the circuit breaker in the kitchen had blown. When none of the switches she hit in the living area or in the master bedroom worked either, she headed for the bathroom. Opening the door, she stepped in and got the shock of her life. There, right in the middle of the lava rock shower, nosing at the drain, was a pig as big as an overstuffed easy chair.

And if she wasn't mistaken, it was the same pig she'd nearly run down when she first arrived.

"Go away," she yelled, trying a shooing motion in the pig's direction. He merely turned beady eyes her way, stared for a minute or two, and then went back to snuffling at the drain.

"Okay, that's it." She marched out of the bathroom, slamming the door behind her, then walked back through the house and out onto the lanai.

Without even pausing to slip on her sandals, she hurried along the short platform walk that connected the cottages. As she drew near, she heard Rick call out, *"Lewa. Ami. Holoholo."*

His words were followed by a burst of laughter and then one of the women giggled, "Rick, show me *exactly* where to put my hands."

Kylee paused just outside the door when she heard Rick reply softly, "The bosom. Remember, it's 'to my bosom I call you.' " His voice, strong and melodic, resonated even when he wasn't singing.

She tried to peer into the window beside the front doors, curious to see what was going on. As she drew closer, Kylee kicked over a basket filled with gardening tools. A small hand spade and a trowel clattered onto the wooden lanai floor.

Inside the house, all talk immediately stopped. Kylee was

struck with a ridiculous urge to run, but instead she straightened, waiting while condensation dripped down the glass of iced tea in her hand. Almost immediately, Rick was at the door, smiling in welcome.

"Komo mai. Come in, Kylee. We'd love to have you join us." He glanced down at the garden tools and added, "I thought one of the cats from up the road was out here making mischief."

"I'm sorry. It was an accident." She found herself glancing around curiously at the tidy interior of his small house as she stepped past him over the threshold.

"Hey, Kylee, I'm glad you decided to take a break and stop by. It looks like that iced tea could be freshened up. Or how about a beer?"

"I'm not here to party," she assured him as he led her into the sparsely furnished, open-air house that was a more compact version of *Hale Hanea.* She was somewhat surprised to see an office set up with all manner of state-of-the-art computer equipment on the screened-in back lanai. There was even a copy machine and a fairly extensive library displayed in assorted plastic stacking crates.

At the bar in the living area, his three female guests were all hunched over open notebooks arguing about bosoms again. As Rick interrupted to introduce Kylee, they looked up in unison and waved just as they had upon arrival.

Rick's hand brushed hers as he reached for the iced tea. When they touched, Kylee felt an instantaneous shock wave jolt her. Startled by her overwhelming physical reaction to him, she looked up and found Rick staring down at her, surprise mirrored in his own eyes.

It was a moment longer before he took a step back and said softly, "Let me see about getting you something to drink."

Feeling a sudden, intense need to put plenty of space between them, Rick hurried over to the kitchen and began offering her a list of drink options.

"I'll just have half a glass of wine," she decided.

He glanced over his shoulder at Kylee. It had certainly turned out to be a day full of surprises. First, not only had she shown up at his door looking like something out of a *California Girl* magazine in short white shorts and a lime green tank T-shirt, but then she agreed to stay a few minutes. Now she was even letting her hair down enough to accept half a glass of wine.

Most surprising of all was the jolt he'd received when he had touched her. Not since he had fallen out of love with Angela, his first wife, had any woman had the power to arouse him so intensely.

Noticing Kylee still standing awkwardly in the center of the room watching the others, Rick pulled himself together, walked around the bar, and handed her the wine glass half full of chardonnay.

She thanked him, took a sip, and continued to stand there, obviously uncomfortable. He stayed beside her and began to explain. "These ladies are old friends of mine."

"Not that *old,* Rick. You want to make us feel bad?" The shortest of the three women looked over at him and smiled.

"You know I don't," he laughed. "Uncle Raymond would have my head if I upset you ladies." Then he turned back to Kylee. "My uncle is a *kumu hula,* a hula teacher, as well as a singer at a local restaurant. A couple of times during the summer he goes fishing off the Big Island and I take over three of his hula classes. These ladies have been learning hula for years now."

"Sometimes I don't feel like we're getting any better," the thin, suntanned blonde quipped.

"You're doing the best you can for not being Hawaiian," Rick teased. Then he turned to Kylee and touched his heart. "Hula comes from here," he explained. She was listening intently. He liked that about her, that when he was talking to her she gave him her full attention. She took another sip of wine and nodded, her hypnotic, blue-eyed gaze locked on his.

He felt himself quicken and abruptly headed for the sofa

where he had left his guitar, deciding he had better have something to hide behind before he let his traitorous body embarrass the hell out of him.

When he invited her to watch his uncle's students hula, Kylee nodded and finally sat down on a chair across the room. He knew that after the thirty-minute session and a beer or two, the older gals would be more than delighted to show off their skills—which were minimal at best—but they all had a good time.

Kylee seemed to relax and sat back to enjoy the dance. He began to play and sing the words to an old favorite, *"Ke Aloha,"* and watched her smile over the rim of her wine glass when he had to call out the English translation that keyed the dance steps. For a moment he was lost in the teaching, reminding the women to draw their hands into their bosoms. When they finished the dance, Kylee set her glass down to applaud and compliment them.

Much to Rick's embarrassment, all three women turned admiring eyes his way and proclaimed him as good a teacher as his uncle. He knew he wasn't anything of the sort and so did they, but Raymond Pau was almost seventy. Rick was sure the ladies didn't do half as much flirting during Uncle Raymond's lessons.

On their way out the door, the women invited him to join them for dinner, an offer he quickly declined so that he could get back to Kylee before she decided to leave. He was amazed to find that she hadn't moved, but had simply curled up in the big chair with one foot tucked beneath her. When he noticed her empty wine glass, he picked it up and headed for the kitchen before she could protest.

"They certainly have a good time," she said.

"They do at that. What a trio." He walked back into the sitting area and handed her the wine.

"If I drink this, I'm not going to get much done this evening." Kylee looked into the pale liquid, swirled it around the glass, and took a sip.

"How's the work going?"

She shrugged. "Could be better, but it's coming along. At least it's stopped raining." Her gaze lingered on the window. Anywhere but on him.

"There's a tropical depression off the islands." He felt himself break into a sweat. The sight of her sitting here just the way he'd pictured her so many times over the past three days had him acting like a teenager in heat instead of a thirty-year-old who should have known better than to let his body take control of his better judgment.

"I think *I'm* tropically depressed." She stretched forward to place the wine glass on the table in front of her. The innocent move gave him a quick glimpse down the front of her T-shirt.

Rick almost groaned aloud. He swallowed the sound and wiped his forehead.

"That's quite an electronic setup out there," she was saying. "What do you do with the latest in high-tech computer equipment?"

He forced himself to concentrate on what she was saying. She was looking at his office.

"I dabble some. In this and that. I just created a home page to advertise this place. And I put a business newsletter together. Television cable stops at Hanalei, so nearly everyone out here is on the Net. Brings the world right to the island. Sometimes I wonder if that's good or bad."

He watched her gaze drift back to him and hold on his eyes. For a moment that seemed like forever, yet at the same time far too brief, they stared into each other's eyes.

Kylee suddenly blinked and then quickly uncurled her legs until she was seated almost primly. "I almost forgot why I came over here."

Rick watched her sit up even straighter, a move that emphasized the high swell of her lovely breasts "Why's that?"

"The electricity is out." She slipped forward until she was perched on the edge of the chair as if ready to run.

"That happens a lot. The county is always working on the

lines. It's probably back on by now." He couldn't keep his eyes from roaming over her face, along her throat, down to her breasts, and back to her eyes again.

"And there's a pig in the bathroom." She folded her arms and waited, obviously expecting him to be shocked.

"What did it look like?"

"What do you mean what did it *look* like? What can I say? It was fat. It was a pig. It was standing in the shower snorting down the drain, that's what."

"Around here, a pig isn't just a pig." He tried to keep from staring at her bare thighs, tried not to imagine what it would be like to run his hands up them. "There are wild pigs that have tusks and they can be very, very dangerous. If you ever see one of those, put something between you and it as fast as you can. Better yet, climb a tree. Then there are domestic pigs that usually end up as the center of attention at a luau. The family on the opposite side of the road has a pet pig named Kiko, which is Hawaiian for Spot."

"It had spots and no tusks. In fact, I almost ran over it the day I tried to find this place." She stood up, tugged on the hem of her shorts, and stared down at him.

"Kiko is a him."

"Whatever. He's in my shower."

"Probably gone by now."

"I hope so." She glanced at the door, then back." "I have to be going."

"Stay for dinner." The invitation was out before he could stop himself.

"I can't." She looked like she was going to sprint for the door.

"You have to eat." He sounded like his mother.

"I should get back. To work." She was decidedly nervous now, looking around as if she just realized how very alone they were.

"What are you afraid of Kylee?" He knew immediately that he had pushed the wrong button.

She tossed back her hair, obviously angry. "Is this your m.o., Rick? You play host to women looking for a summer fling? A thrill? A quick passionate tryst in paradise that'll get them through another year, give them a summer fantasy to cling to? I'm not interested."

"Whoa! Is that what you *think* I do? Sit out here in the country and prey on uptight mainland women looking to get laid? That's not why I invited you to dinner. I thought you might enjoy seeing four different walls for a change." His own fury had been ignited by the fact that he *had* been fantasizing about her.

"I'm sorry." She still looked too furious to be offering a sincere apology.

"You should be."

They stood there staring at each other as tension sizzled in the void between them.

Finally, Rick let out a pent-up breath and decided to try again. "So, do you like raw fish?"

Kylee didn't know what had come over her. All she was certain of at the moment was that Rick Pau had the ability to bring out the shrew in her and she had absolutely no idea why. She tried smiling.

"I like it," she admitted.

"I'm going to make some fresh *ahi sashimi*. You're welcome to join me." Then he added hastily, "No strings attached."

"I'm sorry for that comment," she apologized again. "I've been out of sorts lately. Probably this weather." It was hot and sticky now that the rain had stopped and the sun had spent the rest of the day drying out the soggy landscape. There wasn't a breath of air stirring the palm fronds.

Rick headed for the refrigerator and as she wandered over to the serving bar to watch, he pulled a white paper-wrapped package out of the refrigerator along with a head of cabbage and some soy sauce.

"I'd bet it's your script that's bothering you, not the weather," he said offhandedly as he began to unwrap a piece of dark red fish and set it on a cutting board.

Kylee grudgingly had to admit he was right. "It's been like pulling teeth to get the words on the page," she confessed. A tremor of anxiety hit her stomach and she set her wine glass aside.

"Want to talk about it?" He took a lethally sharp-looking knife out of a wooden block and headed back to the cutting board.

"I'd rather talk about anything else," she told him. "How did you end up way out here running a bed and board?"

"I was born on Kauai. Over on the other side, in Hanapepe. My mom and dad worked for a big sugar company. Dad worked the mill. I went to the University of Hawaii. Majored in business. Sort of followed in the footsteps of one of my uncles in Honolulu. I've been lucky."

Kylee watched him execute a shrug, a casual move that drew her eye to his well-honed shoulder and upper arm. She had an instant visual image of him doing push-ups and looked away, concentrating on the interior of the cottage.

With what he made renting out the larger cottage, she figured he had enough to live comfortably, if not lavishly. Faded tank tops and running shorts seemed to be the uniform he lived in. There was little overhead with him doing all the work around the place himself and that rusted pickup couldn't have cost him more than a few hundred dollars. She envied anyone who could live without all the "stuff" most people, including her, thought they needed.

Although he had mentioned his family, there were no photos in the living area, no pictures of family, or children, old or young people, no one who might be a lover. Perhaps they had more in common than she thought. She thought she was the only person in the world without photographs from her past.

"You don't have any photos around." She tried to sound offhanded, casual.

"Lost 'em all in *Iniki,* the hurricane that hit the island back in '92."

So, unlike her, at least he once had photos and the memories that came with them. Curiosity got the best of her. "Have you ever been married?"

"Yeah. Once." The knife slipped easily through the firm, chilled fish as he cut it into a long row of even slices. "Have you?"

Married? How could she tell him that she had never had a chance to learn how to love? How could she tell him that she didn't know the first thing about love or commitment, for she had never been exposed to it in her young life. Then, later, she had never slowed down enough to let herself learn.

Kylee shook her head but all she said was, "No. Not even close."

He looked up, his dark eyes assessing her, before he turned his attention back to the fish and continued. "Why's that?"

"I . . . I've just been too busy." She was adept at changing that subject. "How did you meet your wife?"

"I met Angela at U. H.," he began. "She was a law student, driven, competitive. Determined to be successful. Her dream was to live on the mainland and run with a fast L.A. crowd, shop Rodeo Drive, rub shoulders with the rich and famous. I went along with it for a while, but my heart wasn't in that lifestyle and her heart wasn't in anything but work. She ended up with a big law firm, Tanner, Wilson and Warrenberg."

"Not the defense lawyers in the Ortega case?" Everyone in L.A. was familiar with the murder case which had garnered more than its share of news time over the past few months.

"Yeah. That's the firm. I guess she's got all she ever wanted now." He looked up and smiled. "Then again, I'm happy, too."

Kylee shifted on the bar stool, rolled the stem of the wine glass between her thumb and forefinger. Lost in thought, Kylee didn't comment. *Determined to be successful.* Rick's description of his first wife hit way too close to home. Kylee had never let herself make time for anything but writing, nor had she ever attempted to nurture any kind of a relationship with a man, lasting or otherwise.

While she watched Rick deftly chop cabbage and mix a soy and wasabi sauce to dip the fish into, she found an odd contentment settle over her. The sound of his voice soothed her frazzled nerves as effectively as a massage and an herbal wrap.

She discovered it was quite pleasant to let a handsome man wait on her, set the table, pour the wine. He lit a hurricane lamp and set it in the center of the table. After she sat down and spread the napkin across her lap, then picked up her chopsticks, Kylee looked up and found Rick staring at her over the rim of his wine glass. His sensuous dark eyes were enhanced by the lamplight. She felt a slow, melting warmth spread through her.

"Here's to getting that script finished," he toasted.

As Kylee lifted her glass, she watched Rick, hypnotized by his exotic dark looks, a perfect, utterly stunning mix of features. Even as she stared at him across the table, feeling the warm glow of the wine and the close, humid night air scented with ginger and night-blooming jasmine, a warning bell went off in the back of her mind. Rick Pau was intriguing, genuinely charming, killer handsome, and every woman's summer fantasy—exactly what she didn't need at this point in her life.

How in the world could she balance a love affair with the script opportunity of a lifetime? Besides that, she would be leaving the island in less than three weeks. Rick was a jack-of-all-trades who could obviously live on a shoestring. Except for the fact that he was divorced, she knew little else about him—which, she noticed with irritation, didn't keep her from wondering all kinds of things about him that had nothing to do with his background.

She watched him deftly ply the chopsticks as he dipped the *sashimi* into the sauce and carry the dripping, chilled slices to his lips. What would it be like to have him kiss her? To have him touch her with those same gentle hands that played the guitar with such emotion, hands that could coax a blossom into an arrangement or tuck a ginger flower into one of the baskets he left in her kitchen?

Forbidden curiosity, feelings she had so avidly avoided for so long, surged inside her like the water flowing in the streambed behind the house.

Somehow she was able to manage the chopsticks and eat the delicious *ahi*. Somehow she was able to keep from staring at Rick, at his lips, his hands, into his eyes. If someone asked her tomorrow what they had talked about, she was certain she wouldn't be able to say. She was functioning as if she were two entities, the Kylee that was smiling and eating and conversing on all manner of subjects, and the Kylee who could only think of one thing and that one thing involved Rick Pau and only Rick Pau.

Thankfully, she got through the meal without embarrassing herself. When he asked if she would stay awhile longer, she told him that she had to get back to her computer.

"I'll walk you back," Rick said, stacking the dishes on the counter and turning away from them.

"No, really, you don't have to." Her heart was hammering, her mouth suddenly dry. She didn't want to have to test her resolve out there alone in the dark with Rick. She didn't want him walking her home as if they were two adolescents on their first date.

"I'd like to make certain Kiko isn't lurking in your shower," he laughed.

"Oh, yes. That pig." She sighed, recalling for the first time all evening why she had ventured over to his cottage. She didn't want to walk into the bathroom and have to face half a ton of porker anymore than she wanted to be tempted by being alone with Rick in the dark.

Her fear of the pig won out.

Rick watched the sensuous sway of Kylee's walk all the way back to the rental house. The white shorts that molded her body stood out like a beacon in the dark.

When they reached the house, he stepped inside and turned on the lights, walked into the master bedroom and then the bath. Just as he'd suspected, Kiko the pig was long gone. Kylee was waiting for him in the living room, standing stiff as a sentry beside the door.

He paused a couple of feet away, reached out, and leaned one hand against the door frame, an uncalculated move that brought him within inches of her. As he stood there looking down into her deep blue eyes, he couldn't help thinking of the ocean again and found himself wanting to drown in her gaze.

It would be so easy to lean a little closer, to press his lips to hers. What would she do if he did? She seemed half-convinced he was nothing more than a gigolo, a *hapa,* or half-Hawaiian beach boy looking for a fling with a rich *haole* girl. Stealing a kiss was just what she expected of him. Trying to start something was what she had accused him of earlier. But looking down into the heated depths of her confused, wary eyes, he realized that he didn't want to risk offending her.

When he did kiss her, he wanted to do it right. He wanted her willing.

"I'm going snorkeling tomorrow." He kept his voice low and soft. He could see that she was nervous being alone with him, so much so that he was half-afraid she would rush out of the house. Her breath was coming rapidly and shallowly. Her cheeks were stained with color, not all of it from the wine.

"Let me know if you change your mind and want to come along," he finished.

"I . . . I have to work."

He wanted to touch her hair, to run his hands through it, wrap it around his fist and draw her into his arms. He wanted to tell her anyone could see that she was pushing herself too hard. He wanted to save her from herself. Instead he said, "It's supposed to be hot and dry tomorrow."

He didn't know how he could feel any hotter.

"I don't think so," she mumbled, but this time she sounded unsure. Her hesitation gave him hope.

"The offer stands." Finally, he pushed away from the door and from her and opened the screen.

"Thanks for dinner," she said, as he stepped out into the night.

Rick bid her goodnight and turned away, heading back to his own place. He could feel her eyes following him as he traveled the wooden walkway that connected their lanais. It took all the strength of will he had not to turn around and go back.

The next day dawned, bright and sunny. Up with the roosters before dawn, Kylee worked until one in the afternoon. Despite the thick, cloying humidity and the sweat running between her breasts and into her eyes, she had written eight fresh pages and had even edited what she had finished the day before.

Confident she was back on track, grudgingly admitting to herself that Rick Pau might have been right when he said she had needed to relax and let the story come to her, she stood up and stretched and stared out the window, concentrating on the taro patch and the highway beyond.

The rumble of the old pickup's engine caused her to start to make her way over to the front door. She stepped out on the lanai and watched Rick toss a mesh bag of snorkeling equipment into the back of the pickup. The area beneath his house looked like a secondhand sporting goods store with racks of surfboards of all shapes and sizes, windsurfing boards, rolled-up sails, and long masts. There was a rusted mountain bike and a shiny new racing bike with a helmet dangling from the handlebars.

It appeared what money he did manage to save he spent on toys. The man was obsessed with fun.

What would that be like, she wondered, not to be so caught up in work? To be able to take the time to learn not to hide behind writing?

She stood against the wooden railing and watched him back

the truck out of the still-muddy gravel drive. When he looked over and noticed her standing there, he leaned out the open driver's side window. If the sun hadn't already been shining, the man's smile would surely have chased away the clouds.

"You sure you don't want to go?" he called out over the deep rattle of the pickup's engine.

Kylee started to tell him no, then a thrush called out from the *hau* bush, its song light and breezy, as if the orange-breasted bird was actually encouraging her to acquiesce. Her clothes were sticking to her; her hair was plastered to her temples and the back of her neck.

"I've never snorkeled before," she admitted.

"I'm a great teacher." No doubt about it, his electric smile could have coaxed the habit off a nun.

"Wait thirty seconds," she said, spinning around, hurrying to change into her swimsuit before rational thought could take hold of her.

In less than five minutes she'd slipped into her suit, tossed an oversized tank top over it, grabbed her sandals, and was riding on the bench seat in Rick's pickup with the window down, her hair unbound and blowing in the breeze He negotiated the sharp curves on Kuhio Highway with such ease she suspected he could drive the road with his eyes closed. She relaxed and stared over the steep embankment, down into the crystal waters and the shore break that pounded the glistening sand.

"Congratulations." Rick downshifted and glanced over at her, one hand on the wheel, the other arm still draped over the edge of the window.

"For what?"

"For walking out on your computer to come with me."

"I'm making headway. Finally." She caught herself actually smiling. The world was looking brighter than it had in weeks.

"Want to talk about the script?"

"No." *Not while it's still in the fragile, first draft stage,* she thought. "Tell me about your island instead."

As they drove the few short miles to a place he called Tunnels, Kylee listened as Rick pointed out the highlights of the North Shore as they drove past them. While she was still staring up at the ebony lava cliff face covered with fern, he pulled into a short, narrow dirt road that ended on a bluff overlooking a beach protected by a coral reef.

The sand was hot enough not only to fry an egg but to blister the soft underside of her toes. Rick told her to keep her sandals on and run for it, tossing her a beach towel while he carried the bag of snorkel equipment to the spot she chose.

"I think I'd be content to sit here and watch the water." She stared at the mound of swim fins and fluorescent-colored masks with long snorkels attached that he'd dumped on a towel.

"No way." He tossed her a pair of medium-sized fins, one at a time. "Carry them to the water," he told her, "but put the mask and snorkel on here to be certain they fit."

Finally, she put everything on just the way Rick wanted it. The water was cool and refreshing, the first relief she'd had from the heat in days. Before she could begin swimming, Kylee felt Rick's hand on her shoulder.

"Wuuhaa?" It was impossible to talk with a rubber mouthpiece between her teeth.

Looking like Neptune come to life, Rick stood in the shallow water with droplets beaded across the rippling muscles of his well-honed chest, his mask riding the crown of his head. When he reached for her and cupped her face with his hands, Kylee's breath caught in her throat.

"Let me adjust this for you," he said, gently pulling her mask up and brushing her hair away from the faceplate.

Her heart was pounding so hard she feared she was going to faint dead away and drown in three feet of water. Where his hands had touched her shoulders, her skin burned. Kylee blinked, trying to see Rick clearly through the water-spotted window of her mask.

Gently, he carefully tucked her hair behind her ears with his fingertips. She shivered. Her skin dimpled with goosebumps. He held on to her shoulders.

"Ready?"

Ready for what? It was disconcerting to realize that his touch could make her forget where she was and what she was doing. When he let her go, she experienced an odd sense of disappointment. Kylee couldn't take her eyes off Rick as he stretched out in the shallow water and began to swim a little ways away.

The minute she put her mask in the water she thrilled to the sight of a shimmering rainbow-hued collection of tropical fish gathered around her. As much as she enjoyed watching the fish, most of her concentration was centered on breathing through the rubber mouthpiece and praying the plastic tube would stay above the waterline.

She heard her heart beating in her ears. For the first few minutes they were in the water, they swam shoulder to shoulder. A shiver wriggled through her as they floated side by side in the warm water, skin to skin. Rick stayed beside her, touching her arm whenever he wanted to point out some underwater wonder.

Within no time at all, Kylee forgot about breathing through the snorkel and began to move naturally through the water. The swim fins gave her the strength and confidence she needed and in no time at all she had left Rick's side to follow fluorescent fish over the dramatic underwater landscape without fear. Time ceased to exist as she floated above the magical underwater world, her mind going in countless directions and yet, at the same time, strangely focused.

While she stared at a little black fish with white spots and shaped something like a box with a tail, she began to envision a scene from her screenplay. Dialogue fell into place, the banter witty, the exchange between the character played by Charese LaDonne and the yet-unnamed male lead was complete from the beginning of the scene until the end.

As a parrot fish spit out a mouthful of sand, Kylee hoped she would remember every word when she was back at *Hale*

Nanea staring at the computer again. A cloud passed in front of the sun and she actually felt chilled. Lifting her head, she scanned the surface for Rick but didn't see any sign of his blue snorkel tube or his fins kicking up water.

She swam around full circle, searching for him and, with relief, suddenly spotted him swimming a few yards away. Thinking it best to let him know she was heading to shore, she took two strokes in his direction and then stopped dead still. A scream lodged in her throat. There, a few feet below her in a deep crevice between the coral shelves, the dark sinister shape of a shark wove its way through the water.

She forgot to breathe. Blood rushed to her head, and for a split second, she was afraid she was going to black out.

Something told Rick that Kylee might be ready to get out of the water. Forty-five minutes was longer than he had anticipated her wanting to stay in, but each time he had looked up, she'd appeared to be swimming confidently over the reef. Now, as he closed in on her, he could see that she was lying perfectly still, floating on the surface of the water. Her long, fair hair was fanned out around her head as she stared downward.

Movement near the ocean floor caught his eye and he felt the hair on the back of his neck prickle. In a second he recognized the dorsal fin and knew why Kylee had frozen. A small sand shark was cruising in the depths beneath them. He knew the shark was harmless.

And he knew Kylee didn't know anything of the sort.

She wouldn't see him out of the side of her mask unless she moved, so he hesitated, not wanting to swim up to her without warning and frighten her anymore than she probably already was. He hovered to the side of her and waited for the slow-moving shark to swim on.

Eventually it did, but the few seconds it took seemed like hours. He could only imagine what Kylee was thinking. He saw her turn and head for the beach. In a few long strokes, he was close enough to reach out and touch her. Before he did, she looked over and pulled back with a start. A strangled squeal muffled by the mouthpiece escaped her.

They were near the shore, floating above a sand bottom. Rick put his feet down. His head and shoulders came up out of the water. He spit out his snorkel and raised his mask. Kylee did the same. The minute her mouth was clear, she started gasping for air.

"Are you all right?" He started to reach for her but she jerked away from his touch.

"Am I all right? Am I *all right?*"

"Kylee—"

"Shark bait, that's what I feel like. Shark bait. Did you *see* that shark out there? Go snorkeling, you said. Nothing to it, you said. You'll see turtles and fish. You failed to mention *sharks,* Rick." She stopped long enough to take a breath.

A shiver shook her tempting frame. He told himself this was no time to notice, but there were just some things a man couldn't ignore.

"Are you actually *laughing* at me?" she shouted.

"No. Just smiling."

She turned away and tried striding through the waist-high water, but the swim fins unbalanced her. So did the shallow waves near the shore. She whipped around to face him again.

"Do you really think this is funny?"

"Not at all. It's just that you were never in a minute's danger. I would never had brought you out here if I thought you could get hurt."

She was trembling all over. Her mask was shoved up on the crown of her head; her snorkel dangled beside her cheek. Chicken skin peppered her sleek frame. Her breasts rose and fell, and the smooth swell above her suit drew his attention.

"Of all the nerve," she railed. "I'm standing here frightened to death and *you* stand there staring at my breasts! Take me backs" she demanded. She pulled off the fins and went struggling through the shore break and up the steep, sandy bank.

"Kylee—"

She didn't stop until she reached their towels. Kylee whipped off her snorkel gear and tossed it on the mesh bag. Glancing up and down the nearly deserted section of the beach, she ignored him while she shook the sand out of her towel and whipped it around her shoulders.

Rick threw off his snorkel and mask and walked up beside her. "Kylee, I'm sorry you were frightened, but you were never out of my sight—"

"Ha. I looked up once and you were halfway down the beach."

"It just seemed that way. When you were watching that sand shark I was right behind you, a little to your right."

"Watching that shark? I was paralyzed with fear. Terrified."

"Kylee, it was a harmless sand shark."

"I don't care if it was *plastic*. It scared the hell out of me." She pulled the towel tighter. Her teeth were chattering now but the sun was blazing once more. He realized she had been more frightened than he could guess.

Disregarding the stubborn tilt of her chin, he closed the distance between them and wrapped her in his arms. She stiffened, but was trembling so hard that she couldn't fight back and quickly sagged against him. As he gently cupped her head and pressed her cheek against his shoulder, Rick closed his eyes and let out a deep sigh. Holding Kylee against him felt so right, so perfect, that he was shaken.

Rick held her, sharing his warmth, willing to stand there until she felt safe again. He looked down the beach, toward Makana Peak, the mountain dubbed Bali Hai after *South Pacific* was filmed. The water was clear, azure blue, the summer waves gentle as toddlers tumbling against the sand.

The beauty of Kauai was timeless and achingly lovely, much like the woman in his arms. Around him spread a stunning scene, one he'd gazed at countless times and would never grow tired of. While he stood there holding Kylee in his arms, Rick realized that everything around him was exactly the same as it had been before he touched her, but now his life was suddenly, irrevocably changed.

She needed him. Whether she knew it or not, she did. She needed him as much as he needed her. Although the sudden surety of the notion had been a shock, he was not a man to question fate.

Three

Early the next morning, Kylee couldn't stop thinking of Rick and the way she had behaved after he brought her back and dropped her off at the house yesterday afternoon. She turned off the water, stepped out of the shower, and wrapped one of the plush guest towels around her. She quickly scanned the landscape for signs of Kiko, the trespassing pig, but there wasn't so much as a snout print near the house. Kylee headed for the bedroom, her thoughts once more on her host.

Her anger had subsided, her fear of the shark replaced by a whole new threat—her mounting attraction to Rick. Lord help her, she didn't want to feel anything for him, didn't want to imagine what it would be like to let herself fall in love. She hated to admit it, but she was so attracted to him that she felt an aching need every time she thought of what making love to him might be like.

She had tried all night long, but even now she couldn't deny the way she had felt when he took her in his arms to comfort her on the beach.

After towel-drying her hair, she slipped into clean shorts and a tank top and walked into the kitchen. As usual, the coffee was already brewed. Hot cinnamon rolls were in the oven. As Kylee sat sipping a cup of rich Kona coffee, she marveled at the turn her life had taken in just a few days' time.

Last night, after she had calmed down enough to sit, she found herself working long into the night. She had thrown out the entire script, changed the setting to the tropics, and begun a love story in which the character that Charese LaDonne was going to portray slowly discovered she was in love with a devastatingly handsome man who lived alone in a jungle paradise.

The story flowed from her fingertips, the words and scenes inspired. She had twenty-one pages by the time she was through for the night. Afterward, she turned off the computer, went to bed, and lay in the dark, listening to the now-familiar night sounds of the geckoes and the bullfrogs, the water rushing in the river. Without a doubt, she knew that Rick had been right about getting out and experiencing life.

Her work had been inspired by the roller coaster of emotion she had been riding yesterday afternoon: her anger at Rick, the fear of the shark, the joy and wonder she had experienced when she first saw the universe beneath the surface of the ocean. For a few hours she had actually let go of the anxiety of not being able to produce. Instead of straining to come up with ideas, she had poured out page after page, experiencing all over again the emotion, the tension, and her own growing need in every line of dialogue and every scene.

The coffee mug was empty. She set it down and traced her finger around the rim and then, her mind made up, she pushed away from the table. She owed Rick Pau an apology. Not only that, but she actually wanted to see him again. Needed to see him again and couldn't wait any longer.

When he had dropped her off last night she was still fuming and she let him know it. Although, at that point, most of her anger had been fueled by her own reaction to him, not by the shark sighting. He had left his place shortly after they parted. Not until the wee hours of the night did she hear his pickup come rattling down the driveway again.

As she crossed the lanai and slipped on her sandals, she reminded herself it would be safer to stay put; get to work, and keep her distance from Rick Pau. It was bad enough that lately he haunted her every waking thought. Her heart had betrayed her last night, beating double-time when she heard the sound of his truck on the drive.

Closing the distance between the two houses, she told herself that she was only going to his place to set things straight. Even though she didn't want the rest of her stay to end on a sour note, she definitely didn't want him getting the idea there was the slightest chance of anything happening between them.

No indeed. Not at all. Not even if there were thousands of miles of Pacific Ocean and countless numbers of sharks between them when the affair was over.

Rick heard Kylee's footsteps on the lanai. He stood up and backed away from the computer, raised his arms and stretched. A glance at the clock told him it was almost ten in the morning. As it did whenever he was working, time had gotten away from him again.

The soft knock at the front door drew his attention. He left the screened-in porch, crossed the living room, and invited Kylee in.

She looked gorgeous standing there with the sun streaming in the open window behind her, highlighting her blonde hair like a halo. He didn't know how it was possible, but apparently just a few hours' exposure to the sun and salt water yesterday had already added new, lighter streaks of gold. Even without a touch of makeup except for a hint of lip gloss, she was naturally stunning. He couldn't help noticing she was also very ill at ease. She looked everywhere but at him.

"So, you doing better today?" He shoved his hands into the back pockets of his shorts for want of something to do.

"Yes. Actually, I am. I . . . I came over to apologize for the way I acted yesterday—"

"You don't know me well enough to know I'd never put your safety in jeopardy."

Kylee reached up and tucked her hair behind her ear. Finally she looked directly at him. "No, I guess I don't."

Rick took a deep breath. "Would you like to?"

"Like to what?"

"Get to know me better."

He could see the idea threw her off balance and inwardly cursed himself for not being able to keep his mouth shut. Kylee wasn't the type to be pushed. She glanced over his shoulder at his office, then looked down at her hands.

"The script is finally coming along," she said.

Rick felt a surge of relief. Maybe he was making some progress after all. Two days ago she would have taken his head off for making the offhanded suggestion that they get to know one another better.

"I'm glad. Can I get you anything to drink? A soda? Iced tea?"

He didn't know when he'd ever felt so awkward around a woman and hoped his reaction wasn't making her uncomfortable. After the way they had parted company yesterday, he had already convinced himself that she'd probably pack up and head out today.

"No, thanks." A half smile teased her lips. "I see you're working on the computer. Are you sure you're not a writer?"

He looked over his shoulder at the monitor and shook his head. "The newsletter keeps me pretty busy."

She shifted her stance, crossed her arms, then dropped them to her sides. "Listen, Rick, I came here to apologize, so I suppose I should quit stalling and say I'm sorry for the way I acted at the beach yesterday."

"I told you I understood—"

"I overreacted. I had no right to carry on so long after you apologized. I just wanted you to know I'm sorry."

"Apology accepted."

"I also came over to tell you that you were absolutely right about getting out of the house and away from the computer. I guess my little adventure yesterday inspired me. I've already rewritten the first draft. Things are moving right along."

"That's great."

"No 'I told you so'?"

He couldn't help smiling at the way she was watching him from beneath her lashes.

"Nope. I've got a suggestion though."

"What's that?"

"How about another inspiring adventure?"

Her brow gathered over her clear eyes. He felt himself quicken when she ran her tongue over her plump bottom lip.

"Another adventure?"

"Why not? Think of your productivity."

"I'm thinking of that shark. What kind of an adventure? Is it on dry land?"

"Nope. Water, but it's—"

She held her hands up in front of her. "No way. I don't think I'm up for another up-close-and-personal encounter. Pigs are one thing, but—"

"River water. No snakes on the islands, no dangerous fish. Just a simple little kayak trip to a waterfall. I'll throw in a picnic lunch." He glanced down at the black Casio diving watch on his arm. "I'll have you home before 3:30. Plenty of time to crank out a few more pages before dinner and then you have the whole night ahead of you to work. What do you say?"

"Kayak?"

"Perfectly safe. A monkey could do it. As long as the monkey swims," he quickly added. Rick watched her sigh and knew he had her. If she had been dead set against it, she would have flatly refused.

"Think of it as research. Think of your script."

"Actually, I am." She was still frowning, but he could see that she was considering the possibilities.

"Can you guarantee no sharks?"

"Absolutely."

"What time?" She looked at her sports watch.

"Change into a swimsuit and bring a towel. Give me thirty minutes to finish up here and throw a lunch together. I'll load the kayak in the truck and pick you up outside the door."

He couldn't believe his luck when she smiled and turned to

let herself out. "I'll be ready. Watch out for the traffic on the way over."

He laughed at her joke and watched her bounce out the door with her hair swinging around her shoulders. Turning around, he headed back to the computer, saved the work on the screen, and switched off the machine. Trying to finish now would be a waste of time when all he could think of was Kylee, her smile, her lips, the feel of her satin-smooth skin beneath his fingertips.

He'd promised her there would be no danger from sharks. That meant he'd have to concentrate on keeping his hands to himself.

Kylee found Rick true to his word. Ignoring her own nagging conscience, she was in the pickup forty-five minutes later. A long, bright green kayak hung out of the truck bed as they rode up Kuhio Highway.

Less than five minutes from his home in Wainiha Valley, Rick was pointing out the Lumahai River when they almost drove past a woman using an emergency call box on the side of the road. At first glance, Kylee thought the woman looked the typical tourist in a T-shirt with I ♥ KAUAI emblazoned on the front, baggy white shorts, a floppy straw hat, and a camera dangling around her neck. But as Rick slammed on the brakes and pulled up alongside the frantic, middle-aged traveler, Kylee could see that the tourist was in great distress. The woman slammed down the emergency phone and ran over to the truck.

"My son's being washed out to sea!" The woman's hands clung to the open driver's window of the truck as she stared, panicked and helpless, at Rick. "Can you do something? I called the emergency number but I'm afraid by the time anyone gets here, Richie will be gone."

The woman choked back sobs and explained that her family was from Ohio and that her son had ridden a boogie board too far out and couldn't get back to shore. Kylee glanced up the highway. The road angled around a sharp curve at the top of a steep grade and disappeared. Aside from two nondescript rental cars coming toward them, there was no help in sight.

"Hang on," Rick told Kylee before he directed the tourist to step out of the way and run back across the highway. He whipped the steering wheel to the left and drove across to the ocean side of the road. Pulling up between tall, ironwood pines with wispy, thin needles, he set the emergency brake and was out of the car all in one swift move.

Kylee hopped out and ran around the front of the pickup. Panting and out of breath, the distraught mother came running with one hand atop the crown of the wide-brimmed straw hat while her camera banged against her breasts.

Kylee's heart went out to this woman who was too scared to cry. Rick quickly commandeered a surfboard from one of a group of young teens loitering by their cars. Kylee took the woman's hand and started across the wide sand beach toward the pounding shore break.

Rick jogged past them with the surfboard tucked beneath his arm as if running in the soft sand took absolutely no effort. After half a dozen steps, Kylee felt as if she were trudging through molasses. The trembling, overweight woman beside her was panting from over-exertion. They were both winded by the time they reached the tide line, where the woman's husband and daughter were waving and shouting to a young boy clinging to his boogie board a good quarter mile out to sea.

"I just don't understand it," the midwesterner said as she held tightly to Kylee's hand. "He swims real good in the pool."

"He's caught in a riptide," Kylee told them. Having gone to the beach in Southern California all her life, she could easily spot the rippling current that was carrying the youth away from the island.

Kylee watched the waves suck away from the shore and then crash with a vengeance onto the sharply sloped sand. Lumahai Beach was nothing like the gentle, protected reef at Tunnels where Rick had taken her snorkeling. As she watched the pounding surf, she didn't know how the inexperienced youth had ever made it out through the rough shore break to begin with.

"I told him not to go in, but he never listens to me anymore." The boy's father was complaining aloud to no one in particular. The terror in his voice overrode his anger.

As Kylee and the family waited, standing in a tight knot of anxiety on the beach, she watched Rick time the waves before he jumped in and began paddling out through the current to get to the young teen. Her heart was in her throat until she realized Rick was stroking with what appeared to be effortless power, cutting swiftly through the water.

When he reached the boy, the two of them were not far from disappearing around an outcropping of rocks on the far side of a river mouth that emptied into the sea. Rick waved and Kylee instantly waved back. So did the tourists, as well as a few other beachgoers who had gathered to watch the unfolding drama.

Just then, the shrill scream of a siren cut the air. Kylee turned around and saw a red fire engine roar into the sandy parking area between the pines. The rescue crew climbed down. One of the men, outfitted in swim gear and carrying a buoy, came running across the sand.

"What's up?" The rescue swimmer ran up to the small crowd on the beach while he scanned the water.

"My son—" the woman from Ohio began.

"I think they're all right," the father cut in. "That man out there on the surfboard got to him in time. It looks like they're both headed back."

Relief shot through Kylee like a jolt of caffeine when she realized Rick was indeed on the way back, paddling and towing the boy and his boogie board behind him with the surfboard leash. Their progress was slow but steady toward the river mouth. Still holding the woman's hand, Kylee turned to the fireman closest to her.

"We were on our way to go kayaking when my friend saw

this lady making an emergency call. He borrowed a board and went in after the boy. There wasn't time to wait."

"Is that Rick Pau?" The fireman was watching Rick's progress. The rescue swimmer stood by, waiting to see if he'd have to go in at all.

"Yes. That's him." Kylee couldn't keep the note of pride out of her voice any more than she could wipe the smile off of her face. Rick Pau, houseboy, chef, gardener, snorkeler, newsletter writer, and self-proclaimed dabbler had just added hero to his list of titles. She turned to the tall blonde man beside her. "Do you know him?"

"Sure. He used to paddle for the Hanalei Civic Hawaiian Canoe Club." The fireman called out to the crew. "No need to stay. Looks like Rick's got it under control. Call in and cancel the rescue 'copter." Then he turned back to Kylee and added in an undertone, "Lucky you two were driving by when you did. Unfortunately, we've lost so many tourists off this beach the locals have taken to calling it Luma-die instead of Lumahai."

Rick was so close now that Kylee could see his smile. His hair was wet, slicked back, and shining blue-black in the sunlight. Without thinking, she waved again. His smile widened when he recognized her and waved back. Her heart managed to trip over itself.

Three firefighters wandered back to the truck while the fourth took down information from the Ohio family. The fireman who had been appointed rescue swimmer stood by on the beach in case Rick needed help getting the boy into shore. Most of the onlookers had wandered back down the beach, one or two hunched over, searching for *puka* shells in the sand.

Finally, Rick was in and the boy was safe. The girl from Ohio volunteered to carry the surfboard back to the boys standing by the cars parked amid the tall pine tree trunks while the wayward Richie, none the worse for his close call, walked away between his parents, who alternately gave him an earful of admonishments and hugged him.

Kylee soaked up every word and nuance when Rick slipped easily into island pidgin English. She didn't mind standing by when he and the firemen exchanged handshakes and 'talked story,' for it gave her time to compare him to the firefighters on the beach. All of them were tall, tan, and fit, but it was disconcerting to notice that she found none of them could hold a candle to Rick Pau. As he laughed with the others, Rick moved up beside her, letting her know without words that he hadn't forgotten her. He didn't so much as touch a shoulder to hers, but he let her know that being with her was important to him. A gentle ache began in the vicinity of her heart.

Finally, the hubbub died down and they walked back to the truck alone.

"I hate to think what might have happened to that boy if you hadn't jumped in to save him," she told Rick.

"It was just luck we came by when we did and he had that boogie board. He would never have been able to stay afloat until the rescue swimmer got out here."

As they got back inside the pickup, Kylee slid onto the bench seat and waited for Rick to get in and close the door. "Don't discount what you did back there," she told him once he was inside the cab. "You saved that boy's life."

He turned the key in the ignition. "Any good swimmer would have done the same thing."

She guessed there had been a number of competent swimmers on the beach, but none of them had wanted to risk going after the tourists' son. Yet Rick had done so as confidently and effortlessly as he apparently did everything else.

Kylee settled back for the rest of the ride to the Kalihiwai River, intending to watch the breathtaking North Shore scenery unfold. It wasn't until she grudgingly admitted to herself that she was actually stealing glances at Rick Pau that she realized she was in real danger of losing her resolve, not to mention her vulnerable, inexperienced heart.

* * *

Rick had been up the Kalihiwai River so often that he knew every inch of the valley. Deciding to memorize everything about Kylee instead, he focused his attention on her. Seated in front of him in the double-occupant kayak, she alternately paddled the long paddle and exclaimed over new sights as they floated over the water. The sun was doing its best to make the noon ride up the river perfect. They had stripped off their T-shirts and then, garbed in swimsuits, slathered each other with sunscreen. It would be a long, long time before he forgot the sensation of her hands slicking the lotion over his shoulders and down his back. Nor would he easily forget the way her fair skin had felt like satin beneath his palms.

"What's that?" she whispered in awe as they drifted by a tall, white bird that reminded her of a small stork. It was perched on a *hau* branch that hung out over the water.

"An egret. They nest in the growth along the river."

Kylee watched the bird until the kayak turned the bend and headed beneath the huge concrete bridge that spanned the narrow valley. Rick watched Kylee, mesmerized by the way she moved. As her gold hair teased her bare shoulders, Rick knew that it would feel like heavy silk. What would she do if he were to reach out, to gently brush the hair away from the nape of her neck, lean forward, and kiss the vulnerable spot behind her ear?

His blood was running hot. He felt himself grow hard and decided to put his energy into paddling. The opaque green water had become more shallow and he knew that momentarily they would be able to see the riverbed beneath them. Not much farther ahead the water would be too shallow to navigate so they would beach the kayak and continue on foot to the falls.

Kylee shifted, drawing his eyes to her cute little bottom as she wriggled around on the wet seat. When the seductive coconut scent of her lotion wafted back to him, he almost groaned aloud.

"We're almost there," he said, fighting to hide the frustration in his tone. He needed to get his feet on solid ground and put some distance between them—fast.

"How much farther to the waterfall?"

"We'll have to walk about a quarter of a mile."

"That's not bad."

He glanced over at the tall grass growing in the field on the valley side of the river. "The field is pretty overgrown, and I don't want to risk running into any pigs or pig hunters, so we'll have to walk upstream through the water."

She immediately stopped negotiating her paddle and smiled over her shoulder. "You don't want to risk running into any pigs and yet you don't mind that I have to put up with one in my bathroom?"

He shrugged and laughed, enjoying the easy exchange. "I told you, there are two kinds of pigs around here."

Kylee laid her paddle down across her lap and continued to look back at him. Her blue eyes were bright, her cheeks flushed with sun and exhilaration. She was the perfect California calendar girl. And she was within arm's reach.

"You know what, Rick?"

"What, Kylee?" He gave up, stopped paddling, and decided to concentrate on her and really enjoy the view.

"I'll say it again. You were right. This is absolutely beautiful. Very inspiring."

It was the perfect opportunity, the perfect opening. He thought of reaching for her, of kissing her. Had it been any other woman, he would have done so and risked her ire, but with Kylee things were different somehow. He didn't want to risk losing her over a stolen kiss.

Instead, he forced himself not to touch her at all.

"You know what?" he asked. "You have a beautiful smile." Once the compliment was out, he expected that megawatt smile to shut down, but today she surprised him.

"Thank you. To tell you the truth, it's been a long time since I've even felt like smiling."

The bottom of the kayak was only a few inches above the smooth, round stones that covered the riverbed.

"Sit still," he said just before he put both hands on the rails of the craft and pushed up and out of his seat. He stepped over the side into the water. Using the nylon rope threaded through the nose of the kayak, Rick pulled it up onto the small area on the sandy shoreline and then reached down to help Kylee out.

She unfolded her long legs and groaned as she stood up. While she stretched out her stiff muscles, she gazed up the hillside that plunged down to the water's edge on the right. The land was covered with thick mango, guava, and umbrella trees, the ground beneath it dank and damp. There was no sound except for the rushing water and the song of a shama thrush hidden somewhere in the nearby trees.

"I can hear the waterfall up ahead," she said.

"Do you want to eat here or take the picnic up to the falls? It's no problem to carry it. I put everything in a backpack."

By the look in her eyes it was easy to guess her answer. He began digging the pack out of the storage bin in the front of the kayak.

"I've never been to a waterfall. Maybe it would be fun to eat up there."

"You got it." He slipped the straps over his shoulders and pointed up river in the direction of the falls. "After you.

Ten minutes later, Kylee wished she had never heard the word waterfall. Up to her ankles in river water, she was certain she was going to break her neck, or worse, one of her arms.

"You know, I have to get that script done and I won't be able to do it in a cast." Her buoyant mood evaporated when her foot slipped for what seemed like the hundredth time. Slowly, she cautiously picked her way over the slick, mossy stones that lined the river bottom. "How much farther is it?"

"Just around the next bend."

She stopped short and turned her frustration on him. The

fact that he was smiling his usual killer smile didn't make things any better.

"You have no idea where the waterfall is, do you?"

"Yes, I do," he nodded. "Just ahead we cross the river and climb up the path."

"Climb up the path," she repeated. "Why do I think there's probably more to it than that?"

He shrugged. "Don't you trust me?"

Kylee stared up into his deep dark eyes, then at that smile that was so impossible to ignore, and shook her head. "Not even as far as I could throw you."

When he laughed, she turned around and started off again. They rounded the bend and, anxious to see the falls, she forgot to watch her footing. The moss was too much even for the rubber-soled water socks he'd given her to wear. Her foot slipped off the surface of a rock. Her arms went wide automatically as she fought to maintain her balance but it was too little too late. She started to topple over. Suddenly, Rick grabbed her arm just above the elbow.

Kylee threw herself at him to keep from falling. In a split second, she thought that they were both going to fall, but crashing into Rick was like hitting a lava rock wall. His arms went around her, but other than that he didn't budge. His legs were braced, his stance surefooted, even on the slippery rocks.

Disoriented, she stood there within the circle of his arms, her cheek pressed against his chest, listening to the strong, steady beat of his heart. Her own heart was racing, and an aching need began to throb deep within her. She nearly groaned aloud.

Pull away, she told herself. *Don't do this.* But she didn't budge. Time seemed to stop. Everything was so perfect: the sound of the river, the birds calling to one another; the balmy trade winds; the soothing, dense green forest all around. It felt so good to just let go, to let down her guard and let someone else be stronger for this one perfect moment.

When his hand slipped to the small of her back, she felt him press her, ever so slightly, closer. Kylee closed her eyes. He was so tempting. Everything a lover should be, but a temptation she definitely didn't need at this point in time.

When? The question instantly insinuated itself into her thoughts. *If not now, when?* Would there ever come a time when she wasn't running as fast as she could to stay in one place, to keep up with her work and her career? Would there ever be a time to learn to let herself love and be loved?

Rick had his hand on her chin. He tipped her face up to his and when he stared down into her eyes, she was powerless to move. He began to lower his head. She watched his full, sensuous lips as they came closer to her mouth. Her heart fluttered. Her mouth went dry. He was going to kiss her.

Kylee closed her eyes for a heartbeat and then quickly pushed away, forcing herself to stand on her own two feet. She took a deep, shaky breath and then tried to make light of the situation.

"That was a close call," she whispered.

Rick shifted the backpack. "Yeah. I guess so."

She wished he looked relieved, but he appeared pained more than anything else. She could read the truth in his eyes. He thought she was a tease.

"That was an accident, Rick. Not some ploy I used just to fall into your arms."

He looked over his shoulder, downriver. There was no sign of any other kayakers coming upstream. In fact, she thought, there was probably no one around for miles.

"I know that," he said. Still, the lightness which had threaded his tone all morning was gone. "You can rest assured I wasn't trying to take advantage of the situation, either. It's just that for a moment there, you seemed plenty content to be in my arms."

She felt herself blush and knew she deserved his anger. She had lingered in his embrace. It had felt so very right.

"I'm sorry you came to the wrong conclusion," she told him coolly.

He was no longer smiling. "Do you want to go back?"

She could take the coward's way out and say yes, but she hated to end the otherwise perfect outing with both of them acting like stubborn children. Someone had to budge. She shoved her hair back off her face and smiled.

"Not on your life. Not without seeing that damn waterfall."

It was just the light touch needed to dispel the tension. Rick's lips lifted in a half smile. His shoulders rose and fell as he took a deep breath. Then he held out his hand.

Kylee looked down at it for a moment, hesitating.

"The stones are slippery," he explained.

She reached out and put her hand in his.

The climb to the pool at the base of the waterfall was slow because the ground beneath the thick forest canopy was virtually untouched by sunlight and slick with moisture from the recent rains. As the afternoon heat intensified, the humidity against the rock wall that formed the base of the valley was stifling. Water thundered down from the pool above, the ceaseless cascade showering the rocks that broke the surface with a refreshing mist.

They climbed over the rocks and stood behind the cascade, then swam across the pool where they picnicked on sandwiches and sodas. When they finished, Rick was content to watch Kylee, seated on the black rock beside him.

"I can't stop staring up at the water as it pours over the ridge. It's hard to believe it never stops."

"You should see it when it rains. It's not safe to be up here then, but it's visible from the bridge. The water flows from upriver and turns red from all the mud it carries in it."

"I could sit here forever."

"Take all the time you want."

She turned to him then, her eyes shadowed with something he could feel but not read. Regret?

"I'd love nothing better than to sit here forever, but I can't run away from my life that easily. I have to get back and work this afternoon to make up for all this time off."

"You *have* to work? Is it worth it, if you love it so little?"

"I guess I put that the wrong way. I want to get back to the script because it's finally coming along. I don't want to lose my pace."

A sadness for her settled in his heart but did nothing to decrease his longing. He wanted to tell her that she was on a fast path to self-destruction if she didn't take time to live, to love, but he would be pushing it, he knew, to say anything of the sort. Especially after she had given in and taken the morning off.

He slipped the pack back on, stood up, and for the second time that afternoon, held out his hand to her. Instantly, she took it and he pulled her up without stepping back or away. Her nearness, her smiles were driving him crazy. As he looked down into her eyes, he made a split second decision.

Time was slipping away. In two weeks, she would be gone and he would be alone trying to figure out how he had let her slip away and wondering what might have been.

He was going to kiss her now and damn the consequences.

Four

Kylee knew what was about to happen before Rick pulled her into his arms. Even so, she was powerless to stop what had been building between them since they met. At first, when his lips touched hers, she refused to be seduced. Then, all too quickly, her will evaporated and she began to soften as he teased the seam of her lips with his tongue. Unable to resist her own hunger for him any longer, wanting more than a quick, stolen kiss, she opened her mouth and let him slip his tongue inside.

His strong arms were wrapped around her. His hands rested at the small of her back. She gasped against his mouth when he lifted her slightly and pressed her against his erection.

It was an instant before she realized she was kissing him back with pure abandon, but obviously Rick noticed, for he moaned low in his throat, slashed his mouth across hers, and deepened his kiss.

She raked her fingers through his long, thick hair and relished the feel of him, all hard planes and angles. The waterfall thundered behind them, just as it had for countless centuries. Locked in the moment, standing in the heat and the mist coming off the falls, Kylee almost wished they could slip back to a time when the island was raw and new and as primitive as the torrent of emotion seething inside her.

What this man's touch could do to her was terrifying. His kiss had the power to be her undoing. She felt his hand slip over her rib cage as he slowly slid it up to cup the underside of her breast through her swimsuit. Compelled, she lifted slightly, pressing her breast against his palm, and felt his fingers tighten, ever so slightly, over her fullness.

She almost cried aloud at the blessed pleasure-pain that blossomed inside her. His fingers closed around the nipple budded tightly beneath the clinging fabric of her swimsuit. For the first time in her life, she wanted more, wanted to feel his fingers strip the swimsuit straps off her shoulders. She wanted her breasts exposed to his warm hands, his teasing mouth. She wanted to feel him over her, around her. She wanted to take him inside her. She wanted to pleasure him, to let him give her the pleasure she had denied herself for so long.

She knew Rick Pau could make her blood sing. That made him dangerous to her—and to her career. Kylee let go of his hair. She drew her arms from around his neck, slipped her hands between them, and pushed against his well-muscled chest until he lifted his head.

They were breathing as hard as if they had scaled the rugged cliff face behind the falls. Shaken by the potency of their kiss, Kylee didn't know how long her trembling legs would hold her or if she could even stand alone. Thankfully, Rick kept her within the circle of his arms. It was a gentle cradling, nothing more.

"It would be so good between us, Kylee," Rick whispered against her ear.

Still too shaken to put her thoughts into words, she shook her head, trying to deny it. She had no experience, no idea how it would be, or should be.

"You know it would," he said, reaching down to tip her face up to meet his eyes. "Tell me you don't want me as much as I want you."

His words terrified her, because they were so true. "What I want and what's good for me are two different things. What about you, Rick? Do you actually think I'd be good for you? You told me about your wife, about how she put her career before everything and that eventually split up your marriage.

Why do you think I'm here on Kauai alone with my computer for company? My work is my life, Rick. It always has been. You'd be making the same mistake all over again, unless you're only looking for a quick affair."

"I think you know me better than that by now."

"Not really," she said too quickly, even though right now she felt deep in her soul that she might have known this man forever.

His arms dropped away from her. Rick took a step back and glanced at the upper ledge of the falls. Kylee followed his gaze and caught a glimpse of brightly colored fabric. As she watched, three tourists with cameras at the ready strolled into view.

"How in the world did they get up there?" Her frustration made it sound as if she were furious at these people she had never laid eyes on.

"Horseback. The stable over the hill offers rides through the countryside to the waterfall." He studied the clouds overhead. "We'd better go. There's heavy rain coming."

Rick had already negotiated the boulders at the edge of the pool and was about to enter the path that wound back to the river through the thick vegetation. The sunshine had disappeared along with the lighthearted mood of the day. Thick gray clouds with trailing rain were gathering over the valley. She had no option but to follow.

They rode back to *Hale Nanea,* the sound of the rain against the roof of the pickup the only disruption of their cold silence. Rick pulled up at the front of the rental house and kept the engine running, his hands tight on the steering wheel. He turned his head to look at Kylee.

With one hand on the door handle, she stared out the window, watching the rain trickle slowly down the glass. Her hair was still damp from the rain that caught them while they paddled down the Kalihiwai River to the park on the bay. She looked so bedraggled and forlorn sitting there wrapped in a striped beach towel with her limp, wet hair dripping onto her shoulders that he wanted to pull her into his arms and hold her until he could coax a smile to her lovely mouth.

"Why don't you come over for dinner tonight and we'll talk about this like two adults?" It was all he could think of, short of locking her in the truck while he tried to convince her to take a chance on love.

"There is no *this* to talk about. You aren't going to change the way I feel," she said without looking over at him. "Besides, I have to work tonight." She pulled on the door handle to let herself out. "I can let myself in," she said when he started to open his own door.

"If not me, then who, Kylee? Are you ever going to let anyone love you? You can't run from your emotions forever. You can't spend your life storing them up just to put them on paper." He reached over and rested his palm on her thigh. Her skin was soft and warm. She didn't pull away. Instead, she turned around and looked into his eyes for a fleeting moment. Confusion, anxiety, intense longing were mirrored in blue before she quickly looked down at the hand he still held on her thigh.

"What's between us, if there is anything at all, is a purely physical attraction, Rick." She sounded uncertain, as if she needed convincing more than he did.

"Maybe that was true," he said slowly, choosing his words carefully, knowing this might be the last chance he had to win her trust. "I knew the moment I laid eyes on you that I wanted you, Kylee. But now it's more than that. I've gotten to know you over the past few days and I want to get to know you better. You've got a lot of love bottled up inside."

She shook her head. "How can you possibly know that when I don't?"

"You do," he said before she could protest. "I saw the way you stood by that poor woman, a stranger, on the beach today when she was terrified of losing her son. You were there for her—"

"Anyone would have done that."

"No, not everyone would have. If you'd just open up, take a chance, you'd find you have a lot of love to give, Kylee."

"And you want me to give it to you?"

He couldn't help but smile. She'd backed him into a corner.

"I'm not going to deny it. No matter what you might think, I'm not looking for a one night stand anymore than you are. It's been a long time since I've wanted to be with someone, Kylee. A long time. I don't want to blow it with you. All I'm asking is that you think about what I've said, think about what we might have together. If you'll take a step in that direction, I'll be there to meet you no matter how long it takes. Will you do that before it's too late? Will you at least think about it?"

Unshed tears shimmered in her eyes. She quickly blinked them back, trying to deny them just as she had her feelings. She took a deep breath.

"I'll think about it," she whispered.

He let go of her thigh and clamped his hand on the steering wheel again. "Promise?"

She nodded, then slid off the seat, stepped out of the truck, and closed the door behind her. In the rearview mirror, Rick watched her walk around the back of the pickup and run up the stairs. He smiled when she abruptly stopped at the top step to peel off her rubber shoes like a local before she stepped onto the lanai. At the door she paused and looked at him over her shoulder. Her eyes were wide, the confusion in them intensified. He waited until she disappeared inside before he pulled the truck the rest of the way up the drive.

He'd stated his case. All he could do now was wait.

Four days later the first draft of the screenplay was finished. Kylee had taken advantage of a deluge that hadn't let up since the day of the kayak trip. She welcomed the gray skies. They matched her mood. Just as Rick had accused her of doing, she had spent the days pouring her emotional turmoil into the script. By the time she wrote the last line of dialogue of the final, moving scene where Charese LaDonne was reunited with the hero of the tale, silent tears were sliding down her own cheeks.

Her burst of creative energy spent, Kylee changed into a clean top and then grabbed her purse and the keys to the Jeep. After staring at the taro patch beyond the window for four days, she was ready for a change of view and felt the need to clear her head. Within ten minutes she had reached the town of Hanalei where she stopped in at the crowded Village Variety for postcards. Without intending to, she ended up buying a piece of tropical print fabric that the clerk guaranteed could easily be tied and wrapped into fifteen different styles.

Then, beneath an umbrella-topped table, Kylee sipped an iced cafe mocha while she watched a new generation of hippies in tie-dyed tees and rubber sandals wander in and out of the Hanalei Health Food Store in the Ching Young Center.

Usually when she finished a first draft, she felt both excited and relieved. This time she felt neither. She knew the script was good, probably some of her best work—and knew she had Rick to thank for it.

Rick. Day and night, even as she worked, she thought of him. Of what he'd said. Of how right he had been about her wanting him. She wanted to know everything about him, what made him laugh, what he dreamed of. She wished she could get inside him for a day and learn everything there was to know of Rick Pau. The very idea that she wanted him so much terrified her. Why Rick? Why now? She had asked herself over and over. What was there that attracted two people from very different worlds?

A young couple walked by the table, arm in arm, wearing bright new sunburns over tender mainland skin. As she watched them stroll along, Kylee decided they must have driven over from the other side of the island or just arrived from Maui, because the sun hadn't shone on the north shore for four days. The couple was in their late teens or early twenties, newlyweds by the way the girl studied the bright solitaire on her left hand when her new husband wasn't looking.

Was there a chance that with Rick she might be able to experience something she had been certain would always elude her? Or was she fooling herself?

Finishing up the iced mocha, she picked up her package and left the shelter of the umbrella. She tossed the empty plastic cup into a recycle bin and made a run for the Jeep, but by the time she got the door open and hopped in, she was soaked.

The rain was coming down in steady sheets as she negotiated the curved highway back to Powerhouse Road. By the time she made it down the steep muddy driveway and parked at *Hale Nanea,* she was thankful she'd rented an all-terrain vehicle. She'd barely cleared the lanai steps when a black pickup truck came sliding down the drive. Her heart lodged in her throat as she watched the full-sized truck swerve around her rented Jeep before it skidded to a stop at her front door.

She'd only seen a flash of the driver as he slid by, a burly Hawaiian with arms the size of ham hocks and a smile as bright as a full moon. He revved the engine of the truck and shouted Rick's name. Two other Hawaiian men were riding in the truck bed, sheltered from the rain by a lumber rack covered with plywood sheets.

One of the men waved when he noticed Kylee standing on her lanai. She waved back, stepped into the house, and laid her package on the sofa. She wandered over to the desk and was about to pick up her script when the truck motor shut off and she heard Rick shout to the men.

She closed her eyes. Her hands tightened on the script. Just the sound of his voice could send a raw ache through her. She paused where she was, arrested by the lilt of his words as he spoke to one of the other men in island pidgin.

"You hear, Rick?"

"Yeah. I hear. Coming dis way, yeah?"

"Looks like, yeah. Plenty beeg, but nutting like *Iniki,* eh?"

"Nutting like *Iniki* evah come again, bra, you tink?"

Kylee couldn't fathom much of what they said, except for the word *Iniki,* powerful hurricane, as she recalled. She set the script down. Walking to the kitchen door, she steeled herself for her first glimpse of Rick in days. Standing just inside the door, she saw him clearly through the screen. He was leaning against the railing on his lanai, his arms spread, his strong brown hands gripping the white wooden rail. The breeze had strengthened enough to where it ruffled his long dark hair and lifted it off his shoulders.

Quiet power and strength emanated from him. She knew in a glance that here was a man who had an iron will. He would wait forever, just as he had said, until she made up her mind to meet him halfway.

It was hard to look at Rick and concentrate on what he and the pickup driver were talking about but she tried.

"Need wood?" the driver shouted.

"Nah. I got 'em. You take care." Rick raised his hand to give the *shaka* or hang loose salute as the truck driver started the pickup, gunned the engine, and threw it into reverse. The wheels spun, sending a shower of mud and gravel in the air before they caught and the driver maneuvered a U-turn in what looked like an impossible space. The truck disappeared up the drive.

Kylee took a deep breath, pushed the screen open, and stepped out onto the lanai. Rick was facing her door and saw her immediately. She watched him smile. Just knowing that smile was for her made her simmer down to her toes. What would it be like to wake up to *that* every morning?

Impossible. The answer came immediately after the question popped into her head. Impossible. Rick was an island boy, his way of life as simple as he could make it. His home was here in this serene valley. Her life was her work. L.A. Hollywood.

Impossible. Impossible.

The word echoed with every step that took her closer to where he stood waiting on his own lanai. As she drew nearer, she imagined walking straight into his arms. *What if she did it?* What if she let herself go to him?

She stopped an arm's length away.

"You went out for a while," he said.

"To Hanalei. Just to get outside. It's a nice little town."

"Everyone talking about the hurricane?"

"Hurricane? No . . . but now that you mention it, there were long lines at the Big Save. I'm so used to L.A., I thought that was normal." She had been too preoccupied with thoughts of him to pay much attention to what anyone around her was saying.

She looked away from him, scanning the thick tropical foliage surrounding the houses. The images of the aftermath of *Iniki* that she had seen on the newscasts in L.A. had been unforgettable. Even though she'd had no connection to the island at all, her heart had gone out to the residents of Kauai. Rick's homes were eclectic and charming. The garden was lovely, so tranquil and lush. She thought of the lost photos, of what it must have taken for him to return this place to its perfection. She hated to think of them being destroyed.

She swung around to face him. "What can we do?"

"Not panic." Again, that heart-melting smile. "Right now, they've issued a hurricane warning. If the storm progresses on course, it will hit within twelve hours. There's always a chance it will turn in another direction, or be downgraded to a tropical storm if it loses intensity."

"Your friends sounded worried."

He glanced up at the dense, gray cloud cover. There was no hint of blue, no patch of sunlit sky. "Everyone here is a little gun-shy of hurricanes, with good reason. What you can do is pack up your computer and printer and put them in the boxes you shipped them over in."

"That won't take me ten minutes. What else? What can I do to help you?"

"I'm going to keep checking the National Hurricane Center on the Net. They're tracking the storm. I've got plywood cut to fit over all the windows stored beneath the house. You can help me put them up, but I hope to God we won't need them."

He was so calm in the face of what might lie ahead that her heart went out to him. As she stood there, hesitant and awkward in the sudden silence, he leaned against the lanai railing. She knew he was waiting for her to make the next move.

"Rick, I—"

The phone in the guest house started ringing. Kylee glanced over her shoulder. No one had called her for ten days. No one but Sylvia knew she was here.

"You probably want to get that," he said, straightening away from the railing.

"It must be Sylvia," she mumbled, taking a step back as relief washed over her. Thank God for small favors, she thought. She had no idea how to put her thoughts into words.

"Tell her I said hello," Rick told her before Kylee turned to walk away.

Sylvia called to tell her that word of the mounting storm headed for the islands was on the news broadcasts in L.A. and then she breezily told Kylee not to worry.

Kylee wished she could have taken the advice to heart. For the next few hours she alternately paced the house and tried to skim her script. Everything that she would have hated to lose fit into two boxes, all of it work related. She'd brought no good jewelry, not that she owned that much, nor did she care about her clothing. It could be replaced far more easily than Rick could repair the fine wood floors, the stained glass windows, or the furnishings in the house.

She felt totally isolated. Without looking at the clock it was hard to tell what time it was by the dingy gray sky. A small pond had formed at the end of the driveway. She couldn't imagine what the valley would be like if the storm blew in with full fury.

Unwilling to wait any longer to find out what was going on, she was about to open the door when she nearly ran into Rick.

He was only wearing shorts. His upper torso was soaked, his hair dripping wet and stuck to his shoulders. "I've been pulling out plywood to put on the windows of this house."

"You said I could help," she reminded him.

"That would be great, but you're liable to get pretty dirty."

If his own mud-streaked shorts were any indication, she knew he was right. "I don't care. Let's go."

She followed him outside and together they waded beneath the house where he began pulling window-sized sheets of pre-cut plywood out from a rack. Her job was simply to prop them up until he could haul them out one by one, and then stand by and lend a hand while he hung them on preset hinges.

When they stooped over to walk into the four-feet-high space beneath the house, Kylee's nervousness in the face of the impending storm came out in giggles.

"What's so funny?" Rick looked down, inspecting the front of his pants, and then peered over his shoulder at the back of them.

His assumption that there was something odd about him only made her laugh harder. "I'm sorry," she finally managed. "It's just that standing here hunched over, ankle deep in mud under a house, waiting for a hurricane, isn't exactly the way I pictured the *serene respite in tranquil surroundings* described in your brochure."

She brushed her hair back off her face and grabbed one end of the last plywood sheet they would have to wrestle up the steps and hang. Much to her relief, Rick laughed, too. "Remind me to give you a refund."

"Oh no. I should pay you. Imagine the amount of fresh material I'll get out of this."

"Do you think I'd get more bookings if I threw in an adventure package?" He laughed.

Kylee found herself smiling at him across the plywood. "How do you do it, Rick?"

"Do what?"

"Keep laughing."

"What's the alternative?"

She thought about that for a moment and then admitted, "I never looked at it that way." Together they moved the last piece of wood and hung it over the picture window on the wall above the desk Kylee had been using. It was almost pitch dark inside the rental house, stuffy and eerie without windows. The rain beat down on the metal roof.

"I'm going to run up to the house across the road and make sure the Makais have enough drinking water and blankets."

Kylee thought of the fragile-looking structure on the opposite side of the hill. "Do you think they should come over here?"

"I'll ask, but they probably won't want to. During *Iniki* they chose to stay put. You gather up all the candles and hurricane lamps in this place and have them ready along with your boxes. When I come back, I'll move you into my house."

She hadn't thought past boarding up the house. The idea of sitting out the storm alone was terrifying enough, but to actually move into Rick's place—

"Kylee?"

"Yes? What?"

"My house is more sheltered in the trees. It weathered *Iniki* just fine, so I'm not going to board it up unless the predictions get worse. There's still time. If you have any reservations about staying alone with me—"

"I don't," she quickly assured him. How could she tell him it wasn't *his* behavior she was worried about anymore, but her own weakness? "I'll have everything ready."

"The storm is projected to hit in a few more hours. It was just barely upgraded to a hurricane, so we can always hope it'll be downgraded again." He started toward the door to leave and see about the family up the hill, then paused. "I'll be right back. Will you be all right alone?"

Kylee nodded. Then she forced herself to smile, stuck out her little finger and thumb and shook her hand, giving him the hang loose sign.

His laughter trailed behind him as he headed out the door.

* * *

Kylee sat on Rick's comfortable, deep cushioned sofa with her feet tucked up beneath her, content just to dwell in the flickering light of the hurricane lamps and listen as Rick strummed his guitar.

She glanced over at the dark hallway where Rick had tucked her boxes far from any doors or windows. It was where they would hide, Rick told her, if one of the windows blew, but he had added that there was little chance of that now.

At the last possible moment, hurricane 'Io, named for the Hawaiian hawk, had veered westward. NHC had predicted it would barely touch Kauai and the island would suffer no more damage than with any heavy tropical storm. It had already generated enough wind to knock out the power, but not until after they had worked together making omelets and hash browns on the electric stove.

As she rolled her head back and forth trying to ease the ache out of her shoulder muscles, Kylee surreptitiously watched Rick. He was intent on his music, seemingly oblivious to the havoc outside.

With most of the windows closed, the air inside the little house was sultry, thick with humidity, but not totally uncomfortable. The music and the lamplight created a romantic atmosphere that overrode the intense tropical storm. They sat like two turtles in the same shell. Despite the weather raging outside the boarded-up house, Kylee felt an inner peace and contentment, even though it left her puzzled.

Was this what it would be like to share a life with someone? Would there often be these comfortable, quiet moments of solitude? All her life she had been afraid she didn't have enough to give to both her work and a permanent relationship. She thought she needed to channel all of her emotion, all of her time and energy into her work if she was going to be the success she dreamed of. As a child, and then a teen, she had never lived with a foster family long enough to learn how a woman, a wife, could divide time between her work and a husband and family. Could she really be equally devoted to all of them?

As she sat there staring at Rick, soaking in the music, the tranquil atmosphere he'd created, she realized there was a solace here that, in and of itself, was rejuvenating. She had also gained contentment from the opportunity to be at ease and laugh with him as they hastily threw dinner together and playfully argued over who should wash and who should dry the dishes.

She had always feared that if she became too content, too settled, she would become complacent, that her work would lose its edge and her career would suffer for it. But that certainly wasn't the case if the new script she had written was any indication.

One thing she had always been blessed with was a clear insight into the quality of her own work and she *knew* that the LaDonne script was as good or better than the Emmy winner she had penned last year.

"You look like you're thinking much too hard. You aren't scared, are you?"

Kylee started and found Rick standing over her. She had been so lost in thought that she didn't know how long ago he had stopped playing, set aside his guitar, and crossed the room.

"Of course not. We're locked up tight as a drum in here." She started to smile, but just then something shuddered against the back of the house that made them both jump.

"Tree limb," Rick speculated.

"What'll we do?"

"Nothing right now, but I'll have plenty of yard work tomorrow. You'll have to get back to your *serene respite in peaceful surroundings.*"

"This is actually the most peaceful hour I've ever spent with someone," she admitted, her voice barely audible.

He sat down on the other end of the sofa and draped his arm along the back. "In the middle of a hurricane you find peace. Care to explain?"

She didn't think she could put what she was feeling into words until she looked into his eyes. He was a man of his word. Somehow, like a disciplined warrior, he had tempered the passion he'd shown earlier. Like her own for him, it was still there. But he had given a promise and he was doing his damnedest to keep it. She could trust him with her innermost thoughts.

"Tonight is a first for me, Rick. I've never spent quiet hours alone with a man, never shared any household chores or just . . . well, sat around sharing quiet hours with a man."

"You've never lived with anyone?"

"I've never let any relationship go that far."

He was watching her closely, intent on what she said. She could almost see the wheels of his mind working and braced herself for the inevitable question.

"Are you still a virgin, Kylee?" His tone was laced with disbelief, as if he'd just stumbled across an archeological wonder and questioned having found it.

Her gaze dropped to where her hands were folded in her lap. "I'm twenty-five years old."

"That's not exactly an answer."

Her heart was in her throat. Her palms were sweating. In a moment of clarity, she thought of what a reflection on society it was that she felt ashamed having to admit it.

"Yes. I am." She crossed her arms beneath her breasts and then met his gaze directly. "I've dated plenty of men, but . . . I just never got around to . . . you know."

"That's nothing to be ashamed of."

"Then why do you look so astounded?"

A half smile slid across his lips and he shrugged. "A woman like you . . . I can't believe you've never been in love before."

"I give everything to my work, Rick. At least I have until now."

"And now?"

"This stay here on Kauai has made me think. I've been able to go out and play and still produce." She felt herself blushing when she thought of what she had just said. "I didn't mean play around, I meant the snorkeling, the—"

"I knew what you meant." He reached over and picked up a lock of her hair and rubbed it between his fingers. She was tempted to lean closer and brush her cheek against his knuckles.

"And tonight?"

"Tonight has been . . . well, nice, despite the storm. I've always thought that loving someone meant putting one hundred percent into nurturing the relationship." She paused, trying to find a way to make him understand.

He found the words for her. "A relationship can nurture you, too. It doesn't just take, but can give something back. Make you stronger. His voice had a mellow, hypnotic tone, as if he were speaking slowly and softly so as not to frighten her.

"Can it Rick? Can it make you stronger? What if it turns out like your marriage? Why take a chance?"

"The human race would end if people didn't take a chance on love and believe it would last."

"Despite all the odds?"

"Despite them all."

"Kiss me, Rick."

"Kiss *me,* Kylee. It's been harder than hell to keep my hands off you all day long. *You* kiss me. That way, you can set the limits."

Five

You kiss me.

For a moment she sat perfectly still. The riot of weather outside was nothing compared to what was going on inside her. Slowly, Kylee unfolded her legs and slid in closer, her gaze jumping from Rick's mouth to his eyes. Reaching up, she cupped the side of his face, paused a moment, then touched her lips to his.

All the pent-up desire, all the hunger and need raging inside her, took over. Kylee moaned and slipped her fingers through Rick's hair, pressing against him until her breasts were crushed against the hard wall of his chest. Her tongue slipped into his mouth, delved, tasted, explored. She shivered as their tongues touched, danced, circled.

With her eyes closed, she was lost in a heady whirl of sensation. She drank him in, the taste, the scent, the hard planes of his well-honed body. She held nothing back and for the first time in her life let her heart take over.

Rick was the first to pull back, to end the kiss. They were breathing as hard as racehorses. Kylee realized she still had his face imprisoned between her hands. She couldn't break contact with his dark-eyed gaze, for in the depths of his eyes lay the promise of fulfillment.

She had never felt so alive, as if every nerve ending were pulsing with life. She was quivering in anticipation. When a bead of perspiration trickled between her breasts, she felt every centimeter of its sensuous slide. Despite the heat in the closed-up house, she shivered. Leaning into Rick, she kissed him again, daring to move boldly against him. Her nipples ached. Deep in her throat, a moan voiced her need.

Rick felt that need, for it was echoed in his own heart. He slipped his hands up beneath her tank top, touched her naked breasts. Her nipples were pebble hard. When he traced his open palms over them, she cried out. Her fingers tightened in his hair.

"Let me love you, Kylee. Let me show you how good it will be between us," he whispered.

She sat up and his hands slipped away from her breasts, down her midriff. He lay his palms on her thighs below the hem of her shorts, watching her intently. She reached down and grabbed the hem of her tank top. Yanking it up over her head, Kylee tossed it over her shoulder. With her breasts exposed to his gaze, she sat there waiting, wanting, but not for very long.

Rick reached out and cupped her breasts gently, lifted them, gazed down at the perfection that was Kylee. He lowered his head to suck on her nipples, one and then the other, back and forth.

She threw her head back, her hands grasping the soft material of his worn T-shirt. She cried out, desperate for release as the incessant throb building in the bud at the apex of her thighs intensified. Burning with desire, her hands tore at Rick's T-shirt. The fabric was worn, thin from many washings. The material ripped away from the neckline with a rending tear.

Beyond control, she jerked the front of his shirt down to his waist, leaving his arms in the sleeves, the crew neck banding his throat. Kylee ran her fingers up and down his abs, just the way she had envisioned doing when she first saw him exercising. He was rock hard perfection.

Rick's hand went to the button at the waistband of her shorts. After two tries at slipping it open, he gave up and pulled. The button popped and flew over the back of the sofa. Kylee squirmed around until he could lower her zipper and slid her shorts and panties to her hips.

In one deft move, he used his strength to hold her close as he slid them both off the sofa to the *lau hala* mat on the floor. Kylee stretched out full length and lay there looking up at him. Her blue eyes had darkened to the color of the midnight sky backlit by a full moon. He reached down and drew her shorts and panties the rest of the way over her hips and down her legs. She kicked them off and reached for him.

Before he moved into her arms, Rick shucked off his own shorts, pulled off the remnants of his T-shirt with a smile, and then raised himself to his knees. He was fully aroused.

Kylee stared up at Rick, the *lau hala* mat beneath her cool and slick. She gazed up in wonder at his erection. Despite her past, despite the wave of trepidation, she felt as she lay there watching him, she wanted Rick Pau, wanted him in ways she'd wanted no other man.

There was no rational explanation for the way she felt about him, other than that he had given her a glimpse into a world she had never known and never would know unless she took a chance.

"Are you sure this is what you want, Kylee?" His words came to her over the sound of the rain lashing the roof and the wind howling outside.

"Yes, yes it is." She reached up, slowly, like a child who has been warned against touching a rare treasure, and stroked him with her fingertip.

Still on his knees beside her, Rick closed his eyes, threw his head back, and let her explore him with her hand until he thought he would explode.

"Stop, Kylee," he whispered. When he had collected himself, he looked down at her again. Panic and confusion pained her expression.

"Did I do something wrong?"

"You are perfect. I'm going to leave you for a minute. I

almost hate to give you time to change your mind, but I think we should play it safe."

"I won't change my mind," she told him. There was a confident certainty in her calm assurance.

Rick pushed up to his feet and left her staring up at the vaulted, open-beamed ceiling of the cottage. *Play it safe.* She shook her head in the semi-darkness. Even though she might have lost all sense of reason, Rick was responsible enough to look out for both of them.

He was back in only seconds, but they seemed like hours. Once more he knelt beside her knees and sat back on his heels. Reaching down, he lifted her hair out from beneath her head and shoulders, spread it around her like a golden halo on the woven mat. Then he ran his hands over her face, traced her lips with his fingertips, continued down along her throat, trailed his hands over her collarbones.

Kylee closed her eyes and bit her lips together to keep from crying out. He was slowly, systematically charting his way down, all the way from her hairline. When he reached her breasts, stroking them slowly, then moving his fingers over her rib cage, she almost screamed with need.

He was molding his hands over her hips, along the outside of her thighs. Her knees, her calves, her ankles, and then her toes were kneaded and caressed in turn. Kylee was writhing now, her head thrashing from side to side.

His hands closed around her ankles. He opened her legs. He drew the left one over his knees until he was kneeling between her thighs.

Kylee's breath caught in her throat. She pressed her open palms on the mat on either side of her as Rick bent forward, lifted her legs, and draped them over his shoulders. He lowered his head and kissed her in that most intimate of places.

Out of control, as if she were being tossed on the waves of the stormy sea that surrounded the island, she bucked and moaned but he wouldn't stop, wouldn't lift his head or stop the intense, soul-shattering torture until she finally shuddered and came.

She could hear herself sobbing his name over and over, and yet was powerless to stop. He had given her the universe and she had yet to give him anything at all.

Rick gently drew her legs off his shoulders. When she lay there pliant and willing, he slid over her, took her in his arms and buried his face against the crook of her neck and felt her frantic pulse until it began to subside.

He reached down, slid his hand between their bodies, and slipped his fingers inside her. She was hot and wet and ready for him. Knowing this was her first time, he didn't want to hurt her. He wanted to take things slowly, to make it perfect for her, but he was ready to explode. Rick moved his fingers along her slippery flesh. She quivered and rose to follow the movement of his hand.

"Rick, oh Rick," she whispered.

"I'm going to come inside you, Kylee."

"Yes," she whispered, urging him on with her hands on his hips.

As she lay beneath him, relishing the feel of his smooth, hard body, Kylee was certain she could feel each and every inch of her skin. Flashing hot and cold, she was alive with sensation, pulsing with the need to have him fill her.

"Please, Rick," she urged, not caring how desperate she sounded, but she was desperate—for him, for his body, for the deep, resonating fulfillment to hit her again. But this time she wanted to share it with him.

Rick withdrew his hand and pressed closer as he positioned himself. He hoped and prayed she was as ready as she claimed. He wanted this to be a special night for her, a memory she would cherish no matter what the future held in store. With aching slowness he pressed into her, further, further until he heard her gasp. She froze, held still, and so did he.

His breath was coming, harsh and fast. Every muscle tensed as he strained to hold back while she accustomed herself to the fullness of having him inside her. She was tight, so very tight, so warm.

He eased in further. She clutched his shoulders and cried out, a sharp, keening sound that lasted only a split second. He plunged into her and withdrew partially.

"No! Don't stop," she urged.

It was all the encouragement he needed. Rick moved, rocking with her, holding back until he could feel her quiver and tighten around him. He carried her up, up and over the edge again. This time he was with her. This time when she called out his name, he threw back his head and let out a cry of his own when his release came.

The sound of their voices was lost in the moan of the wind and the tattoo of the falling rain.

Dawn came all too soon for Kylee, who woke up naked as a newborn in Rick's bed with one leg draped over his thigh. The bedroom was still dim, but daylight was trying to squeeze through the edges of the boarded-up windows. Kylee was content to lie with her hand on Rick's heart while he slept on. She could hear the roosters outside, crowing their little fowl hearts out and wondered how they had survived the wind. When she pictured them in the branches of the *hau* bush stripped naked of their feathers, she couldn't suppress a giggle.

Rick opened one eye and stared up at her. "What's so funny?"

"Naked roosters."

"I'm tempted to make a joke about naked cocks."

"Please don't," she groaned and buried her face against his neck.

They fell silent and he pulled her close. Kylee let her mind drift, lulled by the isolation they shared in the boarded-up house. Once they opened the doors to the new day, once the drapes were opened, they would have to face the sunlight and the world. Not to mention the ravages of the storm. She likened herself to a butterfly emerging from a cocoon, except she was far from certain that she had unfolded her wings.

Last night with Rick seemed like a dream now. She was almost afraid to think about what happened, about how far she had let herself go. Giving herself to this man, to any man for that matter, had been the furthest thing from her mind when she packed up her computer to come to Kauai. The holiday had been a last-ditch effort to hang on to her sanity and get her work moving again.

She had moved more than her work. She had been profoundly changed. Now, she was profoundly frightened. Who was this man she had given herself to? What magic had the sun and the sea, the jungle-like forest alive with birds and flowers, worked on her heart and soul?

She had been seduced by the island and the man. Seduced in such a casual, gentle way, almost as if she didn't know it was happening until she was under a spell.

"You're so quiet," he said.

Kylee started. She'd never woken up with a man before, never had a hard masculine body in bed beside her, never heard the sound of a deep, sensual voice in her ear at the break of day.

"I was thinking."

"About me?"

She could answer honestly. "Who else?"

"Kylee, I want to tell you something and I want you to listen well. I treasure what you gave me last night."

She closed her eyes and could almost feel his hands on her again. After they made love, he had picked her up and carried her into his room. Before the storm, he had filled the sunken tub in his bath with water to save in case they would be without it after the storm. After they made love, he had put her on the hardwood floor, washed her thighs with cool, clear water, wiped away all traces of her lost virginity.

"I feel like such an oddity. A twenty-five-year-old virgin." Nervousness made her laugh. "Sort of like finding the missing link, huh? I hope I wasn't too clumsy or anything."

"Are you embarrassed?" He put his hand beneath her chin,

made him face him. "You might say I was as inexperienced as you last night. I've never slept with a virgin. Angela certainly wasn't one when we met. I hope I didn't hurt you."

"No. You didn't." Kylee shook her head, expecting to die of embarrassment within the next two minutes. The fear she had felt upon remembering was building. She wanted to think about anything but what they had done last night. Without a clue as to where to go from here, she looked over at the clock on the bedside table.

"Power's out," Rick said, stretching his arms wide over his head. His toes wriggled back and forth beneath the sheet. "Maybe we should forget the time and stay in bed all day."

"Maybe we should go outside and see if anything is damaged." She tried to slide out from beneath the sheet.

His hand grasped her upper arm. "Let's do stay here a little longer. What do you say?"

Kylee sat on the edge of the bed with her back to him. She stared at the light passing through the cracks around the boarded windows and then curled her bare toes. Once the sun flooded the house and the day was allowed inside, the magic of the night would end. She would have to think about what she had done and why and where she would go from here.

But for now, they were alone, closeted in the house, comfortably hidden away from the world. Kylee turned and slid back into bed.

Rick had recognized the fear in her eyes the minute they arose and he opened the doors and the screens. All through breakfast, he had kept up a steady stream of talk, outlining the cleanup plan he would undertake once they had the plywood off the windows and stacked away again. He asked her to help him, not so such because he needed it, but because he wanted to keep her beside him so that he could hold her fear at bay.

Making love with Kylee had been more than he had ever dreamed. He had suspected they would be good together, ever since that first day when he had found her standing there like a wet kitten on the lanai—but he had never imagined just how good. The haunting sensation that somehow she had been meant for him since the beginning of time had not lessened as the days passed and he got to know her. If anything, that feeling had grown stronger.

Now that they had made love, he wanted her more than he had ever wanted anything in his life—even more than life itself. Rick marveled at the depth of the feeling he had for this woman who, a little more than a week ago, had been a virtual stranger until he looked into her eyes.

She was fragile and uncertain. He was determined to help her through the next few hours and days, to stay close to her and yet give her enough space to work things through.

"Want a soda?"

Kylee heard Rick call out and watched him throw down the green rake he'd been wielding for far too long. He swiped his arm across his forehead, wiping off sweat. She stopped gathering broken branches from a tall, wild plum tree and piling them at the edge of the lot.

"I thought you'd never ask." She pushed her sunglasses up her nose and started walking across the yard. "I would have hated to see this place after the hurricane," she said, surveying the damage to the yard.

There were leaves and small branches everywhere, thick as a carpet in some spots. They had cleaned most of the debris away from the house, but there was more than a day's work to be done. If anyone had asked her before today if she might have actually enjoyed doing yard work after a storm, she would have said no. And she would have been wrong.

While she watched him rake up the leaves, she wondered what he would say if she told him flat out how much she needed him. It had been downright perverted of her to stop every few minutes and watch the play of the sunshine on his muscular upper arms or the way the sunlight tinted his dark hair with shimmering blue-black highlights as he bagged up leaves.

More than once as they worked together, she wished that he would stop and take her in his arms and kiss her. She felt too shy to initiate any love-play herself, too uncertain of what she was caught up in, or how to go on from here. Each minute that passed brought on more apprehension, gave her more time to wonder about what she had done last night.

On the lanai, Rick grabbed a couple of diet sodas out of the big cooler he'd packed full of ice before the storm, slammed the lid down tight, and then started back to where Kylee was waiting in the shade of a tulip tree.

"Here," he said, handing her a can and popping the top on his own. He put the can to his lips and chugged down a good third of it before he looked over and found her watching.

"What?"

She smiled. "Nothing." She popped her own top and took a few sips, then licked her lips.

Rick stole a kiss the minute her tongue disappeared.

"What was that for?" she asked, surprised.

"Just saying thanks."

"This is slave labor," she sniffed.

"Not thanks for helping, I was thanking you for—"

Just then they heard a terrible commotion coming from behind his house, near the river. The cries sounded half-human. A cold chill of dread snaked down her spine.

Rick immediately started running toward the house. She followed on his heels. They put the sodas on the edge of the lanai as they raced by headed toward the river. The cries kept coming.

Rick ducked and picked his way through the bush, following the sound of high-pitched shouts mingled with loud squeals.

"What is it?" Kylee couldn't see what was up ahead. She forgot to dodge a low hanging branch, bumped her forehead, and cursed under her breath.

"Sounds like Kiko," he yelled back.

She heard someone distinctly call out in a high-pitched wail, "Help me!"

"Kiko can't *talk,*" she reminded him.

Rick stopped short, staring at the edge of the stream. She came up behind him and peered over his shoulder. The Wainiha River, usually a clear running stream, was flowing deep and wild, carrying storm water down from the mountains. The water was no longer clear and bubbling as usual, but a madly thundering, muddy torrent.

They heard the shout again and plunged on to the right. Within ten yards she saw the little boy she'd talked to in the road clinging to a thick branch that hung out over the deadly stream. The child was shouting for help and each time he did, Kiko, happily mired in mud on the slippery bank nearby, would raise his dirt-encrusted snout and squeal in harmony.

"Oh my God, Rick. If he slips into the water—"

"This kid is always getting himself into scrapes. He'll be all right." Rick sounded calm and certain. Kylee wasn't as sure.

"Hang on, Zeb," Rick called out to the boy as he made his way down the last few feet of slick embankment. He grabbed the trunk of the nearest tree and used it to steady himself until he'd tested enough of the tangled undergrowth to find a sturdy branch to hold him.

"Don't come too far down the bank," Rick warned her over his shoulder. "You might slip and get swept under."

She didn't want to think about losing her footing or being tugged along over the rocks in the streambed.

"Help!" Zeb spied Rick and started crying. "I get plenty stuck ovah heah!"

"Hang on, Zeb. I'll get you down but you have to hold on until I get closer." Rick inched his way down the bank, hanging on limbs as he went. He was within arm's reach of the little boy who had shimmied out over the water and wrapped himself around the damp branch.

Kylee's heart was in her throat as she watched Rick work his way down the embankment. "Be careful," she warned.

Her tennis shoes were practically buried in mud. She clutched a dangling tree branch. Her thighs were streaked with dirt, her tank top clinging to her damp skin. At the sound of her voice, Kiko had left the water and was grunting his way over to her. Kylee tried to motion him away with one hand, her attention focused on Rick.

Rick called up to the child in the tree. "Wiggle out this way, Zeb." Patiently, keeping his voice calm, Rick slowly coaxed the child forward.

"Mo' bettah I stay heah." Zeb sounded as if he wasn't going anyplace.

"Mo' bettah you come dis side. I get you down. No mattah." Rick easily slipped into the island pidgin the boy was most familiar with. "Come."

There was a two-second contest of wills while Rick stared down the frightened little Hawaiian boy. Finally, inch by inch, Zeb slowly started crawling toward Rich's hand.

"What you doing deah anyway?" Rick tried to keep the child talking while he inched closer.

"I come get Kiko. Him by da wattah, I get scared. I go up tree, so can hit heem with da steek, den he run back." Zeb had stopped moving while he spoke.

"Keep crawling," Rick urged. The kid was almost close enough for him to grab.

"Did he say he was going to make a *steak* out of this thing?" Kylee asked. She was backed up against a rock, still trying to shoo Kiko back. The porker was obviously smitten with her.

"He said he was going to hit him with a 'steek,' a stick." Rick's hand closed over the little boy's T-shirt. He stretched and managed to get his arm locked around Zeb's waist.

Kylee held her breath.

Apparently, lifting the five-year-old adventurer took very little effort on Rick's part. Within seconds, he was holding Zeb on safe, if not dry, land.

Then he reached out for Kylee, who put her hand in his.

Rick pulled her up the bank and Kiko followed, as tame as a kitten.

Kylee watched as Rick set the child down, cupped the boy's little chin in the palm of his hand, and looked down into Zeb's face. "Don't go by da wattah no more aftah a storm come tru'. You gotta be more *akamai* den dat."

"Okay, Reek."

"You family good?"

"Okay."

"Tell 'em hi. Bettah get home." Rick gave the child a gentle tap on the rear.

"Tanks, Reek!" Zeb called out with a wave and a holler as he scrambled through the foliage at the edge of the river, quickly heading for home.

"No problem," Rick called out before he smiled down at Kylee and pulled her into the shelter of his arm.

She leaned against him, thankful the boy was safe. Watching Rick's natural exchange with the wayward child had warmed her heart and started her thinking thoughts she had never before entertained.

"What did you tell him?"

"To be smarter next time."

They watched as Kiko snorted and then ran after the child, but the animal paused once to look back adoringly at Kylee before he pranced on. She and Rick both started laughing at once. It was the most lighthearted she had felt since they had opened the house and stepped out into the light of day.

"I know what he sees in me," she said.

"And what might that be?" Rick kept his arm around her shoulders as they headed back to the house.

"I'm sure *he* thinks all this mud's attractive," she motioned down at her dirty shorts and mud-streaked legs. She thought Rick might kiss her then, for he was staring into her eyes with a thoughtful look.

Instead, he took a step back and asked, "Why don't we quit for the day? We've been at it since breakfast. With any luck the power will be back on and I can hook your computer up for you. I'll come hose the leaves and mud out of your bathroom so you can shower."

Feeling the need to be alone, Kylee hosed down her own outdoor bathroom, taking pleasure and satisfaction from watching the lava rock turn from muddy brown to black as she worked. Finally, the job was finished and the place was back in order. She'd gathered up a set of clean towels from the closet in the hall, replaced the soap, and even found her shampoo container where it had blown off the lanai.

She stripped down and stepped in, lathered up and let the warm water soothe her aching muscles. Once the layer of mud was gone, she spread shampoo through her hair and let her mind wander.

"Kylee?"

She nearly choked on a mouthful of water when she jumped at the sound of Rick's voice and gasped beneath the shower spray. Blinking furiously, she looked over her shoulder and found him standing there in the doorway, watching her.

"What are you doing?" Her adrenaline was pumping from more than the fright he'd given her.

"Admiring the view." He was still filthy from the yard work, right down to his ankles where his shoes and socks had protected his feet from the mud. "Can I get in?"

"Here?"

"There."

She was still shy around him, uncomfortable with the fact that she was stark naked and his gaze was on her. Before she had a chance to say anything, he dug a condom out of his pocket, stripped off his shorts, and tossed them aside as he headed for the shower.

She turned around, hid her face in the stream of water while he readied himself. Then she stepped aside and let him have the full force of the shower spray, feeling awkward while he ducked his head beneath the jet and came up sputtering. He gave an audible sigh of relief once the water had begun to wash the mud off his skin.

Kylee was practically hugging the lava wall, at the same time taking care the rough rock surface didn't touch her.

Rick picked up a bar of soap. "Come here."

"What?"

"I'll wash your back for you."

"I—"

"It'll be nice, you'll see."

She stared at the oval bar of soap in his hand. Slowly, he lathered it until his hands were soapy, then motioned for her to turn around. Putting aside her reservations, she did and let him rub the ache out of her shoulders and back.

"That feels great," she sighed, closing her eyes as he worked his way down her back to her waist and then her hips. His hands on her skin were water slick, sliding like warm butter above the soap bubbles.

He hadn't said a word since he'd touched her. She didn't want to break the spell as she put aside the embarrassment of being naked in the shower with him and relaxed. Her weary muscles let go under his ministrations, so much so that she soon realized he'd pulled her up against him. She leaned back against his strong chest and felt his erection probing between her thighs.

Kylee stifled a moan and reached behind her to touch his water-slick thighs. He pressed against her again, seeking entrance.

Instinctively she reached out and put her hands against the rock wall to brace herself. Rick was nuzzling his face against her neck, gently nipping the sensitive spot near the base of her throat. His soapy hand cupped her buttocks and slipped between her legs.

This time she couldn't hold back a small cry of longing.

She pressed up against him again, took a step, and opened her legs, bracing herself for his entry.

"I want you, Kylee," he whispered against her neck, then kissed her temple.

The warm water sluiced down their bodies. He eased forward, slipped between her thighs and then, with his hands on her hips, tilted and lifted her until he could enter her from behind.

Kylee cried out again and threw her head back against his shoulder. It was maddening not to be able to touch him, and wonderful at the same time. He filled her, moved in and out of her, possessed her completely. His breath was coming ragged against her ear, his own throat caught on a low, animal-like growl.

Finally, when Kylee was certain she could not bear any more of the sweet ecstasy, he pushed upward, all the way to the mouth of her womb. She convulsed around him, unable to hold back a cry. He began moving faster, thrusting before he drew her closer. As they stood beneath the gentle pulse of the shower, she felt him shudder against her.

They were out of the shower, clean and dry. Rick looked over at Kylee where she stood on the open lanai, lost in thought as she combed out her long wet hair. He didn't want to spook her by making any more assumptions like the one he'd just made when he climbed into the shower with her. Had she ordered him out of there, he would have respected her choice even though he found himself wanting to spend every minute with her.

"I've moved your boxes back into the living room," he told her and watched as her gaze shot over to him. Her eyes were wide, blue, and unreadable. He couldn't tell if the idea thrilled her or not. All he knew was that she had cared enough for him to have given him something very precious, a treasure she had guarded her whole life, and he didn't want to lose her. He'd already decided the best way to insure that was to let her call the shots from here on out.

"I set up the computer on the desk."

She didn't respond at all. Rick waited for her to ask him to spend the night with her, but all she did was look at him. Her eyes were shadowed, haunted, and confused.

"Kylee?"

"Thanks," she said with a start after he prodded her. "I need to polish up a few scenes."

He knew she was confused; he'd seen it in her eyes all day and now that look had intensified. He wanted nothing more than to have her confident and self-assured again.

"Are you all right?"

She smiled, but it didn't reach her eyes. "I'm just tired."

Deciding to give her the time and space she needed, he said, "I'll bring your dinner over as soon as it's ready. It won't be fancy—"

"I'm not too hungry," she said, her gaze not on him, but on the leaves scattered all over the ground off the lanai.

He paused in the doorway, watching her for a moment longer before he headed back to his own house, determined that no matter how much it taxed his will, he was going to wait for her to come to him.

She never showed or called. He slept alone that night.

Six

Kylee's hands shook as she folded the last piece of clothing and tucked it into her suitcase. Tears slid down her cheeks as she told herself to calm down so that she would be packed and ready to go before Rick brought breakfast over.

During a sleepless night, she had come to a decision. Before dawn she had started packing. It took her no time at all to gather her paperwork and magazines, the computer and her clothes.

She had to leave, had to get away from Rick before the sight of him, the warmth of his touch, the sound of his voice could lure her into staying.

Yesterday, when he left her after making love to her in the shower, she had been in a state of shock, not at what they had done together, but at the power he had to make her respond to his touch. How could she have lost her heart and her control? How could this have happened to her so quickly?

Last night she prowled the house alone, not knowing whether to go to him or not. When he didn't show up at her door, she thought maybe he was reconsidering. Maybe he had realized everything had moved too far too quickly and he wanted to backtrack. Worse yet, maybe leaving her alone in the guest house had been his subtle way of saying he was through with her.

She had no idea what the protocol between lovers might be.

All night she had tossed and turned, trying to imagine where they would go from here. She was due back in L.A. in less

than two weeks with script in hand. The first draft was finished.
Editing it in L.A. would be no problem.

She would come to her senses once she put time and space
between them.

While she was lying in bed last night, her heartbeat had been
in tune with the hum of the insects outside, the rhythm of the
surf, the rustle of palm fronds on the trade winds. By dawn,
she was convinced she definitely had been seduced by the island, not to mention the man, and needed to get back to L.A.
where she could clear her head and think about their relationship without Rick around to captivate her with his charm.

Now, in the bright light of a sunny new day, she glanced up
and looked out over the taro patch. Her fingers tightened
around the cotton sweater in her hands.

There was a sound behind her, the hush of bare feet against
the *lau hala* mat. She turned, clutching the sweater against her
heart. Rick moved into the doorway and stopped. His eyes narrowed as he took in the suitcase on the bed.

"What's up, Kylee?" The warmth she had come to know and
expect was missing from his tone.

"I think you know." She looked away.

"You're leaving."

"Yes, I am, I—"

"Why?" He took a step into the room.

She took a step back. "I think you know why," she said. "I
need some time alone, Rick."

"I'm willing to give you that. And space. That's why I left
you alone last night. I'll give you all the room you need."

Her heart fluttered. So last night he had left her alone so
that she could make the next move—and she had been too
frightened by the power of her feelings to do anything but lie
there in the dark, mired in confusion.

"I honestly don't know where we go from here," she said.
"I've never done this before."

"You can't just walk away from what happened between us."

She shook her head. Turning around, she leaned over to lay the sweater in the suitcase. "But it's all happening too fast."

"Why did you do it?"

Kylee straightened. "Do what?"

"Let me make love to you. Now you want to just walk out as if nothing happened? I don't understand. Maybe you didn't take this as seriously as I did. Did you just want to change your status? Open up new possibilities when you get back to the mainland?"

"That's not true—"

"Then why are you running out and turning this into the very thing you were trying so hard to avoid?"

"What are you talking about?"

"A one night stand. A summer fling."

"I'm doing no such thing," she cried.

Rick began to pace, walking to the window and then halfway back. "Then what are you doing?"

"I don't know."

"Are you running because you can't admit you love me? I'm not afraid to say it, I love you, Kylee."

His profession of love startled and shocked her. She felt as if a mighty hand were squeezing her heart. He just said the three words she had longed to hear for a lifetime and all she felt was sheer panic. She had no idea how to respond.

She held her hands out before her, palms up, pleading. "How do you *know*, Rick? How can you be so sure? I've never been in love. I don't know what it's supposed to feel like."

His expression changed, softened. Now he looked more sad than angry. "If you have to ask me that, then you really *don't* know whether or not you love me."

"I want to," she said softly. "I really *want* to love you. This is the very first time in my life I've ever gotten this close to anyone."

"Then why not stay and give this a chance to work?"

She closed her eyes and took a deep, shuddering breath as she clutched her hands. "I'm afraid," she whispered.

When she opened her eyes he was standing there before her, reaching out, about to take her in his arms.

She held up her hands. "No, Rick. Don't. Please. That won't solve anything. I'm going home to finish up the script and do some soul-searching by myself."

"I'm beginning to think that's how you like it, Kylee. By yourself." He ran his hand through his hair and sighed. "Forget I said that. You have about a week's time left here. I'll send you a refund." His tone was void of emotion.

"Oh, Rick . . . I never meant—"

He turned and walked out the door. Two minutes later, as Kylee sat numbly on the edge of the bed, she heard his truck roar out the driveway.

Two hours later, Rick sat on the top step of the lanai. Kiko lay beside him in a pool of sunlight. Kylee was gone when he got back. He'd gone bodysurfing to clear his head and cool his anger, unwilling to ruin any chance they might have had together.

He had hoped she would change her mind, but obviously, Kylee had been too scared to stay and talk things through. As he stared over at the empty guest house, he couldn't believe she was really gone. Rick reached over and scratched the pig behind the ears.

If Kylee needed time, he was going to give it to her, but he wasn't about to let her slip out of his life that easily and certainly not without a fight. He would give her time, but not enough to become wrapped up in her work again and lose herself in it.

Eventually, though, if he didn't hear from her, he was going after her. He'd enlist help if he had to.

Kylee sat across from Sylvia at a table on the patio of The Ivy, one of Beverly Hills' trendiest cafés. Sylvia lifted a tall fluted glass of champagne and smiled over the rim in salute.

"Here's to you, Kylee. *Through Her Own Eyes* is the best script you've ever written." The agent shivered dramatically and then declared, "I feel an Emmy coming on." She took a sip of the sparkling white wine and then nodded to two men who had just walked in, headed for indoor seating.

"Those two are in production at Paramount," Sylvia whispered. "By the way, I think you're ready to try your hand scripting a feature." Changing the subject again, she said, "Did I thank you for meeting me here on such short notice?"

"You know I'll always show up for a free meal. Is anything else up?" Kylee couldn't help noticing that her friend was more unfocused than usual.

Sylvia scanned the patio. "No . . . not really. I just felt like getting out and thought it would be great to see you. We haven't really had time to visit since you've been back."

Kylee settled back in her chair and looked around at the beautiful people who filled the restaurant, those who *were* somebody, those who *thought* they were somebody, those who *wanted* to be somebody, and those who were just there to ogle the rest.

As Sylvia went on and on about the way Charese LaDonne was gushing over the script and the "role of her career," Kylee made a mental tally of the Armani suits, the Gucci shoes, the Tag Heuer watches, Prada totes, Black Fly wraparounds, and Lunor shades and wondered if there was anything under the glittering surface of most of these people.

The entertainment industry was a game she didn't really want to play any more than she had to.

"Kylee? Don't you like your salad?"

Kylee glanced down at the plate filled with the very latest in designer food and picked up her fork. "It's great, Syl. I was just thinking."

"Tell me, tell me. What about? Got a new idea already?" Sylvia leaned forward, engrossed in the role of co-conspirator.

"I've got an idea, but it's not about a script. Charese loves the new one and so does the producer so I was thinking—"

"Love? Darling, they're *raving.*" Sylvia was not really looking at Kylee anymore, but over her shoulder. "Hi, Jerry." She nodded and waggled her fingers in the direction of the white picket fence that fronted the place. "What were you saying, dear?"

Kylee sighed. "Sylvia, if I'm to believe what everyone's saying about *Through Her Own Eyes,* I did my best work ever on Kauai."

"And it was *my* idea to send you over." Sylvia looked like the cat that ate more than a canary. "I just knew it would be inspirational, in more ways than one."

"What would you think if I told you I was moving there permanently?"

She should have waited until Sylvia had swallowed her champagne before she made the announcement. The champagne came spewing out again just before Sylvia fell into a coughing spasm.

"Should I do the Heimlich or call the waiter?" Kylee shifted in her chair and pushed her sunglasses up the bridge of her nose.

Sylvia pressed her napkin to her lips and shook her head.

"Kauai?" she said at last when she could finally draw a breath. "You are going to *move* to Kauai?"

Kylee took a deep breath and voiced aloud the conclusion she had reached weeks ago. "I fell in love with Rick Pau." She had realized it was true after the first miserable days away from Kauai. She waited for the terrible, wrenching pain to pass, hoped that the longing would fade, but instead, her need to see him again, to hear his voice, only intensified over the weeks they were apart. Yes, she admitted to herself, it was true. She loved him. Sylvia, her trusted agent and friend, deserved to know.

Her reaction wasn't exactly what Kylee expected.

Sylvia's hand flew to her throat. Kylee thought she was honestly choking this time and started to get up until Sylvia all but moaned, "Rick Pau? You fell in *love* with Rick Pau? I gave him strict instructions to make sure you had a good time but—"

Kylee's heart dropped to her knees. Her mouth went dry, her palms went damp. "It was a setup?" she whispered.

"Well, it wasn't supposed to be *that* big of a setup. All I wanted was for him to take you out a few times, make sure you got out and relaxed a little. I could see how uptight you were over this script. I've never seen you like that before. I wanted you to loosen up a bit."

"I'm afraid I might have loosened up a bit more than you intended."

Sylvia leaned forward and whispered, "You don't mean . . ."

Kylee nodded. "I'm afraid so. Don't forget it was your idea that I experience a little passion while I was there."

"But, my God, Kylee."

"I must have been crazy for even *thinking* about moving to Kauai. I must have been crazy period." The whole thing had been a setup from the start—a little ploy Sylvia had finagled to get her out of her funk.

"Yes." Sylvia blotted her lips with her napkin, then stared hard at Kylee. "Oh, don't look like that. Have some champagne. I suppose with today's technology, that damned hair-net highway or whatever it is that's bridging the gap to the twenty-first century, you can work anywhere." Sylvia's brow knit and her eyes scrunched, a sure sign that she was mulling over the idea. "Rick Pau is a great guy. I'd be the first to admit that. Besides, it's not as if you can't afford to fly back here whenever you need to. I hear there are quite a few famous writers and celebrities with homes on Kauai."

"I wouldn't know. I didn't get out much while I was there." Kylee was miserable. A few seconds ago, everything was so very clear, so simple. She thought she had figured out what she wanted. Now she knew Rick's undivided attention toward her had been set up by her well-meaning agent.

"Sylvia, what are you doing?" When she noticed the odd motions Sylvia was making, Kylee was tempted to turn around. Her agent was partially out of her chair, half-waving, half-patting her head with a white linen table napkin. "Are you signaling the waiter? What's wrong?"

"Nothing."

"Sylvia, you're the worst liar on the face of the earth. You're up to something. Now what gives?" Kylee turned around and looked over her shoulder. Her breath caught in her throat.

A striking, dark-haired, bronzed-skinned man in a stunning silk Hawaiian print shirt and linen pants was threading his way through the tables.

Rick.

Kylee watched, stunned, as he walked up to Sylvia. His exotic black eyes were hidden behind dark, reflective sunglasses. Kylee's heart stumbled just looking at him. For two months she had thought of nothing but this man and the magical time she had spent on Kauai. The longer she was away from him and the island, the stronger the pull to go back became until, up to a few moments ago, she had been obsessed with returning.

Now, here he stood. Stunned speechless, all she could do was watch while he bent to give Sylvia a quick kiss on the cheek.

"Kiliwia, how are you?" Rick was smiling down at the agent.

Sylvia actually fluttered her lashes up at Rick. "You know how I *love* it when you say my name in Hawaiian. I'm wonderful. How else would I be when I'm with my two favorite people in all the world? Look, Kylee. What a surprise. Rick Pau of all people. Fancy meeting him here."

"Kylee." Rick nodded in her direction as the waiter slipped up to the table with another chair. Rick sat down, smiling at Kylee all the while.

"You look wonderful," he told her.

She didn't say it, but she thought that he looked better than wonderful. He looked absolutely good enough to eat sitting there amid the salon-tanned, carefully outfitted crowd. Neither the men nor the women seated around them bothered to hide the fact that they were trying to figure out who the hell he was.

When Kylee couldn't manage word one, Sylvia quickly began to fill the void. "Rick, we were just talking about you—"

"All good I hope." He turned to the waiter hovering at his elbow and ordered an iced tea.

Kylee refused to smile as she sat there studying her two companions, both partners in crime. "You two set me up again today, didn't you?"

Rick looked at Sylvia. Sylvia shrugged. "All right. I'll admit I went along with Rick when he called last night and asked if I'd have you here by 1:30. But I honestly had no idea things were so serious between you two."

"You told her that things were serious between us?" Rick asked, watching Kylee closely.

Kylee wanted to slide under the table. "That was before I knew she'd asked you to make sure I had a good time on Kauai."

"She just admitted that she was in love with you and that she's thinking of moving to Kauai." Sylvia lowered her voice to a mumble. "I wanted you to be nice to her, show her the sights, but I never expected, I never thought . . ."

Rick was staring hard at Kylee. The waiter came with the iced tea and left before either one of them moved.

Kylee looked back and forth at both of them. Without a word she slowly folded her napkin and set it on the table beside her untouched salad. Her champagne had gone flat.

"Kylee, I was only trying to help." Sylvia laughed.

"So you *were* in on this?" Kylee turned and stared at Rick. She couldn't trust herself to speak. He wasn't smiling now, but watching her closely.

"I think we need to go somewhere and talk. I'm staying at the Beverly Hills Hotel, but if you'd rather not go there, then—"

"I'd rather not go anywhere with you."

Just then, one of the Armani-suited execs walked out from inside the café and came over to the table.

"Hey, Rick. How's it going?" The man stood beside the table nervously jingling the change in his pocket.

"Great, Jimmy. Howzit with you?" Rick smiled a slow smile in Kylee's direction before he looked up at the newcomer.

"Good to see you again, Rick. How long are you in town?" He paused, obviously waiting for Rick to introduce Kylee and Sylvia, but the introduction never came.

"Just two days."

"Still content over there on Maui?" The man either couldn't take a hint, or didn't care that Rick was barely making conversation.

"It's Kauai. Yeah. I'm staying put."

Jimmy nodded at Sylvia, stared a bit too long at Kylee, then said good-bye and made his way out.

"It seems like you still have some connections here," Kylee said, watching Rick as he held the tea glass up to his lips and took a long swallow. How many nights had she lain awake remembering the way his mouth felt against her skin? Was what he had said and done sincere, or had he merely been devoting his time to saving a mercy-case of Sylvia's?

Sylvia tried to fill the silence. "Rick inherited lots of property here in California. He owns the block of buildings where my office is located over on Robertson. He edits and publishes one of the biggest Internet investment bulletins, but then, I'm sure you already know all of that, seeing as how you two . . . well, I just can't believe it." Sylvia stopped abruptly, looking at each of them in turn. Did I say something wrong?"

Rick was far kinder to her than Kylee felt like being at the moment. "No, Sylvia, you didn't. I never got around to telling Kylee any of that before she left Kauai."

"And just when *did* you intend to tell me you were a real estate magnate and investment wizard?" Kylee asked him.

"Would that have made a difference?" He was leaning forward, on his forearms, so closely she could see herself quite clearly in his mirrored glasses. She felt as if she were looking at the reflection of a fool.

"Of course not, but you have to admit it's a pretty whopping secret. Not telling all of the truth is the same as lying," she said.

Sylvia polished off her champagne and signalled the waiter, who hurried over to refill her glass.

Kylee and Rick ignored her. "You fell in love with me when you thought I was nothing but a beach bum who ran a bed and board. So now you know I have some income. I'd think you'd be happy, not furious."

"I'd think you'd have the decency to be just a little embarrassed about not telling me how close you and Sylvia really are and that you knew exactly who I was when I got there. How do you think I feel knowing I was a little mercy project for both of you?"

"I would think you'd be happy Sylvia loves you enough to sense you were in trouble, that she cared enough to want you to get some R-and-R and have a good time. Besides, from the minute I saw you standing there on the lanai, soaking wet, looking mad as a wet hen, you stopped being a duty to Sylvia." He tried to reach for her hand. "You were never a mercy case."

"What about today? You two set me up again."

Sylvia held up her hands in surrender. "I was *totally* innocent this time. Last night Rick called out of the blue and said he had to see you. He thought it would be best if I got you two together."

"I didn't even know if you'd take my call, Kylee. We didn't part on the best of terms and I haven't heard from you for two months," Rick reminded her.

Sipping champagne in the sun had given her a thunderous headache. "I've got to go." Kylee abruptly pushed herself out of her chair.

Rick stood. Sylvia blinked and looked around. "I'll get the check," she said to no one in particular before she drained another glass of champagne.

Kylee grabbed her purse and headed for the exit. She was conscious of how many heads turned while they walked across the patio. She whipped the valet ticket out of her pocket and handed it to the smiling young man waiting at the curb. Handsome enough to be a *GQ* model, he ran down the tree-lined street to get her car.

Totally aware of Rick standing at her side, she tried her damnedest not to react. "Don't do this, Kylee. Not again. Not after you admitted to Sylvia that you love me."

Finally, she looked up at him. A slight breeze played through his hair, ruffling the familiar ponytail.

"You're not the man I thought I fell in love with." She looked him up and down, from the his dark glasses to the toes of his Italian loafers.

"You're not holding a grudge against me because I happen to have money, are you?"

She looked over her shoulder. There was no one close by, but she lowered her voice anyway. "Of course not. I'm upset. For the first time in my life I opened up enough to fall in love with someone and now I find out that person wasn't who or what I thought he was at all."

The valet came roaring up in her low slung, black Corvette, hopped out, and waited for Kylee beside the open door. The engine rumbled.

"I've got to go." Kylee was torn with confusion and anger, her bruised heart aching.

Rick grabbed her upper arm just as she started off the curb. "Kylee, wait."

"There's nothing left to say, Rick."

"There's this." He pulled her into his arms before she could protest. His lips covered hers in an almost fierce meeting, as if he were trying to bend her to his will with his kiss. Stunned, Kylee could do nothing but cling to him. Her purse cut into her right breast, one of her square-heeled mules nearly slipped off her foot. He held her so tightly there was no way she could break his hold, even if she had wanted to.

Just as she had feared, his deep, soul-wrenching kiss moved her more than words. As his tongue teased hers, as his embrace brought back the heady scents and sounds of the island, Kylee felt a rush of longing so deep she wanted to cry. His hands pressed her close as his lips moved against hers. She was clinging to his shirtfront, leaning into him. Drinking in the heady taste of him as chills ran down her spine despite the dry heat of the California summer afternoon.

He raised his head, put his hands on her arms, and set her on her feet. Behind them swelled a round of quick applause and laughter. Kylee glanced back at the café patrons, who were already dismissing the display and getting back to the business of power lunching.

The valet had already given up on his tip and ran to get another car. Rick was watching Kylee intently.

"I love you, Kylee. You love me. Anything else is irrelevant. I've come this far to find out how you feel and now that I know you love me, I'm not going home without you."

He opened the passenger door and stood there waiting. She looked at Rick, then back at the restaurant. He didn't look as if he were going to budge.

"Get in, Kylee."

She didn't move.

"Please." There was nothing but rock-hard determination in his tone.

Kylee slipped into the car and Rick shut the door behind her. She sat without moving, waiting for him to walk around the front of the car and get in. When he did, she spared him a quick glance.

"Where are we going?" she wanted to know.

"Anywhere you say. Someplace we can talk."

Her eyes scanned the street, which was hemmed in by high walls formed by buildings on both sides. A ragged flash of memory came to her.

"Let's go to the beach."

He put the car in gear. The tires squealed as he headed away from the curb.

* * *

The contrast between staring out at the Pacific Ocean from the Santa Monica pier and watching waters off Kauai made it seem to Rick as if he were on another planet. The pier itself was covered with various food stands and amusement booths, a permanent carnival of sights, sounds, and activities.

He and Kylee walked to the end of the pier and stopped a few feet away from a group of fishermen. Bewitched by the sight of her, Rick couldn't take his eyes off of Kylee as she stood there leaning against the railing with her long hair blown back away from her face, exposing her long, slender neck and shoulders. The breeze off the water molded her black silk blouse against her breasts. Her troubled eyes were hidden behind dark glasses, her brow marred by a slight frown. Since it didn't appear that she was going to start any conversation whatsoever . . .

"Sylvia was worried enough about you when you came to Kauai to call me and ask for my help. Are you going to hold that against me?"

She turned slightly, enough to look at him. There was a slight, sad smile on her lips. "This isn't about holding anything against you, Rick. This is about trust."

"Kylee—"

"Let me finish." She took a deep breath. "When I was three, my mother deserted me. She was nineteen when she left me with a neighbor and simply walked out of my life. I never knew my father. As I moved through a series of foster homes, the one constant in my life became books and reading. Later I took up writing. I've never been exposed to a real family situation, never known what it would be like to have a brother or a sister who really cared, let alone a mom or a dad."

As she spoke, Rick thought of his own *ohana,* his extended family of aunts, uncles, cousins. Every month was marked by family celebrations, birthday luaus, anniversaries, holidays. Imagining life without his family was impossible. He wondered how she had survived.

"So," she went on, "my work became my family, my stability. I threw myself into it. I dated some, but whenever I got close to anyone, I felt inept, uncertain." She shrugged. "Anytime anyone got too close, I was afraid that I'd be wanting when it came to sustaining a relationship. I don't know the first thing about day to day give and take."

Rick reached for her hand. He couldn't stand to see her so alone and vulnerable, pouring her heart out to him. She surprised him by accepting the gesture. He stepped closer, until they stood at the rail, shoulder to shoulder, their fingers entwined. For the first time that day, he felt a sweeping sense of relief. She had opened up to him.

"Sylvia is the closest thing to family I have—"

"Which is why she called me in June and wanted me to make sure you were okay," he told her. "That's what family does. They look out for one another."

She swallowed twice. The bittersweet smile crossed her lips again.

"Kylee, I can only tell you what I said before. From the moment I saw you, everything Sylvia said to me flew out the window. I wanted to get to know you. I wanted to show you Kauai. There was something in your eyes, in your smile, that told me you were the one I've been waiting for since my marriage ended. When I got to know you, I knew my intuition was right."

"But—"

He gently squeezed her hand. "Let me finish. I didn't tell you about the extent of my business ventures because I don't really see all of that as who I am. I've always wanted to keep that part of my life separate so that I could walk away from all of it tomorrow and be happy waiting tables in Hanalei. I don't define myself by what I have. As far as I'm concerned, money is just dirty paper that gets you though life. I wanted you to fall in love with me, Rick Pau, without all the trappings. That way, if I ever did decide to drop out and walk away from it all, you wouldn't be disappointed."

"When were you planning to tell me?"

"You walked out on me, Kylee. I was waiting for you to come back. I can't wait any longer."

He could see her struggling. Finally, she shoved her sunglasses up onto her head and looked him in the eyes.

"I was confused. I didn't know if I was in love with you or the *idea* of you, the handsome, island lover, but every day I was away from you, I missed you more. I wanted to go back that first week I was here in L.A. again, but I made myself wait. There was the script to finish, then the meetings with Charese and the producers. I kept waiting for my feelings for you to cool. I kept thinking I would forget the way you make me feel, the way I need you, but it only got worse."

He let go of her hand to slip his arms around her shoulders and hold her close.

"No one told me love was supposed to hurt," she whispered.

"It only hurts when you deny it, Kylee, when you don't nourish it. You know what we had on Kauai, how great it was between us. You were able to write. I thought I knew what your work means to you, but I had no idea that it was all you had. It's your lifeline and I would never ask you to give that up. Not in a million years. All I'm asking is that you think about loving me as much as your writing. Think about what we had this summer and what it would be like to have that love last a lifetime."

With a glance over his shoulder, Rick dismissed the fishermen, tourists, and sightseers on the pier. Placing his hand beneath her chin, he tipped Kylee's face up to his and lowered his head to kiss her.

Kuiho Highway was packed with rental cars, and the humid September air was as thick as pea soup without the trade winds to cool the island. Bumper-to-bumper traffic lined the single-lane bridges that spanned the Wainiha River. Two weeks earlier than she'd planned on arriving on Kauai, Kylee drove with care. She snaked the rental Jeep forward until it was her turn to cross the bridges and then, a few yards farther, she turned left up Powerhouse Road. She laughed when the Jeep hit a deep pothole and mud flew up off the tires. The interior of the small car was packed with a duffle filled with clothing, boxes of computer equipment, a copy machine, a modem, and three phones.

The *Hale Hanea* sign appeared amid the foliage before she expected it. Kylee slammed on the brakes, put the gearshift into reverse, and then swung the Jeep across the road and down the steep drive. There were three cars in the drive already. As Kylee maneuvered to pull up in front of the rental house, a stunning young woman wrapped in a colorful sarong, her long dark hair hanging to her waist, walked across the lanai and waved.

Kylee felt her stomach lurch. The lighthearted euphoria she had been feeling since she boarded the plane that morning quickly dissolved. Rick had said she would know where to find him.

But she hadn't expected to find him with someone else.

Dazed, she sat there immobilized until she realized the brunette was waiting for her to roll down the window. Kylee hit the power button and the window slipped down.

"Hi, are you looking for Rick?" When the girl leaned against the lanai railing, Kylee couldn't help but notice she was very well endowed.

"I was," Kylee said, tempted to throw the still-idling Jeep into reverse, whip around, and head back up the drive before Rick found out she was here and she suffered more humiliation.

"If you're in the hula class, they've already started." The girl shook out her hair and let it dust her shoulders.

"No. I . . . I just came by to . . ." *To have my heart broken into a thousand pieces.*

Just then, a short, paunchy, balding man with a goatee walked out of the guest house, crossed the lanai, and slipped his arm around the girl's waist.

"Hi," he called out with a wave. "I'm Dave Thompson. You a friend of Rick's?"

"I . . ." Kylee's heartbeat accelerated. "Yes," she smiled. "I am. Are you two staying here?"

"Two weeks. We're from Seattle. On our honeymoon." Dave Thompson gave his new bride another squeeze.

"Congratulations," Kylee called out as she popped the door of the Jeep, swung out, and headed for the house at a trot. As she drew near, she heard a recording of a Hawaiian song. Kiko came prancing out of the bushes and froze when he saw her. She laughed aloud when he came lumbering across the lawn, snorting out a greeting. She hurried up the steps, leaving him behind, and kicked off her shoes when she reached Rick's lanai.

Her bare feet made no sound as she crossed the deck and stopped outside his door. She could see him inside, dressed in his familiar tank top and swim trunks, his back to her. For a moment she thought he might be playing the guitar when she saw him sway, then she noticed his arms moving in time to the music. He was doing the hula. Beyond him, seated together on the sofa, his *haole* students were watching intently, mesmerized by the seductive lure of the sheer animal magnetism of an expert male hula dancer.

Kylee slipped inside and stood there watching in excitement and anticipation until the recording ended and so did Rick's dance. The ladies on the couch burst into enthusiastic applause.

Rick immediately turned around, as if he knew someone was watching. His gaze instantly locked with hers across the room.

"Komo mai," he said with a wide smile as he held his hand out to her. "Come in."

She crossed the cool, wood floor and took his hand. "I got away earlier than I expected and decided to surprise you, but you don't look very surprised."

"I knew you were here. I felt it when you walked in, just the way I knew we were meant to be together from the start."

Rick reached for her, ran his hand up and down her bare arm. His smile widened. "It helps to have a cousin at the car rental booth in Lihue, too."

"It looks like I won't be able to get away with anything here on Kauai."

"You won't have any time to try," he said, pulling her close. "Not with all the aunties and uncles and cousins and new in-laws you are going to have in your life."

She felt a wave of anxiety and then drank in his smile, re-assuring herself that Rick would help her adjust. Soon she would have all the family she'd ever wanted and more.

She couldn't resist kissing him, so she stood on tiptoe and pressed her lips to his. When Rick raised his head, he looked over at the women watching spellbound on the couch.

"Class dismissed, ladies. Go home and practice."

It took them a few minutes to gather their notebooks and hurry out the door. Kylee couldn't help noticing the touch of envy in their eyes as she said good-bye from the circle of Rick's arms.

Once they were out of the house and headed up the drive, she turned to Rick with a smile of her own.

"Speaking of practicing—"

"Just what I was thinking." Rick scooped her into his arms. Kylee looped her arm around his neck and was about to smile up at him when someone knocked at the door.

Still holding her, Rick swung around and both of them burst out laughing at the sight of Kiko standing at the door with his nose pressed up against the screen as he made deep snorting sounds.

"Looks like I'm not the only one who's glad to have you back." Rick chuckled.

"I never thought I'd be so glad to see a pig again." Kylee laughed. An overwhelming peace settled over her as she nestled close to Rick's heart. Any last shred of doubt she might have had fled. He loved her. Together, they could see anything through.

His heart was in his eyes as he ignored Kiko's snorts of protest and guided Kylee toward the bedroom.

Early in the Morning

Stella Cameron

A Friday evening in July

"What do you think about sex therapists?" Chloe Dunn held her breath and frowned at the ten of clubs she'd just picked up.

But for the tap of Steven Early's short, clean fingernails on the kitchen table, silence was absolute.

Chloe pulled nervously at the neck of her tank top. A sultry Seattle evening, the kind they weren't supposed to have, stuck the cotton to her skin. "Steven?" She smiled so brilliantly her jaw hurt. "Tell me what you think."

"About what?"

He hadn't even heard her. "I'm discarding the ten of clubs," she said irritably, and glanced at him. He glanced back. The bluest eyes in the world, they had to be.

Chloe sighed. She loved him. He loved her. But if they couldn't deal with their differences they'd lose each other.

Steven retrieved her discarded card, but didn't appear particularly triumphant.

He was every woman's dream—most women's dream. Sensitive, kind, strong, and a slightly-crooked-nose short of being handsome. Dreamy. Steven was the kind of man a woman looked at, then started dreaming about.

And that was the problem. In the ten months since Chloe had met Steven she'd done a great deal of dreaming—but very little else. In the physical sense, that was. In other words: sexually.

Tonight was the night.

She'd made up her mind. Tonight they would find a way to confront this problem.

Tomorrow was their wedding day.

Supposed to be their wedding day.

It would be their wedding day. Chloe jutted her bottom lip and puffed at a strands of hair around her warm face. "It's my fault," she blurted out. "I make mistakes. I'm not good at thinking enough before I act."

Steven turned sideways in his chair and stretched out his legs. "You couldn't be sure I needed the ten of clubs," he said, and he studied her quickly from eyes to mouth, and then not so quickly all the way to her shorts and bare legs.

Chloe's skin prickled.

"I can be pretty sneaky," Steven said.

Now he'd decided she was apologizing over a game of rummy! "You sure can be sneaky." And infuriating.

He was a tall, lean man. Lithe, economical of movement.

Great body.

She'd never actually seen him naked—completely naked. Chloe shuddered.

"Hey, sweetheart." Steven reached across the table and covered her hand. "You're not getting sick on me, are you? I'd hate to have to carry you to the wedding."

Chloe shuddered again. "I'm not sick." He could carry her anywhere. "Not really. Just jumpy about tomorrow. I want it to be the most special day of our lives."

"Me, too." He patted her fingers and withdrew his hand. "And it will be. I'd better get that garbage out for you, and go home. We both need our beauty sleep before tomorrow." His laugh did fabulous things for a wide, clever mouth.

Steven's mouth was very clever.

He could kiss—and kiss, and kiss.

Chloe took a deep breath. Kisses pretty much accounted for the romantic diet Steven had offered her—before, and after their engagement of three months. Not that she didn't turn completely weak when he kissed her. Yeah, she did. Weak, and hot, and shaky, and then hotter, and weaker, and more shaky—and then she couldn't breathe too well, and couldn't find enough of him to touch, and she ached and burned in places that definitely felt good when they ached and burned. But aching and burning demanded more, they wanted much, much more. Sweet, over-the-top pain, and warm, throbbing satisfaction would be good. Uh huh, that would be very good.

Whew, so good. Must be all those days she spent whispering in the Seattle public library. Made a woman need some escape, some release. People thought librarians were automatons, book machines. Well, librarians were librarians because they loved books, and book people's minds were highly tuned to exploring and experiencing. Not just in pages, but in life.

She was wandering. Felt like her brain was fevered. Probably caused by feeling hot so often, and getting to stay that way for too long.

Chloe really did adore Steven.

He was the funniest, most honorable, generous man she'd ever met. She couldn't walk away from him just because . . .

Sex wasn't everything.

But why didn't he show any interest in making love to her? She'd tried to make herself talk about it, and tried, and tried, but chickened out every time. How did you ask your fiancé why he didn't want to have sex?

She wasn't the type men lusted after. Never had been. *You can tell Chloe anything.* How many times had friends said that of her? *Chloe's wonderful—she makes you feel so safe. You can trust Chloe with anything.* Everyone's confidante, everyone's shoulder to cry on—no one's one-and-only. Never the girl who got the boy. Never the woman who got the man—until Steven, and Steven had been the first, the only man she'd ever truly loved. But maybe he was just looking for a confidante, a buddy, someone to trust.

Chloe pressed her temples. Having him as a lover and a best friend was her dream, but if best friends were as much as they were destined to be, then she'd take that.

But she had to know what to expect.

"You look tired, Chloe."

"I'm not," she said. "We need to talk."

Steven smiled again and his blue eyes crinkled at the corners. "After tonight we're going to be able to talk all we want to." His dark, curly hair touched the collar of his navy blue polo shirt. "Last night alone, partner—for either of us. I'll be relieved to move out of the apartment. I'm glad we settled on this house, aren't you?"

"Yes."

He tilted his head and studied her. "No second thoughts about buying so far out in the boonies?"

Woods surrounded the single-story, hilltop house. Their closest neighbors were five miles away on the opposite side of Cougar Valley.

"I like being isolated," Chloe said. "I'm going to love being isolated with you."

Steven gathered the playing cards into a heap, stacked them, shuffled them, set them down in the middle of the table. She was almost sure he'd broken into a sweat. His brow glistened.

He didn't say, "Me, too, honey."

Some people would find an old-fashioned approach to a relationship charming. Most of the time Chloe found it charming. She wasn't exactly a woman of vast sexual experience anyway. But her friend, Barbara, who also worked at the library, but who was going to school at night to become a psychologist, said Steven's behavior was suspicious.

"Tomorrow, the wedding," he said. "Then two weeks alone right here in our own home, sweet home."

Chloe watched his lips form the words.

"Are you looking forward to home, sweet home as much as I am, Chloe?"

She whistled silently and said, "Uh huh. But I think we should talk now."

"Sweetheart"—he took a deep, deep breath—"you mean everything to me. I couldn't face life without you."

His sudden, naked expression disarmed her. She said, "You won't have to face life without me. But, Steven . . . Steven, I want to make love." She felt her blood stand still.

Steven rubbed a hand over his face. "Tomorrow, Chloe."

"Tomorrow, Chloe? Chloe isn't always the sweet, well-behaved little Ms. Dunn. I breathe, Steven. I *feel*. I *want*. I *long,* Steven, I *absolutely long."* She rose to her feet. "I *desire*. I am a *passionate* woman, Steven. *Passionate."*

His eyes widened a fraction, then narrowed. He crossed his arms and muscles flexed. Steven had very nice muscles.

"So?" Chloe said. "What do you think of that?"

"This is tough, sweetheart. Getting married is stressful."

God! "You'd never know it by your behavior. But then, you've done it before, and—" Shoot, she hadn't meant to sound like a shrew.

There was the faintly troubled expression again, the expression she'd seen on the few occasions when the subject of his ex-wife had been raised.

"Garbage out," he said, standing. He was so much taller than Chloe—something that made her feel like a silly, spiteful kid at this moment. He continued, "Why don't you go to bed, honey? Take Merlin with you. He'll cheer you up."

Chloe looked at her white puffball of a Persian cat and felt something within her grow very strained. That was the instant before the "something" snapped. A breath, two breaths. She mustn't shout, or say something she would absolutely regret in the morning. "What will it take to get through to you? I don't think Merlin's quite going to do it for me tonight," she murmured. "If you know what I mean."

She would absolutely regret that in the morning.

"I do take you seriously," Steven said. "Will you just trust me? Go on and get some sleep, Chloe."

He had cold feet. That was it. He didn't really want to marry her. "I asked you what you thought about sex therapy."

Merlin leaped onto the kitchen counter and strolled, high-stepped delicately among a group of canisters. Playing like a naughty toddler . . .

"It's very common for couples to see sex therapists nowadays," Chloe said. There would be no turning back now.

Steven studied her without blinking—or speaking.

"Don't think I'm being critical. Sometimes people have hang-ups about sex."

"Do they?" That clever mouth could thin to an exceedingly straight line. "I don't."

"I wouldn't want you to think sex is all I think about."

"No, you probably wouldn't want me to think that."

"But it does cross people's minds. In situations. Certain situations. People *think* about it."

Steven worked his jaw before saying, "You mean some people are obsessed by it, don't you?"

"I'm not obsessed by sex," she told him, incensed. "But it is an important thing in marriage."

"Yes, it is."

"I'm really not preoccupied with sex."

Steven picked up Merlin and placed him on the floor. The cat promptly jumped up on the counter again.

"Are you listening to me, Steven?"

"You're not preoccupied with sex—just unable to think about anything else."

Her face flamed. "That's nasty. You're trying to shut me up."

"Please go to bed. You'll feel fine in the morning. We'll feel fine in the morning."

This was a side of him she'd never seen before. A cutting, put-you-down side. "We're getting married tomorrow."

He pulled the garbage bin from the cupboard beside the sink. "Yes." And he didn't turn to look at her. "It's just as important to me as it is to you."

"We've never had sex."

"I'm traditional."

Chloe sat down again. Hard. "You're thirty-five."

"Can't I be thirty-five and traditional?"

She had a horrible thought. "Is that why . . . ?" Could Barbara's wild suggestion be true?

"Why what?"

"Didn't you . . . ?"

He set down the can. *What?*

"Barbara says it's possible."

"I've never met your friend, Barbara, but I don't think I'd like her."

"Even though you were married . . . Are you a virgin, Steven?"

Hurt transformed into disbelief. "Good grief."

She did love him, and she couldn't bear to lose him. "Sex doesn't matter," she told him hurriedly. "Really. I can live without it."

"But not without talking about it." His teeth set between slightly parted lips.

"Well," Chloe said, feeling weak. "You're avoiding the issue here."

"You know what they say?"

"No. Are you afraid of sex?"

"Do you know what they say you should do if you're in a hole?"

"No!"

Stop digging.

"Steven, this is important."

"If your horse dies, get off."

"I don't have a horse."

He opened a drawer, pulled out a plastic bag, and headed toward the hall.

It was now or never. Either they found a way to be open with each other or it was over. "You're walking away from an argument."

"I'm going to deal with the wastepaper baskets. I've got to take the goddamn garbage out."

* * *

He shut the kitchen door firmly and closed his eyes. Damn, this was hell. Sex was all she would talk about tonight, and sex was all he could think about tonight.

What would she say if he just opened up and told her what was on his mind?

Sex.

Oh, terrific. And his thoughts on the topic played right into what she'd just suggested—sort of.

Emptying the wastepaper baskets didn't take long. One in the bathroom off the master bedroom and one in the bedroom itself. He stared at the bed, then went back into the black-and-white bathroom. The shower had two gold heads. "A his and hers," the real estate woman had said coyly.

Chloe had moved into the house three weeks earlier. Her shampoo rested on a ledge, and a bar of soap and a razor. He picked up the soap. *Slick skin to slick skin. Water pounding down on them. Steam. Sliding, sliding.*

Steven took a deep breath.

She wanted him.

He wanted her. He didn't want to disappoint her.

Searching hands on his body—touching, testing, holding. Soapy breasts and thighs. Laughter. So easy to lift her, to enter her . . .

Hell, he had to control his mind, then make sure he got everything right when the time came.

He went back into the kitchen and stuffed the bag into the trash bin.

"Steven, please don't do this. We can't base a marriage on avoidance."

He was scared, dammit. His palms sweated. He'd been so sure they'd make it through the wedding without having this discussion. Then everything would be okay—he was sure of it. Almost.

There was no one like Chloe. He hesitated and looked at her, and smiled.

Curly red hair, big, deceptively sleepy-looking gray eyes,

pointed chin, a definite upward tilt at the corners of her mouth. A lovely face made more interesting by the way her moods changed the set of her eyes and lips. The mood of the moment was all watchful irritation.

He widened his grin.

She didn't grin back. Her yellow tank top rested on her pale, smooth skin the way he'd like to rest on it—like warm butter applied with a brush. He tried not to linger too long at the level of her pointed breasts. Her cutoff shorts rode low on her round hips and clipped the tops of bare, well-shaped legs. When she moved just so, her smooth middle showed between the tank top and the shorts.

He was dying.

Death by repressed sex drive.

"What are you thinking?" she demanded.

That he'd like to grab her, kiss her silly, and not stop kissing her until they were both naked and he was so deep inside her he'd forget every hang-up he'd ever had.

"I'm a lucky guy," he said quickly, and swallowed.

He would forget his hang-ups eventually. They weren't worth clinging to. He didn't want to cling to them. Faye had been wrong—she'd cast around for some excuse to hurl at him and suggesting he was a failure sexually had been what she'd found. *"Selfish to the bone. Get what you want and to hell with my needs. Don't ever change your last name, Steven. It suits you perfectly. Early. Always early."* Her voice had risen with each word until she'd shrieked, *"Early."*

"Oh, Steven." Chloe's mouth quivered. She came to him and wrapped her arms around his neck, pressed her face into his chest. "Please talk to me about this."

Beautiful Faye had wanted out of their marriage. When they'd met, she'd known all about his very wealthy family—she hadn't expected to find herself the wife of a high school physics teacher who'd become estranged from that moneyed family.

He was a perfectly competent lover.

Wasn't he?

"Chloe, darling, you're overwrought."

"I am not *overwrought!*"

And now she was crying. "Maybe we shouldn't have decided to make this wedding such a private event after all." He brushed at the tears, kissed her lightly—and felt the expected jolt. "You'd be more secure if your mother was here."

"I don't want my mother," she wailed, hugging him tighter. "I'm thirty years old and I don't want my mother. I want you."

"And I want you," he told her, his heart beating too hard, too fast. "I want you so damn much." She believed marriage was forever. Steven had decided to concentrate on that and trust that once they were married, if there were any . . . adjustment problems, they'd work them out. He couldn't risk losing her on the eve of their wedding just because he finally surrendered in a battle with his zipper.

"You say you want me," Chloe said. Her eyes were anything but sleepy now. "But you're deliberately avoiding what it means for a man and woman to want each other and I need to know why. Do you realize we've never even seen each other undressed—completely undressed?"

Oh, God.

She played the backs of her fingers along his jaw. "I've never been a forward person."

"No. You're just you. Look, I don't want to brush you off on this, but—"

"But you're going to anyway." Chloe stepped back and yanked her tank top over her head. Her skin was very white. She sucked in her bottom lip. "Only I'm not going to let you. Take something off."

He grabbed her wrists as she reached back for the fastening on her bra. "What are you doing?"

"Getting naked. Now it's your turn. Start with your shirt— that would be fair."

Heat followed chill in a race over his body. "This isn't like you."

"No, it isn't. At least, I don't think it is."

Gently, but firmly, he trapped her hands against his chest. "Sweetheart, I'll be by for you around nine in the morning. Tomorrow's going to be a wonderful day."

"Okay, I've got it. I've got the answer. Let's elope."

Steven's mind went into free fall.

"We could get into your car right now and drive to . . . No. What am I saying? That would take longer . . . Oooh, this is awful. I started talking and now I can't seem to stop." She made a sound Steven was afraid might be a choked-down sob. "Why did I say anything?"

"Because you're confused. My fault. I guess I've been sending mixed messages." She had to know how much he loved her, and wanted her, yet every time the signal had been clearly declared, "go for it," he'd said, "back off," without giving Chloe as much as a vote.

"But why, Steven?" She was crying, really crying.

"Chloe—"

"I'm sorry. I lost it for a few minutes." She sniffed and swiped at her cheeks. Her forced laugh made him feel like shit. "I was going to suggest we play strip poker. Can you believe that?"

Steven swallowed. He didn't trust himself to say anything.

Lace trim along the top of her skimpy bra didn't cover the hardened tips of nipples the color of warm honey.

He couldn't look away from her breasts. They'd fill his hands, weigh softly in his palms—and they'd taste sweeter than honey. And he was torturing himself.

"Most men would be having a stag party tonight, Steven."

In other words, most men not only thought about sex at times like this, they acted on the thought. "And you wish I were?"

"No. I hate the thought of those things. But I would like to play strip poker with you. There! Now I've told the truth."

"Chloe!"

"I wish you wouldn't say *Chloe* like that. I've never played strip poker."

"But you think your education's incomplete without the experience?"

"No! But I want . . . Oh, this is horrible and it shouldn't be."

He should tell her, just tell her what was on his mind and trust her to understand. "You aren't ready for this marriage." *Nice job of coming clean.* "I've rushed you."

"We've known each other for months," she told him.

"Not long enough."

She spun away. "You want to call the wedding off?"

"Chloe, I do not want to call the wedding off. What man would want to call off a marriage to you?" He was being so unfair.

The slump of her shoulders smote at him. She said, "I'm so embarrassed."

"You don't have anything to be embarrassed about. You're lovely, and natural, and I need you, Chloe. I can hardly wait for our wedding."

"Then don't." When she faced him again, her cheeks were flushed—and her breasts. "Kiss me, please."

Steven lost the battle to control his breathing, and his heart rate—and other bodily elevations. Her fingers, slipping beneath his shirt, were cool and very, very determined. Chloe wasn't tall. She rose to her toes to seek his mouth and as she rose, she pushed up his shirt and pressed her breasts to his chest. Her lacy bra scratched just the slightest, most infuriatingly sexy bit.

Her breath played over his lips, a soft, warm, sweet puff that sucked him down, sucked him in.

Kissing Chloe was torture of the best kind, but still torture. For months, he'd been kissing her, feeling her, yet not feeling her.

The tip of her tongue sought out his.

He passed his palms up and down her sides. "I love you," he told her. "I always will."

Chloe kissed him hard, closed her eyes and rocked their

mouths together, and rubbed her all-but-naked breasts against his chest until he thought he'd explode. "Keep touching me," she said.

The tremor that hit him tightened his grip on her waist.

She sighed, and her fingers roamed down his spine, inside the waistband of his shorts as far as she could reach, then out again and down to the tensed muscles of his thighs.

He *would* explode.

"I love the feel of your body," she murmured.

The next sound she made was a cry, part surprise, part excitement—all pleasure. Chloe fastened on Steven's penis and she had to know the effect she was having on him.

Getting it up had never been a problem.

Even Faye had said that much. It was what he did with it, and other things afterward, that his beloved ex-wife had insisted left her unsatisfied and frustrated to near-suicide.

"Oh, Steven," Chloe whispered. "You do want me as much as I want you."

"Wrong," he said through his teeth. "I want you more."

"I don't think so."

Gently, but firmly—and not without the pain of loss—he took her hands from his crotch.

"What is it?" Chloe crossed her arms over her breasts. "Tell me what's wrong."

"Nothing." He picked up the garbage bin and went outside into a hot, dark night. He throbbed. His legs didn't want to support him. Even the wind through tall evergreens didn't cool him.

Concentrate on the small stuff and get the hell out of here.

Clouds spun a drape across the moon. The skitter and scrape of invisible, living things seemed louder than it could possibly be.

Small stuff.

They were fortunate to have garbage pickup at all out here. The truck passed on its way between two developments near the town of Issaquah, and Chloe had managed to arrange for it to stop each week.

He heard her footsteps behind him and kept walking down the gravel drive toward the road. The trees rustled and whined on either side of him.

Something white shot past his ankles. Merlin's unexpectedly deep yowl jarred Steven.

Chloe caught up and stood beside him. "I've made up my mind."

For an instant he paused, then carried on. "We made up our minds some time ago, my love."

He dumped the bin into a larger one stashed in a wooden shelter beside the road.

"I've made up my mind to tell you exactly what's really worrying me. We're going to be man and wife. I owe it to my husband to explain what I'm thinking, don't I?"

The cat meowed again, more loudly this time. The sound went on and on. Steven tried to shut the noise out. "You don't have to say anything else," he told Chloe. "You are honest. I'm the one who's been holding out. What's the matter with the cat?"

Chloe shushed the animal and took one of Steven's hands in both of hers. "Never mind Merlin. What do you mean, you've been holding out?"

He drew in a breath so deep it made him cough. "Hell, Chloe, there's something wrong with me." That hadn't been what he'd intended to say, but he couldn't form sentences like, *Faye complained of premature ejaculation.* "I may have a . . . problem."

"Steven! Oh, darling. You should have told me. What is it?" She'd put her tank top back on but her breasts felt just as inspiring when she pressed his hand between them. "What's wrong with you?"

If there was an Idiot of the Year award, he had it in the bag. "I didn't put that very well. It's this possible loss of—or maybe gradual loss of function."

She gasped and whispered, "Paralysis?"

"No, not exactly. Although it could be something like that because I'm not even aware of it happening."

"I don't understand."

No kidding. "Things may sort of . . . *fall off* without my noticing."

Chloe gave a small scream.

Merlin set up a wail and kept on wailing.

A shudder climbed over Steven's back. He was murdering this confession.

"My poor darling," Chloe said, wrapping him in a hug so tight his breath shot from his lungs. "Don't worry about me. I don't care what drops off. You'll always have me here holding things together."

"Chloe—"

"I've always been told that the harder things get, the better I perform. And I'm Jennie-on-the-spot. If there's an emergency, I come through fast."

According to Faye, coming through fast had been Steven's downfall.

The damned cat shrieked for attention.

"Shush, Merlin. Steven's got enough problems without that racket. Sweetheart, lean on me, please. And promise me you'll never try to hide anything from me again. For richer, for poorer. In sickness and in health. Remember."

"I'm not sick."

"Don't give me that brave stuff. Whatever happens, you'll never be alone. If you—if you lose things, we'll find a way to have just as full a life without them. There are always ways to compensate for these things."

Think. Backpedal fast. "Things don't fall off. Not the way I made it sound. It's more that they apparently don't always do what they're supposed to do and I'm not even aware of it."

"Don't give it another thought. From now on I'm in charge. You can put yourself in my hands."

Oh, yes, yesss!

Chloe grew still. She looked past him and said, "Sweetheart, what time is it?"

"I don't know. Ten, maybe."

"Huh. I could have sworn I saw light coming up through the trees. Anyway, as I was saying, I'm in charge. I'll make sure you know if something's not working quite right."

Oh, joy—history about to repeat itself.

"And I'll work with you, my love," Chloe told him, smiling adorably. "If something's not performing up to expectations, I'll just work on it until it does. And I'll enjoy doing it."

If you're in a hole, stop digging. "Thanks, Chloe darling. I don't know about you, but I'm suddenly exhausted."

Merlin, landing on his shoulder—with all claws extended—made Steven shout.

"It's okay," Chloe said, threading her arm through his. "Come on, I'm getting you back into the house. We've got a lot to talk about."

She was gentle and caring, and so special. He owed her complete honesty, and he owed it to her now. "Okay. You've got it, sweetheart. We're going to get everything in the open. Then I'm just going to have to hope you'll still want me."

"There's nothing that could make me not want you," Chloe said.

He started to leave, but held back, turned around. "It is getting light out."

Chloe's grip on his arm stiffened. "Not light," she whispered. "Not really. It's getting bigger. Glowing. Steven!"

The cat's cry died, but the animal placed its feet close together on Steven's shoulder and arched its body.

"Geez. Do you think the real estate woman forgot to tell us there was another house over there?"

"That doesn't have anything to do with a house," Chloe muttered.

"No." She was right. Steven said, "No. Get behind me. And if I say run, do it. Get back to the house and call 911."

"And say what? Excuse me but there's a glow in our woods?"

"Shit," Steven said under his breath. "If I didn't think I was seeing things, I'd say there's a blue light coming this way."

"Make that two of us seeing things," Chloe said. Waves of shivers shook her arms. "A bubble of blue light with green fog coming out of it."

"You see it, too. Maybe it's some sort of atmospheric reaction. Warm air. Cold ground, and . . . Hell, I don't know."

"Nothing's cold right now," Chloe said. "I'm so hot I may melt. Is there something in the middle of the light? Steven! Is it a UFO?"

He laughed. "What happened to your sensible side? I thought you didn't believe in that kind of stuff, anymore than I do."

"Two somethings, Steven," she said in a small voice. "I see two . . . There are two people inside that, that whatever-it-is. And they're coming this way."

Two people. Two tall, slim people wearing silver. Steven closed his eyes for a few seconds, squeezed them tightly shut, and opened them again. His heart made a flying leap into his throat. "Run, Chloe! Now. I'm right with you."

Chloe didn't move. Neither did Steven. He couldn't. He couldn't move his arms and legs at all.

"Run, Chloe!"

"I can't," she said, her words coming in pants. "Steven, I'm scared."

"That's because you're smart," he told her. "I don't believe this."

"Hello," a male voice said, a voice both far away yet so close it might have come from the very air Steven breathed. "How fortuitous. The exact people we'd hoped to encounter"

"I'd faint," Chloe murmured. "Only I can't move, so I can't fall down."

The luminous bubble drew to a halt several yards away.

"A man and a woman," Steven said. "I don't get this."

"We must ensure that we speak most slowly and clearly or they will not understand," the woman said to her companion. Almost as tall as the man, close to six feet at least, the light revealed her black eyes and hair, and pale skin—a thin, sharply intelligent face. "We are so very pleased to meet you. You are lovers, yes?"

Steven tried, without success, to move his legs. "Don't be scared," he whispered to Chloe. His mouth was all that would move. "This is just . . . it's . . ."

"Weird," Chloe finished for him.

"They are lovers," the man said. He bowed slightly. "We're honored to be in the company of lovers. This has been our hope, that we might be granted the extreme good fortune to select precisely the right subjects for our needs. How blessed we are. We are most grateful."

"I want to scream," Chloe said, her voice suddenly loud. "Steven, help me scream. I can't move. I'm glued here."

"Well-favored," the woman said, and the bubble bobbed a little closer. "Are they not well-favored, designated mate?"

The man leaned forward a little. "Quite, I believe. The clothing is primitive, but has a certain antique charm. I've seen pictures of such garments. And their forms are very pleasing."

"I collect they will suit quite well," the woman said. "Clearly we made an accurate interpretation of the messages we harvested from their minds. They are topping."

"Oh, *shit,*" Steven said, then added, "Sorry, Chloe. Slipped out."

"Shit seems about right to me," Chloe said. "This is really happening, isn't it?"

"Yup." The man's eyes were pale, as silvery as the one-piece, body-hugging suit he wore. His short, blond hair took on some of the light's bluish hue. Elegantly handsome, and haughty rather than arrogant. "It's happening," Steven said. "Two aliens just floated out of those woods. They're inside a bubble that gives off green vapor. And they sound like a cross between characters from an English period film and a bad sci-fi flick."

"I couldn't have described them better," Chloe said. "They're beautiful, aren't they? Who are you?" she asked the woman.

The man looked at the woman. "Perhaps we should have done more work on decoding their verbal strings."

"Too primitive," was her response. "And unnecessary. We have identified and isolated those thought topics that are of interest to us. That will be adequate for our purposes. There is no doubt that they have what we require. I do believe they may be afraid—at a purely primal level, of course. They are gentle, I feel that."

"As do I."

"And we have made contact with what was lost by the ones who have gone long ago," the woman said:. "It is here in these two simple creatures."

"Simple creatures," Chloe echoed. "Who is she calling simple?"

"Remember, our data tells us that they can hear us and that they will understand uncomplicated sentences." The man smiled at Steven as an adult might at a young child. "We are friends," he said. "We have need of you for a short time. You will come with us. You will help us. We will not hurt you."

"Fuck off! "

"Steven!"

"Sorry. I'm . . . This is wild. We've got to get out of here."

The woman clapped her hands together and laughed. "Why, listen to their enthusiastic, youthful sounds."

"This could be serious," Steven said.

Chloe snorted. "This *is* serious."

"We would be most happy if you would listen to us carefully," the man said. "You will not be hurt."

"I'm so comforted," Steven muttered. "Don't panic, sweetheart, I'll get us out of this."

"Sure. And I'm the man-in-the-moon."

Steven laughed, and laughed harder when Chloe joined in. She sputtered, "Make that the woman-in-the-moon."

"I am Orchis," the woman told them when they'd subsided to spasms of chuckles. "This is my designated mate, Vigar."

"Let me get this straight," Steven said. "We can understand when you talk—in simple sentences, of course. You can't understand a word we say. And you can read our minds?"

"They do jabber rather, don't they," Orchis commented. "The male is . . . well, he is, rather, isn't he?"

Vigar, or whatever he was called, glanced down the high bridge of his nose at Steven. "Possibly. Some females might find him so, I suppose. Apparently overt sexuality used to be common."

"Precisely," Orchis agreed. "And we must be vigilant. We must grasp this sexuality and make the best of it."

"Over my dead body," Chloe muttered.

Steven managed to grin and it felt good. "Jealous, Chloe?"

"The female is also sexually obvious," Vigar said.

"Gee, thanks," Chloe said.

Orchis and Vigar skimmed even closer in their bubble. Orchis studied Chloe. "One of the old ones told of how the women used to reveal their breasts. I didn't believe her."

"Oh!" Chloe's voice rose. "I want to cross my arms and I can't."

Vigar turned to Orchis. "We should take them to the caposphere at once. It is essential that they be comfortable or they may not be as useful as we require. We agreed that we should ensure their quiescence without restraint before embarkation."

"Caposphere?" Chloe said. "Quiescence? *Embarkation?*"

Steven longed to hold her hand, to draw her close and convince her, even though it would be a lie, that everything was okay.

"I agree," Orchis said. "I am concerned that the required thought patterns have ceased."

"Indeed. Fear—possibly of us, of the unknown—may be the cause."

"Ooh, they're quick," Chloe said.

Vigar laced his long fingers together. "Let us gather them quickly. There is a great deal to be accomplished."

"The thoughts have utterly ceased," Orchis said, also lacing her fingers. "Perhaps we should endeavor to calm them."

"The bubble doesn't touch the ground," Steven said, more to himself than Chloe. "It's floating. They're floating."

"I'm glad I'm not doing this alone," Chloe told Steven. "I'd think I'd lost it if I were."

"Nice to feel needed," Steven said. "Sorry, love. Didn't mean to sound flip. I'm rattled too, I guess. So far all we've got on our side is that they don't understand our speech. We should be grateful for that, I suppose."

"Here it is warm," Orchis said, extending her joined hands. "Come to us."

Vigar echoed her words and actions.

Only when Steven discovered his eyes several inches above the level of the bubble did he realize he'd moved.

"Steven!" Chloe shouted suddenly. "I can move again. Look at me. I'm moving. You're moving!"

He did look at her—an instant before she shrieked and flailed her arms. Steven still held Merlin. The cat made a scrambling leap and left more tracks on his master's back before Steven could draw the cat into his arms.

"We're flying, Steven! I'm going to throw up."

Chloe didn't throw up. Softly, with a sensation similar to sweeping velvet over one's skin, Steven was drawn inside the vaporous globe. With Chloe at his side he touched gently down.

"It is warm," Chloe said, pushing a hand beneath Steven's arm. "But this thing's solid, isn't it?"

He gave the globe a poke. "Ouch! You bet it's hard. And I can't see out—but they could. They could see us." If this was someone's idea of a pre-wedding gag, he wasn't laughing.

"Soothing words, Orchis" Vigar said. "We should try simple, soothing words to ensure comfort, and cooperation. I think we will work on their verbal strings after all, but there will be plenty of time for that after embarkation."

"Just so. These sounds they make are annoying, especially in the absence of readable mind messages."

"If our research is entirely accurate and there are indeed as many of them as we think, then they must be driven to couple."

Chloe's nails dug into Steven's arm. "Driven to *couple*," she repeated. "Do they mean . . . ?"

"Reproduction is their entire purpose." Vigar reached out, brought a single forefinger within an inch of Chloe, and made an outline from the top of her head, down her profile, beneath her chin, to the tip of a breast . . . and to the tip of the other breast. "Exactly as the old ones described. See how she links to him—evidently without thought. So primitive."

"So necessary for our research," Orchis said. "I shall try to communicate with them, then we'll take them to the caposphere."

"Listen carefully," Steven said to Chloe. "I want you to make a lot of noise. They don't like it because they don't understand what we say. Shout and scream and fling your arms about."

"That should accomplish a lot."

"Save the acid tongue, my love. You create the diversion and I'll give our evolved friend an old-fashioned fist. Maybe we'll get lucky and catch him off guard."

"We need you," Orchis said, sounding out her words slowly, carefully. "Our people are dying."

Steven settled a hand on the back of Chloe's neck. "I'm a teacher," he said. "Chloe's a librarian. Not a medical bone between us." He turned to Chloe. "Maybe reason will work."

Orchis continued. "Not dying really. Becoming extinct."

"So much for reason," Chloe muttered. "They don't get a word we say, remember?"

Vigar watched Orchis intently. She raised her finely sculpted chin. "Once, many generations ago, there were young ones—many young ones. Vigar, how will we know if they comprehend us?"

"We will know. Trust, Orchis, we will know."

"Over hundreds of what you call years, the numbers of

young have decreased. Now there are still young, but they are rare and must be carefully guarded."

"The patterns are returning!" Vigar's triumph brought an unexpected smile to his lips. "Do you see them, Orchis?"

"I must continue very rapidly." Orchis brought her face close to Steven's. "This is why we had to return to the roots of Sardo. Sardo is the place we come from. It is very far from here, but you will like it."

"I fucking-well won't," Steven said, and felt every word snap from his lips.

"You are to help us save the planet that grew from the most innovative minds your people ever produced, minds that probed the greatness and founded a better place."

Chloe made a scoffing sound. "She sounds like a deranged evangelist."

"Excuse me," Steven said, with great care. "But you need medical help. We'll be glad to help you find what you need."

"We chose you because your . . . *minds* tell us you will be able to teach us all about what we have lost, what is essential now." The depths of Orchis's eyes shone gold and intense. "If you understand, please move your heads up and down."

"Now what?" Chloe said. "Where are the police when you need them?"

"Pretending we don't understand isn't going to help," Steven said. He nodded up and down. "Maybe if we draw them onto our side, they'll get sloppy and we can make a run for it."

Chloe grabbed his shoulder. "Mushrooms! I put mushrooms in the casserole."

He looked at her.

"This is a hallucination. Oh, thank God, that's it. We're having a hallucination. Whew, I've never been so scared in my life. That'll teach me to think I'm a whiz at picking good, edible mushrooms."

"I think the male understands," Vigar said. "Continue and we'll be certain."

"The *same* hallucination?" Steven said, wishing he didn't

have to snatch away her straw. "The same hallucination at the same time?"

Orchis closed in on Chloe. "You must show me how you do it."

"What does she mean?"

"Let her finish," Steven said, and jumped violently. "Get your hands off me!" Orchis didn't actually touch him, but his penis rose in the wake of her undulating fingers as if she'd used a tire pump.

"Steven!"

He dropped his hands in front of him.

Orchis said, "The ability to produce this protrusion is no longer enough. That is functional but has ceased to be effective since none of our people spend time in such shallow pursuits anymore. But you must show me how to want this to happen, and then how to make my designated mate want this to happen. You must both show us the steps. We would learn what we have forgotten."

"Exactly," Vigar said. "We would learn how to begin the repopulation of our planet."

Orchis spread her arms, closed her eyes, and executed something akin to a slow-motion backward dive. Vigar moved gracefully beside her.

"We're going," Chloe squeaked. "Hold my hand. We're going!"

"Like Mary Poppins," Steven said through his teeth while they all sailed along. He couldn't see beyond the green gas. "Or Peter Pan. I love you, Chloe, so much."

"And I love you, Steven. We can't lose each other now."

"If we get out of this alive, we're never getting out of bed again."

"What?"

"Never getting out of bed," he shouted over a roaring sound that grew and grew. "We'll hold each other forever. Sex, sex, and more sex. Morning, noon and night. Wall-to-wall sex. I'll only come out of you to—"

"Yes," Chloe sang out. "If we live, we'll be naked all the time and never—"

"Perfect," Vigar announced loudly. "You have done perfectly, Orchis. They understand. They can hardly wait to begin."

"Indeed, Vigar. Two rudimentary minds, but with a single thought. Remarkable."

"A single thought," Vigar agreed. "Coupling."

"Yes, coupling. What one of them seems to catalog as *fucking their brains out.*"

The same Friday evening in July—but later

Just because they'd never heard of two people having the same hallucination at the same time didn't mean it couldn't happen.

"Steven?"

"What?"

"Nothing. I was just checking."

"Checking what?"

"Oh, this doesn't prove it one way or the other. Us—talking, or me thinking we're talking. For all I know, I'm the only one having a hallucination. If I am, then I'm passed out somewhere imagining we've just been captured by two aliens who look like spectacular humans—"

"Chloe."

"And I'm so delirious I think they've floated us to their spaceship and taken us aboard, and left us—"

"Chloe."

"And left us in a room—or whatever this is—that looks like something in a movie about a Roman orgy, and smells of incense. The mushrooms were so strong they're making me think you're with me and talking to me. And I'm only imagining there are two silver weirdos who want us to show them . . . No, the mushrooms were so strong I've dreamed up some craziness about these creatures knowing all about how sex works, but nothing about wanting it in the first place."

"Chloe!"

"Yes!"

"You've just described exactly what's really happening to us."

"I was afraid of that." She stepped between two green satin-covered divans, peered at a multitiered golden centerpiece dripping too-brightly colored fruit, and stood shoulder to shoulder with Steven. They faced a sliding panel in the wall—also silk-covered, but in deep blue—of the semi-circular chamber. Vigar and Orchis had left through that panel.

"Their people originally came from earth." Steven picked up Merlin and stroked the cat absently. "But they don't understand what we say. They're so damned smart, or *evolved,* they think they don't have to know what we say—that seems dangerously arrogant to me."

"I'm glad they don't understand us." Chloe stared at the place where Vigar and Orchis had last stood. "They just drifted away, didn't they? But they said they'd be back?"

"Probably before we're ready for them," Steven said. "As soon as they've dealt with 'necessary tasks.' They are so cold."

Chloe surveyed the silk- and satin-lined chamber. "We've got to try to think up a way out of here."

"Yeah, and before this thing takes off." Steven arranged Merlin around his neck. "From what I gathered, the ship, or sphere, is less visible to any interested parties by day, so they'll wait for morning light. That gives us a few hours. Did I imagine it, or do they lose contact with our so-called mind patterns if we're not thinking about sex?"

For a man who'd been avoiding the subject of sex for months, Steven Early was showing very little reticence now. "That's what I understood. So don't think about it."

Chloe slipped a hand into his. He laced their fingers together and squeezed. "They picked us because we're always thinking about sex. That's what they said."

A faint smile flitted over his features.

"That means you, too." She tapped his arm until he looked at her. "Were you really thinking that?"

"What exactly?"

"What they said. You know."

His lips parted. He watched hers.

"Steven?"

"They say people under stress want sex for various reasons."

"Spare me the scientific discussion. We're about to be whisked into space, probably never to return."

He shook his head. "We're not going to let that happen."

"How will we stop it?"

"By giving them what they want before morning."

Chloe frowned.

"Can you sum up what you think their problem is?"

She thought a moment. "They've become all brain and no heart."

"Uh huh. In other words, no emotion. And they've become remote from their bodies."

Chloe felt suddenly exhausted. She dropped to sit on the nearest divan and pulled Steven down beside her. Merlin complained, but didn't budge from Steven's neck.

"Maybe you were the one thinking it—what they said," Steven suggested.

"Thinking"—Chloe turned to him—"I've never even *thought* that word. You even said it tonight. Several times."

"Extreme circumstances," he said, avoiding her eyes. "Anyway, it's a guy thing."

She dug an elbow into his side. "I don't believe you just said that. But you actually thought it, huh? What they said?" He still avoided looking at her. Chloe poked him again. *"It. You know. That?"*

"I seem to remember telling you pretty clearly what I intend to do if we ever get out of here—as long as you don't mind, that is."

"Fuck my brains out?" She clapped a hand over her mouth and felt herself turn red.

Steven laughed. He tipped back his head and laughed and laughed.

"Stop it. I'm embarrassed."

"So you should be." He choked, and cleared his throat—and looked at her very closely now. "I can't believe you said a thing like that, either. But I forgive you. Excessive stress causes inappropriate behavior."

"Gee, thanks."

He stopped laughing. "They've forgotten how to love, Chloe."

Her heart seemed to stop beating. She should be too scared for such things, but she wanted to hold Steven. "Poor souls," she murmured.

"I love you, Chloe."

"I know. I love you, too—so much."

"We've got to make it to the church on time." His great grin made another fleeting appearance. "As the song goes.

"And we're going to show these—no, we're going to convince them we've given them all the information they need before sunrise, and then they'll let us go.

"Do you have a better idea?"

She felt hot all over—yet again. "Sounds like a fantastic idea. I just wish it didn't have to be here." A new thought struck. "This doesn't mean we have to . . ."

Steven raised his eyebrows.

"Well, you know what I mean. In front of them?"

He grimaced.

"It does?"

" 'Fraid so."

She eyed him suspiciously. "You wouldn't."

"Wouldn't I? Outrageous circumstances call for outrageous measures. Isn't that what they say?"

"But . . . We're going to . . . in front of *them?*"

"Not exactly."

The surge of disappointment Chloe felt shocked her. "Oh."

"We're going to think about it—in detail." He rubbed her thigh and Chloe jumped. Steven really grinned this time, and said, "Sorry, love. But it could work. I don't think they'd respond to a visual demonstration. It would probably be purely clinical to them. They've already let us know they view sex that way, and that's why their people aren't interested enough to . . . Geez, this is bizarre. We've got to teach them to *feel*. They'll only do that if we get at their minds. At least, that's my take on this."

"I'd rather work on the mushroom theory. I think I feel sick."

"Could I kiss you, sweetheart?"

The tenderness she heard in his voice overwhelmed Chloe. He lifted her to sit on his lap, chafed her bare arm, stroked her neck, settled the tip of a thumb beneath her chin, and covered her lips with his own.

Merlin yowled and flew to perch on the back of a sumptuous amethyst-colored chair.

Steven's kiss was gentle, but desperate. She let the pressure of his mouth tip her head back.

He slipped a hand inside her tank top, inside her bra. Chloe drew in a sharp breath but kept on kissing him. The sensation of his big hand supporting and lifting her breast, caressing seared skin, made her press against him. Beneath her bottom she felt his solid erection.

"We ought to be looking for the door out," she murmured between brief, hard, urgent kisses. "I wonder what time it is."

"Mmm." Steven kissed her to silence. "This is going to be tough."

She slipped a hand down to fondle the outline of his penis through his shorts.

Steven groaned. "So tough."

"Explain."

"I'm only human. It's going to be murder to stop."

"You never found it murder before."

"Didn't I?" He raised his head enough to see her eyes. "Take it from me, I've been dying from the moment I set eyes on you."

Chloe gripped his shoulders. "You've been *dying* since you set eyes on me? What are we talking about here? You wanting to make love to me? Or the falling-off things? You should have told me about that. I don't know how you could have thought it would change my mind. Why would you think I wouldn't want to just because you thought you were about to lose something?"

"I've been dying to make love to you," he said with no hint of a smile. "And I've been terrified I'd disappoint you."

She sat absolutely still. "Disappoint me?"

He exposed her breast.

Chloe followed his long look at her flesh, caught the flicker of his tensed jaw. With his thumb he circled her nipple, drew closer to the center until she panted with need. "Steven? Please don't stop."

"I'd better until we know exactly what we're doing."

"Oh, we know exactly what we're doing. I can tell we do."

"We've got to"—he bent to lick the soft rise of her breast—"We've got to plan how we're going to do this." His breath wafted over her peaked nipple.

"We're doing fine." Chloe wiggled.

"Don't do that, honey," Steven groaned. "I should have explained something to you a long time ago. I haven't been fair."

"We could find a way to convince them we need absolute privacy to . . . *do* this." They had to do it or she would faint. If Steven didn't take her in his mouth she'd probably faint anyway—but she would faint with ecstasy if he did.

Fainting might be a fabulous thing about now.

"That's what I thought, too," Steven said. He moved to the top of her other breast.

Chloe moaned. "Does that mean we have to try to get them back in here now?"

"Given what's happening here, I'm surprised they haven't come rushing in already." The stubble on his chin grazed her skin. Wonderful. "We've got to be sure what we intend to do. Then we'll attract their attention. And we can accomplish that pretty simply, I think."

"How?"

"Concentrate really hard on—you know."

At another time and in another place, this might be funny as well as incredibly arousing. "Are you sure we aren't already doing that?"

"We're going to organize the process. Make them think we'll give them some sort of step-by-step blueprint. That's the kind of thing they'll understand. They're short in the emotion department, remember."

"Short in the basic sex drive department, too," Chloe said brusquely, and thought that, until now, she'd been fearing Steven might suffer from the same condition.

"We'd better hope we can do something about that. If we can get them . . . Well, ideally we want them to . . ."

"I know what you mean," Chloe finished for him. "We want them making mad, passionate love and too busy enjoying making mad, passionate love to think about either flying this thing to Sourdough—"

"Sardo."

"Whatever. And we also want them to forget we even exist, at least for long enough to let us escape."

Steven said, "You've got it. But we start by getting them here, then we concentrate on wanting—no, needing to be alone to, to make love? We rudimentary beings can only make love alone."

He still bent over her breasts, still tasted them with lips and tongue. His hair was very black against her pale skin. Other hair on his body would be black against her pale skin. Chloe's belly jerked tight. She felt herself grow wet.

"We've got to excite them," he murmured. "Then hope we can get out while they're too busy with other things."

"If I can still think at all," Chloe said.

"That'll make two of us. You've got beautiful breasts."

She filled her hands with his hair. "You've got a beautiful mouth. I've always thought how clever your mouth is."

"You make it clever." He skimmed the very edge of one of her areolas. "Chloe, I'm already self-destructing here. Let's get this show on the road."

She avoided considering the possibility of their lovemaking becoming a show. "An audio," she said vaguely.

Steven barked a laugh. "You're quick, love. Yeah, let's get the audio on the road." He straightened her top and shifted her beside him. "Concentrate on the first step."

Chloe closed her eyes, waited, opened them again. "The same first step as you?"

"Hell, yes, the same . . . Sorry. Okay. Think very hard about . . . about us holding a baby."

"A baby!"

"That's the end result they want," he told her with enough pained care to let her know this was costing him as much as it was costing her. "So we visualize what they want first. Then back up to the natural starting point."

"Holding the baby wouldn't have been my idea of the first . . ." She let the sentence trail off. "Okay. Babies. Then what?"

"We keep on thinking about babies until they show up."

"The babies?"

"Chloe! You know I mean Vigar and Orchis."

"What if they don't show?"

"They will."

"Then what?"

He sat straighter. "Think about starting to make love, then stop."

Chloe giggled and said, "Coitus interruptus."

"We're not getting that far," Steven growled. "Don't be difficult."

"Be grateful I'm not screaming and throwing myself at the walls."

He smiled faintly. "That may come later. Close your eyes and see babies."

The incense-like scent that loaded the air made Chloe's nose itch. She squeezed her eyes shut and thought.

How ironic. They'd never as much as discussed having children—probably because they thought, without comparing notes, that they were marrying too late to start a family.

"You're thirty and I'm thirty-five," Steven said suddenly. "This would be a great time for us to have children. We'd make good parents, too. I know we would."

She stared at him. "Stay out of my mind."

"Huh?"

"You read my mind about being too old to start a family."

"I didn't. It's just that we haven't discussed having children and I don't know why. I'd like some, wouldn't you?"

Chloe hunched her shoulders and hugged herself. "Yes. Yes, of course." She felt soft inside, and very in love. "Our children."

"Think about them."

"I was."

"Good."

"Steven."

"Yes."

"What color is their hair?"

"How would I know?" A faint hiss preceded the entrance of Vigar and Orchis. "They've got red hair like you."

"The timing is inconvenient" Orchis said. "I would prefer to complete flight preparations. But they're actually relaxed—and sexually oriented. Amazing, but probably a function of their simplicity."

Chloe gritted her teeth.

"Exactly," Vigar agreed. "As we assumed, they have an extraordinary drive to procreate. We will proceed as we planned, only somewhat earlier."

Steven wanted children. In the midst of madness, Chloe savored that one crystalline, one charming thought. What more could she ask for than a man who loved her enough to want children with her?

"Think," Steven said under his breath. "Visualize."

Chloe did as she was told. Not red, but black hair. She smiled to herself. Lots of black hair.

"This process is not as we envisioned." Vigar sounded peeved. "Seated one beside the other. Thinking only. A more physical, less mindful approach would have seemed in character. On the other hand, doubtless this will make our job of instructing the others easier."

Steven's fingers, stealing over hers, broadened Chloe's smile. With him she could do anything, be anything. He wanted her for herself—and for himself. She was first with Steven, not someone who made a good distraction until he could have someone else.

He pressed her hand. "Are you thinking of the other now?"

"The other?" Her voice emerged as a hoarse croak.

"The *other*. About starting to make love. Then stop when I press again. Go blank then."

She concentrated. Sometimes sensation was everything. In the months since she and Steven had met, she'd spent more time than she should admit just imagining sensations. After they'd been together, the memory of how his lips felt on hers lingered, and how they felt on her neck, her ears, her closed eyes.

Steven always took his time. He could take forever just kissing her hands, nipping them in unexpectedly sensitive places. She'd never guessed that a nibble between finger and thumb could pull tight all the little muscles between her legs, or that the tip of his tongue on her knuckles might tense her nipples.

"So," Vigar remarked. "Do we agree that stripping away all clothing is the first step?"

Chloe's eyes opened instantly.

Steven squeezed her hand and she closed her eyes once more, but with difficulty.

"This is the male's perception?" Orchis said. "Interesting. With the female I saw only hands—but that does not mean the premise is not identical. However, there was a certain . . . something. No matter."

"Stripping off clothes?" Chloe muttered. "You animal."

Steven cleared his throat. "Think of nothing."

"I can't."

His sigh was audible. "Music then. Play something to shut out anything else."

"Good idea. Beethoven's Ninth."

" 'Masquerade' from *Phantom,*" Steven said. "Great music."

"Beethoven's Ninth," Chloe insisted.

" 'Masquerade' is—"

"The sexual progression has ceased."

Chloe heard Vigar, but schooled herself not to look at him.

"No." Orchis sounded different, less certain. "There was some sound in the female. Very primitive music. One of the little-known composers preserved on the history disks."

"I told you to think of nothing," Steven said.

Chloe moved her hand to rest on top of his wrist. "You told me to hear music. I did, and so did Orchis."

A noise caught Chloe's attention and she did open her eyes—to glance at Orchis. The beautiful creature returned the look steadily, but with a frown puckering her smooth brow. Chloe had the disquieting notion that the woman might have recognized her own name on one of her "rudimentary" captives' lips. She'd definitely heard the Beethoven.

"Leave this to me," Steven said shortly. "Count backward or something."

Obediently, Chloe began counting backward from a hundred.

"Ah," Vigar said at last. "Once more he has removed her clothes."

"Not even a kiss?" Chloe murmured. "No finesse."

"Please don't say that."

The hard edge in Steven's voice held something more—anger? She bowed her head and remained silent this time.

"Anger," Vigar told Orchis. "Fading anger, but he's taking off his own clothes. How very outmoded."

These people had outsmarted themselves. They'd lost the best parts of being human, and being men and women in love, men and women loving.

"Gone again," Vigar said with more than a touch of annoyance. "They approach each other and stop. Then nothing but meaningless shapes. He is thinking of us."

"She is thinking of him."

Chloe looked at Orchis again. The other woman stared back intently.

"He sees us leaving and they're alone again," Vigar reported flatly. "Once more he is removing her clothes."

"Into undressing me, huh?" Chloe asked.

"Can't think of anything I'd rather do."

"He sees us leaving again. He waits for us to be gone. And he undresses her again. And she begins removing his clothes. He plans for them to produce a child."

"She feels something very deep for him."

"Feels?" Vigar's tone was sharp. "These creatures are not capable of feeling. They are too primal. They are not evolved enough to feel."

"Evolved," Steven muttered. "I think I hate the stupid, cold-blooded bastard. His kind have forgotten how to feel and he doesn't even know it. He's looking for some sort of technique to solve his problems."

"Surely they'd have sex manuals among all the data they boast about." Chloe recalled her own reading of the volumes Barbara had so generously picked out.

"Vigar," Orchis said. "If it were as simple as what goes where, we should not require help. The manuscripts would have provided the instruction we seek. Our difficulties are deeper—perhaps even older."

"Naturally I consider your opinions of the utmost value," Vigar said. "However, it occurs to me that you may be fatigued from the intensity of our recent efforts. We did not have sufficient time to make complete preparations for this mission and I know your passion for detail."

"You are generous, Vigar. But I declare that our inability to converse—"

"We would gain nothing from conversing with inferior minds."

Chloe stopped Steven's fingers from curling into a fist. "I think we're getting somewhere," she whispered. "Be patient."

"I should still find it interesting to attempt communication. There is something in her that is familiar—something that stirs a recollection in me. One of the old ones spoke of certain *sensations.*"

Chloe's spine stiffened.

"You must rest, Orchis. After we embark for Sardo you shall leave matters to me until you are recovered."

"His images of our leaving them," Orchis said as if she hadn't heard Vigar. "Could it be that our physical presence inhibits their coupling?"

"Hardly. The requirement for privacy at such times is not documented at their primitive stage of—"

"Evolution," Steven said explosively.

"At their primitive stage," Vigar continued. "Their communication is rough. I doubt we could decode the strings without some years of study. He is imagining us leaving again. And again. Taking off her clothes. No, we're leaving."

"Come, Vigar, we are going to the outer chamber."

"But we've known there was no certainty of getting the help we must have. If we fail to grasp this opportunity for knowledge—at this very moment—they may pass out of season."

Season? Like dogs and cats? Chloe wondered.

"We will not miss the opportunity. I believe that they are ripe to couple and that they will do so, but not unless they are physically alone."

"But—"

"But what, Vigar?"

Chloe squinted at them through slitted eyes. Orchis inclined her lovely face to watch Vigar. Unlikely color rose in his cheeks. "I merely thought that as reproduction specialists and designated mate counsellors it might be instructive for us to observe them coupling."

"Since we have never experienced spontaneous coupling ourselves?" Orchis walked past Vigar. "Open your mind and come with me. This is the moment we have dreamed of throughout our studies. We may hope that we are about to learn what our people need to know."

Vigar followed her in silence.

Orchis said, "We must be receptive to their mind images. I believe I fully understand what we must do to optimize this extraordinary opportunity."

"As you say," Vigar said neutrally.

"I'm glad you agree." Orchis preceded him through the open panel. "I assure you that we shall increase our teaching potential immeasurably by engaging in a practical application."

"I fear your meaning is obscure, Orchis."

"Trust me, Vigar. I have always been considered a remarkable instructor. Allow me to demonstrate. We shall begin with your removing my clothing."

Even later on that Friday night in July

Moments of truth.

The moments that punctuated every life, and this was one of those moments, probably the biggest Steven had ever faced.

As the panel closed behind Orchis and Vigar, Chloe remained seated beside him.

A diffuse glow washed the room with multicolored beams, which shone through a border of glass floor tiles. The beams gradually dimmed.

"I thought they didn't know anything about creating moods," Chloe said.

Steven glanced at her long-fingered hands where they rested on her thighs—he glanced at her thighs, as far as the knee, and back to the hem of her shorts.

"Steven?"

"Hmm?"

"Did you hear what I said?"

"Moody people?"

"I said I thought Vigar and Orchis didn't know anything about creating moods."

Chloe wasn't very tall, but her legs were long and well-shaped. She clasped them just above the knee.

"Steven?"

"Yes." He met her eyes. "No, I'm sure they don't know anything about the kind of moods we're used to."

"You aren't concentrating—on anything but my legs."

Her smile brought a matching one to his mouth. "I like looking at your legs."

The faintest blush stole over her cheeks. "Good. That's very good. But what about the dimmed lights? They left us alone, then they dimmed the lights in here. That's mood-setting stuff."

"It sure is. You're observant. Just a minute." He bowed his head and concentrated.

"What are you doing?"

"Making sure they don't pop back in here to see what's holding up *the sexual progression.*"

"Do you really think they're somewhere out there waiting for us to load them to . . . *It.*"

"Uh huh. The lady definitely is."

A large table, low to the floor and made of a transparent medium shot through with gold flecks, claimed Chloe's attention. As if suspended, the contents of drawers in each side were clearly visible: shimmering crystals artfully arranged.

Chloe attempted to push her springy red curls away from her face. She anchored some of them behind her ears, managing to produce an appealingly fragile, elfin appearance. "They know what goes where but they can't be bothered to put it there," she said, scowling. "How do they think we can change that?"

"Not how, why. Because they figure we can be bothered, that we want to be bothered. They touched that truth when they touched our minds, and now they expect us to make them care, too."

"She's much more open than he is."

Steven propped his elbows and massaged his temples. "She seems to be."

"Or smarter, maybe."

"Possibly."

"Only to be expected, though."

"I'll let that pass—this time. I need to concentrate here."

"Women are more into some things."

He turned to see her. "Like sex? Dream on, Chloe."

"Because you're so into sex, you mean?" she asked sweetly.

"Let me deal with this, then I'll let you know what I mean."

Chloe hummed the melody to "Masquerade" from *Phantom of the Opera*. Her voice became gradually louder until she stood up and spread her arms with a flourish.

Steven sighed. "What's that all about?"

"Orchis reacts to music. She heard mine before. And I think she's the one who dimmed the lights because she's more evolved than he is."

"Chloe," Steven said, striving for a patient tone. "Would you mind avoiding that word?"

"Which . . . Oh, evolved." She sniggered. "Sure. But since you voted for 'Masquerade' I'll assume it's some sort of guy take on a sensual trigger. Maybe Orchis will hum it for Vigar and it'll turn him on."

"Good luck, Orchis," Steven said. "I wonder what's in Vigar's mind about now?"

"Taking off Orchis's clothes if you've been doing your job."

He thought about that, then tried not to think about it. "Lucky Orchis. That should be a thrill a minute with the ice man."

"Vigar is quite a man," Chloe said. "To look at, anyway."

"Is that right? I wouldn't have pegged him as your type."

"He isn't. I prefer darker, more obvious men."

"More obvious?"

She plucked a handful of red-blue grapes from the top tier of the golden centerpiece. "Much more obvious. The kind with primal instincts. Preferably downright primitive."

Just the sight of her, more than slightly mussed and rumpled, excited him. "Anyone in mind?"

"Yes."

An amusing, intelligent, red-haired dynamo. "Want to share his identity with me?" Her breasts had tasted slightly salty and totally intoxicating.

"Not yet. At this point I have to check him out to see if he really fits all my criteria."

He studied her. "What made a woman like you fall for a man like me? Seriously?"

"Seriously?" She dropped her arms to her sides. "Wow, you mean it, don't you? You're actually asking the question, and you aren't even fishing. That's amazing."

"What does that mean?"

"Let me tell you—later." Chloe dropped to sit on the silk-carpeted floor at his feet. She wrapped her arms around her knees and rested her chin. "You may have bought us the time we need to escape. At least I hope so. But they are out there waiting for us to repopulate their planet."

"Yeah. Big job. We'd better move ahead. They could be getting chilly by now."

Her big gray eyes sought his.

"Without those silver suits, I mean." He grinned. "You aren't scared, are you?"

"Sure I am. But we're going to pull this off, or croak in the attempt."

There was something so magnetic about her, about everything about her. "You're something, Chloe Dunn. You're fabulous. Seeing your smile every day. Talking and laughing and being with you every day. Lying with you every night—and any other time I can tempt you—I want those things. I haven't thought about much else since we met."

"Neither have I. I'm forever going into the stacks in the library and forgetting why I'm there. Goodness knows how many people I've left standing at the desk until they gave up and went away."

"You're kidding."

She scooted closer, propped her cheek against his thigh. "It's tough to concentrate on *A Guide to Potty Training Your Iguana* when I'm imagining you naked."

Even to him his laugh sounded self-conscious. "Women don't do that."

Her open mouth on his leg, the edges of her sharp little teeth against his skin, made him jump. She pulled back her lips in a mock snarl, then grinned up at him. "Men are backward. Have I ever told you that? Well, they are. Backward and pig-headed. Bad combination. They think they're still hunters for the poor little woman back in the cave—which would be fine with me from time to time. They also think sex wouldn't exist if they didn't spend their lives thinking about getting it, trying to get it, and getting it. Now that's really a laugh."

"It is?"

She did bite him then, lightly—and ran her fingers up the inside of his thigh and beneath his shorts.

"Hey!" He jumped and jackknifed forward. "Unhand me."

"Sure you want me to?"

"No."

"Neither is Vigar."

"So now you're reading their minds?" His shifting on the divan only allowed Chloe to slip her hand farther inside his shorts. He said, "Have pity on a man who needs to concentrate."

"Concentrate. Think of this as the next step to getting out of here."

"And I thought you were feeling me up because you're obsessed with getting inside my pants."

"I am obsessed. But I'm already inside your pants and you feel so good, Steven." She rose to her knees and contrived to work her nimble-fingered way to his bare, throbbing flesh. "I'd like to have you in my mouth. Does that shock you?"

The jolt she caused snapped him. "It's going to make me lose it—right now if I'm not very careful." He covered her hand at his crotch. "You're killing me—but don't stop."

"Okay," she breathed, and undid the waist of his shorts. "I want to watch what I'm doing. I've seen you like this in my mind. Now I want to really see you."

"You aren't joking, are you?"

"No more than you would be if you said you'd imagined me naked."

Heat flashed, in his body, and in his brain. "We both know I've done enough of that."

She lifted his shirt and blew softly on his belly. "I do now." Again she blew, and kissed the rim of his navel, blew—and kissed.

Steven fell against the back of the divan. "It's about time I let you hear the ways you get to me. Hear me count them. Didn't someone write about counting the ways?"

"Elizabeth Barrett Browning. How do I love thee? Let me count the ways," she said against his tensed stomach. "Hear us, Vigar and Orchis. Think about love. Show each other how you love."

"Every man should love at least one librarian. They know important stuff."

"Uh huh. One librarian. You only get to love one, Steven Early. Me."

Why had it taken an outrageous probable disaster to make him open up to this woman? "Faye said she was divorcing me because I was a lousy lover." He averted his face and held his breath.

"Shows what she knew." The splayed fingers of one of Chloe's hands skimmed each of his ribs, each muscle she could reach without raising her head.

Slowly, Steven turned back and looked down at her tangle of red curls. "Is that it? All you've got to say? You don't have any questions about why she might have said that?"

"I may sometime—but not now. I'm busy."

"Chloe, I couldn't bear it if I lost you."

"You aren't going to lose me." The calculated adjustment of her grip on his most sensitive parts brought a groan to his lips—and a smile to Chloe's. "I've got you, my love, and I'm not letting you go. Not ever. Not that we aren't in imminent danger of getting lost together."

"Not funny. Chloe, I've been afraid to try to make love to you in case I disappointed you."

She hesitated, her drowsy expression clearing. "How could

you disappoint me? Did you think I was going to rate your performance or something?"

"Or something. I didn't exactly do a great job of explaining, but when I said something stupid about *falling off,* I meant . . . Hell, some things are hard to say."

"So don't say them."

He had to, for both of their sakes. "Look, let me just tell you, okay? What I meant to say was that I'm not sure how my performance is—if it's frustrating enough to drive a woman mad."

Chloe regarded him solemnly. "When you kissed my breasts I thought I'd faint. Then I thought I'd faint if you didn't . . . well, if you didn't finish."

"I'd rather never finish. Not entirely."

"You are one sexy man." Swiftly, she parted his thighs and scooted on her knees until she could rest her head where he sure wasn't going to forget it. "You're so masculine."

"Thanks, but—"

"Hush, I'm counting the ways. You're elegantly powerful. The way you move. I've seen women watch you, and I want to tear their hearts out."

He heard his own, not very convincing laugh.

"You've got fabulous hands."

"So have you. And you're very good with them. God, are you good with your hands."

With her pointy chin resting on the underside of his erect penis, she hooked her fingers inside the waistband of his undershorts.

Steven quit breathing altogether.

"Your hair drives me crazy," she told him. "All of it. The way it looks against my breasts. Thinking about how the hair here"—she squeezed him—"how this hair will look—and feel—on my thighs."

His hips came off the divan.

Chloe laughed and edged his pants down another inch. "Your watch on your wrist. Against the bones in the back of your hand. The fine black hairs there, too. I watch your hands when you drive. And when you stroke Merlin—who is besotted with you, y'know. But I bet you never guessed that looking at your hands makes me feel heavy inside, did you?"

"Uh uh." He squirmed. "Have mercy."

"Never. You've got long, long muscles. Everywhere. I imagine the ones in your thighs holding me down, and I think of them heavy on me when I wake up."

"Chloe."

"No man ever had bluer eyes than you. Sometimes, when you're thinking about something else, and you turn your head just so—and look at me—I'm jelly inside."

Every word she spoke packed a one, two punch. What she said destroyed him and made him want to stay destroyed, and the jut of her chin pumped his already stretched male parts even tighter. He risked a downward glance and saw that the head of his penis was free of his pants and only a couple of inches from her mouth.

"Our two neophyte lovebirds had better be getting this out there," Steven said. "I can't go on much longer."

"Sure you can. The first time I saw you was at that new library dedication. You were looking at the mayor. Every woman in sight was looking at you—watching you."

"No they weren't."

"You kept running your fingers under your collar. Your hair was long—it still is."

"You'd like me to cut it?"

"Don't you dare."

"The first thing I remember about you is how you could make me laugh," Steven said. "You do that, you make me laugh. And you make me feel important. You listen to me, Chloe."

"Now I ought to feel shallow." His pants, with Chloe's help, worked even lower on his hips. "I do feel shallow. You were thinking about how I made you laugh while I was thinking about things like this. Just call me Sidewalk Puddle Chloe—the shallow one."

"You aren't shallow. You're—" His breath jammed.

Chloe extended her tongue and delicately rested the very tip on the distended head of his penis.

"Aaah." He blinked several times, slowly, and worked his jaw. "Chloe, sweetheart."

Her response was the slow curling of her tongue around him. She freed him entirely of his pants and supported him with both hands while she took him into her mouth.

Steven turned fiery hot, then cold. Sweat broke on his brow, his back. His hips surged upward and he was helpless to control the violence of the thrust.

Panting, he sank down. "Stop." He clamped his hands on her shoulders. "I don't care what our evolved friends are getting from this, I know what I'm getting. It's got to be a two-way street. You and me together. You want that, don't you?"

The curls around her face were damp. She drew her lower lip between her teeth and pressed her eyes shut. He hadn't noticed how heavily she was breathing until now.

"Chloe?"

"I do want everything to be a two-way street, but that doesn't have to mean I can't do things for you sometimes. Don't you think I'm enjoying this?"

He'd never known a woman who showed pleasure simply at giving him pleasure. "I think you're enjoying it. Can I tell you what I want?"

For a moment she looked into his eyes, then she gently rested her face where her mouth had been and slid her arms around his waist. "Tell me. Everything." A faint shudder went through her.

Steven brought a hand within inches of her hair and hesitated. "You're pretending, aren't you? Faking it because you're feeling sorry for me. Tell me. Be honest, for god's sake."

Her skin drew tight over fine bones. "I wouldn't know

enough to fake it. And I'm not pretending about this—this with you. But I'm scared. We're helpless."

"No, we—"

"What time is it?"

He checked his watch. "Midnight. Chloe—"

"What if they're getting the caposphere ready for take-off? What if they're not paying any attention to us at all?"

"They're missing some great mind pictures."

She didn't laugh. "As soon as it starts to get light they intend to start their journey. Under early cloud cover, they said."

"Yeah, I know. General galactic concern about Earthies' preoccupation with UFOs. An agreement to eliminate as many sightings as possible. They called us Earthies! This is so off-the-wall. I heard everything they said to each other. They talk like machines—antiquated machines."

"They aren't machines, just people who've lost their way because their society put too much emphasis on—well, not on wrong things, I guess. But they ignored important things until they went away."

"Kind of like the sign in Harwick's office."

She nuzzled deeper in his lap. "Who's Harwick?"

"My dentist. Great dentist. Great guy—if you like being made to laugh with a mouthful of cotton rolls. The sign says, 'Ignore Your Teeth. They'll Go Away.' That's what these people from Sardo have done with their emotions. But they aren't happy."

"No. And it isn't just because they're afraid of their race dying out. There's a wistfulness in them. Obviously they've got at least a notion of what's missing. They call it drive because they're dedicated to their science, but they selected us to help them because they felt something powerful in us."

Steven sighed. "Yeah. Frustration run amok. Two people ready to chew doorjambs if they don't get some sexual satisfaction—with each other."

"You were thinking about making love," Chloe said, sounding smug. "All that time when you were acting superior because I was trying to get some sort of reaction out of you—you were, well, you were doing it in your head. When you watched me, you thought about . . . Well, you did."

"Spit it out, love. You really turn me on when you say the words."

"Do I?" She pulled his shorts down to his ankles. "You were thinking of sliding your unbelievably sexy penis inside me."

"Hey!" He attempted to cover himself with his shirt. "And I always thought you were such a nice girl. What if our host and hostess decide to pay a visit?"

"He'll be jealous. So will she. And I am a nice girl."

Steven closed his eyes. "Nutty, but the nicest." He bent over her and kissed the back of her neck. "Your hair reminds me of red silk in the sun. You smell like sun, sun on warm, wind-swept grass. Hell, now I'm turning into a bad poet."

"Were you a good one once?" she asked innocently, and kissed that other area of dark hair she'd mentioned.

"Witch. You know how to make a man feel ten feet tall."

"And bulletproof?"

"That, too." The shudder coursed her spine again. He stroked her hair and rubbed the nape of her neck. "We're going to get out of this. Give it another hour and we'll find a way to get their attention."

Chloe sat up abruptly. Her eyes had widened and become too bright. "Why would we do that? I think we should work hard to distract them, then try to sneak away."

"And if we do that, and fail, they'll probably be able to find a way to keep us restrained until they get off the ground."

"Off Earth, you mean." Chloe's voice rose. "We don't even know if their timeframes match ours. What if it takes two hundred of our years to get to Sourdough?"

"Sardo. You're right. We don't know a thing about their reality. If you can use a word like reality for any of this. The way I see it we've got one chance—to follow through with what we started. I can do it if you can." Even with the end of their world knocking at the door.

"We're just beginning our life together," she told him, and he felt her tears hit his legs. "I'm not ready for it to be all over."

"Sweetheart." Steven kissed her neck again. "I'm never going to be ready for it to be all over. But it's not going to be yet. A few more strong mind images and we'll raise enough ruckus to get them in here. Then we find a way to plead our way out."

"They don't understand a word we say."

"We'll make them understand. One way or the other."

"But what if we can't?"

"Leave it to me." The jaunty grin he assumed even felt good to him. "They can let us go quietly, or I'll knock the shit out of good old Vigar."

"Steven!"

"Sorry. Didn't mean to be sexist. We'll knock the shit out of both of them."

She actually giggled, and sat up to show him her flexed muscles. He peered at her slim arms and wrinkled his nose.

Chloe examined her muscles. "No fat there," she said.

"No muscle either. You're a wimp."

Without warning, she launched herself from the floor and landed, sprawled, on top of him. Steven grappled with her squirming, quicksilver body. She was all over him.

"No fair tickling," he gasped. "Stop it, No, not that." His struggle pulled his feet free of his pants. Chloe sat astride his hips, hauled his face toward her, and instantly took advantage of the opportunity to yank his shirt over his shoulders until it cleared his head.

She yipped, and bounced, and squealed—and tickled each vulnerable spot he exposed in his attempt to keep hold of his shirt.

The shirt hit the floor.

"This isn't the way it's supposed to go," he said, breathless. "You're ravishing me."

"Uh huh. Your turn to ravish me next. When we get out of

here. This is important. Orchis is obviously going to have to take the lead with our snow king, so this is the way for now."

"Oh, don't give me excuses. You're aggressive. You're a sex fiend."

"True. True. Steven Early, I'm crazy for you. I'm going to have my way with you, so you might as well give up."

"Give up and what? I'm sitting on a silk divan, in a spaceship in the middle of some woods on the top of a hill. In the buff. With a beautiful woman on my lap. What am I giving up, anyway?"

"Choices. I'm in charge. I'm a ball-breaker." Her lips drew back in a sharklike leer. "Lie down."

"The hell I will."

"We've got one hour. Less than an hour now."

"Yeah. What does that mean to you?"

"Ooh, I'm going to experiment. And while I experiment I'm going to think of every little nuance I can come up with."

He grasped a tasseled cushion and batted her lightly with it. "You're going to do this for an hour? And I'm going to lie still for it?"

"Not still." The toothy grin grew wider. "No, I'd much rather you didn't lie still."

"Enough," he told her, and felt the tensing of his features. "You've forgotten one detail, ma'am. I'm a hell of a lot bigger than you. So now it's your turn."

He lifted her and swung her to lie stretched out between him and the back of the divan. "An hour can be a long time, Chloe, a very long time."

Her bravado faded. She touched his lips with trembling fingertips. "Then we beat the shit out of them?" she whispered.

"If we have to—only I still say we won't. I've got a plan."

"Another plan?"

"Yup. Another one."

"What?"

"This part is going to have to be a surprise." To both of them, since he didn't have the vaguest idea what he'd do. "It'll be important for you to behave as if you're shocked, too. Let me see. What shall I do to you first?"

"Steven—"

He swallowed whatever she'd meant to say with his lips. Rolling half on top of her, pressing her into the divan, he closed his mouth over hers, surrounded her slight body, and ran his hands the length of her spine, over her round bottom, beneath the legs of her shorts to her warm cleft—and he smirked when she wriggled and squealed. He worked a single forefinger farther forward between her legs until he found what he wanted to find. Touching the hot, slick little nub of flesh made her gasp, and forget to press her legs together.

He slipped back and forth, back and forth, still kissing her even when she forgot to kiss him back. "That first night we met," he said, clicking his jaw in concentration, "you took such pride in showing me around that library. I couldn't believe my luck that you were the one appointed to me."

Sweating, he rolled to his back, pulled her on top of him.

"Er—Steven. Oh, Steven, oh—God." Her hips rode his thigh. She used her knees to lift herself enough to make his job easy. "Oh. I—wasn't. I wasn't appointed to you. I—oh—yes—yesss."

She was so wet, so ready. A little maneuvering and he unzipped her shorts to plunge inside the front of her panties. Chloe bucked. Her eyes glazed.

"You weren't appointed?"

"I—erased the name of the person who was supposed to show you around."

"You didn't."

Her body closed tightly around the two fingers he inserted, then the three. "Don't stop," she demanded. "Please, don't stop now."

"You wouldn't erase someone's name just to walk me around a library." He wanted her damn clothes off. He wanted inside her, and her breasts where he could fill his mouth, his hands, where he could slide them over his chest, his belly.

"I'm not stupid," she murmured. "I'd have shown you around the silly library twice if I could have got away with it. Just standing close—Steven, don't stop! Just standing close to you made me shake."

"Funny. Standing close to you gave me some interesting feelings. But I didn't shake."

"Tell me about the feelings." Her urgent pressure against him sent the message that she wanted more, much more.

Steven clamped her to his thigh with one hand and eased her tank top over her head with the other. "Geez, Chloe. If we can stand up after this it'll be a miracle. Walking's probably going to be out of the question."

Through her teeth she said, "Because you're going to fuck my brains out?"

"Don't say that."

"Not ladylike, huh?"

"Not ladylike. Rub your breasts against me, against . . . Yeah, move down. Rub them there. And think about me coming into you till you think you're going to burst."

"Oh, burst me. Come on. Now."

"Not yet."

Her breasts spilled from the cups of her tantalizing lace bra. Slowly, she rubbed them back and forth over his penis. She lifted it and rubbed again, on top of his balls. And he imagined what he and Chloe looked like, or would look like to someone watching. He made the fucking mind images and didn't have to do a thing to add all the sensations that went with them.

Take that Vigar, brother. Do something about it. Your lady's ready.

"What were you feeling in the library?" Chloe asked.

A prize, a damned prize for self-control, that's what he had coming. "I was glad I was wearing a dark suit—with the jacket buttoned—and that I had a book to hold in front of me."

"No!" Her face came up. "Steven, no! That first time we met you . . . you know?"

"Uh huh. But all you felt was cold. A pity." The bra straps

were easy to pull from her shoulders. He lifted her breasts from their accommodating pieces of nothingness and flattened them to his belly—and held her there.

Chloe scooted rapidly up his body until she could take him in her very capable hands. She said, "What I felt was that I had a more or less tamed wild creature at my side. You were all male energy hiding in that business suit and I wanted to unwrap you."

He laughed, undid the bra, and contrived to toss it aside. "You'd better watch what you do down there. I'm hanging onto control, barely."

"You won't be."

"Oh, don't—"

"Don't tell me what to do. Just be guided for once. We're working here, remember? Weren't you in the middle of something?"

"Oh, I haven't forgotten. Let's change positions—Chloe, stop."

Ignoring him, she took the tip of one of his flat nipples between her teeth while she used her closed hand to stimulate him.

Seconds. A second and it would be over. "Chloe, sweets. Please." Up and down, up and down. And her hard nipples dug into his skin—her thighs spread wide over his.

"I can't," he groaned. "No. Let me do this for you. I can wait."

"Sure you can."

He didn't know when she shed her own shorts and panties. He did know when she slid his aching penis between her legs and squeezed.

"Chloe."

"Just think."

"Are you just—thinking? Nothing but thinking?"

"Hmm—mmm?" She used him to bring her own pulse thundering on top of his own. "Mmmm. All those months of not letting ourselves go. Not even talking about—this. What a waste."

He intended to more than make up for the waste, Steven decided.

Music, blasting from every side of the room, battered his eardrums.

Chloe covered her ears and kept on moving.

"Masquerade" grew louder.

Steven winced and turned his head aside. "God, what the hell is that?"

"It's your—your 'Masquerade.' You created a monster."

Voices rose, crescendoed, fell, rose again. Voices throbbed. Steven felt nothing but Chloe—and the pain in his ears.

"Ooh!" She rose to her hands and knees. "How could they do that? They wouldn't know a piece like this and they couldn't just scare it up."

"That's exactly what they've done—they've just scared it up."

Chloe climbed off him. She breathed heavily, her breasts rising and falling. When he reached to cover one of them she placed a hand on top of his and ground it closer.

"Do you suppose they're watching after all?" Steven said, speaking his thoughts aloud. "And trying to help us along with the music, maybe?"

"Don't say that." Shooting to her feet, Chloe grabbed up her clothes. With quick motions, she stepped into her panties.

Steven rose to an elbow to watch her breasts swing with each move. "Lovely, my love."

She glared at him, grabbed up what appeared to be a plum, and stuffed it into his mouth.

He bit into very sweet flesh and wiped juice from his chin—and didn't take his eyes off Chloe's next hopping-from-foot-to-foot routine as she put on her shorts.

"Where's my bra?" She spun around, searching the floor. "What did you do with it?"

He waved a hand airily and pointed toward a ledge high on

the curving, silk-covered wall. "Is that it up there? I threw it aside, I'm afraid."

Chloe backed away to look, then went close and jumped, reaching for the shelf. She jumped, and jumped, feeling along the edge of the shelf.

"You have a fantastic little body, my love," he said, taking another bite of the plum. "You have no idea what it does to me when you show it off like that. What legs. What buns. What a sweet waist. And your breasts." He kissed his sticky fingers. "Bring them here and I'll see if they like plum juice."

"I'm going to ignore that," she yelled. "How can you stand that music blaring?"

He knew the moment when she sighted the bra—beneath the cushion he'd also dropped. She glowered at him and strode to retrieve it.

Steven whipped up the bra and tucked it behind his back.

"Give it to me. They're watching us, I know they are. I'm so embarrassed."

"Come and get it, Chloe. Come on. I won't eat you. Not much of you, anyway."

The attempt she made to grab the bra landed her on top of him again. "Please," she said, gasping as he tweaked her nipples, one by one. "You promised we'd only give them so long before we caught their attention."

"I thought you said we'd already caught their attention."

Her peaked nipples made him long to take them in his teeth.

"You are completely horrible, Steven Early." Chloe captured her bra and leaped away from him. "A badly behaved, immature, tormenting . . ."

"Go on." He frowned his disappointment as her breasts were covered—sort of.

"Why pretend? You're wonderful. This has been the most frustratingly fabulous experience of my life—and it's probably the best experience I'm ever going to get in my life." She donned the yellow tank top and tried, pointlessly, to smooth out wrinkles. "Get dressed. I don't want her looking at you like that."

Steven laughed aloud, and grimaced again at the deafening volume of the music. "I never thought you were selfish. Wanting me all for yourself."

"Put your clothes on," she shouted.

He did, not hurriedly, but leisurely—starting with his thongs. Next, his shirt.

"Be quick," Chloe begged, glancing toward the panel and twining her fingers together. In her agitation, she rose to her toes and jiggled. "Steven! Put on your pants. *Now.*"

"Well, I would, but they're in such a twist." They hadn't been, but by the time he wound them together, and half inside-out, they sure were.

Chloe marched in front of him and snatched the shorts away. "You're impossible. Steven!"

"Yes?" he asked innocently, gripping her hips while he backed her across the chamber. "What is it you want to say? We hadn't finished what we were doing, y'know."

She flapped his shorts, slapped his hands away. "Here. Put them on and let's see if we can get out of here before we're launched into space. Now I know where some of those so-called missing persons who were never found went. They were stolen by aliens and never returned."

Seemed very logical. Steven sighed and put on his pants. He knew he must be as wildly mussed as she was.

"Now we've got to make them let us go," Chloe said. She cradled her arms across her middle and paced. "How are we going to do that?"

"Shout?" Steven said tentatively.

The pacing ceased. Chloe stared at him with huge, accusing gray eyes. "You said you had a plan."

"I said . . . Yes, I did say that. I lied."

The next breath she exhaled seemed to drain her. "I see. All right. We'll shout. *Let us out!*"

"Masquerade" drowned her words.

"Come on, Steven. Help me." She climbed on the table and jumped up and down. Her bare feet made scarcely a sound. "This is useless."

"Completely," he agreed, studying the door panel. "I vote we try to figure a way through that."

He helped Chloe down and they approached the panel. She said, "They obviously have some sort of device they use to open it. Do you see a control pad or something?"

"No. And we'd better be careful. We haven't seen any sign of force—not conventional force—but I haven't forgotten that they can physically stun us without lifting a finger."

"They did lift their fingers I think." Chloe drew close to his side and they took another step forward. "But they might be able to knock us unconscious the same way they stopped us from moving. Then we'd wake up somewhere out there." She raised her eyebrows at a ceiling draped with swags of blue and gold silk.

With a chirrup, Merlin strolled past them and went to the panel. He pressed his nose against the edge and waited while it slid open.

He walked out and disappeared.

Speechless, Steven looked at Chloe, and back through the opening to a space where colored shadows hovered and shifted. He saw the sheets of illuminated buttons he'd been too apprehensive to study when they'd been brought aboard the circular ship. Some of the buttons blinked. The shadows coalesced into wisps of vapor tinged with green, purple, magenta, silver. The wisps passed like flags born by invisible runners.

"Will you look at that? All we had to do was walk out."

He felt Chloe back away. "I think I'll sit down and think a bit first," she said.

"I think I'll just walk out," he said. "I'm going to find our hosts and figure out a way to let them know keeping us is a lousy idea."

"We ought to decide what we're going to say first."

His reassuring smile went unnoticed. Steven bowed his head.

"Stay there, honey. There's no point trying to plan anything. I'm going to go on instinct. Anyway, I've got to find Merlin."

"I'm not letting you go alone." Chloe scrambled to her feet and followed him into a very cool gallery.

Once they'd walked past several banks of controls, the gallery became a catwalk over chambers that opened to the top of the vehicle.

"Weird," Chloe whispered. "Like a big, plush, divided bowl."

At the center of the bridge span, the soaring notes of the music became eerily sibilant and rose to echo between the curved, shining struts overhead.

Silently, Steven pointed to the outer shell of the caposphere. Here it assumed the quality of glass. Beyond they saw the night sky with clouds still skimming the moon, and the faint outlines of tall, wind-pressed evergreens in the woods so close to their house. These were the woods that shielded the ship from Sardo.

"And if we do get out, we'll never be able to talk about it," Chloe said, her voice filled with wonder. "They'd say we'd lost our minds."

Steven didn't mention that he wasn't sure he hadn't lost his mind. "The music's softer here."

"More open space . . . Steven"—her voice dropped again— "look. Over there."

He followed the direction of her pointing finger, and edged forward. Suspended across the open dome was a huge and definitely swinging hammock. Made of black gauze studded with gleaming specks, and loaded inside with gold satin pillows, the hammock wasn't empty.

"Those silver suits ought to be burned," Steven commented. "What a waste to cover that."

Orchis had the kind of body movie stars went under the knife to achieve. Supple, full, firm—talented. Showing the effects of a lot of activity, her black hair curled. And she could move— God, could she move.

She moved suddenly, differently, breaking the steady rhythm

she'd employed on top of Vigar's matching nakedness. In fact it was Vigar, drawing her rapidly beside him and sitting in front of her, that caused the change in action.

Vigar reached to put a large pillow on top of Orchis. "Stay, my dearest," he said. "I will deal with this. Do not overset yourself."

"Oh, my," Chloe murmured.

Steven snorted. "They never got past English 1700 or whatever that is."

"Oh, my," Chloe repeated breathily.

Steven frowned at her, and discovered she was staring, open-mouthed, at Vigar.

"Sorry to interrupt," Steven called. They shouldn't be standing here like a couple of voyeurs. "Excuse us. We had no idea. Come along, Chloe."

Chloe gripped the spun-glass ropes at the side of the catwalk. "He doesn't understand. But he is gorgeous."

"Don't look! Come on, let's get out of here."

A laugh, husky and suggestive, grabbed Steven in sensitive places. Orchis laughed and sat up, holding the pillow to her. "Listen to them, Vigar, my beloved. Their language is distorted, but they do converse in an ugly form of English. He is as jealous of her as you are of me. How quaint."

Chloe planted her fists on her hips. "Our English is ugly?"

"Oh, indeed," Orchis told her. "Quite vulgar in fact. But if I am most patient, I can take your meaning."

Vigar made no attempt to cover himself. He did appear to concentrate intently.

"Look," Steven said. "We're glad to see the two of you having such a—stimulating time. If it's okay with you, we'd like to get home now."

"Egad," Vigar said slowly. "I do not understand each word, but I believe they wish to leave us."

"Gorgeous, and quick, too," Chloe muttered.

Steven chuckled, but sobered instantly. "You've got it, Vigar, old buddy. We'd like to blow. The lady and I are tying the knot in a few hours."

A blank stare was his reward.

"We shall need time to . . . to consider those comments," Orchis said. Her tone became petulant. "Tell them we'll join them when we're finished, Vigar."

"Good grief," Chloe said. "Does she mean what I think she means?"

Vigar's smile, the heavy-lidded expression that softened his features, made Steven turn away. "That's what she means."

"We shall not detain you long," Orchis called. "We're becoming most adept at these matters." She snaked an arm around Vigar and engaged in an activity too fresh in Steven's mind for comfort.

Vigar tore the pillow aside and rolled over Orchis.

The strains of "Masquerade" rose to pummel the onlookers' ears.

With Chloe's hand in his, Steven hurried back the way they'd come. At least the two overachievers weren't preparing the caposphere for departure. Cooperation and reason seemed as good an approach as any to diverting them from their plans.

The chamber where Vigar and Orchis had left them remained open. Chloe dashed ahead and threw herself down on the green divan. She drew up her legs and crossed them.

"They said they won't be long," Steven told her awkwardly.

"Adept at these matters," Chloe commented. "Incredible. I've heard of quick studies, but those two are something else."

Steven cleared his throat.

"Something else," she said again. "Did you see him?"

"I saw him." There were things a man shouldn't have to swallow. "Here's Merlin."

Chloe showed no sign of hearing—or listening. "What a body."

"Orchis isn't so bad either," he said, and didn't regret the jab.

Evidently Chloe still wasn't hearing a word he said. "I'd say they've put it all together, wouldn't you?"

Striving to flatten his own possessive urges, he said, "I guess."

"Oh, they have." Her little frown was the most endearing, the sexiest thing. "Steven, we did it. They not only know where to put what—and how. They want to!"

Saturday morning, not early enough

He was sulking!

In a darkly brooding, tummy-knottingly fascinating way—but sulking nevertheless. "What time is it?" Chloe asked.

"Almost six." Steven set out on another measured circuit of the chamber. "How long can it take, for crying out loud?"

She snickered, and sniffed, and managed to cough.

"Did I say something funny?" The full force of his blue eyes turned on her. "I'm glad your sense of humor is still intact. If I wasn't angry enough to eat aliens I'd be unconscious. I'm exhausted."

"Maybe I'm too hysterical to be exhausted."

"You aren't the hysterical type."

"No, I'm not," she agreed. "You just amused me when you asked how long making love could take. That's funny, Steven. Think about it."

He stopped pacing and came to sit on the edge of the table with its suspended store of brilliant crystals. Jutting his beard-darkened jaw close to her face he said, very softly, "I am thinking about it. I haven't stopped thinking about it—making love. Making love to you."

"Neither have I." Chloe poked his knee. "It was wonderful, wasn't it?"

"What there was of it was wonderful."

She couldn't look at him. "I thought there was a great deal of it."

"You didn't think we sort of missed the main point?"

"Nope." Chloe shook her head. "We got the main point, Steven."

He rubbed the back of her hand. "Are we talking about two different main points here?"

"I'm talking about how we learned that we're very good for each other. That we really are meant to be together. That each of us is going to bring an entire person to our marriage so it's two hundred percent of everything it can be."

His sigh moved her hair. "Yes," he agreed. "We did learn that. You just said it better than I would have."

"You weren't talking about the same thing. You were talking about sexual intercourse."

"Oh, *Chloe*."

"*Oh, Chloe*," she mimicked.

"Do you have to be so blunt?"

"Fucking our brains out is blunt. Sexual intercourse is clinical."

"And they're both inappropriate," he said shortly. "On your lips, anyway. I was talking about making love—really making love."

Softly, without a sound, Vigar and Orchis entered the chamber. Vigar hung back. Orchis, her arms crossed, stepped forward and stood, swaying slightly, with her eyes averted from Chloe.

Chloe cleared her throat and when Steven glanced at her she inclined her head. He turned around.

The silver suits were securely in place again.

Vigar clasped his hands behind his back and studied his silver boots from all angles.

"You do understand our speech?" Orchis asked, and when Chloe nodded, she added, "We owe you our apologies."

She and Vigar flushed faintly and lowered their heads as if they were bashful teenagers.

"Most certainly," Vigar added. "Sincere apologies. Most inappropriate."

Steven filled his lean cheeks with air.

"Think nothing of it," Chloe said. "I mean you certainly don't owe us any apologies. Whatever for?"

"How about snatching us away from our own garbage cans and taking us prisoner in this box of tricks?" Steven said as if he were remarking on an unremarkable wine. "Not giving us any choice but to give them lessons in how to make love?"

"Shush," Chloe told him. "You didn't enjoy that, huh?"

"Oh, but I did." A smile flickered, but quickly died. "But we have to keep things in perspective here. Don't apologize for a thing, folks. Just let us go home."

Orchis looked at Vigar. "I know our dear helpers will want to come to Sardo when they fully understand the importance of what they are to do there."

Steven shot to his feet. "The hell we will," he said explosively. "From what we saw out there you don't need any more help from us."

"No," Chloe said quickly, trying to send him signals to tame his comments. "You will be more than capable of teaching your people about emotion."

"Emotion." Orchis's dark eyes became intent. "Explain yourself, if you please."

"What you felt when you were together in that hammock. Emotion and passion—and plain old physical lust. And love. Great foursome. Feelings. The elements you were missing in your sexuality and your behavior together until tonight. They go together perfectly. You can build on them. First as a couple, then as a family when you have children."

"There will have to be practical examples of these things to share," Orchis said. "We certainly are not in a position to do more than facilitate your lectures on the subject."

"Oh, shit," Steven muttered.

Chloe glared at him, and asked Orchis, "Why would we be in a better position than you?"

Vigar came forward. The blush on his face intensified his fairness. "You have achieved this coupling. You have sealed your agreement to mate. Therefore you are ready for the next phase."

"We damn well haven't achieved this coupling," Steven said fiercely. "So we aren't ready for the next phase. But you've achieved this coupling. A number of times, or my name isn't Steven Early."

"We have a dilemma," Orchis said. She extended a hand to Vigar and he hesitated only a moment before lacing his fingers through hers. "All that you have said is true. Your unselfish sharing accomplished exactly what we had hoped it would accomplish. We have achieved a remarkable ability to create and enjoy satisfaction together, but we were precipitate."

"You mean you've only just met?" Steven suggested helpfully.

Vigar raised his handsome jaw. "We met as exceedingly young Sardines. Our parents approved our designated match whilst we yet suckled."

Sardines? "I see." Chloe didn't dare look at Steven. "How fascinating. An arranged designation."

"Naturally."

"But now you've discovered you don't dislike each other after all."

"We never did," Orchis said, haughty once more. "We are well-matched."

"Exceedingly well matched," Vigar said.

Steven slid out a drawer in the table and selected a hunk of dark red crystal to examine.

"Then why would it be . . . be . . . precipitate?" Chloe asked. "For you to do the job you told us you have to do? Because you're these coupling experts?"

Vigar and Orchis swung their joined hands and studied the carpet.

"Yeah," Steven said, looking up sharply. "Why would you need us to do your job?"

Chloe saw the dangerous set of his jaw and her stomach turned. He was barely holding his temper.

"We have already told you we may have been very hasty in succumbing to our impetuous urges."

Steven rose to his feet and squared his considerable shoulders. "Spit it out."

"Pardon me?" Vigar's blank expression mirrored that of Orchis's.

"Speak plainly," Steven said. "How could you possibly have been hasty?"

"It is my season," Orchis announced.

Silence followed, then Vigar gathered her awkwardly into his arms and kissed her eyes shut.

Chloe murmured, "Aah."

"It is not unreasonable to suspect that we may have propagated. A slip may have been fertilized."

"Only one?" asked Steven.

The innocence in his voice made Chloe grin.

"This would be inconvenient," Orchis said, and sniffed. "We should not have succumbed to primitive drives. My fault. I incited—*lust.*"

"By no means, my love," Vigar said, his back even straighter. "If to be yourself is to incite lust, then it is so. But you are simply a female of great attraction. This is to be celebrated. There is no fault—certainly not on your part."

"I thought all this was exactly why you were here," Steven thundered, flexing his hands. "You've lost touch with your damn primitive urges and your people are dying out. Now you've got the urge again. So go home and multiply. And teach all the other—whatever you are, to multiply. *Sardines.* Young Sardines in every home—that should be your aim."

"We do not as yet have the dwelling we require." Vigar held Orchis's face against his shoulder. "Or all the accoutrements appropriate to our station and the comfort we desire. The exceptional quality of instruction our young would require has not yet been provided for. Naturally the fund has been initiated, but it is by no means adequate.

"And we have yet to visit all the more desirable aspects of

our planet. Then there is the diversionary dwelling on the sand
flats to be secured. Diversionary equipment also, of course, and
we should certainly require vehicles suitable to our changed
state. We had planned to accomplish these things prior to attempting fertilization."

Assimilating this long speech took time. At last Chloe said,
"Some things aren't so different on Sardo."

"But the two of you are this—designated mate thing?" asked
Steven.

Orchis nodded.

"Then why can't you have your young while you work together for these things you want?"

Orchis wrinkled her perfect nose. "Once it was done that
way. The old ones have spoken of reading about these things."
She considered. "It does hold a certain appeal."

"Perhaps," Vigar said thoughtfully. "A most daring appeal,
and we are daring people. However, we are designated, but not
sealed."

With her eyes downcast, Orchis stepped away from him. "I
would never compromise you."

Steven made owl eyes.

"You are not compromising me, my dear one," Vigar insisted. "You never would. But, if you should agree, I would
like to embark upon this course the earthies have suggested.
At once."

"What does your sealing involve?" Steven asked casually,
not casually enough to fool Chloe. She'd noted his frequent
glances at his watch. "Anything we can help with?"

Ignoring Steven, Vigar lowered himself to one knee before
Orchis. "I would seal the agreement of our parents, Orchis."
He took her hand in both of his. "If you would seal it also, if
you would accept their wishes—and mine—as your own."

"Gives hokey a whole new slant, don't it?" Steven said under
his breath.

Chloe shushed him softly. "It's sweet."

"I would seal the agreement of our parents," Orchis said to

Vigar. She pressed her lips to the top of his head, to his brow, to their joined hands, and, finally, to his mouth in a chaste kiss.

"Let it be so, then," the man at her feet said. "We are sealed."

"And that's it?" Chloe's groom-to-be put his glittering red rock back in the table's drawer. "What happened to good old you-may-now-kiss-the-bride? Excuse us folks, but we've got a sealing of our own coming up."

The kiss ceased to be chaste.

"Excuse us," Steven repeated. "Hey, don't forget to breathe."

When the happy couple turned toward them, Chloe smiled and hunched her shoulders. "That was beautiful. So simple, and special. Congratulations."

"Yeah," Steven said. "Congratulations. You two need to be alone now. So, if you'll excuse us?"

The kiss resumed.

The still-open panel revealed the faintest shimmer of rising sunshine through the sphere's outer skin.

"Okay," Steven said to Chloe. "There's nothing for it. We're not going to Sardo to meet the rest of the Sardines, or any other place we don't want to go. We're getting married. This morning. This is it. Stand back. I'm going to beat the crap out of him.

"And you stand back, too, Orchis. This is going to be ugly. I'm going to have to fight your new mate."

Rather than move away from Vigar, Orchis drew him up and held him tightly. "Fight with Vigar?" Lines of confusion crumpled her face. "Why would you fight?"

"Because you two won't let us out of this thing. We don't want to go with you to your planet."

"But such missions bring honor. Our brother and sister Sardines will delight in honoring you."

"Honor we don't want," Steven said, advancing with raised fists. "Honor we won't have. Honor we'll fight rather than accept. This is going to hurt you more than it'll hurt me, but you asked for it."

"Oh, Steven, I can't let you do this for me," Chloe said. "You don't know what he can do to you."

"It doesn't matter what he does to me. I want you safely back in our house and I'm not letting them take you anywhere."

Vigar shook his head and smiled. "Such devotion. You are an inspiration."

"I am pissed!" Steven said. "We want out. Do you understand? Out. We want to go."

"Then go with peace," Vigar said, as he led Orchis to a divan. "You have our gratitude and the gratitude of all Sardines. All who wait there now, and all who are to come. You will be renowned among our future generations."

"The fruit of our first couplings shall bear your names," Orchis said. "Steven-the-generous. Chloe-the-wise. Never to be forgotten."

Vigar bowed and made a humble gesture. "We shall always remember you." He watched Merlin run his neck against the scarlet crystal and said, "We have no knowledge of such creatures as this one, but, since it appears of importance to you, our third slip shall be named Merlin-the-magnificent."

There were no words!

Sunlight burst across the chamber. "It's getting late," Chloe said, visualizing the dress she'd planned to wear to her wedding—visualizing the dozens of tiny buttons she'd have to fasten. "It's going to be a terrible rush making it to Bellevue. How on earth are we going to get there on time?"

"Vigar, I fear they are very anxious to depart."

"So it would seem." Vigar led the way to the catwalk. "Proceed across. On the other side lies the way of passage to the outer places. The way will open to you."

Grabbing Chloe's hand, Steven broke into a run. "We've got to hurry."

"Orchis, my love," Vigar said. "They are generous, but they lack logic. Why didn't they tell us at once that they did not wish to leave their home?"

Early Saturday morning

Steven slammed Chloe's car door. Rather than go into the house, she walked slowly down the driveway toward the road.

"Hey!" He flexed his arms within the confines of his suit-coat sleeves. "I'm ready to carry my wife across the threshold."

With her ankle-length white gauze skirts billowing, she turned and smiled at him, but continued walking backward.

"Come on," Steven said, wiggling his fingers. "Champagne and strawberries in bed? Or plums, if we've got some?"

Moving as easily as if she wore tennis shoes rather than low-heeled white pumps, Chloe spun around and ran. She ran, and reached the road before Steven gave up expecting her to come back.

Rubbing the back of his neck, he started after her. Women could drive men slowly mad. Chloe was more woman than most. She might accomplish the task quickly.

"Chloe!"

He knew his shout reached her.

She ran faster.

Steven ran too. "Chloe! Hold up, dammit. What's with you?"

By the time she stumbled awkwardly down the dip on the opposite side of the road, Steven was right behind her. Her outstretched arms wobbled as she struggled to keep her balance.

"Could we talk about this?"

"No. Go back. You're tired. You should sleep."

Very quickly mad.

She reached the bottom of the slope and started up toward the woods. He'd as soon never go near those trees again but he wanted his bride. He wanted her now.

With each short gasp of breath Chloe made a raw, rasping sound. She entered the trees and surged ahead, dodging trunks, her white shoes flashing with each awkward leap over an obstacle.

They both knew where she was going.

The surprisingly small clearing lay several hundred yards from the perimeter of the woods. Surrounding Douglas firs had cut out light for a hundred years. Not grass, but springy moss covered uneven ground. Fallen branches hosted tender ferns, the same type of ferns reflected in a single shallow dew pond captured by an age-smoothed hollow rock.

"It seemed much bigger," Steven remarked quietly of the caposphere. "Too big to fit here."

Chloe tipped her face up toward the distant circle of sky.

"I suppose it could have been much bigger really," he said. "It could have been anything. Our perception wouldn't necessarily hold true for them."

"You sound like a confused physics teacher."

He smiled and nodded. "I am a confused physics teacher. And you're a confused librarian. You're also my wife."

"It wasn't a hallucination."

"No. It all happened."

"And we'll never be able to convince anyone else it did."

Her stiff posture warned him not to approach. "I don't think I want to. I like the idea of sharing something like that with you and no one else."

She glanced at him, and instantly lowered her gaze to the ground.

Very softly he asked, "What is it? Regrets?"

Her wedding band shone. A random scatter of little flowers were very white in her red hair. The simple lace-trimmed cotton dress she wore made of her a picture reminiscent of a Regency girl in a morning gown.

"Chloe?"

She shook her head.

"You've been through too much, love. Too much in too short a space of time. You need to rest."

"I don't." The shortness of her reply surprised him. "But you do. Go and get some sleep. We'll talk when you wake up."

"Sleeping alone isn't what I've got in mind."

"You're honorable."

"Where did that come from?" He attempted to put an arm around her, but she stepped away. "Are you already wishing you'd never married me?"

"No," she flashed at him. "Are you?"

"No. What's the matter with you?"

"I'm embarrassed."

Whatever he might have expected her to say, that she felt embarrassed wasn't it.

Plucking at handmade lace around the cuff of one long sleeve she said, "That wasn't me. Not really."

Steven sensed he should wait rather than respond.

"I'm not like that. Barbara used to say I was sexually repressed and that's why men always saw me as a buddy rather than a potential lover."

"Barbara's a pain in the ass," he told her explosively. "I knew I wouldn't like her and I was right." Cold-eyed Barbara—the psychology hopeful—had been Chloe's witness at the brief wedding and she hadn't hidden her disapproval of Steven and Chloe's choice of a simple ceremony, no reception, and a honeymoon at their new home rather than in some exotic locale.

Chloe didn't defend Barbara.

"What do you mean by 'not like that?' " Steven asked.

"I don't want to talk about it. They've gone as if they were never here."

He looked around the clearing. "Not a trace left behind."

"I wonder where they are now."

"On their way back to the rest of the Sardines." He chuckled. "I thought they were joking about that at first."

Chloe didn't laugh. "So did I. I hope they'll have lots of children."

"If they don't, it won't be because they haven't tried."

Still Chloe didn't laugh. Instead she turned pink and fiddled with her hair. "I was so forward."

Stunned, he took a moment to respond. "Forward? I haven't heard that term in years."

Chloe rocked back and forth and her filmy skirts swayed about her slim ankles.

"Please tell me what this is all about. You were quiet at the wedding but I thought that was good, old-fashioned jitters. I had them, too."

"I don't blame you."

Steven frowned and grasped her arm. She tried to pull away but he wouldn't let go.

"You're a man with normal urges, but you're traditional."

Not so traditional. Very normal urges. "What's your point?"

"You're too kind to admit I horrified you."

"Horrified me! You couldn't horrify me if you tried. You're wonderful. Natural, sweet, passionate."

"And pushy."

He narrowed his eyes and considered. "I am tired. I concede that much. But the rest of this is garbage. Could we cut to the chase and talk about your hang-ups? And get on with our lives?"

"I don't have any hang-ups."

"No? You believed a would-be psychologist when she tried to line you up as a future client."

"She didn't."

"Is she going to specialize?"

"Yes," Chloe said slowly.

"Please say she isn't planning to be a sex therapist."

Chloe turned a shade more pink.

"Uh huh. I rest my case on that. But what's all this stuff about you being forward, and my being horrified?"

"I don't want to talk about it."

Steven took off his jacket and trailed it over one shoulder. "I like thinking of you as my buddy."

Hurt flashed in her eyes.

"My buddy, and my lover—my everything. That's what this was all about. But I'm an honest guy. I thought about the loving before I considered how fascinating your mind might be."

"Did you?"

"Sure did. You must have been right when you called me an animal."

She smiled faintly. "I was way off base."

"Even though you found out I fantasize about taking your clothes off."

"You were doing that for Vigar and Orchis's benefit."

Steven laughed. "Sure I was." The flowers in her hair made him itch to push his fingers into her curls.

"I can't believe I was so aggressive. And I said all those things to you."

This really bothered her. "You were assertive and you said some sexy stuff."

"And I . . ." She turned up a palm and made vague, airy gestures toward him. "I . . . *touched* you."

If she wanted to call that just *touching,* he'd go along. Steven closed his eyes and murmured, "Oh, yeah."

"I took your clothes off."

"Terrible ordeal."

"You didn't invite me to do that."

Hadn't he? "I should have."

"I was the animal. You must have been too shocked to react."

She thought he hadn't reacted? "It was pretty shocking."

The region of his belt claimed her attention—and lower. She fashioned another, more descriptive gesture. "I never did that before."

"No?" Steven sucked in the corners of his mouth, where the smile threatened. "Don't worry. No one would ever know."

"Uh, Steven, I know you wouldn't share any of this." The earnest pucker of her brow all but undid him. "I just don't want you to think I'm going to make excessive demands on . . . well, you know. *Demands?"*

"I'm not sure I understand." He shouldn't be enjoying this so much. He shouldn't be enjoying it at all.

He was only human, and she did look so lovely when she was earnest.

"Okay, I'm going to stop tiptoeing around and just come right out and say what needs to be said."

"If that's what you want to do, that's what you should do."

"You're too generous, Steven."

"I believe in allowing people to exercise free will."

She nibbled at the light-colored lipstick she wore. "But I can't be weak. I can't let you allow me to abuse you the way I did, then not insist that I explain myself."

"No. No, I see that."

"I'm surprised you still married me."

He'd pushed her far enough. "I love you."

"Yes." When she inclined her head a single white flower drifted to the ground. "I know you do and that makes it all even worse. I took advantage of your love."

Despite his best resolve his curiosity went on overload. "How do you feel you did that, Chloe?"

Her gray eyes shifted away, then back to his. "You're right to make me look closely at my behavior. Last night—before—I felt as if I were going to blow up from frustration. I wanted you to want to make love to me."

"I did," he said, with more force than he'd intended. "I did, and I do."

"You told me you're a traditional man. You meant you wanted to wait until after we were married and I should have honored your wishes."

He shrugged but didn't point out that the actual deed had yet to be done.

"I've had such a time of it keeping my hands off you, Steven."

Men dreamed of having a beautiful woman say those words.

"Every time I look at you"—her mouth remained open before she went on—"Every time I look at you it happens. It doesn't matter what you're wearing. Most of the time I couldn't tell you afterward. But every time I look at you I see you naked."

"Really?" Conveniently, the rock containing the pond was big enough for him to perch on an edge. He did so and crossed his legs. "That's really something."

"I imagine what you look like. Without anything on. At all."

He recrossed his legs in the other direction and gave her an encouraging smile.

"Men are supposed to say they're leg-men, or . . . whatever."

"Boob men?" he suggested helpfully.

"I guess. Among other things."

"Hmm." Where she was concerned, he was an everything man.

"When you wear shorts, I'm a leg-woman." Her nervous giggle softened the tension in her eyes. "But when I see your shoulders—in my mind—then I'm a shoulder-woman. Then there's your chest. Steven, you've got a fabulous chest. And shoulders, of course. And your back. Oh, Steven, even when you've got a shirt on I look at your back and my legs go all jellyfied. And I get this feeling inside." Her hand went to press low down on her belly.

Steven clasped his hands in his lap.

"And I used to visualize your *buns.*" She covered her mouth. "I feel *awful.* Like a dirty old lady."

"You can't be a dirty old lady at thirty."

"You know what I mean."

"I don't want you to give this another thought."

"I know—but I don't think I can stop myself."

In other words, his wife lusted after him? "There are times when we need to accept things the way they are and be grateful for our blessings."

"I'm sorry," Chloe said. "I will never, ever, say fuck your brains out again."

He all but swallowed his tongue.

"And I'll make sure you never have to tolerate my losing control of my appetites the way I did. But when I actually saw your"—once more she drew a hand picture—"Well, I'd sort of seen the outline. And I'd felt you get hard. But you always controlled yourself because of your principles."

"What I told you about being afraid of disappointing you was true," he said with complete honesty. "I wanted you as much as you wanted me. I'm a lucky guy."

"You told me our lovemaking had to be a two-way street. What I did stopped you from participating as fully as you wanted to—as you needed to. I could blame that on the stress of what happened last night, but it would be a lie."

"Really?"

"Yes." Chloe turned her back on him. "A complete lie. I used extraordinary circumstances to serve my own purpose. I exploited you and it was so wrong. I took away your right to make up your mind how far you wanted to go."

"We didn't have much choice, sweetheart," he reminded her, while he admired the straight line of her back, her narrow waist, inside her lace bodice. Dozens of minute buttons closed the back of her sweetly informal wedding dress. "We either had to convince Vigar and Orchis we'd taught them all they wanted to know or they were going to blast us into space with them."

"I still took advantage of the situation."

"You don't think I did, too?"

"Not the way I did. I . . . It's so hard to say it, but I've got to be brutally honest with myself. I pulled down your shorts and, and, and I took you in my mouth."

Steven barely bit back his moan.

"I forced you to get physically aroused."

"Chloe, I don't think—"

"I'm sorry. I know this must be horribly embarrassing to listen to. But this is why I'm not going to allow you to cater to my whims anymore."

If his belly sucked in much more it would scrape his backbone. "You're not?"

"Absolutely not. We love each other and that's a great start. It's more than most couples have to build on. But I obviously have to bring myself under control. You'll have to help me, Steven. You'll have to take me in hand."

"It'll be a pleasure." He cleared his throat. "I'll give it my best shot. Why don't we go back to the house now? If we move it, we can be in bed by eleven." That was not the way he'd intended to put the suggestion.

"Still trying to make me happy. Oh, Steven, I'm afraid that if you allow my lust for you to run wild I'll eat you up—I'll use you all up. I never thought I'd say such a thing, but now I don't have to imagine what you look like without clothes anymore, and just the memory of you makes me all hot and sweaty. Isn't that disgusting?"

"No."

"Yes, it is. I'm addicted. Addicted to you—to you and sex. I've read about people like me. There are support groups for sex addicts."

"Yeah. And I'm sure they do a great job. You won't need one."

Her shoulders hunched. He didn't dare think what that made him think of. Her pointed breasts pressed together were a sight he'd better not dwell on just yet.

"Let's make love, Chloe."

"Just to make me happy?"

The joke was over. "I want to make you happy. I also want to make me happy."

"You won't have to lie awake at night worrying I'll attack you," she told him. "I won't give in to it."

"Would you like to undress me again?"

She looked at him over her shoulder and whispered, "Yes. I can't lie. I would like to, but I won't. This has been a hard time for both of us. Would you mind leaving me alone to think? I won't be long."

This was his fault. His insecurities had led to her insecurities.

And he'd also deprived them both of a whole lot of great love-making. No more.

Steven undid his shoes and slipped them off. He tossed his socks aside, and loosened his tie to pull it off and drop it on top of the shoes.

Chloe wandered a few yards away. She crossed her arms on the trunk of a tree and rested her face.

A beat, an insistent thrum began in Steven's chest and re-verberated to his gut. His thighs tensed rock hard. So did his penis.

Sweat broke on his brow and ran down his temples. His shirt buttons defeated him and he wrenched them open. White linen hit mossy ground and would never be the same. His new belt resisted his efforts but finally fell apart. The zipper was easy.

"Sweetheart," he said, his throat so dry it ached. "Sweet-heart, I want you."

"I'll always want you."

"Chloe, look at me, please."

Rather than face him, she turned her head just enough to see him. She blanched, then flushed. "Oh, you dear man."

Dear man hadn't been quite what he'd hoped for.

"What will it take to prove to you that you don't have to do this for me unless you're in the mood?" she asked.

He pushed his slacks down. "I'm in the mood."

"Oh, sure you are. You didn't sleep all night and you're standing outside in the woods." She hid her eyes once more.

The slacks went the way of his shirt, and his underpants followed. "Take another look, Mrs. Early, and tell me whether or not I'm in the mood."

After what felt like a very long pause, Chloe peeked at him with one eye. Starting at his face, that eye made a downward visual—then widened.

"Well?"

"You're cold."

"I am not cold!" Shouting was completely out of line. "I'm sorry, love."

"You want to make love with me?"

"This isn't a mirage." He planted his feet apart and waited until he had her attention. He pointed. "Thinking about you, about your body, and about making love to you did this."

"It's lovely."

Steven blushed.

"Barbara says a lot of women think they're ugly. Those things. I think they're beautiful."

He wasn't sure how he felt about the group classification.

"Not that I've seen too . . . well, not in the flesh, anyway. Barbara gets a magazine with pictures."

"You're kidding! And the two of you look?"

"I sort of glance." She remained where she was, the side of her face nestled on her crossed arms against the tree. "After all, men have always had their girlie magazines."

"I haven't."

"Barbara says—"

"I don't really want to hear what Barbara says."

"No. Steven, none of those men look as good as you do—without clothes."

A breeze wafted around his rear quarters. The same breeze flattened Chloe's skirt to her derriere. As impossible as it seemed, he grew even harder. "We can use my clothes as a blanket if you like."

"You're doing this to try to make me feel better."

"I'm doing this to make"—he swallowed the retort that he was the one most in need of feeling better—"I'm doing it for both of us."

"I put you between my legs. I used you."

The next shudder all but brought him to his knees. "It was wonderful," he told her, "and this time's going to be better."

"What if someone comes."

"Who's going to come?"

"The garbage people?"

"Into the woods? Come on, Chloe. Loosen up."

She dropped her hands to her sides but stayed by the tree.

"That dress has so many buttons."

"I know."

"They're going to take a long time to undo."

"I know."

He considered, then said, "I'm not going to undo them."

The breeze sharpened, whipped her skirts sideways. Her long legs curved from thigh to knee. The soft cotton wrapped over her calves, tucked closer yet to her bottom.

"Did you hear what I said?" Steven asked, drawing close enough to smell the light lily-of-the-valley perfume she wore.

"You aren't going to undo my buttons," she said clearly and reached behind her neck to fumble with them. "I'll do it."

"It'd take too long."

Steven knelt on the ground behind her. Slowly, he smoothed her dress upward, smoothed his way over her calves, made circles behind her knees with his thumbs.

Her sigh thrilled him.

Lacy white stockings ended halfway up her elegant thighs. Satin garters, each one trimmed with coy pink bows, secured the scalloped tops of the stockings. The skin between was soft. Steven kissed that skin and smiled when he felt Chloe brace herself against the tree.

When her skirts were bunched around her hips, high-cut white panties revealed her buttocks. She rocked a little from side to side and reached back to seek him, but he opened his mouth wide on her taut muscle and she cried out, grabbed to brace herself once more.

"We ought to go in." Chloe panted now, and she was wet— Steven felt how wet she was and employed what it took to make her legs sag while she helplessly sank onto his probing fingers.

"Still think we ought to take time to go in?" The delicate puffs of breath he sent into the swollen folds between her legs maddened her enough to make him grin. But he needed more. He found her center and stroked, stroked with increasing pressure and speed. "Let go, my love. I've got you. Let me take you."

"I want you," she murmured urgently. "Come to me, please."

"But—"

"Come to me."

Blindly, he pushed to his feet, ducked to find the entrance to her body, and, gently at first, eased into her from behind. She cried out and pushed away from the tree with both arms as he bent at the waist.

He couldn't hold back.

Chloe felt him fill her, withdraw, fill her higher, deeper, wider. With each lunge, tension built. "Yes," she said, not knowing for sure why. This couldn't be her, Chloe Dunn—Chloe Early, now—little Chloe the librarian. Standing in the woods with Steven making love to her. Behind her, making love to her. Steven naked while she wore all her clothes. He hadn't even taken off her panties. She had the disjointed thought that they would be shredded. Then she saw the vision of the two of them against the tree, the abandoned image she must make—the amazing, erotic picture of his penis penetrating her beneath the white dress, of her deliberately enticing garter belt, the parts of her that were exposed, yet adorned just enough to arouse.

Her feet were torn from the ground. With a large hand fondling each of her breasts through the dress, Steven swung her around and tipped her further forward until she gripped his hips with her thighs and absorbed the violence of his release, the echoing ripple of her own. And the onward echoes that trembled through them but died even as she wished they would never cease.

Beneath her dress she wore a thin chemise and no bra. She didn't need one and she'd wanted nothing to spoil the smooth lines of the gown.

Her husband's sensitive fingertips—her lover's hands—caressed the tips of her tingling nipples. She jerked against him and cried, "No," but laughed. "I can't stand it, you sadist. It's too much."

Steven laughed with her, and collapsed. He went to his knees with Chloe straddling his thighs. "Your stockings are never going to be the same."

"I don't care."

"I've ruined your panties."

"If I put on some more will you do that again, please? All of it? And again?"

He buried his face in her neck. "Don't you ever change. I love you just the way you are."

"Does that mean, yes, you will do it again?"

"Could I have time to recover? Just a few minutes maybe? You wouldn't want to kill me on our wedding day."

Carefully, she managed to clamber to her feet and straighten her dress. Steven promptly slipped his hands up her legs once more, threw her skirts over his head and shoulders, and sought her pouting clitoris with his tongue. Clever Steven—his tongue was inspired. He sucked, then blew again. Each breath whipped her to the breaking point.

Chloe batted at the back of his hidden neck. "Enough! Come out at once."

"Come out . . . Come out wherever you are." His muffled voice reached her between his deliberate and irresistible torment.

He managed to push his hands upward beneath her chemise and the bodice of the dress to claim her breasts. Another climax broke over her. This time he barely caught her.

Chloe rallied quickly. He'd scarcely lowered her in front of him before she made a dive and dealt him return attention he didn't attempt to fight. His release came very quickly.

Entwined in each other, they lay, panting, on a bed made of Steven's clothes and clumps of moss. He gazed into her eyes, kissed the tip of her nose. "You'll have to stop doing this to me."

"*Me!* Steven—" She gripped his shoulders and strained to

hear a sound that came, faintly at first, from somewhere that might be near, or far.

A familiar yowl joined strains of music and Merlin bounded into the clearing. He landed on Steven's chest.

"Music," Steven said, apparently oblivious to the cat walking over his face. "It can't be. Chloe, it isn't, is it? You don't hear music?"

"I do," she told him.

Merlin returned to Steven's chest, sat and raised a hind leg to begin a thorough wash.

" 'Masquerade,' " Steven whispered. Gently, he lifted Merlin to the ground and sat up. His rumpled slacks were more or less intact and he pulled them on, then his shoes, but no socks.

"It's getting louder," Chloe said, alarmed. She looked toward the sky, expecting to see the caposphere racing down.

Merlin dropped low to the ground and crept forward, his tail flicking. He made for the rock pool, leaped on top, and disappeared behind.

"Stay here," Steven told Chloe. "I'll get Merlin. Then we'll get out of here."

She let him get a few steps away, then followed.

"Masquerade" grew louder and louder.

The cat's tail showed above the rock. Steven went close and bent to see what Merlin had found. Chloe did the same.

Something silver glinted through the fronds of a fern. Steven moved the greenery aside and lifted a silver box. On top of the box rested a tiny green ball that pulsed with the musical notes.

Steven turned to Chloe. "You think they left this?"

"Who else?" She went to pick up the ball, but Steven stopped her. "The music's coming from that thing, not the box," she pointed out.

"I think we were supposed to come and find it."

Chloe glanced skyward again. "They know we're here."

"They're probably a million miles away by now. How could they know?"

"They did before. They connected with our minds and came here. I think they connected with our minds again just now—while we were making love."

He looked at her. His ruffled black hair turned him from Steven Early, physics teacher, to Steven Early, untamed lover. Perspiration still glistened on his shoulders and in the hair on his chest. The blue of his eyes was almost navy.

"Maybe this is a wedding gift," she told him.

He shook his head. "A sealing gift, you mean."

The music had softened to a faint chorus. Steven picked up the ball, that is, tried to pick it up. The instant his fingers met the surface, it crumbled. Tiny flecks of green sparkled and flew away in the breeze.

"S, and C," Steven said, brushing the lid of the box. "Our initials."

"They left it for us," Chloe said. "I feel sad. Isn't that stupid? I feel sad because they've gone, but they scared me when they were here. In a way." She opened the box and gasped. "Oh, my goodness."

Inside the box nestled the red crystal Steven had taken from the drawer in the chamber aboard the caposphere.

"Wow." He rested a single finger on its beautiful surface. "Who knows what it is, but it's great."

"Great proof," Chloe commented.

Steven rested his forehead on hers. "For you and me."

"Of course for you and me. If I ever want to get you locked away, I'll get you to try to make someone else believe that we were kidnapped by a couple of Sardines."

They laughed together and Steven looked at his watch. "Still time to be in bed before noon. Let's run."

"Run? You've got to be kidding."

"Would I kid my new bride? We've got to see how many times we can make love before we collapse."

"Steven!" she complained as he took her hand and pulled

her along behind him. "We've got all day. All night. The rest of our lives."

"Sure we do, but I believe in living for the moment. And this is my time of day. I always was a morning kind of guy."

Sultry

Anne Stuart

One

Whoever named the high desert town of Sultry, Wyoming, must have one hell of a sense of humor. In the blaze of high summer heat the creeks dried up, the grass withered, and there wasn't an ounce of humidity in the air. It was fiendishly, hellishly hot.

But it was certainly not sultry.

Which just went to show how easy it was to dupe gullible easterners, Carolina thought wryly. If Dennis hadn't heard of a town called Sultry and thought longingly back to their lost home near the Louisiana bayous, they never would have left New Mexico. By the time they reached Sultry, Dennis was too ill to travel further, and they had just enough money left to buy the old saloon. It seemed like a sign.

Now Carolina Cunningham wasn't so sure.

She noticed him the moment he walked into the barroom of the Queen of Diamonds Saloon on a hot summer night. That wasn't saying much—Carolina noticed everything, every seemingly useless detail, and there wasn't one man who'd walked through the swinging doors that night that she hadn't seen, judged, and filed away for future reference. So far none of the tinhorn gamblers and horny cowhands, none of the traveling drummers or lonely ranchers or timid farmers meant trouble, and Carolina had learned to smell trouble over the stink of spilled whiskey and unwashed bodies, leather and tobacco and things she didn't even want to think about.

This man was trouble. More trouble than Carolina had ever seen, and she'd seen more than her share in her twenty-four years. She glanced around the crowded room for Dennis, but he was nowhere to be seen. He might be upstairs with Dora, but she doubted it. Dennis hadn't bean interested in much more than his bottle of whiskey and his cards for the last year, and had only enough energy to sustain those two pursuits and little else. The lung sickness was getting worse, and he was going to die. And there wasn't a damned thing Carolina could do about it.

She let a grim smile curl her mouth, savoring even the mental use of the word damn. Her mother would be spinning in her grave. But then, doubtless Suzanna Emerald Lassiter Cunningham had been spinning for years, ever since they first laid her in the ground next to her husband. Or maybe she had no idea what had befallen her children. Carolina hoped not.

The odd thing about the stranger was that no one else seemed to notice him. Granted, on a Saturday night the Queen of Diamonds was bustling with activity, and everyone there was pretty well liquored up. Carolina's daddy had always told her that a man who couldn't hold his liquor was no gentleman. Carolina hadn't seen a gentleman since she'd come west.

He was a tall man, in a land of tall men. He wasn't burly like most—whipcord lean, dressed in dark clothes, his black hat still sitting low on his head. He was clean shaven, but his dark hair was too long. She couldn't see his eyes.

She didn't need to see his eyes. The other people in the Queen of Diamonds might not know they had a rattlesnake in their midst, but Carolina couldn't afford to make mistakes. The man wore two guns, big and nasty, and she expected he knew how to use them.

There was an ordinance in Sultry, Wyoming, that you weren't allowed to wear guns into the saloon. Too much chance of someone acting foolish. If they had to wait to get their weapons there was always a good chance they'd have time to cool off. Or at least sober up.

But the last sheriff had died, badly, shot by an irate husband, and there was no one to enforce the law. No one to keep Billy and his gang of cutthroats away from them if he decided to return to his childhood home outside of Sultry. No one to keep dangerous men from wearing their guns into Carolina Cunningham's saloon.

The man had a rare ability to blend in. He moved through the crowded room with an almost feral grace, and no one even glanced in his direction as he brushed past them. It was a rare gift, to be able to blend in like that. A dangerous gift.

He was about ten feet away from her when he stopped. There were two tables and at least a dozen noisy men between them, but he looked up, pushing the hat off his head to stare directly into her eyes. He'd known she'd been watching him.

That realization hit her at the same moment she looked into his eyes. She didn't know which was the more disturbing: the knowledge that he was just as observant as she was, or his eyes themselves.

They weren't rattlesnake eyes, that much was certain. They were gray, smoky, with an intensity that seemed to reach out and grab her. She didn't let men touch her, though many tried. This man managed to get past her guard just by using his eyes.

It was a hot summer night, and she was sweltering in her tawdry satin dress. Her hair was piled in outrageous curls on the top of her head, and her makeup was starting to smear, but she'd been born a Cunningham and no two-bit gunslinger was going to make her back down.

That was what he was, of course. Maybe not two-bit, but a gunslinger through and through. Carolina had seen enough to know one.

She also knew not to let him get the upper hand. She moved through the crowd, putting a hand on one man's shoulder, pushing past another, putting just the right amount of sashay in her hips as she approached the stranger, her cool, welcoming smile curving her painted lips.

A lady never used paint, her mother told her. But her mother was dead, the money and house and land were gone, and Carolina Cunningham survived. And she wore paint, lots of it. The more she wore, the safer she felt.

She came right up to him, standing just close enough to show he didn't scare her. "You're new to Sultry," she said in her cool, clear voice. As a conversational gambit it lacked something, but she'd learned that the men out west were totally devoid of subtlety.

He watched her out of those smoky eyes. "Yes, ma'am," he said. Giving nothing away.

"Well, it's a nice enough place if you're looking to settle down, and if it's fun and relaxation you have in mind you can't beat the Queen of Diamonds. The women are clean, the games are honest, and the whiskey isn't watered. Make yourself welcome, Mr. . . ."

"O'Malley," he said. "James Patrick de Cordoba O'Malley." He glanced around the crowded room, seemingly at random, but Carolina suspected he didn't miss a thing. "You must be Carolina Cunningham."

She didn't let her surprise show. In fact, she wasn't that shocked that he knew who she was. She'd already figured out he didn't miss much. She simply nodded. "I own the place," she said.

"You and your husband." It wasn't really a question, but she nodded again, the lie second nature to her by now.

"And where would I find him?"

"He's busy, Mr. O'Malley. I'm certain I can help you."

His eyes drifted over her, and she looked back, unflinchingly. She didn't see the lust she got from drunken cowboys, or the practiced wiles of the gamblers. His look was veiled but thorough, and her discomfort grew. As did her determination not to show it.

After a moment he nodded. "What's the going rate for the girls working here?"

Just another horny cowboy, she thought contemptuously.

"Slavery has been abolished, Mr. O'Malley. There was a war fought over that very issue a few years ago."

"And I can tell which side you were on," he drawled. "You're from Louisiana, aren't you? I recognize the accent."

She thought she'd wiped away every bit of the Creole softness in her voice. Dennis still spoke with a strong accent, particularly when he was drunk, and since that was most of the time most people knew he came from the South. They just assumed he'd picked up Carolina somewhere along the way west.

"A lifetime ago, Mr. O'Malley."

"And the women? Don't tell me their company isn't for sale? Or should we say rent?"

"You'll have to deal with them directly. They handle the arrangements themselves. But don't assume that they have no protection. My bartender sees to it that no one's allowed to hurt the girls, and he gets mighty riled if anyone tries."

Sam would be no match for Mr. O'Malley if he decided to get ornery. She doubted few men would be, but she made it a practice to let potential customers know that the girls were looked out for. In a world too full of compromise, it was one thing she insisted on. No woman even marginally under her roof was going to be hurt.

He was looking at her again, with those far-seeing eyes of his, and she found herself wishing she'd applied the rouge with a more lavish hand. She had to make do with attitude. Attitude, Grandmere Lassiter had always told her, was everything.

"And just what do you charge for your time, Mrs. Cunningham?" he asked.

She was used to it by now. Men thought that any woman who worked in a bar sold her body, and there was no reason this man should be any different.

"I don't, Mr. O'Malley. I'm afraid I'm not for sale. My husband wouldn't approve." As a matter of fact, Dennis Cunningham probably wouldn't notice, but O'Malley wouldn't know that until he met him.

"Would you have a drink with me then?" He didn't look the slightest bit chagrined, as if he'd known the answer all along.

She should tell him no. She seldom drank with the customers—she simply moved through the crowds, exerting a civilizing influence while she made sure no one got too drunk, too rough, too out of control.

"Why?"

His smile was slow and wicked. "Because I expect you don't drink with many of the customers, and I'd like it known that I'm no ordinary newcomer to town."

"You care that much what others think of you?"

"It can be useful."

"And why aren't you an ordinary newcomer to Sultry?"

"I'm the new sheriff."

It stopped her cold, but only for a moment. "You don't look like a lawman," she said flatly.

"What do I look like?"

"A gunslinger."

"They're often the same thing. It just depends who's paying their salary."

She nodded. "You drink whiskey or beer?"

"Whatever you're having."

What she'd be having was a glass of dark amber liquid from her own private bottle. Cold tea, strong as sin and twice as nasty, and no one ever knew the difference. "Whiskey it is," she said. "Come with me."

The others were beginning to take notice of the newcomer. By the time she sat down with him at the table in the corner, most everyone there had looked him over and made their own judgment. Carolina was willing to bet most of them underestimated him. She had no interest in making that same mistake.

He held the chair for her. Even Dennis had gotten out of the habit of those particular courtesies, and she could have wished the new sheriff wasn't adept at them. She gave him her cool, practiced smile before taking a healthy drink of her tea.

"Aren't you going to ask why I'm here, Mrs. Cunningham?"

he said after a moment, leaning back in the wooden chair. He was a man who was far too comfortable in his body, lounging gracefully opposite her, as if certain he had everything under his control. He probably did, she thought dismally.

"You told me you're the new sheriff," she said. "The town council hires one every now and then, and they hang around, trying to keep the peace, until someone shoots them or they get a better offer and move on. Which one will it be with you, Mr. O'Malley?"

"Just call me O'Malley," he drawled. "And I don't intend to get shot."

"Are you going to settle down then? Find a good woman and get married, raise a family?" The faint lilt of mockery was so slight most men wouldn't have noticed it. O'Malley wasn't most men.

"No, ma'am. Not here. I've come to do a job, and when it's done I'll be moving on."

"Sounds about typical," she said, leaning back and trying to match his lazy grace. She was so tightly corsetted it was hard to be relaxed, but she made the effort. "What makes you think your job will get done?"

"I'm here to kill Little Billy Gaither."

So much for trying to appear at ease. The very name of Sultry's own homegrown monster was enough to put starch in her backbone. "What makes you think he's going to show up here? He hasn't been home for a couple of years."

"And he killed three men and a woman when he was here."

"Yes," she said flatly. The woman had been Joanna, one of the older girls who had worked the saloon, a big, foolish, kind-hearted woman. Every time Carolina thought about what Billy had done to her she wanted to vomit.

Ah, but Grandmere Lassiter would have told her a lady never vomited. Maybe she just hadn't seem some of the stomach-turning things Carolina had.

"A lot of men have tried to kill Little Billy," she said in a deceptively casual voice.

"Yeah," he replied. "But they're not me." There was no arrogance in his voice, just a flat statement of truth. And she found she believed him. If anyone had a chance against Billy Gaither's vicious speed with a gun, it would be a man like O'Malley. Unfortunately, she didn't believe that anyone had a chance.

"Let's hope for your sake that Little Billy doesn't suddenly get homesick," she said, taking another drink of her tea, matching his whiskey intake. "You're too young to die."

His smile was slow, mocking, though she couldn't be sure whether he was mocking her or himself. "Trust me, ma'am," he drawled. "I'm not."

She looked into his eyes. Dark, smoky eyes that had looked into the face of hell and hadn't flinched. They were bleak eyes, but beneath the chill there was banked heat that seemed directed straight at her. It was probably another one of his little talents. An ability to make every woman feel wanted, needed, special.

She didn't want to be wanted. Too many people needed too much from her, and she was mortally tired of it. But she couldn't keep from looking into his eyes, and she wanted to move closer, she wanted to touch him.

The shouts ripped her attention away from him. A fight had broken out in one corner of the barroom, between Fred Myers and one of Loot Cassidy's cowboys, and both of them were wearing their guns. Carolina surged to her feet, cursing her inattentiveness. She was usually able to stop things before they got this far, before two drunks were staring each other down, getting ready to draw their guns. But she'd been too busy looking into O'Malley's pretty eyes to pay attention to her job, and now someone might die.

She started forward, only to have an arm shoot out in front of her, barring her way. O'Malley pushed her back into her chair with a rough lack of ceremony, and then crossed the saloon to move directly between the two combatants.

She didn't like being shoved. She didn't like being out of

control in her own place of business, and she didn't like the ease with which O'Malley calmed the volatile situation. Fred Myers sat back down, shaking his head, and the cowboy stumbled drunkenly out the door, muttering underneath his breath. A moment later everything was back to normal for a Saturday night, and O'Malley was temporarily forgotten by everyone in the bar but Carolina Cunningham.

She glared up at him as he approached her. "I don't like being manhandled," she said in a chilly voice. "And I can take care of trouble in my own saloon."

"Seems like you were about to miss your chance, Mrs. Cunningham," he said slowly. "Another half a minute and you'd have had some nasty bloodstains on your floor."

"It wouldn't be the first time," she muttered.

"No, I suppose not." He spun the chair around and straddled it, picking up his whiskey and downing it before looking at her. "And I don't make a practice of pushing women around. But if it's going to save your life I can shove with the best of them."

"My life wasn't in danger."

"It would have been if you'd stepped in the middle of a gunfight. Or do you think they would have been gentlemanly enough to listen to your sweet reason and drop their guns?"

"What did you do to stop them?" she asked, belatedly curious.

"I told them I'd cut off their balls and feed them to the hogs if they made a scene in Mrs. Cunningham's presence."

"How . . . charming," she said faintly.

"Not very. But it worked."

"What about when Fred leaves? Won't that cowboy be waiting for him?"

"I doubt it. If he is, he'll probably have passed out."

"Leaving Fred a clear shot."

"Is he someone who'd murder an unconscious drunk? He didn't strike me as that kind of man."

She glowered at him. He was absolutely right, of course. All both of them needed was some cooling-off time. And she would have seen they'd gotten it, if she'd been paying attention and not been distracted by a pair of smoky gray eyes.

"Touch me again," she said in an even voice, "and Sam will shoot your hand off."

He didn't even blink. "Who's Sam? Your husband?"

"The bartender. He's got a gun under the counter and he knows how to use it. One sign from me and you're out of a job. There's not much call for a one-handed gunslinger, now, is there?"

She was wasting her time trying to intimidate him, and she knew it. "Sam takes good care of you," he said. "Protects your virtue and keeps you supplied with cold tea. Do all the girls here drink tea while their customers get drunk?"

"It's their choice," Carolina said coldly.

"Their choice? They set their own price, they decide the rules? You aren't like any other madam I've run across, and this sure is a strange whorehouse."

She didn't dispute the name he called her. He'd said it with a certain amount of admiration, and that was what she wanted him to think.

"As I said, slavery was abolished. I'm not going to tell them what they can or can't do. They have to make a living the same as the rest of us, and it's up to them how they want to do it. I'm just not going to let anyone hurt them."

"Neither am I," O'Malley said soberly. And then he smiled slowly. "Just part of my job, Mrs. Cunningham."

She didn't like the way his slow, deep voice lingered over the Missus part of her name. He knew her whiskey was tea, he knew who she was and that she'd been watching him. Just how observant was he?

"It's nice to see a man devoted to his work," she said sweetly.

"I always put my best effort into anything I set out to do," he said.

There was no reason why those simple words should have sounded so dangerous. He hadn't leered at her, hadn't touched her except to shove her down in the chair. His asking her price wasn't even necessarily a sign of interest; he might have been simply curious.

And yet she knew. With an instinct she hadn't even known she possessed, she knew he wanted her. And he was a man who got what he wanted.

Not this time, though, she reminded herself. There wasn't much she could protect from this wild land, not her gentility or her looks or her dignity. But she could protect that basic core inside her, the center of Carolina Emerald Lassiter Cunningham. And no man, no matter how smoky his eyes, no matter how enticing his mouth, no matter how elegant his strong hands, could ever, ever touch it.

She rose, and he rose with her. There was no practiced politeness about the gesture; he moved with an instinctive grace that she'd never seen before. "I'd better get back to work. Welcome to Sultry, Mr. O'Malley. I hope you make it out alive."

He smiled down at her, a slow, lazy smile that made her stomach do odd things. "I intend to, Mrs. Cunningham. I purely intend to." And he took her small, strong hand in his and kissed it.

Two

Carolina Cunningham had the hands of a lady. James Patrick de Cordoba O'Malley pressed his mouth against one, repressing the urge to bite her. She had to be the prettiest damn woman he'd ever set eyes on, and he'd set eyes on a few. He liked women, and he'd loved a few, Good, strong women with their own sense of decency and honor. Most of the women he'd loved had been whores and procurers, and it looked like he was following true to form. Because he could love a woman like Carolina Cunningham. He'd known it the moment he'd caught her watching him from across that smoky barroom.

It wasn't that he couldn't love a schoolmarm or a farmer's daughter. He didn't mind good women, as long as they didn't pass judgment on the bad ones. But for some reason most of the good women who'd strayed within his sights had very firm notions on who was saved and who was damned, though they didn't seem to mind trying to reverse the process in his case. They didn't like sex, didn't like kissing, didn't seem to like to do much else besides cleaning.

They did say cleanliness was next to godliness, and he probably spent a hell of a lot more time in the bath than at church, but there were limits. There was more to life than a well-swept floor.

He stepped back from her, and Carolina practically ran. Not that anyone else realized he had rattled her. She did a good job of hiding it, and he expected most everyone there took her at face value. He was too smart a man to make that mistake.

Besides, he wanted her. And she was going to be a hard one to get. He was going to have to be very careful in how he handled her.

Paco would have laughed at him. In town for less than twenty-four hours and he'd already picked himself a woman, a married one, no less. Except that he had the uneasy suspicion that he wasn't the one doing the picking. He was a pragmatic man, but every now and then fate dealt a hand. He had the feeling the Almighty had been dealing off the bottom of the deck.

First off, he had to find her husband. He hadn't heard much good, or much bad either, about the man, but if the lady loved him then he'd step back and ignore the itch that had started the moment he looked into her troubled brown eyes. He'd always been a sucker for blondes with brown eyes.

Sultry, Wyoming, was a nothing little town. It had one saloon, one church, two stores, a jail, and a barbershop that doubled as an undertaker's. The townspeople were an uncomfortable mix of saints and sinners, ranchers and farmers, but they'd learned to rub along together so far and he didn't anticipate any problems during his short stay.

And it would be short. Just long enough to put a bullet between Little Billy Gaither's mean little eyes, and then he'd be on his way, alone, like he always was.

He glanced across the room at Carolina Cunningham. Her bright pink satin dress was cut low across the back and front, and she had smooth, creamy skin that ached to be touched. But she didn't look like a woman who'd been touched enough in her life.

He needed to find her husband.

Dennis Cunningham was in the back room, a bottle of whiskey by his side, a cigar in his mouth, playing cards with a group of men. He recognized the mayor, Walter Slicer, and Jed Roberts, the most powerful rancher in the area, among the well-dressed gamblers. This was obviously where the real money changed hands.

Slicer looked up at him, a welcoming smile on his crafty face. "Wondered when you'd be showing up, O'Malley. Boys, meet our new sheriff. James O'Malley, from Denver."

Cunningham barely glanced at him. He was wraith thin, pale, and drunk. He was also dying of lung sickness; O'Malley could spot that at a glance. The others made suitably welcoming noises, and opened up a spot at the table for him.

"Haven't I heard of you?" one of the men, a narrow-eyed, paunchy older man demanded.

"I don't know," O'Malley replied evenly. "Have you?"

"There was an O'Malley from Denver who was a gunfighter. Killed the Durango Kid during a shoot-out, then wiped out his gang. Killed five of them with six bullets."

"There were only four," O'Malley said, pouring himself a drink. Carolina was right, they didn't water their stuff. It might have made it taste better.

The men at the table were looking at him uneasily, as if a hungry mountain lion had wandered into their midst. He raised his head and gave them his most innocent smile. "What are we playing?"

"Five card stud," Dennis Cunningham said with a lazy drawl. He coughed, fumbling for his handkerchief. It was spotted with blood, but his initials had been carefully embroidered by a woman's loving hand. His wife's?

"I've met your wife," O'Malley said, not inclined to waste any time. "A fine woman."

Cunningham lifted his eyes, and O'Malley got his first shock. Beneath the thinning blonde hair they were warm and brown, almost identical to the woman he'd married. "I think so," he said pleasantly enough. "Though folks around here can tell you not to rile her. She can be mean as a snake and twice as ornery."

"Hard to imagine," O'Malley said. "What is it particularly that riles her?"

It was Cunningham who answered him, Cunningham who was fully aware of the undercurrents of their conversation. "She doesn't like men touching her, kissing her, trying to take advantage."

"That must be real hard on a husband," he drawled.

"Don't you worry about me, sheriff," Cunningham replied. "Concentrate on what you came here for."

"Good advice," O'Malley drawled. "After all, the lady has you to look after her."

"She doesn't need me. Carolina is more than capable of taking care of herself. She doesn't like temperance lectures, she doesn't like anyone hurting the girls, and she sure as hell doesn't like people talking about her behind her back."

O'Malley laid down his pat hand. A royal flush. He had no doubt that Cunningham had dealt it on purpose, though he couldn't figure out why. The others cursed, throwing their cards in, but Cunningham merely smiled faintly as he poured himself another glass of whiskey.

"O'Malley's here to take care of the Gaither problem," Slicer said, leaning back and relighting his cigar.

"I didn't know we had a Gaither problem," one of the other men, a storekeeper named Benson, muttered. "Only one around is young Pete and the grandma, and she's dying."

"Young Pete reckons to be as bad as Little Billy," Slicer said. "He already killed the Watson boy last winter, and the two of them only sixteen years old. Little Billy was seventeen before he started killing."

"Word has it that Little Billy is headed back this way," Slicer said. "Wants to see his dear old granny before she passes onto her final reward. She raised those six boys, hellions all of them. It's just a damned shame Little Billy didn't die with Virgil and Elroy."

"If he shows up back here, he's dead," O'Malley said.

Cunningham gave him a shrewd glance. "That would suit most of us. But killing him's easier said than done. You gonna give him a fair chance? Let him mend his ways?"

"He raped and killed a rancher's wife in Tucson. He burnt three Indian women and their children to death in a cabin outside of Nogales just for the sport. He shot his own brother in the back. I think he's about ready to meet his maker," O'Malley said calmly.

"I don't care how you do it," Slicer said hurriedly. "Just get him before he turns this town into a graveyard."

There was no mistaking the sudden, muffled explosion from overhead. O'Malley kicked his chair over, starting for the door. "Sounds like it's too late," he drawled.

"It came from one of the girls' rooms." Dennis Cunningham had made no pretense of rising, and O'Malley suspected it was because he was too weak. "Check there first. And make sure Carolina keeps out of the line of fire. She's likely to charge in first and ask questions later."

O'Malley could move fast when he wanted to. The customers in the main barroom seemed totally unaware that a gun had been fired in one of the overhead rooms—chances were they hadn't even heard it over the noise of conversation and music. Carolina Cunningham was nowhere in sight, and O'Malley knew a sudden, instinctive dread.

He took the steps two at a time, moving swiftly, his gun already drawn. A group of half-dressed women were milling around an open door, but they parted willingly enough to let him through.

The bedroom was plain, small, and hot as hell on the steamy summer night. A woman lay curled up in a corner, naked, bleeding, barely conscious. A man lay dead in the middle of the floor, face down. And Carolina Cunningham stood over him, holding a gun, a stunned expression on her carefully painted face.

She should have known her troubles weren't over. No sooner had she gotten rid of the unnerving new sheriff when who should saunter in her door but young Pete Gaither. He knew damned well no one wanted him there, but he also foolishly thought no one would be brave enough to stop him. Everyone knew what kind of shape Dennis was in, and most everyone made the mistake of thinking that just because Carolina was a woman, she wouldn't be a threat.

Carolina didn't move, watching him carefully. She could have gone after O'Malley for help, but that was the last thing she wanted to do. She didn't want to rely on any man. She had a gun and she knew how to use it, and Pete Gaither was only seventeen years old, for god's sake. He was a bully and a killer, even at that tender age, but he could surely make it through a night at the town bar without getting into too much trouble.

She hadn't seen him go upstairs with Daisy. But she'd heard Daisy's scream, and by the time she made it up the stairs, her small but serviceable Colt revolver in one strong hand, it was almost too late. Daisy was cowering in the corner, her eyes glazed, as Pete Gaither drew bloody patterns on her skin with the blade of his knife.

"Get the hell away from her!" Carolina said in a cold, deadly voice.

Pete had looked up at her, hair flopping down over his forehead, hanging in his strange eyes. And he'd laughed at her, surging to his feet and coming toward her, that huge knife aimed straight for her heart.

She hadn't even had time to think. She pulled the trigger, twice, and he went down like a stone, lying still on the floor, the blood flowing out from underneath him like a dark river.

A large pair of hands covered hers. She realized she was still holding the gun, pointing it at Pete Gaither's body, and that her hands were trembling. She looked up into O'Malley's dark eyes, but he seemed to be far away.

"Are you all right?" he asked."

Hell, no, she wanted to scream at him. *I've just killed a man. How do you think I feel?* But she didn't give in to the temptation. Strength and endurance had been beaten into her over the long, hard years, and she squared her shoulders, releasing the gun into his hands and stepping away from him. "Fine," she said in a deceptively brisk voice. "He was trying to kill Daisy."

The other girls had already gathered around the wounded woman, fussing over her, and O'Malley simply nodded. He looked down at the body. "Who is he?"

Suddenly the whole, awful reality of the situation came crashing down on her. She hadn't just killed a man. She'd killed the baby brother of one of the nastiest, most vicious killers in the whole Wyoming territory and beyond. A man reputedly headed home to visit his dying grandmother. He might even make it in time for his brother's funeral.

"Pete Gaither," she said.

He was leaning down, examining the body, when his head jerked back. "Little Billy's brother?"

"His favorite," Carolina said. She looked up at O'Malley. "I'm a dead woman," she said simply.

For a moment he didn't move. And then a slow, devastatingly sexy smile curved his mouth. "Honey," he said, "you're forgetting. You have me looking out for you now."

It rattled her, that notion, even more than the possibility of her impending death. This man rattled her. She didn't want anyone looking out for her. He'd abandon her in the end. She didn't want to count on a man to protect her. They were too easily distracted. Too easily seduced, inebriated, and generally made useless.

She'd learned to count on herself. But this time it wasn't going to be enough. Even a dangerous man like James O'Malley wasn't going to be enough to stand between her and a blood-crazed madman.

"And what happens after he kills you?" she demanded tartly.

"Hell freezes over," was his lazy reply.

"It must be nice to be so sure of yourself," she shot back.

"It has its uses." He glanced around the crowded room. "We need to get you out of here."

He was going to put his arm around her, she just knew it, and if he did she'd scream. She gave him a warning look, and he came no closer, wiser than most men. "All right," she said, moving past him, holding her tawdry satin skirts close to her body. They brushed against him anyway.

He followed her, closer than she would have liked, but he didn't touch her. He followed her down the long hallway, through the closed door, down three steps into the back of the building. It looked different back there, but she was in no condition to worry about it. Let James O'Malley form his own opinion about the lack of red-flocked wallpaper, the clean austerity of their living quarters. Let him form his own opinion of the small parlor she led him into, with the lace curtains and flowered pillows, with the old settee that was so comfortable she often fell asleep on it. Let him wonder why she had watercolors of western flowers and old family portraits instead of voluptuous nudes on the walls.

She stood in the middle of the room, momentarily confused. She couldn't remember why she'd brought him back here, or what she intended to do with him.

O'Malley made it easy. This time he did touch her, and before she could struggle she found herself seated in her rocker, a patchwork quilt of soothing colors tucked in around her.

He took a seat on the settee, far enough away to set her mind at ease. "Where's your husband?"

"Playing cards, I expect," she replied in a low voice.

"He heard the gunshots. We all did. Didn't he want to check and make sure you were okay?"

"Dennis knows I can take care of myself."

"Not always." He frowned. "Where I come from a man looks after his womenfolk."

"Dennis is sick." She didn't know why she bothered defending him to this cold-eyed stranger. It didn't matter what he thought, of either of them.

"He's dying," O'Malley said flatly.

He probably hoped to shock her. But she'd faced that truth long ago, and she didn't flinch. "Yes."

"You think he'll be any good against the likes of Little Billy Gaither?"

"Not anymore. He used to be a champion marksman, but I don't think his hand is steady enough to hold a gun anymore," she said calmly.

"Champion marksman? Oh, that's right, you're from the South. If I didn't know better I'd think there was a genteel southern lady beneath all that paint and satin."

Only the second time in his company, and he was already seeing a lot more than most people who'd known her for half a decade. She didn't know whether she'd been adept enough at schooling her reactions, and she didn't care. "But you know better, don't you, Mr. O'Malley?"

He let his eyes run over her. There wasn't much to see. On this hot, dusty night she was cold, shatteringly cold, and she huddled beneath the bright quilt she'd stitched herself. "I surely hope so, Carolina. Because a southern lady wouldn't have a snowball's chance in hell against Billy Gaither. She wouldn't survive one year out here. This land is rough, and the people don't come with social graces. You don't mind if I call you Carolina, do you?"

In fact, the sound of her name on his lips was unsettling. "My husband might."

"It doesn't appear that your husband has much interest in you at all."

"I told you he's sick."

O'Malley glanced around the parlor. His eyes didn't linger on anything in particular; it was a simple perusal, and yet Carolina had the grim feeling he didn't miss a thing. Especially when he noticed the small oil portrait behind her.

She wanted to stop him when he rose and crossed in front of her, moving to examine the picture more closely, but she couldn't move. Her bones felt like ice, and there was no way she could keep him from doing whatever he wanted.

She should have had the sense to keep that portrait locked away. But then, she never allowed strangers into this room, any more than she let them into the small bedroom alcove that lay beyond the closed curtains. If she hadn't been so overwrought she would have been more careful.

He was staring down at the charming portrait of two blonde-haired, brown-eyed children. The girl was undoubtedly a beauty, in rose-colored frills, and the younger boy looked handsome and innocent and safe in his riding clothes. They belonged to a world that had vanished in a welter of blood and guns and war, never to return.

"That must be you," he said. "You haven't changed much in twenty years. Who's the little boy next to you?"

It would have been stupid to deny it, and Carolina had learned that though lies were sometimes necessary in order to survive, the fewer you told, the less likely you were to get caught up by them.

"That's my brother," she said flatly. "He died young."

O'Malley glanced over his shoulder at her. "You looked very much alike back then."

The phrase "back then" was a loaded one, and she didn't know whether she dared ask him what he meant when Dennis pushed open the door.

"Are you all right, Lina?" he demanded in his ruined voice. "Someone said you shot a man. Not that busybody new sheriff?"

He hadn't noticed O'Malley standing in the shadows. It was little wonder—Carolina had never had a man other than Dennis in her rooms.

O'Malley moved into the light. "It would have been better for her if she had. Unfortunately, I didn't give her any cause."

Dennis gaped at him. It was just as well—in his current condition the family resemblance was almost nil, and that astonished expression made it even more remote. "What the hell are you doing in my . . . wife's room?"

Carolina heard the very slight hesitation and she wanted to cry. O'Malley was already too smart, too knowing, and even slight hesitations would give them away.

"Looking after Mrs. Cunningham, since you were nowhere

around." He glanced once more at the portrait, then back at Dennis. "She shot Pete Gaither."

Dennis would never have cursed in front of a woman, whether it was a hooker, a grand dame, or his own sister. "Is he dead?" he managed to ask.

"Yes."

"We're leaving," he said flatly.

"No." Carolina wasn't about to let her life be dictated by a pair of men. "We've come too far to just give up everything and run. This is a good town, we've got a thriving business—"

"This is a hellhole, and our thriving business is a bar and whorehouse," Dennis said brutally. "I promised Mama I'd take care of you and I will."

She wanted to tell him to hush his mouth. O'Malley was already far too observant, and she didn't want to give him any more clues. "We'll be all right, Dennis. After all, we have the big, strong new sheriff to protect us, now don't we?" She let her voice be slightly mocking, but O'Malley was impervious.

"That you do, ma'am," he said. "Little Billy Gaither will be dead before he comes within sight of you."

She looked up at him. In this case she had no choice but to put her fate in his hands, much as she hated the notion. She was no match for a crazed killer, and Dennis was too sick to be of any help. She would have to count on James O'Malley to save her life. She wondered what kind of payment a man like him would expect.

"You'd better be prepared, then," she said calmly enough. "Because he's coming, and he's coming soon."

"I know it, ma'am," he said softly. "That's why I'm here."

Three

Little Billy Gaither and his gang didn't arrive back in the town of Sultry, Wyoming, in time for his baby brother's funeral. He was too late for his grandmother's funeral three days later. Not that there was much wait between the dying and the burying. In the heat of high summer it wasn't wise to keep a body around too long.

It was a shame, because a funeral would have been the best place to waylay Little Billy. Not that Billy would relax his guard one tiny bit, but in the confusion and the weeping and the wailing O'Malley might have a better chance getting the drop on him.

O'Malley had no delusions of grandeur. Killing Little Billy Gaither was going to be a damned tricky business. He'd waited ten years for this chance, and he wasn't going to let it go by. He owed it to Alice. He owed it to Paco. And he owed it to himself.

He'd seen what Little Billy could do to a whore who'd displeased him. Alice's savaged body was a vision he'd never been able to rid himself of, no matter how hard he tried. Billy's baby brother obviously shared his twisted tastes—the girl he'd been tormenting had died the next day. No one had been able to stop her from bleeding to death.

As for O'Malley, he was just biding his time. Waiting for Little Billy Gaither.

The Queen of Diamonds Saloon was busy on this hot summer day. As far as he could see it was always busy. He'd taken a room at the hotel across the way, one with a good view of the swinging doors on the front of the bar, and once the place opened, about midday, it kept going until the small hours of the morning.

And he kept going with it. He had a table of his own now, in the far corner where he could sit with his back to the wall, seemingly absorbed in his newspaper or a hand of cards, all the while he was watching. Watching everybody, everything. Listening. The sound of the horses out in the street, the distant thunder of a summer storm that would never come. The way Carolina Cunningham moved through a room, the way her lush hips swayed when she knew someone was watching. The way they didn't when she thought she was unobserved.

The lady was a puzzle. She was like no hooker he'd ever known, and he'd known and loved a few. She went upstairs with no one, and while her manner was friendly and welcoming, none of the patrons, from the town fathers to the most drunken cowboy, dared touch her.

He leaned back in his chair, stretching his long legs out in front of him, and took a drink of his coffee. He could hold his liquor as well as any man, but he had no intention of giving up even the slightest edge when it came to a showdown with Billy Gaither. At night he drank the same dark tea that Carolina did, and everyone was too preoccupied with their own drinking to take notice.

He saw her watching him from across the room. Not Carolina, but the pretty girl who'd wept so bitterly over Daisy's grave. Dora, her name was. She'd been talking with Dennis Cunningham a few minutes ago, and O'Malley couldn't decide whether she was asking permission to approach him, or whether Cunningham was sending her. He'd find out soon enough.

She smelled like cheap perfume, and her painted smile was tentative when she came up to his table. "Can I join you, sheriff?"

He'd already risen, and she looked up at him in surprise. "Certainly, Miss Dora," he replied, holding the chair for her.

He wasn't going upstairs with her, even though she was the kind of woman he usually couldn't resist, with womanly curves and a sweet smile. He wasn't going upstairs with anyone but Carolina Cunningham.

"I thought you might be in need of a little companionship," she said with great delicacy. "It must be lonely, bein' new in town and all. I'd be more than happy to fill some of those empty hours."

Women were sensitive creatures, easily slighted. "I thank you for your kind offer, Miss Dora, but—"

"I meant for free. No charge," she said hurriedly. "You don't strike me as a man who has to pay for it."

He let a brief grin light his face. "I have no objections to paying, but I think I'd better not let myself get distracted right now. I've got a job to do."

"Carolina's distracting you," she said shrewdly.

"Is that why her husband sent you over to distract me?" he murmured lazily.

It always surprised him to see an experienced woman blush. "The idea was mutual," she said. "He's very protective of Carolina. We all are."

Now that got his interest. "You're protective of her? Why?"

"She looks out for us. Look what happened three days ago— she killed a man to try and save one of us. Not many women would give a damn about what happens to a group of whores," she said bitterly.

"You work for her. She makes her living off your bodies— don't you think she'd want to protect her investment?" He kept his voice deliberately cynical, waiting to see what would happen.

Dora reacted just as he thought she would. "She doesn't get any of our money. We work for ourselves, the group of us. We set our own fees, we take care of each other, we decide if we want someone new to join us. We rent rooms from the Cunninghams and that's it."

"Sounds pretty noble of them. I hadn't realized Miss Carolina was such a saint."

Dora rose, looking down at him with stolid disapproval. "Maybe I don't like you after all," she said sternly. "Just one thing, Sheriff. Keep your hands off Miss Carolina. And make sure Little Billy doesn't get anywhere near her."

"That's my job, Miss Dora."

She glowered at him. "Do it."

It didn't take long for Dennis Cunningham to take her place. He didn't smell a whole lot better—whiskey and sickness clung to him like a cloud. He was almost a skeleton, and O'Malley, who'd seen a few men die this way, figured he had a month at the most.

"You've offended Dora," he said diffidently, taking the seat she had vacated. "That's not easy to do."

"I needed some information. She provided it." O'Malley said lazily.

"Why do you need information about my wife?"

"Why did you send Dora over? You afraid I'm going to be the man to Carolina that you aren't?" he countered.

Dennis looked at him out of red-rimmed eyes. "She's not what you think she is," he said finally. "She's a fine, true woman, better than the likes of you or me. She deserves better than living in this hellhole, but it was the best I could do under the circumstances. The sickness got so bad I couldn't move on, and she wouldn't leave me. She had the foolish notion she could take care of me when I could no longer take care of her."

"Why are you telling me all this?"

"Because I want you to understand the kind of woman you're dealing with. I want you to respect her, and to keep your goddamned distance," Dennis said.

"And if I don't?"

"I'm not dead yet, O'Malley. And I can still shoot straight."

O'Malley nodded. "Point taken. But if you're so damned worried about her, why'd you bring her out west in the first place?"

"Hell, it was her idea," Dennis said, wiping the sweat from his brow with a brown stained handkerchief. "Our land was gone, our home, our money. All of our kin. We had nothing back there, but out west was a world of possibilities. Or so Lina said. I hate it out here, but I truly think she could have been happy. If she hadn't . . ." He let the words trail off. "You're real good at making people say too much, aren't you, O'Malley?"

"It's a useful talent. If she hadn't what?"

"Been tied down to me." Dennis had brought a bottle of whiskey and a glass with him, and he poured himself a shot. "This is the only stuff that keeps me from coughing my brains out," he murmured absently. "Or maybe I just don't notice that I'm coughing." He swallowed the shot, then looked at O'Malley out of bleary eyes. "Believe it or not, I like you, O'Malley. If I could choose a man for Carolina, you'd be the kind of man I'd want her to end up with."

"She already has a husband," O'Malley drawled.

"You know that's bullshit as well as I do. And you know I'm going to be dead before long. Maybe before Billy Gaither if he doesn't get his ass here soon enough. You'll take care of her for me, won't you? You'll keep her safe from Little Billy?"

"Yes," said O'Malley.

Cunningham rose on unsteady feet. "And you'll take her with you when you go?"

"Yes," said O'Malley.

Cunningham nodded, satisfied. "Treat her well," he said. "Or I'll come back and haunt you."

At first it had seemed like a smart idea, posing as husband and wife. A brother didn't seem as much protection as a husband, and Dennis had always been frail and sickly. As Mrs. Cunningham, she found that people thought twice about offering her disrespect. Dennis might look weak but he was fast with cards and people rightly assumed he was just as fast with a gun.

And it had worked fairly well during the long years of their sojourn from Louisiana to the wilds of Wyoming. She'd never regretted it. Men seemed to fall into two categories: the sweet, weak ones who needed to be mothered, and the nasty ones who needed to be kept at bay.

James O'Malley was neither. Well, he definitely needed to be kept at bay, but it would make things a whole lot easier if he were just the slightest bit nasty. If he pawed at her, leered at her, tried to pinch her butt or touch her breasts or make smutty comments. He didn't.

Neither did he treat her with the deference and charm she'd been brought up with. He didn't regard her as a fragile ornament, a flower to be sheltered. When he looked at her there was something in his eyes she didn't remember seeing before. Something that made her go hot and cold inside. Something that called to her, deep inside, called to a wildness she hadn't known existed.

She didn't have time to be distracted by a tall, dangerous man in black. Her brother was dying, and if Billy Gaither found out the truth, she'd be joining him. She could count on O'Malley to keep her alive for the time being. But the Gaither gang was a wild bunch, and sooner or later they'd come after her, and no single man was going to stop them. And she doubted O'Malley felt like dying for her.

It was so blessed hot in the saloon. Not a breeze strayed through the swinging door, and outside the cottonwoods were still. Her body felt itchy from the stifling clothes, her lungs were clogged, and she thought if she spent another hour in that place she would scream. With everyone watching her, half of them writing her obituary in their brains, the other half too concerned with getting drunk or rich or laid to bother about Carolina Cunningham.

Dennis was deep in conversation with the new sheriff. That in itself was surprising enough, but Carolina wasn't about to waste her chance wondering about it. She whispered a word to Sam behind the bar and then took off before the old man could protest.

She was good at slipping away without being caught. If she hadn't figured out a way to do it over the years she doubted she could have survived her narrow, limited life for so long. By the time she got to her room she'd already managed to unhook the long row of buttons that ran down her back, and she stripped off the satin dress, the layers of short, frilly crinolines, the garters and garish stockings, the gaudy necklace and feathered headpiece. It took her no time at all to wash in the cool clean water she kept in her room, to scrub the makeup from her face, to take her long, thick hair from its artful curls and braid it in one thick plait down her back.

Within half an hour she was dressed in Dennis's cast-off clothes and her old riding boots, her horse was saddled, and she was racing through the midday heat, the wind rushing against her face as she headed toward the foothills. It would be cooler up there. It would be quiet and peaceful and safe, with no eyes watching her, no one passing judgment, no one wanting something from her. She wouldn't have to think about a smoky-eyed gunslinger who made her forget who and what she was. She would steal this afternoon for herself, because God only knew when she'd get another one.

The sun was blisteringly hot overhead, and she slowed her pace, not for her sake, but for Bucephalus's well-being. Bucephalus had come west with them, and he was old now, too old to be treated with anything less than gentle respect. He appreciated a good run as much as Carolina did, but in this heat he could wear out his old heart in no time. And she couldn't afford to lose him as well as her brother.

She was right, it was cooler in the mountains. The pines and aspens grew tall and thick as they climbed the narrow trail, and overhead a hawk made lazy swirling loops in the bright blue sky. She tilted her hat back to stare upward. She wanted to be that hawk. To fly away, free and wild, no one to worry about, no one to take care of.

Another hawk soared past, close, and she found herself wondering if they were mates. They flew together, in concentric rings, dipping and gliding, almost dancing on the air. She wanted to dance on the air with another hawk. She wanted freedom, but she wanted love. She wanted . . .

She shut off that line of thought with a sharp exclamation, one that made Bucephalus jerk in surprise, then stumble over the rocky trail. "It's what I get for daydreaming," she told him, leaning over and stroking his neck. "I promise to keep my eye on the trail and not on the sky."

Even the icy mountain pool was warm today. She never took long with her swimming—though she never saw anyone on her trips into the foothills, she couldn't feel comfortable frolicking in the deep, still water without her clothes on. But it felt so blessedly good today, rippling against her skin, combing through her hair. For once she almost hated to get dressed again.

She left her shirt, Dennis's old fancy dress shirt, unbuttoned to let the breeze waft against the thin white chemise she wore. She left her boots and socks off, letting her toes delight in the sunlight as she sat on the grass by the pool and combed her long, thick hair.

She hadn't been sleeping well. It was no wonder—every time she closed her eyes she saw one of three things. Pete Gaither's expression of shock when she shot him. Dennis, fading more and more each day. Or James O'Malley's smoky gray eyes, watching her, watching her. Calling to her.

She lay back against the thick cushion of grass, spreading her hair around her. She was safe, hidden, blessedly alone for a short, precious time. She could close her eyes and revel in it. In another hour she'd ride back down to town, put on her satins and her garters and her face paint, twist her hair on top of her head, and swing her hips through the crowd of men. In the meantime, she had this moment of peace.

To be herself once more.

He knew it had to be her, but for a moment he couldn't believe it. As soon as O'Malley realized that Carolina had slipped away he went after her. She was a magnet who would draw Little Billy Gaither to her, and O'Malley had no intention of losing that edge. Just as he had no intention of losing Carolina.

The girl who lay sound asleep beneath the bright Wyoming sunshine looked years younger than the gorgeous creature who strode through the barroom with such majesty. Skinnier too, without all that crinoline and satin. She had long, thin legs, small breasts, a narrow waist, and hair the color of a wheat field. He knew it couldn't be anyone else but the woman whose horse he'd tracked up into these hills. But he still had a hard time believing it.

He could sneak up on just about anyone, and she didn't even move when he crept down the narrow path to the deep pool of water. She was barefoot, and her long hair was still damp, so he realized she'd been swimming, and he cursed himself for taking so long to find her. It would have made life a lot simpler and more direct if he'd come across her naked.

He sat down beside her, moving with utter silence, stretching his long legs out in front of him. She slept deeply, a bad thing to his mind. Any kind of rattlesnake could sneak up on her, him included, and she'd be helpless.

Carolina Cunningham had never struck him as helpless, but right now that's what she looked like. Her lashes were long and thick against her cheeks, and they were gold like her hair, not black and spiky with paint. Her lips were soft and pale, not bright red, and there was a sprinkling of freckles across her pretty little nose. Her chin didn't look stubborn, and her eyes were closed so he had no idea whether they were uneasy or not. She lay in the sweet grass, asleep, oddly innocent-looking.

He didn't like innocent women, never had. They were devious, manipulative, afraid of everything, and always wanting their own way. He shouldn't be sitting there, finding Carolina Cunningham almost irresistible when she was looking so sweet. He wanted her when she was tarted up and dressed for business, wanted her with a hot, hard need that had been driving him for days.

That need had boiled over, not at the sight of her erotic smile or swaying hips, but the sight of her looking small, pale, and vulnerable.

He didn't like it. If he had any sense at all he'd get back on his horse, ride like hell back to the Queen of Diamonds Saloon, grab Dora and hustle her upstairs for some hard and fast sex and see if he could screw Carolina out of his brain. If Billy Gaither were anywhere near Sultry, O'Malley would have heard.

But he had no sense, at least not right now. All he had to do was look down at Carolina's pale, sleeping face, and any common sense went directly to his cock.

He wondered if the Cunninghams had named their saloon for Carolina. The Queen of Diamonds, sharp and hard, bright and beautiful. She didn't look hard or sharp, lying in the sun. She looked soft and sweet and he knew he wasn't going to wait until her brother was in his grave to have her.

She felt sinful, lying in the sun. She drifted in and out of sleep, knowing she should force herself to wake up, then drifting back down into the warm, lazy spot where everything was safe and wonderful. The sun warmed her without scorching, she could smell the grass and the wind and the dampness of the water. She could smell leather, and bay rum, and coffee, and she moved restlessly, dreaming. Dreaming of a man with hard hands and smoky eyes, with a mouth that promised all sorts of wondrous things. A dangerous man who stood between her and death, and yet could be the end of her.

But a dream was safe. In a dream she could reach out for him, have him, take him, and there was no rush. She didn't have to worry that he'd know too much, she didn't have to pretend to be anyone other than who she was. Carolina Cunningham, formerly a lady, now a lost soul from Sultry, Wyoming.

What would it feel like to kiss his mouth? She wanted to know. What would his skin feel like beneath her hands? What would he feel like on top of her. Inside her? Would he hurt her?

She stirred, imagining his hand cupping her breast through the thin layer of cotton. Big, strong hands, hot against her cool flesh. Her breath quickened, even in sleep, and she wanted more of him.

Images were flickering through her mind, remembered scenes she'd stumbled upon, whispered conversations she'd overheard, old dreams returning in a welter of hot desire. Bodies arching together, skin burning, and she felt a fierce dampness between her legs, and she wanted more, so much more.

Her body convulsed, quickly, sharply, waking her from her erotic dreams. Waking her to look up into James O'Malley's smoky gray eyes as he took his hand from between her legs.

Four

"Seems like you've been needing a man real bad, Miss Cunningham," he murmured.

She moved so fast he was unprepared: rolling away from him, grabbing the six-shooter from her pile of clothes, and ending in a crouched position, aiming the gun directly at his head.

He sat up, slowly, warily. "You don't want to shoot me, Carolina," he murmured.

"Yes," she said, "I do."

"Why?"

She knew her cheeks were flaming, and she decided to blame it on the hot sun that had been beating down on her while she slept. "You put your hands on me."

"You wanted me to," he said calmly.

"I was asleep, damn you! I was dreaming."

"Who were you dreaming about, Carolina? Surely not your husband?" He seemed perfectly relaxed, yet she could sense the wariness in his dark gray eyes as he watched her. And the gun.

"And why shouldn't I?"

"Because your brother and I had an interesting talk before I came looking for you."

She could feel a clenching in the pit of her stomach as one of her strongest defenses was ripped away. She wasn't going to shoot him, much as a part of her wanted to. She wasn't going to shoot anyone, ever again. Pete Gaither's shocked expression still haunted her dreams, and she hated even holding the cold metal gun in her still hands. It was already growing warm against her skin, like a poisonous snake curling up beside her. Taking on her heat, leeching the life from her.

"He wouldn't have told you," she said sharply, gripping the hated gun even more tightly.

"I already knew. And he was smart enough not to underestimate me. I guess good sense doesn't run in the family."

"Go to hell, O'Malley."

He made the mistake of smiling at that, and if she hadn't killed a man three days ago James O'Malley would have been history.

"If you shoot me, who's going to keep you safe from Little Billy?" he asked in a reasonable voice.

"I'm not sure if I agree with your definition of safe," she said.

He shook his head. His hair was too long, his mouth too wide and mocking, his face too taunting. "You're acting like an outraged virgin, Carolina," he drawled. "I think you're taking this entire situation much too seriously. I came looking for you when you disappeared from the saloon, saw you lying in the sun, obviously having one hell of an erotic dream, and I decided to give you a hand. Literally." He smiled at her.

Carolina cocked the gun. The clicking sound was loud in the still, hot afternoon, and his mocking eyes narrowed. "You shouldn't point a loaded gun at a man unless you're prepared to use it," he said in a cool voice.

"I've killed one man this week," she replied. "What's to stop me from making it two?"

He moved so fast she never saw him coming. He sprang across the narrow space that separated them, and she only managed to throw the gun out of the way at the last minute before he hit her full force, knocking her flat on the hard ground, covering her.

The sensation was so shocking it left her momentarily breathless. She stared up into his eyes, closer than they'd ever been before. She had never lain beneath a man's strong body, felt his hipbones against hers, his long legs, his arms imprisoning her, his body bearing down on her. She'd been around the women in the saloon enough, heard them talking, to know exactly what that ridge of flesh was that pressed against her belly. She knew all the mechanics, and she knew what he wanted. What she didn't know was whether he planned to take it.

He rose up on his elbows, staring down at her. "You're lucky you didn't shoot me," he said. "I'm too damned big to bury, and you wouldn't have wanted to haul my body back to town."

"I could have left you for the wolves," she said bitterly.

"They don't eat their own kind."

He was too close. His mouth, his entire body. He was invading her, crushing her, drawing her into him, and she couldn't fight back.

"Please," she said, not quite sure what she was asking for.

"All right," he said. "I'll behave myself. I'll keep my distance." And then he kissed her.

She stiffened, expecting brute force. What she got was much, much worse, a slow teasing of her lips with his, soft and tempting, nibbling, taunting. He slid his hand behind her neck and cradled her head, slanted his mouth against hers, and deepened the kiss. She was too lost to stop him, though she knew she should.

She didn't know kisses could be like that. Slow and sweet and drugging. For all that she'd just held a gun on him, threatened him with certain death, he seemed content to take his time, to explore the taste and texture of her mouth.

He tasted of coffee and hot, sweet sin. He tasted of warmth and forgetfulness. God help her, he tasted of love.

O'Malley didn't want to stop kissing her, but he figured he had no choice. She lay still beneath him, though he could feel her hands fisted in the back of his leather vest, and she made no more attempts to fight him. He didn't know whether he'd worn down her resistance or whether she was coming to appreciate his mouth. He lifted his head to look at her, but she quickly turned her face away.

He should get off her, he knew it, since he wasn't about to have her in anything but a warm, soft bed, but for the moment he couldn't move. "I guess you don't like kissing much," he murmured. "Either that, or you're way out of practice. How long has it been since a man kissed you?"

She jerked her head around to face him, and he froze. There were tears in her eyes, holding such an ancient sorrow that he was at a loss to understand it. "Get off me," she said in a raw voice.

He rose, catching her hand and hauling her up beside him. She looked thinner in her boy's clothes, less curvy, less sinful. Even more desirable. "I'll take you back to the saloon," he said. "And then we can go to your room and finish what we started."

"Don't count on it," she said in a husky voice, turning away from him. He stood and watched as she pulled on her socks and boots, picked up the gun and carefully uncocked it. She was lucky it hadn't gone off when she'd thrown it instead of shooting him. He was even luckier.

Except that luck had nothing to do with it. He lived by his instincts, and it was instinct, not arrogance, that told him Carolina Cunningham was just as drawn to him as he was to her. The problem was, in her case she was fighting it tooth and nail, and the lady was a fighter.

He couldn't figure out what her problem was. She had no man to look out for her, no one to be jealous. She had to know her brother wasn't going to be around for much longer, and if she had the sense most women had she'd be looking for someone else to take care of her.

Except that Dennis Cunningham hadn't been doing the taking care, Carolina had. She took care of her dying brother, the bar, the hookers, and the crazed cowboys who came to town to carve up whores. She wasn't used to being taken care of.

Maybe that had something to do with why he was so drawn to her. She had the fine-boned elegance of a lady and the grit of a hooker. The fierce strength of a mountain woman and the delicacy of a schoolmarm. She was a mass of contradictions, and if he didn't stop puzzling over them they were both going to be in a hell of a lot of trouble.

He came forward to help her mount her horse but she was already ahead of him, climbing up into the saddle with effortless ease. He looked up at her, a wry smile on his face. "You might have let me help you up," he said.

"I don't need help, from you or anyone else," she said tightly.

"You need my help to stay alive. Little Billy Gaither is one of the fastest guns in the Wyoming Territory. You're no match for him."

"And you are?"

"Yes." He held the reins for a moment. "If you stopped to think about it you'd realize I don't mean you any harm."

"Don't you? Then keep your hands and your mouth off of me. I don't like it!" She jerked at the reins, her horse skittered nervously, but he held tight.

"Liar," he said, very softly.

Carolina Cunningham was made of stern stuff. She kicked him in the ribs, hard enough to make him release the reins, and a second later she was off, riding too damned fast for the rocky path, not bothering to look back.

He caught up with her at the edge of town. She looked deceptively calm, her face pale, her eyes bright. Somehow she'd managed to braid her long hair while she rode, and it hung over one shoulder in a thick golden plait. He wanted to reach out and touch it, to touch the breasts beneath her hair, to kiss the base of her throat and work downward.

He gave her a crooked smile. "I don't want you to go riding without me," he said when he came up to her.

"I don't want your company."

"I don't want your corpse on my conscience. Ride with me or keep your sweet little fanny at home."

She glared at him. "I'll take my sweet little—"

"Miss Carolina!" The distraught voice caught their attention, and O'Malley's eyes narrowed as Sam ran toward them. He was panting, sweating, out of breath. "He's here!"

O'Malley didn't give Carolina a chance to respond. He was already off his horse, grabbing Sam by his shirt. "Where?" he demanded.

Sam shook his head. "He's staying at the family place. Just got there, I guess. He sent word that he was coming for Carolina and she'd better say her prayers."

"Like hell," O'Malley snarled. "How long ago did the message come?"

"No more'n a couple of hours. But that's not the bad part, Sheriff. Mr. Dennis took off. Just lit out the moment he heard Little Billy was around. Gave me a message for you. Said to remember your promise, and take care of Miss Carolina."

O'Malley was adept at keeping his reactions well-hidden. "Which way did he go, Sam?"

Sam shook his head. "I don't rightly know. South, I'd guess. Away from the Gaithers."

"No, he didn't," Carolina said in a raw voice. Her horse was sidling nervously, closer to O'Malley, and he coiled his muscles, ready to move. "He went after Little Billy himself. The stupid fool! I've got to—"

He reached up and hauled her off the horse, taking her by surprise. She kicked and struggled, screaming insults at him, and he absently noted that even in her desperate rage her language was a hell of a lot more delicate than that of any woman he'd ever known. "You can't stop me," she screamed. "I'm going after him, you yellow-bellied son of a Yankee whoremonger—"

He didn't really want to hit her. He avoided hitting women if he could help it, but Carolina Cunningham was leaving him no choice. He clipped her neatly on the jaw and she collapsed, stunned, onto the hard, dusty ground.

"Tie her up, Sam," he said tersely. "I'll go after Cunningham."

"I can't tie Miss Carolina up!" Sam protested.

"If you don't she'll follow me and she'll get us all killed. Tie her up and keep her at the bar until I find him."

"You think he really went after Little Billy?"

"Yeah," he said grimly. "And I don't think he had a chance in hell against him."

It took him a couple of hours to find Dennis Cunningham's body. He was spread-eagle on Pete Gaither's freshly dug grave, and O'Malley stood over him, concentrating on not puking his guts out.

He'd seen other bodies in the same kind of shape, but not often, and the sheer viciousness of it always made him sick. At least Dennis Cunningham had died fast. He couldn't have withstood that kind of torture for very long in his weakened condition.

That might be part of the explanation for the shape his mortal remains were in. Little Billy liked to linger over his killing, drawing out the pain for his own pleasure. Dennis Cunningham would have cheated him of that particular delight, and Billy's rage would have increased.

He wasn't going to let Cunningham's sister see what was left of her brother, that much was certain. He grabbed a blanket from his pack and wrapped the body in it before he tossed it over the back of his horse. It was only half a mile from the small cemetery into town—he could walk it easily enough. He could use the time to think.

Little Billy was nowhere around at that particular moment. O'Malley trusted his instincts—if there was any danger he'd know it. But that reprieve wouldn't last long. He'd killed Cunningham, and next he'd come after Carolina. And if past history was anything to go by, the entire town of Sultry, Wyoming, would go up in flames in the next twenty-four hours.

He wasn't going to let that happen. Little Billy Gaither had come to the end of a short, nasty life, and he wasn't going to take anybody else with him, with the possible exception of any family members he happened to drag along with him for the ride. He was going to die. And O'Malley was going to think of Alice and Paco, and Dennis Cunningham, and he was going to take pleasure in killing him.

"Don't look at me like that, Miss Carolina," Sam said pitifully. "I ain't gonna untie you, no matter what you say, and it won't do you no good to get all round-eyed and weepy."

"What if I get mad?" she shot back, still struggling against the bonds.

"You already did. I'm following orders."

"I'm your boss, not O'Malley."

"The law's got the final say," Sam said stubbornly. "Besides, in this case he's right. You go tearing out after Mr. Cunningham and you'll get killed, sure as shooting. You just settle down and wait."

"I don't have much choice, do I?" she said bitterly. Sam had lashed her to a straight-back chair in one of the deserted back rooms. The place smelled of whiskey and cigar smoke—it smelled like her brother, but she wasn't going to think of that. She was just going to concentrate on how she was going to get free and go after him.

Stupid, noble, high-minded southern gentleman! He was going to die, they both knew it. There was no reason to rush things. Especially since he usually had the shakes so bad he couldn't hold a glass of whiskey still, much less a gun. His eyesight was failing as well. He'd committed suicide, that's what he'd done, and for no good reason. It wouldn't keep Little Billy Gaither from coming after her. It would just whet his appetite for blood.

"Please, Sam, untie me," she pleaded, one more time. And then she saw the shadow at the door.

She couldn't see O'Malley's face. She didn't want to. "Get out, Sam," he said in a rough voice.

Sam didn't even stop to ask the logical question. Maybe he'd seen O'Malley's face more clearly, and knew the answer. Maybe he'd always known.

O'Malley sat next to her and began undoing the convoluted knots that Sam had tied. His eyes were averted, his face utterly still, and his sleeves were rolled up, exposing tanned, muscled forearms. He'd just washed his hands. She wondered what he'd been washing off them.

The fight had gone out of her. Vanished, leaving her empty, aching, lost. "He's dead, isn't he?"

"Yeah." His voice was cool and emotionless as well. "I left his body at the undertaker's."

"I want to see him,"

"No, you don't," O'Malley said, still working on the knots. She didn't argue. "Did he suffer?"

"I don't think so."

"Couldn't you lie to me and put my mind at ease?" she demanded, a brief moment of pain piercing the numbness.

His eyes met hers. They were cold and bleak, emotionless. "It wouldn't do any good. Pretty lies aren't worth spit out here. He's dead. He was going to die soon enough, and he died trying to save your life. For what it's worth, I think he's happier going that way than choking to death on his own blood."

She didn't flinch. "Yes."

The ropes fell to the floor. "Are you going to do as I say? Or are you going to keep fighting me?"

His voice seemed to be coming from far away, and it took an effort to make herself look at him. "I'll do what you say," she said quietly.

He stared at her for a long, grim moment. "I think I liked you better when you were fighting."

She was going to point out to him that she didn't care

whether he liked her or not, but somehow she couldn't summon the energy. She just looked at him.

He cursed, a phrase she'd heard but never used. She wanted to use it now, but she was too tired. He rose, but she stayed still.

He put his arms around her, but she ignored him. He picked her up, holding her against him. "I'm putting you to bed," he said in a muffled voice.

She didn't answer. Bed seemed like a good idea. She wanted to sleep. Maybe she wouldn't have to wake up.

Where would they bury him? In that desolate graveyard at the edge of town? She didn't want to leave him there. She didn't want to leave him at all.

She closed her eyes and leaned her head against O'Malley's shoulder. No one had carried her since she was a little girl, and it felt strange. She didn't want to be a child again—her earliest memories were filled with the war. But she wanted her mother and father back. Most of all she wanted her baby brother.

He laid her down on the bed, pulled off her boots, threw a quilt over her body and tucked it around her. This was the second time he'd taken care of her, she thought distantly. Another death. Who would wrap a quilt around her and tuck her in when he was gunned down?

"Sleep," he said, touching her face with his long, gentle fingers, pushing the wisps of hair back.

She felt the darkness drift down around her. "Will things be better when I wake up?" she asked very quietly.

"No."

And she turned her head and closed her eyes, giving in to the darkness.

Five

Sultry, Wyoming was preparing for a siege. Little Billy Gaither had already killed one of their own, and the Gaither gang wasn't known for halfway measures. If they ran true to form there wouldn't be anything left of the Queen of Diamonds Saloon or most of the town by the time they got through with them. Little Billy believed in impartial vengeance.

The so-called good people of Sultry were making themselves scarce since O'Malley had returned with Dennis Cunningham's body, but at least no one had come up with the smart notion of simply tying Carolina to a stake at the edge of the Gaither property and hoping that would satisfy Little Billy's bloodlust. It was lucky for them, O'Malley thought grimly. They had only to look into the eyes of their brand-new and very temporary sheriff to know how far they'd get with that notion.

They were probably smart enough to know it wouldn't do any good. Nothing was going to stop the Gaithers but a bullet, and O'Malley aimed to make sure he had plenty of them.

For the first time since O'Malley had come to town, the Queen of Diamonds was empty. It was late, and it was more than clear that no one was coming. Sam was busy piling chairs and tables in front of the plate glass windows, and the women huddled in a corner, talking amongst themselves, ignoring O'Malley as he sat by the bar, keeping watch.

Carolina hadn't emerged from her room. It was past midnight, a hot, still night, and in the hills he could hear the coyotes howling. Everything else was silent.

The piano player hadn't shown up for work, but that didn't matter since they had no customers. The hotel was closed and locked tight, but that wasn't a problem either. O'Malley had no intention of sleeping until he finished what he came here to do.

He had his back to the women, his eyes on the front door, but he knew the woman who approached him was Dora, knew it with the same instinct that told him Little Billy wasn't coming that night.

She took the seat beside him without asking, and she looked like holy hell. She'd cried all her heavy makeup off, and she looked sad and old and weary. "You have to do something about Carolina," she said flatly.

He swiveled around to look at her. "There's nothing I can do right now. She's asleep, and Little Billy is out there somewhere. If I go looking for him I'll get a bullet in the back of the head before I can even turn around, and then you'd be up shit creek without a paddle."

"She's not asleep. Look at this." She shoved a piece of paper at him, and he glanced at it with seeming disinterest. It was a bill of sale for the Queen of Diamonds Saloon. From Miss Carolina Cunningham, sole proprietor, to Miss Dora Hunnicutt, Miss Sally Jo Spendling, Miss Altalou Hanon, Miss Betsey O'Bannion, Miss Erma Roberts, and Mr. Sam Jackson for the sum of one dollar.

Miss Carolina Cunningham's signature was neat and flowing. Three of the women could sign their names, the others used crosses to signify their agreement.

He dropped the paper back on the scarred table. "It won't even be worth a dollar if Little Billy has his way."

"But he's not going to, is he, Sheriff?"

"No." He rose. "What's she doing?"

"Sorting her belongings. Preparing to die. You gonna reason with her, Mr. O'Malley? Are you gonna give her a reason to fight?"

"Why should I care?"

"Because you promised Dennis. Because I've been in this business most of my life and I know what it means when a man looks at a woman the way you look at Carolina. And I know the difference between lust and something that's a lot deeper and lasts a lot longer. You got it bad, O'Malley. Just make sure it doesn't get in the way of killing Little Billy Gaither before he kills all of us."

He scowled at her. "There's nothing worse than a smart hooker," he said.

Dora grinned at him. "We're businesswomen, sheriff. You have to be smart to survive out here. Now you go and make sure we still have a business to support."

He didn't bother knocking on Carolina's door. There was no light underneath the crack, no sound of anyone moving around on this hot, still night, but he knew she was awake. Dora's words were like a burr in his side. He wasn't a man given to introspection, to pondering his choices, to hesitation. He wasn't about to hesitate now.

The room was hot and still when he opened the door, with only the moonlight sending fitful shadows across the floor. He closed the door behind him and walked quietly across the wooden floor to the alcove where she would be sleeping.

The brass and iron bed was empty. She sat in a chair by the dresser, still and silent, and he had the sudden, horrifying fear that she was dead, that somehow Billy Gaither had managed to sneak in through one of those open windows without O'Malley being aware of it and put a bullet in her brain.

But Little Billy wouldn't be that subtle, or that neat. She blinked, watching him in the moonlight, unmoving.

"Is he here?" she asked calmly.

Her lack of emotion was beginning to piss him off. He unfastened his gun belt and dumped it on the end of the bed. "No, he's not here," he snapped. "Did you think I'd come to fetch you for your execution?"

"It would probably be the smartest thing you could do. I've already deeded the saloon over to the women and Sam. My affairs are in order, and I don't really mind. I just don't want anyone else to die."

"Well, they will," he said. "Little Billy isn't going to be satisfied with one or two of you, he's going to kill anything that moves around here. He'll go through your girls real slow and painful, probably make the others watch. He'll burn people in their houses and laugh while they scream. And you showing up like a holy martyr isn't going to change it."

He'd managed to get a trace of color back into her cheeks, and he continued, sitting on the bed and pulling off one boot. "I hate to disappoint you, Carolina," he said. "You were probably planning on wearing something white and virginal, and smiling bravely as he shot you. But death isn't pretty and noble. It's bloody. It stinks. And it's real."

"I know," she said. "I saw what he did to my brother."

He froze in the act of taking off his other boot. "You weren't supposed to," he said after a moment.

"I needed to." Her eyes were clear and calm. "You didn't need to spare me, you know. I'm stronger than you realize. I can take care of my—"

"You can take care of yourself, yeah, you told me." He rose, and shrugged out of his leather vest. "And I believe you. You can probably take care of yourself better than most women and half the men I know. Maybe I need you to take care of me. Did you ever consider that possibility?"

Her eyes narrowed in the moonlight. "I don't think so, O'Malley," she said softly. "You're invulnerable. You don't need anybody or anything."

"I need you."

He'd managed to shock her out of her damned calm.

"Bullshit," she said, and from the expression on her face he might have thought that was the first time she'd ever used the word. "Bullshit," she said again, as if she were savoring the taste of that forbidden word. "I don't know what game you're playing, but it won't work. If you want sex I'm sure one of the women will be more than happy to oblige."

"I don't want sex, I want you. Take off your clothes and get on the bed."

She stared at him in patent disbelief. "Don't you think you ought to wait for a better time?"

"There might not be one."

"I'm not going to sleep with you, O'Malley," she said fiercely.

He came around the bed, right up to her, and cupped her face with his hands. She didn't try to pull away from him, she just stared, speechless. "That's right," he said in a harsh voice. "You're not going to sleep with me. You're going to bed with me. I'm going to give you the ride of your life, lady, and when it's over there won't be any question about who you are and where you belong."

"Who am I? Where do I belong?"

"With me."

"You mean you've fallen desperately in love with me?" she mocked him. "You're offering me your heart and hand, you want to marry me and set me up in a cottage with a white picket fence and—"

He slid his hands down her shoulders and hauled her up, stopping her flow of words. She wore a white cotton night dress, something suitably martyr-like, and he almost would have thought it was funny. "I'll explain it to you, real simple-like," he said in a slow drawl. "I'm going to take you to bed and make sure you have no doubts at all about where your future lies. Then I'm going to kill Little Billy Gaither and any other member of his verminous family who happens to get anywhere near my gun. And then I'm taking you out of here."

"Where?"

"Someplace cool and clear and quiet. You'll like it there."

She shook her head. "No," she said, "I won't go—"

He was getting tired of her yammering. Kissing her seemed the best way to shut her up, and she was too surprised to fight him. Her mouth was already open and he took advantage of it, and her, sliding his arm around her hips and pulling her up tight against him, letting her feel him. She was right, it was a hell of a stupid time to let his cock dictate his actions, but until he took her she was going to keep figuring a way out.

He knew her. She'd fight like crazy to keep from getting involved with him, whether she wanted him or not. But if he took her it would be too late. She'd be bound to him, by her own code. Even if he let her go, she'd still be his.

And he wasn't about to let her go.

He ripped open the tiny row of buttons traveling up the high collar of her night dress. She let out a quiet sound of protest, but he ignored it as he moved his mouth down to the side of her neck. "It's a stupid nightgown," he muttered. "You won't be needing it again."

"Don't," she said, trying to pull away.

But the white cotton was caught in his fist, and she couldn't move. "What are you so afraid of, Carolina?" His voice was low and sensual. "You can't tell me you don't want me, because I know that's a lie. Isn't it?" He feathered his mouth across hers and her lips reached for his, almost by instinct. "Isn't it?"

"I want you," she whispered.

"Then what's stopping you?" He kissed her behind her ear, the soft, sensitive spot that made her shiver.

"I don't want to love you," she said bleakly. "I don't want to belong to you and watch you die."

"I'm not going to die," he said. "And you don't have to love me. Just stay with me."

If she'd put up any more arguments he would have let her go. But she didn't. She looked up at him, her eyes full of sorrow and a frightening acceptance. "I don't think I have any choice in the matter," she whispered. And she put her arms around his neck and kissed him.

Like a virgin martyr going to the stake, willingly, she kissed him, with set enthusiasm but no expertise, and he had a sudden, chilling thought that maybe she wasn't as experienced as he'd assumed she was. But she was too soft, too sweet, and he wanted her too badly to let it stop him. He scooped her up in his arms, and she was lighter than he would have thought, almost fragile for such a tough young woman.

She didn't look tough, with her clean, tear-cleansed face, her thick braid of hair, her wounded eyes. She looked lost and vulnerable, a waif, and he'd never been one to mess with waifs.

Things were about to change.

She wasn't going to think, she was only going to feel. She'd been crying too much, hurting too much. In a few short hours she'd be dead, and the man holding her might be dead as well. There was no way to stop it, nothing she could do to change things. But she was going to move through the last hours of her life experiencing things she never thought to experience.

She felt the softness of the mattress against her back, the slight coolness of the night air as he pulled her nightgown away from her. She wasn't afraid, she told herself. Not of death, not of him, not of his big, strong body and the thing he would do to her. She'd been through a lifetime in the last few days. It was only right that she go through this as well.

He stood over her, stripping off his shirt, and his chest was hard, tanned, smooth-skinned. He reached for his belt and she closed her eyes, her courage only taking her so far. She didn't want to watch him. She didn't want to participate. She wanted him to take her, make love to her, just once before she died.

She heard the rustle as he stripped off his clothes, and the bed sagged beneath his weight. He lay beside her, his skin hot, silky smooth, and he touched her face with surprising gentleness, turning her to face him. She opened her eyes, tentatively, looking into his, and when he kissed her she moved closer, unable to help herself.

He seemed to know just what she needed. The night was hot, so hot, and her skin was on fire. Wherever his mouth touched hers it soothed and aroused. She didn't know why she shivered when she was burning up; she didn't know why her heart clawed against her chest when he kissed her mouth. He didn't speak, and she was glad. She didn't want words, she wanted his hands, rough, tender hands, stroking her fevered skin, cupping her sensitive breasts. She wanted his mouth tasting her skin, kissing her stomach, sucking at her breasts until she thought she would explode. His long hair fell over his face, and in the darkness she couldn't see. She was in a hot, sweet cocoon of touch and taste and feeling, and she surrendered to it, willingly, joyfully, fully alive for the last few hours of her life.

She let her hands touch him, let her fingertips trace the cool planes of his face, dance through his long hair, brush against his mouth. He kissed her fingers, sucked them into his mouth, and she felt the flames burn hotter.

He rolled on his side, taking her with him, taking her hand and placing it on his body. He was very hard, much larger than she had expected, but she said nothing, letting his hand guide hers, stroking him, learning the rhythm as his hand clamped around hers.

He put his hand between her legs, and she forced herself to relax, not to fight him, but when he moved away from her, and put his mouth there, she panicked, struggling.

He ignored her silent protest, holding her hips with his elegant hands, using his mouth on her. She could feel tears running down her face, she wasn't sure why, and the cocoon turned darker, smothering. She caught his strong shoulders in her hands, trying to push him away, but instead her fingers dug into his flesh, clinging to him, as she felt a terrifying spark shoot through her body.

She tried to jerk away, but he wouldn't let her go. "More," he said, and put his mouth against her once more, touching her with his hand. Another spark shot through her, stronger this time, and her body convulsed tightly.

And then he was moving up, over her, covering her with his big strong body, spreading her legs apart and lying between them. It was going to hurt, she knew that, it was going to hurt like bloody hell, but she no longer cared. He thought she was an experienced woman; he wouldn't worry about being gentle, about being careful. He would take her, and it would be done.

She thought there would be more resistance, but she was wet from his mouth, from her own need, and he pushed inside her, filling her, with no pain. No pain, she thought dazedly, until she realized he was frozen above her, his body invading hers, and even through her tightly shut eyes she knew he was staring at her.

"Open your eyes, Carolina," he said.

She didn't want to. She wanted to stay in this dark tunnel of private pleasure, but his will was as strong as hers, She could hope the darkness of the room would shield her, but when she let her eyelids flutter open the moonlight spread across their bodies, and she could see his smoky eyes clearly.

"That's better," he whispered. "I don't want you dreaming. I don't want you thinking this is some handsome prince, some noble southern gentleman. This isn't a fairy tale, Carolina. This is me. James Patrick de Cordoba O'Malley. Mixed blood gunslinger with nothing to offer you but himself. You tell me you don't want me and I'll leave you, and you'll still be a virgin."

She didn't know how he knew. She didn't care. She reached up and cupped his face, and his long hair flowed over her hands. "Don't leave me," she said. "Ever."

And he pushed past the barrier of her innocence, taking her, his eyes burning into hers.

She cried then, just a little, and he licked the tears from her face. His first thrust was tight, painful, the next not so bad. She told herself she could endure, for him, and she caught the white linen sheets beneath her in her fists and held on, prepared to suffer.

The darkness came back, swiftly, but this time she wasn't alone. He was with her, surrounding her, inside her, and she could see him, breathe him, taste him, smell him invading every part of her. And she wanted more, needing something more, something his body promised, his eyes promised, his mouth promised.

Her body learned the rhythm before her mind did, and she was moving with him, reaching for him, struggling for something she could only begin to imagine. Her breath was caught in her throat, her body was a mass of pinpricks, and she trembled, lost.

"Now," he whispered, putting one hand against her mouth, the other between her legs, and he thrust, hard and fast, and it hit her with the force of an earthquake, a wash of reaction so powerful she thought she would explode.

He was with her, around her, and she screamed against his muffling hand. And she pulsed, with his life and hers, surrounding them both.

The first light of dawn was edging slowly across the floor of her room when Carolina awoke. O'Malley lay facedown and sideways across the bed, seemingly asleep, and she lay curled up beside him. She was tired, aching, sticky, and glowing. She thought she'd be ready to die when Little Billy came for her.

Now she found she wanted to live.

She slipped from the bed, careful not to wake him. She didn't want to die, but even more, she didn't want James O'Malley to die for her. No one had managed to stop Little Billy in his bloody career, but no one had Carolina's fearlessness.

She almost regretted washing the traces from her body, her legs. Her white nightgown lay in a torn heap on the floor, and a faint smile lit her face. O'Malley knew her too well. She'd pictured herself a saintly martyr, dressed in white, going to her death. And now the bastard had made her want to live again.

She dressed in Dennis's cast-off clothes again, hoping they'd stiffen her resolve. She was rummaging around the bottom drawer where she kept her gun when a shadow fell over her.

She almost screamed in shock until she realized it was O'Malley. He was wearing his black pants and nothing else, and he was looking down at her with far too much wisdom in his gray eyes.

"I . . . er . . . didn't mean to wake you up," she said, biting her lip nervously.

"I enjoyed watching you dress," he drawled. "What do you think you're doing?"

"Running away?" she suggested brightly.

She didn't expect him to believe her, and he didn't. "I don't think so," he said. "You looking for anything important?"

She shoved the drawer closed. "You took my gun."

"Yes."

"Why?"

"So you wouldn't go thinking you could kill Little Billy yourself. You can't. He's deadly."

"So am I," she said fiercely.

He reached down, caught her arms, and pulled her up against him, holding her tightly. She didn't even bother struggling, not when it was what she wanted most in this world.

And he released her, spinning away and heading for his discarded clothes. "I want you to stay here," he said, pulling on his shirt. "Little Billy's on his way."

"What makes you so sure?"

"Instinct," he said, reaching for his boots. "And knowledge. Little Billy likes to start out his day killing. He also knows that dawn is when people are least observant. He'll be here, any time now."

"You're sure?" Carolina said, picking up the antique porcelain vase that had once belonged to her Mama. It was heavy, one of Suzanna Emerald Lassiter Cunningham's most prized possessions, and Carolina had carried it safely out west, through more than a decade of travel.

"Absolutely," he said.

He didn't make a sound when she brought it down over his head. He simply pitched forward onto the bed, unconscious.

She found her gun under the mattress where he'd hidden it. She looked at him for a moment, wondering whether she'd killed him. She shrugged. She wasn't likely to make it out of her encounter with Billy Gaither alive, though she had every intention of taking Little Billy with her. If James O'Malley was already waiting on the other side it might make things easier.

Though his ghost would be mad as hell.

She checked the gun. Six bullets, enough to finish off Little Billy Gaither and maybe some of his brothers.

And maybe, just maybe, she might come out of this alive.

Six

The Queen of Diamonds Saloon was still and deserted as Carolina walked through the hallways. The women were asleep upstairs, most likely alone. Dora had told her there were no customers—for once the fear of the Gaither Gang overwhelmed the citizens of Sultry and their lust for various carnal pleasures.

Just as well. If most everyone was tucked safely in bed then maybe the carnage would be slight.

It was going to be a hot day. Even at that early hour, with the sun barely up, the air was still and sluggish, and Carolina could feel faint beads of sweat forming between her breasts. Sam had a shotgun behind the bar, and she went looking for it, ducking down to search among the bottles, when she heard the horses.

She rose, very slowly, unwilling to give in to her initial fear. Part of her had wanted to cower behind the bar, to pray that they wouldn't find her there. That they'd give up and go away. But Billy Gaither wasn't going to give up.

They were already at the door, and she stood very still, waiting for them to see her behind the bar. It wasn't a reassuring moment.

He hadn't come alone. The two surviving Gaither brothers, Perley and Hammond, were with him, small, mean-looking men. Their cousin Albert was there as well, his starched suit a glaring contrast to the filth of the Gaithers.

But the three of them were nothing compared to Little Billy Gaither himself. Six feet seven inches tall, more than three hundred pounds of pure evil, Little Billy towered over his kin like a crazed grizzly bear.

He was the first to see her, his small, dark eyes lighting on her behind the bar. She'd set her six-shooter down when she'd started looking for the shotgun, and it lay in plain sight, hopelessly out of her reach.

"Well, lookee who's come out to meet us, boys," he announced. "The lady herself. Must be she's in a hurry to meet her maker. What do you say, Hammond?"

"Don't know, Little Billy," Hammond muttered.

Little Billy moved closer, and even from halfway across the bar she could smell him. "It's just a damned shame though, isn't it, boys? Because I don't like to hurry these things. I like to take my time when I kill a whore, don't I, boys?"

"Yes, sir." Perley said.

"Then again, maybe she's the kind who likes pain. There are whores like that, Perley. You're too young and sweet to imagine such things, but there are women who get real pleasure from being hurt. You one of them, Miss Carolina?"

"No."

Little Billy chuckled. "She talks, boys. I thought she was just going to stand there and stare at us like we were ghosts. 'Course, that's what she's gonna be before long. A ghost, just like my poor little brother Petey."

"Just like my brother Dennis," she said, lifting her head to stare at him.

Little Billy scratched his jowly, unshaven cheek. "Well, there is that. You kill my brother, I kill your'n. Some folks might say we're even."

"Some might," Carolina said carefully.

"But you know, I don't see it that way. Your brother was a walking corpse anyway. I just hurried things along a bit. You might say I was doing him a favor. Doing you both a favor." He looked around him. "Now where's that new sheriff that's supposed to be protecting you?"

"He doesn't have anything to do with this. No one needs to

be involved but me. You don't have any argument with the rest of the town—they didn't kill your brother, I did. And I'm here to face you for it. But I want you to leave the town alone."

Little Billy stared at her for a long, thoughtful moment. And then he let out a bray of laughter. "She's real cute, ain't she, boys? Innocent for a whore." He moved closer, the stench of his unwashed body growing stronger. "You don't understand, Miss Carolina. I'm gonna kill you, real slow and painful-like, and while I'm doing that, my brothers are going to be taking care of the whores you got upstairs and anybody fool enough to be with them. And then we'll find your sheriff and have a little fun with him before we blow his brains out. Then we'll start on the town. You'll probably be dead by then, but if I'm lucky you might hold out for quite a while. I surely do like to take my time."

She didn't know whether it was his words or his smell that made her want to vomit. She looked into his mad, dark eyes and knew she'd made a very grave mistake. He was going to do everything he said, and the one person who could stop him was lying unconscious, maybe dead, in her back room.

"Go on upstairs and enjoy yourselves, boys," Little Billy said amiably. "I'm itchin' to get started with this one."

She felt a stray ounce of hope. If she was alone with Gaither she might have a chance.

But dapper cousin Albert stayed where he was, leaning against the piled-up chairs and watching as Billy advanced toward her, making no move to follow the two brothers upstairs.

"Isn't he going too?" she asked, wishing to God she wasn't trapped behind the bar, that she hadn't been fool enough to put her gun down. She had nowhere to run to, nothing to fight back with.

"Naaah, not Albert. He doesn't like women, leastways, none that are past ten years old," Little Billy said. "Don't be shy, darlin'. He just wants to watch. He'll have his fun later when we get to the children."

The Gaither brothers had disappeared upstairs. Carolina

heard a door slam, followed by a muffled scream, but she didn't dare look up. She'd led them all into death and disaster, and it was too late to stop them.

"Come on out from behind that bar, little lady," Billy crooned. "There's nothing going to save you, and the longer you make me wait the more I'll be obliged to hurt you. Come on out now and face justice."

She saw the shotgun. It was at the very end of the bar, just by the opening, and she supposed there was a very thin chance she could get to it, pull it out, and shoot it before either Albert or Billy put a bullet through her head.

It didn't seem likely.

The gunshots came from overhead, five of them, and Carolina couldn't keep from letting out an anguished cry. Little Billy looked at her and scratched his head. "Now that's downright odd, ain't it, Albert? The boys usually like to enjoy things a bit before they start shooting."

"Wouldn't be the first time they enjoyed things afterwards," Albert said in his soft voice.

Little Billy let out a wheezy chuckle. "Now that's the truth. Them boys ain't too particular about how fresh the meat is. Maybe I'll let 'em play with what's left of Miss Carolina when I finish with her."

"Maybe you won't." O'Malley's voice, cold as ice on this hot morning, came from out of nowhere.

Carolina's first thought was to dive for the pistol, but Little Billy could move shockingly fast for such a huge man, and he leapt behind the bar, catching her before she was halfway to her gun, hauling her up against his body and pointing a gun beneath her chin just as the explosion rocked the room. Carolina froze, wondering if she were already dead, when her vision cleared and she saw Albert, his dapper clothes speckled with blood and brain, slump to the floor.

"You must be O'Malley," Little Billy said after a moment. He was standing in the doorway, a smoking gun in his hand.

His long hair framed his narrow face, and he looked foreign, deadly, as dangerous as she'd always known him to be.

"That's right," he said. "And you're holding my woman."

Carolina could feel Little Billy's chuckle deep in his huge belly as it pressed against her back. "Now do you think it was wise of you to tell me that? I already had enough against her as it is, and you just kilt my favorite cousin. So I gotta avenge Petey and Albert, and this little lady will do the trick very nicely." He shoved the barrel of the gun tighter against her chin as he started dragging her down the length of the bar. Toward the opening, where Sam's shotgun lay. "Drop the guns, or she dies fast and bloody."

"Hell," O'Malley said in a lazy voice, "you can kill her if you've a mind to. If you don't, I probably will. The bitch hit me on the head with a vase."

"Sounds like you don't have very good luck with women, friend," Little Billy said amiably. "Drop the fucking guns."

"Luck's not with me today. But you know, Billy, I think you'd better let her go."

"Do you, now? Well, sheriff, I don't know if I rightly care about your opinion. I'm gonna kill her, and I'm afraid I'm just going to have to kill you as well. A matter of family honor. You understand these things, I'm sure," he said affably.

The pressure of the gun against her throat eased, and Carolina breathed a sigh of relief, only to have the cold steel barrel press against her temple instead.

"I understand you're going to put down your gun and let her go," O'Malley drawled.

"Naah, you don't understand any such thing," Billy replied. "But we've got ourselves a bit of a dilemma, now don't we? If you try to rush me, shoot me, I'll blow the little lady's brains out, and you don't want that."

O'Malley shrugged. "Women come and go. You have a price on your head, Billy, and I need that money. I have a sweet little piece of land up north where I aim to live out my days in peaceful retirement, and I need the ten thousand dollars they'll give me for killing you. You think I'm gonna let a woman stand in the way of that?"

Carolina believed him. Unfortunately, Billy Gaither didn't. "Yeah, I think you're gonna let this woman stand in the way. You got bite marks on your neck, boy, and I don't think they came from wrestling with a mountain lion."

"Let her go." There was no emotion in his voice. "You can leave, you and your brothers, and no one will come after you."

"I don't think so, O'Malley."

"Then fight me like a man. You're fast, and so am I. I didn't think you were the kind to hide behind a woman."

"I'll hide behind anything that'll shield me," Billy said with a rough laugh. "I don't have to worry about being noble, Sheriff. I just have to worry about staying alive. Now me and my brothers, we're getting out of here all right. And we're taking the lady with us. And if she lasts long enough, and gives me enough enjoyment, then maybe we won't come back and burn this hellhole to the ground." He spat. "Then again, maybe we might."

O'Malley took a step toward him, and Little Billy cocked the gun. "I'll do it," he said sweetly. "You know I will." He jerked his head toward the stairs. "Boys! Perley, Hammond, you come on down here now!"

There was no answer. No sound at all from the rooms upstairs. "Perley Bob Gaither, you get your sorry ass down here. We got a dead man to bury, and a woman to enjoy. Hammond, you hear me?"

No answer. Little Billy dragged Carolina to the end of the bar, shoving her up against it, pressing her face against the cool wood as he rubbed up against her. "I'm telling you for the last time, sheriff. Drop the guns. And then I think you better go find my brothers," he said softly. "Them boys know better than to ignore me when I call them."

Carolina's arms were trapped against the hard edge of the bar. Her hands hung down, desperately, tantalizingly near where she last saw the shotgun. She had no idea whether it was loaded, whether she could reach it before he shattered her brain with a bullet.

"Drop 'em," Billy thundered, and Carolina listened with dread to the sound of O'Malley's guns hitting the rough wooden floor of the saloon.

"You know, Sheriff," he said in a musing voice, "I might just have to kill you right now. Seeing as how you don't have a gun." And he aimed his pistol at O'Malley, still keeping Carolina's face pressed against the bar.

It was her only chance, and she took it. She reached blindly underneath the bar, caught the cold steel of the shotgun, and jerked it backward, into Little Billy's armpit, and pulled the trigger.

The force of the explosion knocked him halfway across the room. He lay facedown in a pool of blood, jerking slightly, and Carolina fell back against the wall, still clutching the shotgun.

O'Malley slowly walked across the barroom, took the shotgun into his hands, and went to stand over Little Billy Gaither's twitching body. And then he shot him again, point blank, and Billy stopped moving.

Carolina's knees gave way. She wasn't even aware of it happening; she simply sank to the floor behind the bar, wrapping her arms around her body and shivering.

"Is it over?" Dora's voice floated down from upstairs, more optimistic about the outcome than Carolina had ever been.

"They're dead," O'Malley said.

"What about Carolina?"

"She's all right for now. Until I beat her. Where are the other Gaither boys?"

"They met with a little accident," Dora said, her voice rich with satisfaction. "Looks as though someone better go for the undertaker."

"Yeah," O'Malley said. He moved behind the bar to stand over Carolina, and she could barely bring herself to lift her head and meet his accusing gaze. When she did, it wasn't reassuring.

"You think you know best, don't you?" he said in a cool, mocking voice.

"It was my fight, not yours," she replied, her voice a mere thread of sound.

"It was our fight," he said. "You need to learn that you are not the Queen of the Universe. You're not responsible for everything that happens. You understand?"

"Yes."

"Good. Because next time you hit me on the head and go tearing off with a gun I'm gonna beat you black and blue."

She sat curled up behind a bar in a room filled with carnage, and yet strangely enough she felt like smiling. "You aren't the kind of man who beats women."

"I might be willing to make an exception in your case." He pulled her up into his arms, and it didn't matter that her legs couldn't hold her. He could. And she let him.

He was right. She didn't have to do everything all the time. Sometimes she could just let someone else take care of things.

His hands were gentle, comforting, his mouth hard and possessive as he kissed her. "We need to find a preacher before we take off," he said. "We got some burying to do."

"Take off?"

"You sold the bar, remember? You don't have a job anymore. I think you're going to have to concentrate your efforts on reforming me. I drink too much, gamble too much, get in too damned many gunfights. You need to domesticate me. Show me how to be a good husband. Up in the mountains of Montana, where it's not so damned hot all the time."

"Are you asking me to come with you?" she said carefully, holding her breath.

"No. I'm telling you. I don't intend to give you any choice in the matter."

"Then what are you saying?"

"I'm saying," he paused to kiss her mouth, "that we need to build a house, and raise babies, and get married. Not necessarily in that order."

"Preachers can marry as well as bury."

He grinned down at her. "Are you asking me to marry you, Miss Cunningham?"

"No," she said. "I'm telling you."

He threw back his head and laughed, and even among death it sounded right. "Damned if I don't love you, Miss Carolina Cunningham."

"That's right," she said, sweetly, cupping his face with her hands and looking up with love shining in her eyes. "You'll be damned if you don't."

About the Authors

Janelle Taylor, an award-winning novelist who has tackled everything from historical to futuristic romance, has had six *New York Times* bestsellers. She lives in Appling, Georgia, where she is busily at work on her next two romances, *Wild Winds* and *By Candlelight,* a historical and a contemporary which will both be published in August 1997.

Jill Marie Landis, a national bestselling author, lives with her husband in Long Beach, California. Her many historical romances include *Last Chance, After All, Until Tomorrow,* and *Day Dreamer.*

Stella Cameron has written successfully in every genre in romance. She's made the Walden and *USA Today* bestseller lists for several weeks with *Pure Delights, Sheer Pleasures,* and *True Bliss.* Stella's a multiple award winner from Romance Writers of America and *Romance Times.*

Anne Stuart has won multiple awards for her romances—a Gold Medallion from RWA, Reviewer's Choice Award, Career Achievement Awards, and a RITA. She has written gothics, historicals, series romances, romantic suspense, and, in her words, "various hybrids of all those romantic forms." She lives in Vermont.